Ranulf swung her around to face him.

Morgana's eyes were wide and dark in the half-light.

"You must set the pace for your people if I am to win them to me, as I fully intend to do," he said in a deep, low tone next to her ear.

"And how do you propose I bring this about?" There was a soft catch in Morgana's voice, and her cheeks were flushed.

"By example. You must show them you accept me. As your lord." His eyes were blue as sapphires. "As your husband." His grip tightened, his powerful fingers kneading the tension from her shoulders.

There was no way she could mistake his meaning. Morgana was unable to meet his eyes. She looked away. Ranulf pressed closer, one big hand slipping down to rest at the curve of her waist. She was unable to move, to breathe.

It was not Ranulf she feared now, but herself.

Dear Reader:

Harlequin offers you historical romances with a difference. Harlequin Historicals have all the passion and excitement of a five-hundred-page historical in three hundred pages, and stories that focus on people—a hero and heroine you really care about, who take you back to and make you part of their time.

We have some great books for you this fall. I've highlighted a few, and I'm sure you'll want to look for these and our other exciting selections. Here's what you can look forward to in coming months: *Rose Red, Rose White* by Marianne Willman is a passionate romance set in medieval England. *Texas Heart* by Ruth Langan is the story of a young woman who goes in search of her father and finds love along the way. *Apache Summer* is the third and final book in Heather Graham Pozzessere's miniseries, and it features Jamie Slater. Lastly, in December, look for *Chase the Thunder* by Patricia Potter, which is an exciting Western romance and a sequel to *Between the Thunder*.

We appreciate your comments and suggestions; our goal is to publish the kinds of books you want to read. So please keep your letters coming. You can write to us at the address below.

Karen Solem
Editorial Director
Harlequin Historicals
P.O. Box 7372
Grand Central Station
New York, New York 10017

Rose Red Rose White

Marianne Willman

Harlequin Books

TORONTO • NEW YORK • LONDON
AMSTERDAM • PARIS • SYDNEY • HAMBURG
STOCKHOLM • ATHENS • TOKYO • MILAN

Harlequin Historical first edition September 1989

ISBN 0-373-28629-5

MARIANNE WILLMAN

is an established author in both the historical and contemporary romance genres. Born and raised in Detroit, she now lives close by with her family.

As a child, Marianne haunted the local libraries, and she still manages to read volumes of history as well as fiction of all kinds. When her hobby for collecting antique inkwells finally forced her to acknowledge that she wanted to be a writer, she gave up her critical-care nursing career and turned to writing. She's been busy ever since.

This book is dedicated (of course!)
to "Roses"—my beautiful daughter-in-law
Rosemary Ormsby Willman,
with thanks and much love.

Chapter One

The Tower of London

I will wait for you until the moon rises, and no longer.''

The boatman's voice floated over the surface of the Thames, muffled by the tattered banners of low-lying fog that shrouded the water. His lone passenger nodded but did not reply, holding the edges of the heavy black cloak together to keep out the chill air. The voluminous folds of fine wool hid all signs of sex or age and the draping of the hood concealed the person's face. Still, the boatman guessed more than his passenger suspected: only courage or desperation would bring a woman to such a place at such a time, he mused.

But then, these were desperate times. In the recent abortive rebellion, the Red Rose of Lancaster had been brutally crushed. Once again the White Rose of York reigned supreme under Edward, the King; yet the taint of treason lingered in the restless air.

The boat slipped alongside the Tower walls to the gate, lamps extinguished, and came to rest, bobbing gently. A slender white hand darted from one of the arm slits and dropped a coin into the boatman's outstretched palm, then vanished again.

"Best to hurry, milady," he whispered, and saw the anonymous passenger recoil in surprise. A moment later the disguised form stepped out upon the stone landing, briefly outlined against the darker shapes of the massive keep. Then the black cloak was engulfed by mist and melded into the somber shadows along the Tower wall. The boatman cast off his craft and his curiosity and pushed away, seeking the safety of the shifting fog.

As the boat vanished the figure slipped furtively around a corner of the immense wall, soft footfalls masked by the steady lap-slap-lap of waves against the stone. Faint and far away, a shrill cry pierced the silence. A cry of pain. The figure paused, startled, then ran across the cobbles of the small inner court and tapped thrice on the stout oak door. Already unbarred, it slid halfway open on freshly oiled hinges to admit the clandestine visitor, then shut with fearsome finality.

"Keep yer hood on till yer there," a harsh whisper said. Then the shutter of a lantern was scraped upward and the shadows jumped back. The doorkeeper was a dark wiry man, with a long nose knotted in two places and wary, yet indifferent eyes. He took the proffered coin and tucked it in his pouch without looking at it, then turned and led the way along a dank stone corridor.

The cloaked caller followed closely as the man ascended a stairway, turned right, and went up a winding flight until they reached the top. An iron-barred door with a sliding panel over the peephole faced them on the narrow landing. In the wavering light, chain mail shone in one corner. A guard lay on the floor, snoring softly.

"Don't worrit. 'E's asleep, and will stay that way awhile yet. But a handful of minutes is all ye have. I'll rap when 'e starts to stir." The jailor slid the iron bars back and the bundled guest slipped inside.

The brightness was dazzling after the tunnel-like corridors and dim stairwell. A large branch of candles stood in the center of the cloth-covered table where silver dishes were laid, showing the remains of a sizable dinner. A gentleman sat at the table in burgundy doublet and hose, lingering over a gilt goblet of wine. He was tall and well-proportioned, with the stamp of Plantagenet blood in his golden locks and bright blue eyes. The brilliance of those eyes did much to draw attention away from the weak and dissolute mouth, somehow shocking in one so young and otherwise handsome.

He gestured and his serving man discreetly retired to the small connecting room. The gentleman rose and strolled forward. "You must forgive me, my lady. As you can see, I did not think to entertain company tonight."

When the door closed he made an exquisite bow that mocked the menace of the surroundings. "Should I say, my dear, that I am touched by your solicitude—late though it is?"

Reaching out suddenly, he pulled the hood away and his mouth fell open in surprise. The woman's face was delicately molded beneath a wide white brow, with masses of gleaming rose-gold hair carefully confined in a black silk snood. Her eyes were the pure clear color of aquamarines.

"Morgana!" He seemed unable to speak after that one exclamation. Whomever he had expected to see, it clearly was not his wife.

Despite the tremor in her limbs, Morgana moved toward the table and pulled a small bundle from under her cloak. Her hands shook as she set it down. "I have brought some things for you, Robin, and this cloak for a warm covering. Spring seems unwilling to come to England this year."

She slipped off the heavy, fur-lined garment to reveal a lighter one of plain green wool beneath, then glanced quickly around the chamber. It was meanly furnished with only a small slit for a window, yet not at all the horrid cell she had envisioned. A feather mattress covered the pallet, carved chests stood against the wall and a small table held a game board with playing pieces of ivory and ebony. Food was evidently both good and plentiful, judging from the traces left on the dishes. The situation could not be as dire as she had feared.

Robin watched her examination of his prison and bowed with something of the careless charm that had won him so many fair hearts. "Welcome to my kingdom, milady Hartley. While it is neither so large nor so wealthy as the one I sought to rule, it is my own."

She ignored his caustic tone. "You are treated well, I see."

"As well as any traitor who is kinsman to the King." His mouth twisted cynically. "Perhaps Edward remembers that I am as gently born as he. But I forget my manners. Would you care to tell me the reason you have honored me with this visit?"

Morgana eyed him gravely. "Things have come to a sad pass when a husband must ask such a question. As to why I am here, I am still your wife despite everything."

To a person of her upbringing the answer was obvious, but then it was Morgana's family motto that said "Loyal unto Death," while the Hartley crest was equally descriptive of its heirs: "I seek, I take," suited Robin well. She reached into an inner pocket and set a small parcel and a prayer book wrapped in dark silk upon the table.

"I have brought you these few things and if you will tell me what you lack, I shall contrive to bring it with me when I return on Tuesday next."

"Then you haven't heard?" He looked at her hard. "Strange that a traitor so far removed from the life of the Court should know already what a confidant of the King does not."

"Heard? Heard what?"

"That Edward, my dear cousin, has signed my death warrant. On the morrow at high noon, I shall have my rendezvous with Madame Block on Tower Hill."

For a moment Morgana could not comprehend his meaning. She stared blankly at him as he went on. "Poetic justice, is it not?" Robin said scornfully. "We were wed at the King's command, and now it seems that we will be divorced by his Chief Executioner's sword. Or will it be the traitor's hatchet for me? In either event, I shall wear my new scarlet doublet—the bloodstains will then be less noticeable."

Morgana felt suddenly ill. "Do not jest of it, Robin! There is some mistake. Edward would have told me..."

His face flushed dark with spite. "You have always loved him well, have you not? Your loyalty would be touching if the circumstances were somewhat different."

"My love for the King is the love of a loyal subject and ward. As for loyalty, I have always been true to my vows with you."

"Have you, my dear? How amusing. For I have never been true to you. But then you have always known that."

She flinched beneath the lash of his disdain as she had flinched so many times before, and despite good intentions her temper flamed. "You would not be here today, Robin, were your sword as sharp as your tongue."

"Let us pray the headsman's axe will be equally sharp, then."

Morgana flushed. "I am sorry for my quick words. Pray forgive me."

Robin strode to the window and stared out the slit, one foot high and two inches wide. "I can see two stars tonight. My little kingdom has expanded twofold. Before I could only see but one. And after tomorrow I shall see them all— or perhaps none. Do you think there are stars in hell?"

"I am sorry, Robin," she repeated dully.

With a sudden movement he turned back to her, and for once his face was bare of mockery or deceit. "It is I who should be sorry. Not just for my words now, but for so much else. I have sought power and pleasure all my life, and see where it has got us both..."

He came to her and placed his hands on her shoulders. His face was filled with an uncharacteristic seriousness. He looked into her eyes, as if searching for something, Morgana thought. Condemnation? Absolution?

Their marriage had been a political one, providing Robin with Morgana's fine Welsh lands to make up for those he lacked, and giving her estates the benefit of his protection. A sensible and prosperous exchange—or at least that was how King Edward had considered their contract. At first she had hoped to make a good marriage from the ashes of her own hopes and dreams; but Robin had gone straight from their marriage bed to the arms of his mistress. He had dispersed the bounty of Morgana's lands to finance his treasonous rebellion and almost brought her estate under attainder. And now, it seemed, he would reap the empty harvest of his ambitions.

Robin's fingers pressed into her soft shoulders. "Mayhap Edward will choose you a better husband the next time."

"I shall never marry again. I would rather enter a nunnery."

He went on as if she had not spoken. "If I was not the husband you deserved, understand this: it was only that I loved another, and had wished to wed her instead."

"I know," Morgana said softly.

"You know that I wished to marry Lady Anne, yes. But you cannot know the pain of wanting one person and having to wed another."

Her eyes flashed and anger made her indiscreet. "Did you think you were the only one who loved?"

The look on his face would have been humorous in another time and place. It had never occurred to Robin that Morgana had been equally ill-pleased with Edward's matchmaking. The effort to make the adjustment in thought was written clearly on his face, and the blow to his masculine pride, as well. "It seems that I have not been as good a husband to you as you have been a wife to me."

Silence filled the chamber. He picked up the decanter from the table and poured wine into his empty cup. "Will you tell me his name?" he asked without looking at her.

"It does not matter now. He wed another. He is dead." She was surprised to discover the truth of her words. The old pain, that had seemed so much a part of her, was gone.

Robin set the goblet down, his thoughts already taking another direction. "I am surprised you are still at the Court. Surely it would have been less embarrassing for you to retire to your Welsh estates until this sorry affair is over."

Morgana flushed. "I was brought to Court five weeks ago as a 'guest' of the King. A precaution, until they were sure I bore you no heir."

"Yet he gave you permission for this visit."

"He did not."

The stretch of silence that greeted her words indicated the measure of his surprise. "You defied the King's command?"

Her chin tilted up. "When we wed I vowed to give you comfort all your days. I keep my vows. And I hoped to set aside some of the anger and the distance that has been between us all these months."

This time the pause was longer. Odd, Robin thought, how little he knew her after three years of marriage; but then they had only been together for less than six months of that time. Taking her right hand in his, he raised it to his lips. "Ah, my wife, had we only known one another better!"

Morgana searched for the old sarcasm in his eyes and found nothing but bafflement and a dawning respect. A light tapping on the door made her start. "I must go."

Withdrawing her hand from his, she reached into a deep pocket in her gown, removing a small flacon of rock crystal. The dark fluid within shimmered against the glass. She had kept it by her these past weeks, believing all the while that it was a foolish precaution. Now she knew how terribly wrong she had been.

Morgana held the vial out, unable to put its use into words. There was no need. Robin's brows rose. "Even this you have thought of," he said, taking it from her. "Is it very potent?"

"Not enough to... to spare you from the headsman, but enough so that you would feel no pain or fear."

The crystal vial lay in Robin's hand, a glass diamond with a brown and bitter heart. He bent his head and examined it as if it were indeed a precious gem. Then his back straightened and he thrust it back at her, smiling so his face was transformed.

"I thank you, but I shall not require it. You have defied the King to bring me solace, and thus have given me all the courage I need to die with dignity."

Again he raised her hand to his lips and kissed it, then suddenly pulled her into his arms. He kissed her long and thoroughly, taking comfort and pleasure in the act. Morgana felt nothing but sorrow and surprise. It was the first time he had ever kissed her without imagining she was another woman.

He released her abruptly. "Godspeed, Morgana."

She hastened to the door and, turning back once, saw Robin still watching her. As she stepped through the archway the jailor glanced ahead worriedly. "We mun' be careful. There be strangers about in the Tower tonight. King's Men."

If he noticed her cloak was now dark green instead of black, he made no comment. Perhaps, she thought, the dim light masked the change in colors. He led the way down the winding stairs without a backward glance. Morgana fumbled along behind him, blind with unshed tears. She could not love Robin, but she did sincerely pity him.

When they reached the narrow corridor on the ground floor the jailor stopped so suddenly she almost ran into his back. He held out his hand wordlessly and she placed the small purse of coins into it. In a flash the pouch had vanished inside his leather weskit.

"Our ways part 'ere, lady. Put yer 'and out and follow the wall. Where it ends, take ten paces forward, two to the left and ye will find the door. 'Tis unlocked."

Before she could protest he shuttered the lantern, quenching the light, and vanished in the blackness. Morgana stood in the damp corridor for long seconds and blinked back the tears, hoping her eyes would soon adjust. It was dark as the inside of a tomb and far more eerie. *God's Eyes, what I would not give for a lamp,* she thought.

Reluctantly Morgana put her hand on the damp wall and went forward. Her fingers tangled with a clinging web and she snatched them away, wiping them on her cloak. By the time she reached the end of the wall her palms were damp and her upper lip filmed with cold perspiration. There was a soft squeak nearby followed by a scrabbling sound. Morgana remembered hearing that a prisoner had been found gnawed to the bone by a pack of rats.

She hurried down the hallway, caution effaced by rising fear. The air was dank and musty and water dripped somewhere to her left in the engulfing blackness. Perhaps this narrow tunnel would be flooded by the incoming tide. The watery gurgling sounded closer. Now she was running quietly, desperately. The door was only a short way ahead. And then she collided with a large, hard object that knocked the wind from her.

Arms closed around her like the jaws of an iron trap, and a callused hand clamped over her mouth, shutting her breath in her throat. "I have him! Give me a light," a male voice commanded roughly.

Light burst on Morgana's eyes like a rocket's flare, blinding her temporarily. Someone chuckled behind her. "Not him, master! 'Tis a woman!"

She was pinned tightly, her cheek pressed against a doublet of sapphire silk brocade, but beneath the fabric she could feel hard links of chain mail. A hand caught her chin and forced it up until she looked up into the face of her captor. The wavering light gleamed on fair hair and a stern warrior's visage, all sharp angles and planes. Above wide cheekbones eyes as blue as indigo regarded her narrowly but without any sign of realizing her identity.

Morgana recognized him instantly. She had seen him from a distance many times, although they had never come face-to-face before: Ranulf the Dane, called by some the Golden Knight. The comrade-in-arms and close friend of the King.

Ranulf felt no such sense of recognition. The harsh shadows and half-light made a deceiving mask of Morgana's features. He saw only a pale, frightened face with lips blanched white, and lines of strain seemingly etched deep around her pale, red-rimmed eyes. Dust and streaks of cobweb grayed what little showed of her hair and the sharp contrast of light and dark made her features look gaunt and hollow. Morgana appeared twice her actual age.

"Why do you go in darkness, lady?" Ranulf asked sharply without releasing her. Her ribs felt bruised and she had no breath to answer. His grip tightened. "Have you lost your way, or only your tongue?"

"Please...I cannot breathe," she croaked hoarsely. Ranulf slackened his hold slightly, and she drew a grateful breath. "Let me go. I beg you, sir..." She stopped just in time.

"Then tell me what you are doing in the Tower at this hour. Are you employed on some errand by your mistress or are you about some mischief of your own?"

Relief poured through Morgana: he had mistaken her for a lady's maid or serving girl in her unadorned clothing. She took advantage of his error, adding a quaver to her voice. "Good sir, I . . . I am bent on no harm. I have been to visit my . . . my lover."

Ranulf chuckled. "He must be spry indeed to make you seek him out on such a cold night." The other man laughed aloud and the tension eased. Ranulf's hold slackened further.

"Go home to your own bed, lady, for there is much business afoot here tonight. In future let your lover seek you out instead. It would be much safer."

He released Morgana abruptly. Heart pounding wildly, she wheeled around and sped to the door without a backward glance. She pulled the handle, half afraid to find it locked. The door opened easily and she slipped out.

The fog had thickened and seemed as impenetrable as stone. Only the faint translucency above told her the moon had risen. She hurried into the thick of it, heading for the boat landing, unmindful of the commotion behind her.

"Wait! Detain that woman!" The Captain of the Guard came rushing down the stairway.

Ranulf strode outside, followed by the others, but the visibility was too poor. Then the murmur of oars came from the river, magnified and distorted by the fog.

"Too late, Captain. Your little bird has flown. Who was she?"

"I only glimpsed her from the window, but she looked to be Lady Morgana Hartley, wife of the condemned traitor. When the king hears of this . . ."

Ranulf's face was grim. "Is the prisoner secure?"

"Yes." The Captain began to sweat heavily in the chill damp.

"Then no harm has been done. Tomorrow Hartley will be dead, and no one will interest themselves in the affairs of a corpse. Meanwhile, I suggest you review your procedures and your men."

"Thank you, Sir Ranulf." They parted, the Captain to savor his relief, Sir Ranulf to wonder how the young and handsome Lord Robin Hartley had borne marriage with a woman so plain and so much older than himself. An heiress, no doubt. That would explain it. Whistling beneath his breath, he went back the way he had come. After all, the poor woman was no concern of his.

The King leaned back in his chair at the head table on the raised dais. While the musicians played in the screened gallery dancers swirled across the floor, jugglers tossed leather balls into the air and mimes cavorted on the sidelines. "Life is good!" he declared to no one in particular.

Ranulf, dressed in a red velvet doublet and hose of deep blue, sat at the high table on the King's right hand and viewed the scene before him with growing dissatisfaction. He would gladly exchange his fine feathers for leather and armor. The soft light winked on the sapphires of his wide gold collar and more than one fine lady thought his eyes were bluer and more sparkling than the gems.

"A ballad. We would have a gentle ballad of sweet, requited love," Edward called out when the music ceased. The King was resplendent in yellow satin worn with white hose, and a gold and diamond collar worked with his sun-in-splendor emblem hung low upon his breast. The caressing light of torch and candle shone on his bright hair and handsome face, hiding the early lines of dissipation.

Although the Queen, near term with another child, had retired from court activities, the gaiety of the post-Lenten festivities was unabated. The gleam of rich tapestries upon the walls, the Saracen rugs spread over the rush mats, the gold and silver plate, the silk livery of the pages and the brocade and gold-encrusted costumes of the lords and ladies created a pattern of color and richness to rival the great stained glass windows. The air was thick with the scents of rich perfumes and incense, compounded by the aroma of the dozens of dishes and confections that had made up the evening meal.

Edward never tired of the feasting, the dancing, the amorous intrigues, but their novelty had long since palled on his companion. Ranulf was no courtier at heart. A harper struck the chords of a poignant ballad and Ranulf felt an old familiar emptiness. Leaning his arm upon the table he stared into the shadows of the gallery. There had been a time long, long ago when he had studied in Ireland to become a bard, but circumstance had forced him in another direction: his strong hands, once trained to conjure rippling music from a harp's strings, had been molded instead to wield a sword. At the time there had been a sense of loss and bitterness. Now he was a warrior, first and last.

The closed rooms, filled with the press of perfumed bodies, made him long for the feel of the wind in his hair and a galloping horse beneath him. He sighed without realizing it. Perhaps he should go north, away from it all, where he could feel like a man again, a soldier and not some mincing fop. He would petition Edward to do so.

Several pairs of feminine eyes watched Ranulf's every move, but he was as oblivious to them as he was to his surroundings. The King had noted his friend's increasing restlessness and abstraction over the past months and an idea had been forming in the back of his mind. Now his Plantagenet-blue eyes danced as he cuffed Ranulf lightly on the arm.

"We find you dull company tonight, old friend. You have been frowning into your cup all night like a heartsick lover. Has some fair lady of the Court finally melted your iron heart, Sir Ranulf?"

"Nay, my Liege."

"Then the problem is likely of an opposite nature." Edward examined Ranulf with a calculating expression. The

Dane's face was strong-featured and somewhat grim in repose, but that seemed to attract rather than repel women. Clapping an arm around him, the King leaned closer.

"Your welfare is always of great concern to Us, Sir Ranulf, and the cure for your restlessness is simple: it is time you took a wife and settled down."

An abrupt recoil of Ranulf's hand overset his silver cup, sending a small river of deep burgundy liquid across the table. Immediately one servant was there to wipe away the spill, another to upright and refill his cup.

"Nay, my Liege! Settling down was not bred in my bones and a wife is the last thing I do need or want."

"But you are restless and filled with sighs, like a forlorn lover."

Ranulf smiled. "My thoughts are most unlover-like, Sire. Except for bringing in your rebel Lord before Eastertide, I have seen no action these past six months. I confess that I am longing to be in the saddle and away again. I have been thinking I should like to go north with the border patrols."

"Now I am sure it is a wife you need, one who will make home and hearth so attractive you will have no wish to leave." Edward leaned back and waved his hand over the glittering assemblage. "Is there not one woman here who has caught your fancy?"

Ranulf looked out wearily over the banqueting hall. "The ladies are beautiful, but too painted and powdered for my taste. Too ambitious and sharp-edged, I fear. I prefer a softer armful."

"Your ideal wife would not be a Court lady, then."

"No." Ranulf shifted his large frame uneasily. There were undercurrents to Edward's voice he could not fathom.

"A beauty, of course."

"By all means."

"Country bred?" the King persisted.

"Perhaps . . ."

"And an heiress, I imagine."

Ranulf tried to pass the moment off with a joke. He mistrusted that impish gleam in Edward's eye. "Oh, most certainly. If you could find one foolish enough to marry an unlanded knight with no fortune but the strength of his two hands. Do you know of a woman so beautiful and rich and foolish?"

"That, you will soon judge for yourself." The King murmured something to the page cleaning up the spilled wine and the youth hurried away. Edward turned back with a small secret smile. He looked like a boy about to perform a conjuring trick, filled with gleeful anticipation and satisfaction at his own cleverness.

Ranulf felt the first stirrings of panic. He brooded, nursing his fresh cup of wine. Edward had some deviltry afoot and Ranulf had no doubt it concerned him. He had been the butt of the King's jokes before. Likely the page would return with a heifer on a leading string, or some poor, aged fishwife in tow, to be presented to him as a potential spouse. On the other hand... Taking a healthy swallow of wine, Ranulf eyed the doorway warily.

Some half an hour later, just as Edward was growing restless and testy, the page came scurrying back. The boy looked frightened to death, and Ranulf chuckled beneath his breath. Edward's prank was going awry. He relaxed a bit, ready to enjoy what came next, now that the boot was likely to be on the royal foot instead of his own. The page stumbled to his knee before the King.

"Speak, boy! Why have you failed in your errand?"

The page trembled. "My Liege, the lady will not come."

"What!" At the sovereign's roar of disbelief the musicians faltered, then strummed their lutes more loudly and blew their flutes and krummhorns with greater vigor. Edward's pale eyes bulged with anger and his complexion, already florid, grew more ruddy.

"God's Teeth!" The royal fist came down with a solid thud that rattled the gold plate and sent the wine sloshing in its cups.

"Guards!"

The boy's mouth puckered and his face crumpled. Two armed men stepped forward to flank the page. The boy began to shake like a bowl of suet pudding and his face was much the same color; but the guards were not for him. Edward pointed at the youth. "Follow this page. He will take you to a lady's chamber. You will bring her to Us, at once."

The guards bowed as the page scrambled to his feet and they went out. Whispers of speculation filled the hall like the sound of wind sweeping through a grove of trees. After a short interval the guards returned with the relieved page and another figure; a slight form, robed in a long hooded cloak of mourning with a heavy black veil obscuring the face.

A collective gasp rose from the assemblage and Edward slammed his hand upon the table with a violent oath. He was rigid, his face suffused with choler. Glancing over, Ranulf saw that Edward had grasped the bowl of his silver goblet with such force the sides were bent inward. This was no jest.

Watching the figure's silent and graceful approach, Ranulf waited for the next act of the drama with great interest. The King stood abruptly and strode to the front of the dais. The funereally draped newcomer came forward and dropped into a low curtsy fifteen paces away.

"Rise, Lady," Edward said in a controlled fury, "and say why you ignored Our command for your presence."

The voice was soft, feminine, but not without a thin wire of tension stringing the words together. "Sire, I thought it a request, rather than a command. I did not wish to dampen the festivities with my mourning."

"Approach Us."

Edward gestured to the guards. "Remove the cloak."

A lovely young woman stood before the King's wrath, straight and slender as a lily in her trailing black silks. Her bodice was tightly fitted to her figure and trimmed at the low neck, cuffs and hem with sable. A low, vee-shaped headpiece of black silk held a matching veil of transparent gauze that still obscured her face.

"God's Eyes, you are bold to come so before us!" Edward snatched the veiled coif from her head and threw it to the floor.

The blaze of light from the branching candlesticks fell full upon her and Ranulf watched with mounting interest. The woman was as beautiful as she was bold, although her face was pale as death with the force of her emotion. She looked familiar, although he could not remember where he had seen her before. That she was an aristocrat and wealthy, he was sure, from both her proud carriage and rich manner of dress.

Her shimmering red-gold hair was bound by a simple fillet of gold and pearls and confined on either side of her temples in nets of silver thread. The face they framed was delicate with finely arched dark brows and lashes framing eyes of light blue-green, high cheekbones and a full and rosy mouth. A luscious, tempting mouth now set in defiant lines.

Edward smiled suddenly and reached out his hand. The courtiers and servants began to breathe normally once again. "Come, Lady Morgana," the King said pleasantly, "and join Us in a cup of wine."

Ranulf was startled. There was only one Lady Morgana at Edward's court: the wife of the condemned traitor, Lord Hartley whom he himself had brought in chains to London. He could scarce believe it. Except for those incredible eyes, clear as aquamarines, she did not look like the same woman he had encountered in the Tower. And what had Lady Morgana Hartley to do with him?

Morgana took the King's outstretched hand and joined him on the dais, her heart racing wildly. She had seen Edward's anger before, but never directed against herself. For the first time she feared she had stepped over the line of what would be forgiven. Still, as she came to stand before him, her carriage managed to convey the proper mixture of deference and pride.

The King eyed her, strangely enough, with a secret amusement. "What is the meaning of these dismal weeds? You are no widow yet, Lady Morgana."

Morgana faced him bravely. "I shall be widowed tomorrow, Sire, and by then my garments will be more appropriate."

"We disagree, Lady Morgana. You shall have no need for such somber clothing. It displeases Us greatly."

Although Edward tried to look severe, there was devilment dancing in the depths of his eyes. He gestured to Ranulf, who rose and joined them, with a hunted look in his eyes.

The two men stood together, tall and golden as angels in the torchlight. More than one Court lady caught her breath at the sight of them. Edward took Morgana's hand in his and clasped Ranulf's in the other, startling them both.

"Lady Morgana, you are headstrong and in need of proper guidance. In addition, you have vulnerable lands that need the protection of a strong man."

He turned to his old companion at arms with a triumphant air, as if unaware of the growing consternation on the knight's face. "Sir Ranulf, you have fought well and mightily in Our just cause. It is not good for man to live alone, the Bible tells us. You have need of a wife, one with estates and fortune of her own."

Edward took their hands and joined them. "It is a blessing that your needs mesh so well, for We have a mind to see you safely wed to one another."

Ranulf's fingers closed involuntarily over Morgana's. There was a look of such unguarded horror on his face that she could almost have laughed out loud; but there was nothing humorous in the situation. She was shocked and deeply angered. To go from one unhappy marriage to another, with no say in the matter!

The King scanned Ranulf's stunned face and Morgana's angry one and smiled with satisfaction. Along with the heavy burdens of kingship there were some compensations. Playing God was one of them.

"It is Our Royal pleasure that the marriage take place soon," Edward announced to the expectant stillness. "The formal betrothal will take place on the Feast of St. Elgin."

Morgana felt trapped and breathless as she and her intended husband glared at each other in mutual dismay. St. Elgin's feast was less than six weeks away.

Chapter Two

Ranulf's keen eyes scanned Tower Hill for a glimpse of rose-gold hair, to no avail. The perimeter was packed with an eager audience of richly dressed merchants and master craftsmen, and more drably appareled shop assistants, journeymen, apprentices; even fishmongers, tavern girls and stable boys, hiding the one small figure he sought. His jaw squared. *No sign of her yet. But, by God, when he found the wench . . .*

From across the way Desmond, his cousin and second-in-command, gave a signal that meant they were bringing the prisoner out of the Tower. A moment later the jostling, noisy throng fell still and silent as the solemn drum beat echoed clearly across the green.

Ranulf pushed his way through the densely packed bodies. "Make way in the Name of the King." Two young clerks stepped hastily out of his path, noting the dragon-prowed ship embroidered in gold upon his blue-and-white doublet. They whispered together, recognizing him: Sir Ranulf, born in the Orkneys, of Norse and Irish stock, and called the Dane. The Golden Knight.

Sunlight flashed off the pikes and halberds of the guards and Ranulf saw Morgana, not twenty paces from him. His brows met in a frown. She was discreetly cloaked in the dull brown of a serving maid, her hair carefully covered and had not yet been recognized; but it was only a matter of time. Morgana could no more hide her proud carriage and aristocratic features than Ranulf could his wide shoulders and towering height. And one glimpse of the flaming, telltale hair would give it all away. There were a hundred shades of red and russet in this crowd, but only one would have that unique rose-gold hue.

Against his will and despite his simmering anger, Ranulf felt a reluctant admiration. The Lady Morgana's act of defiance had already caused him a good deal of trouble and would likely cause a good deal more; still there was something touching about this slip of a woman braving the King's wrath to attend her husband's execution.

Her chin was high, soft lips firmly clamped together and eyes straight ahead as the dismal procession came to a halt before the block. The thought came to Ranulf unbidden: she must love the traitor greatly to display such steadfast devotion. Loyalty was a virtue he prized highly. Foolhardy defiance was not. *And,* he thought grimly, *this is nothing a gently bred woman should witness.*

"Make way!" He thrust his way past a gaggle of shopkeepers who had closed their stalls for the event, and elbowed aside a stout merchant in a velvet coat. The man started to protest but took one look at the Norseman's size and held his tongue.

Ranulf forced his way through the densely packed throng, but his progress went unnoticed by Morgana. Her eyes were fixed on the terrible tableau before her: the Guards marching past in their striped garb and burnished helmets; Robin in their midst in crimson satin slashed with cream, diamonds winking in the lace at his throat and the cockade on his jaunty cap; and in bleak contrast, the headsman waiting in his sinister black hood.

There was a look of insouciance on Robin's pale face and a murmur of approval rose from the throng. His reckless air and handsome features had won the crowd's sympathy, as they had earlier won him an army of traitors. At a word from the Captain of the Guard, Robin removed his cap and handed it to his servant. He stepped forward and as he did his eyes met Morgana's. The faintest of smiles touched his mouth and she saw that all the mockery was gone from his face. They both realized there would be no last-minute reprieve.

Morgana knew that every detail of this horrible day would be with her for many years to come, but she would not turn away. The blood of Celtic kings flowed through her veins and she had inherited both their pride and stubborn courage. The marriage had been a terrible failure, but she was Robin's lawful wife until his last breath, and something within her could not let him go to meet his end alone.

The drums kept up their ponderous beat as the priest stepped forward and gave absolution to the condemned man. In the past the traitor's axe had been exchanged for the sword for certain noble prisoners. No such courtesy would be extended to Robin. The axe glittered cruelly in the headsman's hands, drawing her eyes.

Morgana could never quite remember what happened next. Robin knelt and placed his head upon the block and the executioner swung his axe up high. The blade seemed poised for an endless moment, blazing with captured sunlight. Then it blurred into movement, swinging downward in a bright, glinting arc.

Before it reached its fatal destination she was seized by powerful arms and swung around bodily, her face pressed against an embroidered jacket that smelled faintly of sandalwood. She could not see but she could hear. The axe thunked solidly into the wooden block and a great murmur went up from the surrounding mob. Morgana felt dizzy and sick. Her knees buckled and for a moment she was grateful for the support of the arms that held her close.

When the faintness passed she tried to wrench away and her cheek was pressed even more tightly against the wide

chest. She was now aware of hard muscle and bone and of
fine metal mesh beneath the jacket. Again she tried to
wriggle free, but her struggles were subdued by effortless
and implacable strength. She knew the identity of her captor even before she saw his face: Ranulf the Dane. Damn his
eyes.

Suddenly she was let go, and she turned away only to be
spun around to face him again. He moved so quickly she
had no time to react and was caught off balance. Ranulf
pulled the hood of her cloak up to hide her face and put his
arm about her waist, then half carried, half pushed her toward the back of the crowd so that her feet barely touched
the ground. Her attempts at protest were stifled by his hard
palm against her mouth. Incensed and frightened, her sharp
teeth clamped down on the edge of his hand.

All Ranulf's sympathy vanished. "Hellcat!"

He set her down with her back against a wall and examined his hand. The skin was broken and bleeding. Morgana
pushed back her hood and stared at him defiantly. "How
dare you interfere! How dare you lay hands upon me!"

"Be still and you may yet come out of this escapade with
a whole skin, my Lady!" Before she could reply, Ranulf
picked her up and tossed her over his wide shoulder. The
wind was knocked out of her and she hung head down behind his back like a prize catch of fish.

When she caught her breath again she pummeled his back
with her fists, bruising her hands against the mail beneath
his tunic. "Let me go! Put me down at once!"

Ranulf ignored her and did not stop until he had her well
away from the crowd. Then he set her down abruptly. Morgana stood within a ring of six stern-faced horsemen. She
felt a sudden spurt of apprehension and her thoughts were
turned from Robin's tragedy. King Edward had not only
denied her request to attend the execution, he had expressly
forbidden it. She looked at the horsemen fearfully. Al-

though they wore no livery and carried no standard, they were obviously soldiers. King's Men, every one of them.

She recognized Desmond of Orkney holding the bridle of a black gelding, and wheeled on Ranulf. "What is this? You have no right . . ."

"Think again!"

Ranulf lifted her off her feet and tossed her up before the gelding's saddle, then swung up behind her. The others surrounded them in tight formation. They rode briskly through the streets and the Londoners, usually so inquisitive, took one look at their military posture and set faces, and stepped back. *King's Men,* they murmured and went about their own business.

Morgana felt the rigid steel of Ranulf's arm about her and knew she could expect no mercy from him. He had made very clear the fact that he did not wish her for a wife; but she was sure her rich estate and lands were quite another matter. Likely Edward would send her to a nunnery and confiscate her estates, bestowing them upon Sir Ranulf.

When they turned toward the river her unease grew and as they stopped at the one quiet place on the busy docks it coalesced into a cold knot of terror. In the commotion and shouting, the presence of one small woman would not be noted. Perhaps her body would be found when next the tide surged up the Thames from the sea. . . .

Ranulf dismounted, pulled Morgana down from her perch, and bundled her aboard a waiting barge. It was not a commercial barge but one built for pleasure, with sapphire velvet pillows and gold-trimmed privacy curtains rigged around the passenger area. As the bargeman poled the boat away from the dock Morgana looked around in panic.

Ranulf loomed over her, blotting out her view of the passing shoreline. "And now, my lady . . ." He put his hands on her shoulders, then slowly slid them inward until her white throat rested between his calloused palms. Trembling, she still caught at his hands and tried to pry them away.

"Will you hold still, woman?"

She twisted free. "And let you strangle me where I stand?"

Ranulf stood so close she felt the heat of his body. "God's Eyes, but the thought is tempting! You are the most troublesome wench it has been my ill fortune to meet."

The wind blew his gold hair away from his face and Morgana stared at him. She had never known eyes so blue or any that could hold so much menace. As his hand came up she shrank back involuntarily.

With one quick motion he ripped the ties of her cloak and tore it away, then tossed it over the side. It floated briefly on the gently lapping waters and sank like an autumn leaf. The wind ruffled her sea-green dress and Morgana drew herself up with dignity.

"How dare you, sir! That belonged to my maid-in-waiting."

"I shall give her another. Attend to me! We do not have much time. When we reach the palace you will follow my lead in all things: you will say that we have been out together on the river since morning, becoming ah . . . better acquainted."

Her voice dripped with disdain. "No one who saw us together in the banquet hall last evening will believe that."

"Will they not?" Ranulf's slow smile did not reach his eyes. Without warning he caught her in his arms and a moment later she was lying flat on her back atop the velvet cushions. Ranulf pinned her down with his length and pulled the ivory pins from her hair. The heavy rose-gold tresses fell about her shoulders and spilled over the deep blue velvet like ribbons of silk.

"Stop! What . . . oh!"

She struggled but he held her down ruthlessly. "Madam, you do not understand your danger. The King was greatly angered when your absence was noted. If you are to survive this reckless escapade, Edward must believe you have been in my company all morning and not on Tower Hill."

As Morgana digested his words Ranulf turned his attention to her dress. He grasped her bodice with one hand, intending only to rip the embroidered trim along the top, but did not take into account his own great strength. With a sound like a sigh the center panel parted from its seams all the way to the waist, baring Morgana's breasts. They were round and high, pink-crested and white as doves. Ranulf's breath came out with a rush.

Morgana recoiled, cheeks flaming, and lashed out at him with one hand, while she clutched her torn bodice with the other. "Beast! Lecherous barbarian!"

He rolled away, aghast, as a wave of heat and color flooded his face. He scarcely felt her nails as they raked bloody lines along his cheekbone. Ranulf was mortified; he had never been a ravisher of women. And he had never seen such naked loathing in a woman's face before.

"Lady Morgana...I did not..." His tongue knotted with chagrin.

He reached out to help her close the fabric and instead his fingers brushed against her bare skin. The resulting wave of desire robbed him of speech and action. He froze with his hand resting on the curve of her breast. She slapped his hand away and her bodice gaped open widely, revealing even more pearly flesh than the first time. By now Ranulf's face was as red as hers.

Near tears, Morgana crossed her arms over her breasts and backed farther beneath the canopy, looking around for anything she might use as a weapon. She was sure he meant to force himself upon her, and equally sure he would die for his insolence.

Ranulf stared after her, unmoving, his face flushed with embarrassment and the swift rush of desire that had caught him unprepared. She was very beautiful. He looked away hastily but the image of her half-naked body seemed imprinted on his eyes. Painfully aware of her enticing charms, he tried manfully to clear his thoughts as the barge moved in nearer the riverbank. They were almost at the palace, and a welcoming party waited at the landing. Danger sharpened his wits.

Pulling off his own cloak of blue silk lined in white, he handed it to her. "Put this on. Quickly."

Morgana wrapped it around herself, hiding the torn gown; but there was no way she could hide her disheveled hair or the red scratches on Ranulf's cheekbone. Even before the barge drew up to the landing she could hear the laughter and comments.

Ranulf drew her out from the canopied area. "Come. We must act the part of lovers, if you would escape the consequences of your actions."

Pulling her close again he put his arms about her as the barge bumped gently against the moorings. Without warning Ranulf bent his head and kissed her on the mouth. Morgana was rigid with anger and humiliation: first Edward had married her to a traitor, and now she would be wed to a savage who forced her to play the fool in public. And all because she was a woman. A man would not be treated like a parcel of goods to be bartered and sold off without any say in the matter!

Ranulf moved to help her alight but Morgana tried to step out alone, and tripped on the dragging hem of his cloak. He caught her up in his arms and stepped onto the landing. As he stood, still holding her in his arms, the small group in front of them parted before a tall, golden-blond figure.

Morgana gasped and felt Ranulf's arms tighten around her. *Edward.* There was an uncomfortable silence as the King surveyed them with hard, searching eyes. Morgana had never seen Edward's face so regal or so cold. She realized Ranulf had not exaggerated her peril: she felt the shadow of the Tower pass over them and shivered. The courtiers bowed and the King moved toward the barge, fixing the "lovers" with a baleful stare. "Well?"

Ranulf set Morgana down but stood so close to her their arms touched. "Your Majesty." She lowered her eyes and dropped into a curtsy, aware that she was blushing.

"My Liege." Ranulf bowed and she felt the tension of his body beside her. He put one hand on her shoulder. Morgana derived an unexpected measure of comfort from the contact. They must outface Edward's suspicions together or face his wrath. The knight gave the King a smile that seemed both conspiratorial and guileless.

Edward unbent slightly. "We trust you shared a pleasant day upon the water?"

"Yesterday Your Majesty advised me to seek to know the Lady Morgana better. Like a dutiful soldier, I have been out this morning following your orders."

There were titters of nervous laughter at his words, as the courtiers and servants awaited the outcome of the little drama. Edward examined the angry marks on his comrade's cheek, Morgana's disheveled state. His expression lightened.

"Sir Ranulf, you must school the lady in meekness and obedience, it seems, while she must teach you to be more gentle in your wooing." He smiled slyly. "A suitable task for the balmy summer nights ahead."

Edward moved apart from the spectators, taking Ranulf with him. Morgana stood alone in her embarrassment until Bronwen, her young Welsh lady-in-waiting, suddenly appeared at her side. "Come, my lady. Let us slip away into the garden and I will fix your hair."

Making their escape, the two women soon found a stone bench among the herb beds, where bits of green that would grow into spikes of fragrant lavender, parsley, borage, dittany and thyme grew. Morgana had no eye for the horticulture as Bronwen smoothed her tresses into a semblance of order. Suddenly Morgana turned. Her sharp ears had picked up the sounds of footsteps approaching, and a moment later the King's voice carried clearly on the still air.

"Aye, Ranulf, the Lady Morgana is a Welsh firebrand, no doubt, but there is many a man who would enjoy warming himself in her bed. If you are wise, you will get her with child and secure your new estates, even before your wedding day."

Morgana gestured to Bronwen for silence. She could see Ranulf now, through a parting in the hedges, as he answered. "My Liege, I have never pretended to be a wise man. I am only a warrior with a soldier's ways and little taste for the shackles of wedded life. I had liefer wait to claim my bride after the exchange of vows." He grinned and explored the deep scratches on his cheek with his index finger. "And after my wounds have healed."

Edward laughed and the two men disappeared around a corner of the hedge. Morgana jumped to her feet the moment they were out of earshot. "Aye," she muttered beneath her breath. "When your wounds have healed. And when all the fires of Hell freeze to stone!"

Wrapping Ranulf's cloak more tightly over her ruined gown she ran up the path toward the palace, seeking the sanctuary of her own chamber. Bronwen followed her mistress with concern. Lady Morgana was a good mistress and a true lady. But when she lost her temper anything was likely to happen.

Meanwhile, Ranulf was not faring well, either. He had just reiterated his request to go north with the patrols. "Although the company at Court pleases me well, I grow lazy through too much ease. A few months' exercise in the North Country would shake the cobwebs from me."

Edward sent him an impatient look. "You are ungrateful, Sir Ranulf, when We have already provided you with a pretty Welsh mare to ride. A few nights in the Lady Morgana's bed will cure you of this restlessness."

Ranulf fell silent and Edward was lost in his own thoughts. Suddenly he turned to his companion. "There is an abbey of nuns, Ranulf—a very profitable abbey, it might be said—which draws its revenues in part from the patronage of Lady Morgana's estates."

Tactfully, Ranulf bit back the fact that he had no interest in either Lady Morgana or her resources. If Edward thought to make a marriage between them more palatable with such tactics he was wasting his breath.

The King was unaware of his companion's train of thought. "The Archbishop is to bring a petition before Us this afternoon. Perhaps there might be an exchange of favors. What do you think?"

Ranulf shrugged his massive shoulders uneasily. "I do not know what abbeys or archbishops have to do with a simple knight like myself, my Liege."

"The Welsh are a volatile people and prone to rebellion. We have need of your strong arm there. We deem it best to settle the matter of your nuptials in a timely manner."

The faint uneasiness in Ranulf began to grow into something solid and tangible. Once Edward took the bit between his teeth, there was no stopping him. "Within the twelfth-month?"

The King clasped his arm around Ranulf and smiled brilliantly. "Aye, my old and trusted friend. Well within. If the Archbishop will waive the banns, you shall be a bridegroom before sundown!"

The wedding took place in the palace chapel, with the bride given away by the King himself and Bronwen as Morgana's attendant. Lord Hastings and Lord Rivers came as official witnesses and the Archbishop presided at the exchange of vows. The groom, dressed in a doublet of mulberry cut velvet lined with white satin, was handsome if somewhat grim-faced. The bride was ethereally beautiful, with a face as pale as her gown of cream-colored brocade.

The two stood stiffly, like wooden marionettes, while candles burned and incense filled the air. The Archbishop read from his book of holy offices.

"...gathered together here in the sight of God and man..."

While the priest murmured softly, Ranulf glanced at Morgana for the first time since entering the chapel, and sucked in his breath. *How beautiful she is!*

"...joined together in Holy Matrimony..."

Now that the inescapable moment was upon them, he found the idea less intimidating. If a man must marry, it was as well to marry a desirable woman—and dressed in her finest raiment, the Lady Morgana was certainly that. Embroidery of gold thread sprinkled with amethysts and rose-pink pearls adorned the deep hem and cuffs and the low-cut bodice of her gown.

Her hair was the only blaze of color, cascading from a pearl coronet in loose red-gold waves down her back, as befitted a bride. He had never seen such glorious hair. It would slip through a man's fingers like gossamer.

"...from this day forward..."

The Archbishop waited expectantly and Ranulf realized he had missed his cue. "I will," he responded automatically.

"...Lady Morgana, will you take this man..."

This is not happening, Morgana thought. *This is not real.* But it was. The idea of refusing to cooperate danced briefly through her brain, only to be dismissed. It was a luxury she could not allow herself. As Mistress of Castle Griffin she had not only privilege but responsibility. As a traitor's wife her estates might have been forfeit to the Crown, but Edward had been more than generous; if she angered him now, he could still confiscate her lands under the Bill of Attainder. No matter what her own personal feelings were, she could not betray her people so. She repeated the words as if they had nothing to do with herself.

"...until death us do part."

She found her hands swallowed up in Ranulf's as he placed a ring upon her finger. It was an enormous sapphire set with pearls and the weight of it brought her back to the present.

"Then by the power invested in me, I now pronounce you man and wife."

It was done. She looked up into the face of her husband—a quick, intelligent face with a wide mouth and keen, hawk-like lines. He smiled, then slowly raised her hand to his lips and kissed her fingertips. Something ran up her arm and sent chills along every nerve. Something that was half pleasurable and half alarming. And below the surface of her waking mind stirred a deep unease that there was danger to her in his smile, and in his fierce blue eyes.

Bronwen hovered over her mistress, an ivory-backed hairbrush in her hand. "Do sit still, my lady, for I cannot brush your hair while you fidget so."

Instead Morgana rose and angrily paced the width of her inner chamber. Candlelight sparked red and gold on her loosely flowing hair and sent her shadow moving across the paneled walls. "It is barbaric! To make me a widow and again a wife between sunrise and sunset!"

"Hush, my lady! They will be coming soon."

Morgana's eyes were drawn to the high bed set within a curtained alcove for the hundredth time in the past half hour. The sheets and hangings of pale green satin reflected the shifting light. She twisted her fingers together nervously. Tonight, for the first time in almost three years, she would not sleep alone. Beyond that fact she would not let her thoughts go.

Suddenly there was a commotion in the corridor outside, growing louder by the second. Laughter, singing and a few coarse shouts swelled as the revelers escorted the new bridegroom to his wife. Morgana held out her hand and stared at the ring Ranulf had placed there hours earlier. A few words, a ring, a wedding feast, and she was expected to reveal the most intimate secrets of her body to a man who was almost a stranger. She did not know if her new husband would be lusty or cool, indifferent or cruel. But from the intensity of the approaching merriment, she would soon discover this and more.

A trumpet blasted outside her barred door, dreadfully off-key. It was followed by hoots and shouts of laughter and several thumping knocks against the panel which rattled in its frame. "Open, for the bridegroom is come to claim his fair bride."

Morgana slipped off her robe. Her face was alabaster pale above her gown of sheer embroidered linen. Bronwen was almost as white as she handed her mistress up into the bed and arranged the coverlet modestly. Now the pounding was so loud it seemed the door might split in two. Bronwen caught Morgana's fingers in her own and set her face bravely. "Only say the word, my lady, and I shall tell them you are taken ill."

Morgana's expression softened. She leaned forward and kissed her companion on her cheek. "It will be all right, Bronwen. Let them in."

The girl curtsied and unbarred the door. When it swung back, she was almost pinned between it and the wall for her trouble. Torchlight sent the shadows fleeing as a rollicking crowd of musicians and courtiers poured into the room. They filled every corner and cranny with swirls of silk and satin and turbulent eddies of sound. Margot de Maurais laughed and smiled, although neither action was reflected in her hard, jealous eyes.

The uproar was deafening: snatches of song, crude jokes, drunken howls and cheers, chuckles and giggles and titters assaulted Morgana's ears. Even the usually staid Lady Southly was caught up in the madness of the celebration and romped into the chamber, her elegant coif knocked askew.

Trumpets blared again, this time on key, and the noise subsided to a more tolerable level. Blessed silence fell as the King made his entrance, one arm linked through the bridegroom's. Ranulf was garlanded with flowers, his eyes sparkling and his face flushed. He was speaking in answer to some sally of Edward's, but stopped in mid-sentence when he spied his bride.

Morgana was propped up in the bed, a pale green satin coverlet drawn up to her shoulders. With her light red hair tumbling about her shoulders in the torchlight, Ranulf thought she looked like a rose nestled in a bower. Perhaps this hasty marriage was not so bad an idea, after all. Her skin was creamy, her throat a graceful column. He suddenly wanted all the others to leave so he could touch that soft throat with his mouth, let his lips explore down it until they found her ripe-peaked breasts. All at once, he was dizzy, but whether with the wine Edward had pressed upon him or with desire he did not know.

Morgana saw the change on Ranulf's face, the dark color that stained his cheeks, and chills ran up the back of her neck and arms again. She did not understand her reaction and mistook the sensation for fear. She moved to the opposite edge of the bed as Ranulf was guided to it by his groomsmen. He disrobed quickly and slid beneath the covers, but not before the spectators had witnessed his readiness.

Morgana looked away, ignoring the laughter and jokes as the mattress dipped beneath Ranulf's weight. He was much taller and heavier than Robin. There would surely be other physical differences. Her mouth was dry and the palms of her hands were damp.

In what might have been minutes or hours, the ritual witnessing was conducted. Ranulf placed his bare leg next to hers and as their skin touched the spectators cheered.

And then, as suddenly as they had come, the merrymakers left to continue their carousing in the Great Hall. Bronwen barred the door with nervous fingers. After serving the newlyweds each a cup of spiced wine, she curtsied and retired to the small adjoining chamber.

Ranulf tossed his wine down quickly, then turned to look at Morgana. They were alone. In bed. Together. She *was* very beautiful. And that fiery red hair...

He reached out his hand. "Come here, wife."

Morgana set her silver goblet down on the candle stand but remained where she was. She remembered what it had been like to be pressed tightly to his mighty chest earlier, how it had felt to be held by his powerful arms as he had ridden with her to the barge. He was enormously strong, and she would be no match for him in a physical struggle.

He moved closer and his weight brought her sliding down the feather bed toward him. Ranulf's fingers combed through her silky hair, then wound the shining strands around his palm. With his other hand he cupped her face. Morgana's lips parted and her breathing was quick. Slowly he brought his mouth down upon hers and began pressing her inexorably back upon the pillows. His lips were firm and warm. Morgana's arms went about his neck automatically to keep from falling. Ranulf groaned and deepened the kiss so quickly she was overwhelmed with sensations.

He was ardent and experienced in the ways of pleasing a woman. She had not expected that. And she had been so long alone. His embrace was stirring and she felt a shiver of answering response. Heat grew deep inside her, spreading like honey along her veins. For a moment her resolution wavered.

She felt her body melting against his, yielding to his passion and her fear began to grow. His strength, his size, the very warmth of his body overwhelmed her. He was surrounding her, suffocating her. Ranulf's large hand loosened the ties of her gown and slipped inside, seeking and finding the softness of her breast. He cupped it in his hand while the tip of his thumb stroked her nipple erect and throbbing. Passion and need welled up within her, almost blotting out all thought. When he pushed aside her bodice and bent his head to touch her breast with his open mouth, Morgana gasped and jerked away.

While surprise held him immobile she scrambled off the bed. Ranulf threw the sheets back and sprang out to reclaim her, disregarding his nakedness. "What nonsense is this, woman?" he roared.

She quivered before his blaze of anger and surprise and turned her eyes from the sight of his magnificent, battle-scarred body. Her voice came out huskily, but she spoke with a pretense of calmness. "My lord, I know it is your right to do as you will with me, but . . . but . . . I was another man's wife only this morning."

She threw herself down upon her knees before him, her bright hair cascading over her body like a shimmering cloak.

"Please, my lord . . . I have not even been given time to mourn. To pray. I beg of you, give me this one night to spend in prayer for Robin's soul and surely God will bless you all your days. Only until daybreak, my lord!"

She glanced upward at him. There were tears darkening her aquamarine eyes, but they did not fall. They rested upon her lashes like dewdrops, sparkling in the candlelight. Ranulf struggled with his desire for her. He had always been able to resist convenient floods of tears; it was Morgana's restraint that swayed him. He wanted her, no doubt of that. But what she said was true. Surely it was not too much to ask, and it was already well past midnight.

Ranulf grabbed up his discarded garments. He could bide a few more hours while she made her prayers. She would never be able to accuse him of dragging her from her late husband's grave straight to his own bed.

"Very well. Call your maid to you. I will spend the night on her cot, and she may keep vigil here beside you."

A short time later, Ranulf lay upon the narrow bed in Bronwen's small chamber, trying to quench the fires of his arousal by warming himself with the glow of his good deed. It was small comfort. The ache in his loins, as he envisioned Morgana's naked body in his arms, was a sweet torment at first and then an agony of unfulfilled passion. He thought of her shimmering hair, her full mouth, her breasts so white and tender. He wanted to touch her, to know the mysteries of her womanly body, to feel her beneath him as he finally claimed her.

Despite his discomfort the wine began to take effect. Ranulf felt his tension ease, but only after forcing Morgana from his mind by going over military drills in his head. His thoughts grew hazy and at last he slept.

When he awoke it was to sunlight spilling across his face from the uncurtained window. For a moment he did not recognize his surroundings, but then memory came seeping back. His head pounded and his tongue was a piece of wet wool. Bad wine, no doubt. Throwing back the sheet, Ranulf staggered to the window and looked out. It was long past dawn.

Despite his throbbing head he was eager to settle his unfinished business with his new bride. Even the most saintly woman must be prayed out by now! There were no sounds from within the sleeping chamber. He knocked twice and got no answer. Opening the door he stepped into the dim room.

The curtains were drawn over the windows, the bed hangings still closed against the treacherous night breezes. An emerald silk robe was folded across the back of a wooden settle and an ivory brush and pomade jars stood upon the flat top of a carved wooden chest. All seemed as it should be, yet his warrior's instincts were alert.

He strode to the bed, then paused only a moment as he spied the outline of a figure beneath the coverlet. "What, a slug-a-bed? And all this while I thought you still in prayer. Lady wife, this is no way to greet the first morning of our wedded life, unless I join you beneath the covers."

The figure did not stir. Realization hit him. Ranulf grasped the covers and pulled them free with a flick of his powerful wrists. A heap of clothing, artfully arranged to simulate a sleeping form, met his gaze. He strode to the window and threw back the curtains. The casement was open and a telltale length of twisted cloth trailed down to the narrow balcony below. His beautiful bride, whom he had imagined on her knees in tearful prayer, had fled rather than share his bed.

With an ache in his loins and something close to murder in his heart, Ranulf cursed fluently in every language he knew.

Chapter Three

"Make way! Make way!"

A double column of twelve armed men rattled down the west road with the speed and single-mindedness of a pack of wolves. The walls of London were far behind the tireless riders, as were half a dozen villages and market towns. The land lay open and green before them and Ranulf's mighty black gelding led the way, impelled by his master's urgency. Desmond of Orkney spurred his own gray until he finally caught up with his cousin.

"God's Teeth, Ranulf, slacken your pace. The horses will be blown by midday—if they don't drop in their tracks first."

Ranulf frowned, eyes keen upon the road ahead, but eased his horse to a more judicious canter. "I mean to catch up with her as soon as may be. The fewer who know of this, the better for all."

"Two women alone will be easy to spot, and such frail creatures cannot ride as hard as we." Desmond grinned in mischief. "Fear not, Ranulf. Before sunset you shall have your sweet wife back in your arms."

"Rather a nest of hornets, than that Welsh she-cat!"

Then Ranulf was off again, riding like the devil on All Hallows' Eve, and Desmond had only himself to blame for it. He dropped back to the rest of the retinue. "Be easy.

He'll have to wait at the tollgate and stop to water his mount at the Four Plumes. We'll not be far behind.''

Several of the men-at-arms nodded. Well did they know Ranulf's temper, which fortunately always died away as quickly as it sprang to life. Desmond was the opposite: easygoing and slow to burn, but when once the mind beneath the fiery hair ignited, he was a madman. By God's Grace, this happened only rarely. And whatever the two cousins' faults, their men would follow them willingly into the jaws of hell, especially Perry, Ranulf's young, flaxen-haired squire.

In the distance, Ranulf rode out his fury—thundering westward in a way that made sensible men jump to the side into the hedgerows, and those less prudent shake their fists and mutter curses beneath their breath. It was only the women, young and old, maid and grandmother, who stopped to watch, mouths open and eyes dazzled; and to carry home to their private dreams the vision of a sun-bronzed knight riding past like an avenging angel, shimmering gold and blue and silver in the morning light.

Ranulf scarcely heeded them at all, except to avoid accident or injury. In his mind was an image of Morgana, all rose and white in among the pale green satin sheets, and he beguiled the miles with cheerful thoughts of strangling her with his bare hands. His long fingers curled around the bridle as if it were her slim swan's neck. But despite these cherished thoughts of murder in his heart, he began to relax, feeling the wind against his face, whipping his golden hair and blue cloak out behind him.

He was in the open country, riding away from the stifling etiquette and simmering intrigues of the court, shaking off the cobwebs of boredom and forced inactivity. His own man. Unfettered. Free.

He was almost grateful to Morgana.

Galloping over a gentle rise he saw the dark line of hills to the west. The hills toward which the Lady Morgana was surely headed. For where else could she be fleeing, but to her own lands and Castle Griffin along the Welsh shore? He smiled tightly. Well, she was in for a great surprise when he came upon her, for she would not travel there alone but in his company. He had covered her disappearance and gone to the King with a report of an uprising near Castle Griffin, requesting most urgently that the newlyweds be allowed to set out for the Welsh border with all due haste.

Edward had graciously given his permission, and a large party had set out, including two women inside a painted litter. But once past the walls of London the "women" had thrown off their outer garments to reveal Perry and one of the other, slighter built soldiers, both ill-pleased with the indignity of their impersonations in feminine disguise. The ruse had succeeded, and no one within the palace guessed that the Lady Morgana and her maid-in-waiting had slipped out alone during the night watch.

And, thought Ranulf, *no one would ever know. But Morgana will learn, to her eternal regret, that it is not wise to cross swords with her avowed husband.*

His blue eyes glittered with anger and injured male pride, but slowly his mouth curved up in the beginning of a smile. Once he caught up with Morgana she would grow used to his company, for she would find him at her side waking and sleeping until they arrived at the castle. And then—then it would be he who called the tune and she who danced to the piper.

His most urgent deed as Lord of Castle Griffin would be to bed his reluctant wife. Edward had the right of it. The sooner she was with child, the sooner his own position would be consolidated, and with a child to occupy her time she would be less likely to chafe and mope. He imagined a brood of strong-limbed sons and perhaps a few daughters with rose-gold hair. Yes, he must take this wife to bed and teach her who was master.

Ranulf's smile grew wide. He was looking forward to it with great pleasure, and this time he would not be swayed by tears and falsehoods. It would be much easier to keep an eye on his fractious bride within the walls of Castle Griffin than among the courts and corridors of the King's palaces or the narrow winding streets of London. Far easier within the confines of the curtain wall to teach Morgana her wifely duties—as he would, by All That Was Holy! In a happier frame of mind, he reined his horse's pace to a brisk trot and crested the next hill.

The road wound down to a small village with a good-sized inn on the outskirts. Four white plumes were painted on the wooden sign hanging over the door. Ranulf smiled his satisfaction. This was the only place she could have stopped for rest and refreshments. He rode into the innyard expectantly. The air was redolent of horses and hay, and the pungent scents of good wine and strong ale blended with the aroma of a roasting joint wafting from the open kitchen door. Ranulf's mouth watered. A good hot meal would be welcome, but he could not tarry while it cooked. He nudged his horse toward the stables at the back.

The yard was empty and silent except for the clatter of pans from the kitchen. A boy in a tunic of brown homespun came running out to catch Ranulf's bridle, but there were no other signs of life. No satin-curtained litter, no ladies' palfreys and grooms tending to them. And no errant wife.

Ranulf swung down from the saddle. "Lad, have you seen aught of two ladies passing through here this morning?"

The boy only stood and gazed at Ranulf and his splendid garments wonderingly. The question was repeated with no other response.

Ranulf waited, brows drawn together and arms akimbo. "Are you deaf, lad?"

"Aye. That 'e is, good sir."

A knotted old woman had entered the courtyard from a small gate, a square of dull cloth over her shoulders for a shawl and a covered wicker hamper on her arm. She pointed at the boy with an arthritic finger.

"The Good Lord in 'is wisdom left out somat when 'e put poor Nolly together. But the lad's quick-witted and knows what the 'orses like, for all 'e was born deaf and mute."

Ranulf flushed. He dipped in his purse and found a small coin. He tossed it to the stable boy, who caught the piece in one grubby hand and stared at it, goggle-eyed. Ranulf turned to the woman and bowed his head courteously.

"Forgive my ignorance, good wife. I came here seeking two young ladies of good birth, who are on their way to the Welsh border."

The woman set her hamper down and appraised him. There was something, almost an inner light when she focused on his face, and he thought she was seeing through— or perhaps *beyond* him.

Suddenly she chuckled. "Runaways, eh, Sir Knight? Sisters? Or perhaps you 'ave ill-treated yer wife, and she 'as fled to 'er lover?"

His face flamed. Her impertinence angered him, but not nearly as much as her implications. A man would challenge another man for such insult, but Ranulf set his square jaw and swallowed his outraged dignity. A knight did not bring forth his anger on women or the defenseless.

"My business is my own. And I am not a man to abuse any woman, especially one under my own protection."

The crone nodded. "Ah, I was mistaken. For I did think I saw murder in yer eyes."

Ranulf started, caught off guard, but the woman did not seem to notice. "Come inside, Sir Knight, and ease your parched throat with some of our good ale. 'Tis not what ye're used to, no doubt, but 'twill quench yer thirst."

Still chuckling, she entered the inn, leaving him standing there, red-faced and again so furious with Morgana he could feel his pulse beating at his throat and temples. That she should put him in such an awkward position, expose him to such insolence, such malign misinterpretation! By God, when he got his hands on her...!

But there was no use cutting off his nose to spite his face. He *was* thirsty, after all. Ranulf strode across the innyard and entered the taproom. The ceiling was low, the once-whitewashed spaces between the big beams long blackened with soot. Although the day was growing warm, it was quite cool inside and the fire burning cheerily in the massive hearth warded off the damp of the mud-plastered walls.

Ranulf found himself alone, but almost immediately a buxom serving girl came out from the region of the kitchen carrying a tray with a mug of ale, a chunk of cheese and a fragrant loaf of fresh bread. Her blue eyes were bold and merry as she approached him, and filled with such blatant admiration that Ranulf's bruised pride was soothed. Now, he thought, here was a wench to meet a man on his own terms: she'd not run away from her lawful husband on their wedding night.

The girl set the tray down on a tough trestle table and wiped her reddened hands on her clean apron. "Sit yerself down, my lord, and 'ave at it. The way ya come gallumping down t' road ye'll have need of some food in ye."

He sat on a three-legged stool and accepted the mug from her, then raised it for a healthy swallow. It was wonderful ale, rich and full-bodied. In other circumstances he would have lingered over several tankards, but if he meant to catch Morgana soon he dared not tarry too long. Tearing off a piece of the warm bread, Ranulf attempted an encouraging smile.

"I am in search of two ladies, traveling alone and in haste." He stretched his long leg out so the coins in his leather purse chinked loudly. "And there is a reward for any who can provide me with information."

The wench shook her head sadly. "No ladies come by 'ere today, sir. None, at all."

Ranulf frowned. Could he have been wrong after all? Could Morgana be heading somewhere other than her own estates? Or, a dark voice whispered in his head, could she indeed be fleeing to the arms of a lover? A surge of something welled up in his chest. He had never been prone to envy or jealousy and did not recognize the feelings now. Instead he mistook them for anger.

He brought out a handful of silver and examined the play of firelight on it idly. "That is too bad. I would have paid dearly for what I want to hear."

The girl drew in her breath. His wide palm held a year's worth of her hard-won wages. Enough for her dowry, enough so she could marry Alwyn, the miller's handsome son, and give up this drudgery. For a moment she was tempted to lie, but her conscience—and her awe of this giant of a knight—would not let her. Ranulf saw the flicker in her eyes. She knew something, if only he could pry it out of her. Fear might work where bribery would not. He gave her a scowl that would have sent his soldiers scurrying for cover.

"I will deal harshly with any who cross me in this matter. Tell me what you know."

The girl was frightened now. "Nay, sir. I do wish as I 'ad seen 'em. Naught come by 'ere the morning but two young lads. Pale as death they were. Servants or 'prentices, I misdoubt, running from their master."

Ranulf rose so abruptly the stool tipped over backwards. "These lads. Did one of them have hair like a firebrand?"

"Aye, my lord." She crossed herself quickly and backed away. How could he know such a thing, unless he be in league with the Horned Man? She had a mind to hold her tongue until the handsome knight smiled and scattered a few silver pieces on the table carelessly.

"How were they mounted and where were they headed?"

"On a brindle mare and a gray, sir. 'Eading east they was, and so they told me more times than one.''

"East!" He laughed aloud. "How long ago?"

"Not longer than it takes to collect 'en's eggs and bring a pot of water to boil to cook 'em."

Ranulf threw another coin on the trestle. Before the wench could catch her breath he had vanished into the stable yard, leaving her to speculate that he might be an angel in disguise rather than one of the devil's own couriers.

Out in the glare of sunlight Ranulf was still laughing. She was clever, this wife of his, disguising herself and leaving false trails with the tavern wench. But Morgana would soon discover he was more clever than she. He was looking forward to the moment with great pleasure.

He was in his saddle and riding beneath the archway into the road when Desmond and his crew arrived at a fast trot. Desmond's stomach rumbled at the smell of fresh bread and he thirsted mightily for a tankard, and Perry exchanged bold and interested looks with the tavern girl, but it was not to be. Ranulf wheeled out before them, waving them onward.

"They are but a few miles ahead. We shall catch up with them first, and feast later." Ranulf rode off in a cloud of dust. The chase was on, the quarry near and his blood was up. He hadn't felt so alive in months.

Perry, after one mournful glance at the inviting inn and the more inviting wench, spurred his horse and followed.

"Oh, my lady, I do not think the mare can carry me much farther."

Bronwen, dressed unwillingly in boys' garments, tried to urge her mount forward. It obeyed, but sluggishly.

Morgana bit her lower lip. "Then we shall have to leave her behind and ride double upon mine."

Bronwen was near tears. "But your steed cannot carry us both. Not for long."

"Then we shall have to go afoot," Morgana snapped. Instantly she was sorry for her burst of temper, but the strain was wearing on her. They had made a good start, and left false trails all along the way; still she could sense Ranulf somewhere on the road behind her, feel his breath almost upon her shoulder.

"Oh, my lady," Bronwen said again, hoarsely. "What if we should be discovered to be women before we reach the border? We would surely die of shame."

"Nonsense. You are made of sterner stuff than that!" Morgana fingered the hilt of the dagger stuck crosswise in her belt. Unlike her young lady-in-waiting, she felt neither shame nor embarrassment at the tunic and hose she wore. She had paid a pretty penny for the garments, although they were patched and mended in a dozen places and much too large. Still, their very bagginess was a blessing, hiding the feminine contours of her body well. Best of all, they harbored neither fleas nor lice, and where two women alone could not go unmolested, two lads could venture unremarked.

She had no doubt they would reach the sanctuary of her estates in safety, although her muscles and bones already ached with the hard riding. Court life had softened her in a few scant weeks, but she was country bred and knew she would toughen soon. Meanwhile, she had a purse of gold and silver coins hidden beneath her tunic to ease their way, and trusted to God and her own quick wits to see them home without undue difficulty.

Morgana felt that things were progressing as planned, and was rather pleased with herself. For all her womanly attributes, she had grown up wishing she were a boy, free to seek adventure away from the restricted sphere of a woman's life. Now, unexpectedly, her wish had been granted. With Bronwen at her side she had led the way from the postern gate at cock crow, while the light was pearly gray upon the cobbles and the Thames a misty sheet of silver. The road ahead was long and dangerous, but Castle Griffin lay at the end, and once inside her fortress with her own men-at-arms to protect her she could defy any attempt to drag her back to London. Even the King's.

They had entered a verdant valley an hour before and gone through a small woods, but now the sun was high overhead in a burnished summer sky and her stomach grumbled its discontent. The bread and cheese they had obtained at the Four Plumes was long gone, but just past a fork in the road she spied a farmstead atop a hill in the distance. The past years had been prosperous for England, and the farm, with its new thatched roof and freshly whitewashed walls, showed that it had shared in nature's bounty. Pigs rooted contentedly in their pen and a plump cow grazed the lush grasses. Thoughts of spicy sausage, rafters of crisp bacon and pots of fresh cream lured Morgana on. She turned to Bronwen.

"If there were any in pursuit of us we have surely lost them by now. Let us proceed to that farm for food and rest."

As they topped the hill, Morgana looked back over her shoulder. At the far end of the wide valley feathers of dust rose up through the trees. Horsemen, riding hard and fast. She could not see them but she knew who they were.

A party of armed men and Ranulf. Her husband.

There would be no rest or supper for them now. She struck the rump of Bronwen's mount with the flat of her hand, startling it into a gallop, then spurred her own horse on.

Considerably less than an hour later Ranulf and his party arrived at the farmstead. The tracks of horses mingled, both coming and going down the side fork of the road leading to it, and at first he thought they were from the same two beasts. Close examination of the hoofprints showed that the shoe of one of the animals coming toward them had a small but distinct nick. He straightened up. "I knew they would tire and take refuge somewhere along the way. Women are frail creatures, and fond of their comforts."

Ranulf smiled and Desmond felt a chill run up his back, for it was the same smile his cousin wore when he had the enemy hopelessly cornered. Despite his loyalties and the code of man-to-man, Desmond could almost pity the reluctant bride. Still, if one man's wife ran away and was not brought back, who was to say that the same idea might not take hold of other wives, and then there would be the devil to pay.

They rode up to the farmhouse and one of the men dismounted to bang his fist upon the closed door. A straw-headed woman came out, rosy-cheeked and plump, as befitted the wife of a successful man. She waved her arms and shook her fist in the soldier's affronted face.

"Mind the sow, now! Mind the shoats!"

Piglets snuffled and snorted at the man's boot and he hefted one away deftly with his toe. The woman shrieked and scolded and all hell broke loose. A fat pink sow came snorting out from behind the house, intent on defending her young, the shoats scattered and squealed and the horses stamped and sidled. Desmond's curses added to the noise, but whether directed at the woman, the pigs or the soldier, none could tell. Then Ranulf moved forward, his steed quiet and controlled. He raised his hand and the melee ceased. Even the sow backed off.

"If there is any harm to the shoat you will be justly recompensed. We come seeking two—" Ranulf covered his brief pause "—two lads, who have run away from their apprenticed master. And we will pay for information concerning their whereabouts."

The woman's eyes lit. "Two lads, you say? Why only this noon two lads came here asking to buy their supper. I fed them well—lamb and turnip stew, salt bread and apple tartlets with cream—and sent them on their way with full bellies not many moments past. And such good lads they did seem.''

Ranulf threw her a coin. ''Which way did they ride, good wife, and how long ago?''

She caught the coin greedily. ''The west road, to be sure, on a dun mare and a brindle gelding. And no longer since than it takes me to milk my spotted cow.''

Desmond rolled his eyes. He had no inkling of how long it took to milk a cow, spotted or otherwise. But Ranulf did. The Knight turned to his men with a hard blue glitter in his eyes. ''Ride on. They are almost in our hands.''

With only a brief regret for the lamb stew with turnips and the apple tartlets that might have been theirs, Desmond and the men-at-arms wheeled into position behind their leader and followed him back to the fork in the road. There was no hurry now. The fugitives were just ahead. And perhaps they could stop by the farmhouse on the way back to London.

The farmer's wife watched them leave in great satisfaction. Such hair-raising tales as those two lads had told her of doings in the house from which they had escaped. Poor boys! She was not one to interfere between a man and his bond servants, but evil she would not put up with in any shape or form. And the master, the tall golden-haired knight, for all he looked so noble, was the worst of all according to the redheaded lad.

Meanwhile, Ranulf and Desmond continued after the fugitives with their party. Somewhere around the next bend or in the next valley they would come upon their quarry. Then matters would become very interesting. One of the soldiers, John Bowman, laughed to a companion as they came to the fork.

''The farmer's wife squealed louder than her sow. A body would have thought I'd kicked her.'' He grumbled. ''Such a fuss over a wee pig.''

Ranulf heard and turned in the saddle. '' 'Tis not merely a pig, but likely their food for the long winter ahead. They do not forget the famine years." His tone was even and low, but the soldier was not deceived. He had been rebuked and he accepted it. He would not make the same mistake again.

Ranulf led them past fields and meadows, streams and woods at a steady but less frenetic pace. There was no sign of Morgana and her maid, but they would come upon them at the next bend in the road. Or the one after. Now that victory was at hand and his anger damped, he had time to analyze the matter. His pride was injured. He was certain Morgana looked down upon him because his status was not equal to hers.

That rankled deep. He was not a vain man but he knew his own worth in the eyes of a woman as well as the eyes of the world. True, he had neither title nor fortune, but he did have a strong right arm and the ability to command. His lineage was excellent, for the blood of Norse princes and Irish chieftains had fertilized his family tree. His body was vigorous and healthy, with no more scars than many other warriors carried. His teeth were white and sound. He kept himself and his clothing clean. Other women found him pleasing. But not his wife. He ground those strong white teeth.

He had not wanted a wife. This wife, in particular. A traitor's widow with estates in troublesome Wales, home of rebellious Celts like his own fractious, fighting kinsmen. But somewhere between the wedding vows and the bedding ceremony he had become a bit more reconciled to his fate. He was, at heart, a godly man and would have liked to believe it was during the solemn exchange of vows. Honesty compelled him to acknowledge it was more likely that first moment in the chapel when he had wanted to touch her hair and let the shining locks flow through his fingers like satin streamers. Or when he had seen her lying against the silken sheets of their marriage bed, with her hair spilling around her like flame.

What magic there was in her glowing tresses and the curve of her soft white throat and coral-tipped breasts! She was a beautiful woman and she was his wife. He had been filled not only with lust but with a sense of pride. And then the silly chit had run away.

He did not stop to consider that Morgana had pride of her own. Still rankling under the humiliation of a runaway bride, they entered the market town of Little Nodding. The upper stories of the half-timbered buildings hung over the streets, which were narrow and cobbled. They had just passed the central square, ignoring the curious eyes of the townsfolk when he spied a dun mare and a brindle gelding, their slight riders swathed in their brown homespun cloaks despite the warmth of the day.

"Well, Lady Morgana," Ranulf said beneath his breath, "the time has come at last. Now you shall learn it is the cock who rules the roost and not the hen."

He nudged his horse and clattered over the cobbles beneath the overhanging second stories after his quarry. His speed saved him from the indignity that caught Desmond and one of the men-at-arms, as a housemaid emptied a chamber pot from the apartments above the chandler's shop, spattering them liberally.

"By St. George, look what you are about you miserable wench!" Desmond cried out. The maid gave him a saucy look and disappeared inside. Hungry, angry and in need of a washing, they nevertheless rode after their leader like the good soldiers they were.

There was even some excitement to these last seconds of the chase. What would Sir Ranulf do? Would he beat his wife? Would he bind her hand and foot and carry her back to London like so much baggage? Would he repudiate their vows and leave her at some nearby nunnery while he applied for an annulment?

Ranulf was fifty yards ahead when he caught up with the truants. Both riders were huddled in their garments, the tops of the drab cloaks pulled low over their faces like demure pilgrims. Still, a lock of red hair was visible on the nearer one. Ranulf grabbed the reins of that rider's horse and brought the beast to a stumbling halt by sheer force.

"Why do you hide inside your robe, lady, on such a beautiful day? You must share your beauty with the world."

He reached out his hand and tore the cloak away—to reveal the frightened face of a freckled, red-haired farm boy.

Ranulf's men joined them in a jingle of harness and spurs. Desmond pulled off the cloak of the second cowering figure. A boy of not more than ten, though large for his age, and clearly a brother to the first.

Desmond was confused by the evidence of his eyes. His first thoughts were of magic arts and shape changers, and he hurriedly made a sign to ward off the evil eye. "What witchery is this?"

Ranulf, however, knew exactly what had happened. It had taken him less than a split second to realize he had been duped, and how. Morgana and her companion were far ahead now on the other fork of the road leading away from the farmhouse, while they had been following this false trail of her design.

The older lad saw the sparks in the golden knight's eyes. "Please, my lord, the lady said 'twas only a jest and vowed you would do us no harm!"

Releasing the boy, Ranulf shook his fist at the bright blue sky. "By God and all the Saints in heaven," he roared, "was ever a man cursed with such a troublesome wife?"

Chapter Four

How much farther must we go tonight, my lady?" Bronwen asked again.

"Only until we find shelter." Morgana's voice was patient, though her soul chafed, for Bronwen had asked the question with maddening regularity for the past two hours. True, the maid had not only come with her mistress voluntarily, she had actually insisted, pledging her undying loyalty. But that was before mile upon hot, dusty mile of rutted road and tortuous track. Now the road led them through wild, rock-strewn country as barren of shelter as it was of comfort. Even Morgana was wilting under the anxiety and effort.

She suggested leaving Bronwen with some kindly farmer's wife until she could send a more proper escort to take her to Wales, but the girl would not hear of it. Although only seven years separated them in age, she had been under Morgana's wardship for most of that time and would have walked through fire for her.

By nightfall, Bronwen was too dispirited to talk, Morgana too tired and hungry to want anything but a bit of supper and a place to lay her aching head. She had given the last of her bread and cheese to her maid, as much to quiet her as to nourish her stomach. Now they were both shivering with cold, for the air had chilled and the rain, threat-

ening for the past hour, was making good its promise. Sheets
of water, gray as lead, fell from the murky sky.

Skirting the foot of a truncated hill, they saw a glimmer
of welcome lights in the distance. An inn or hostelry of some
sort. They rejoiced at the sight like pilgrims arriving in Je-
rusalem, and urged their horses on with rekindled enthusiasm. The place was simple, unadorned and none too clean,
but the wiry landlord greeted them fulsomely. Yes, there was
room for the night, and the remains of simmered hare with
onions and barley if the young lads felt peckish. Surely,
Morgana thought, manna in the desert could not have been
more savory—or more welcome.

They ate in the kitchen while a sleepy scullery maid and
kitchen boy cleaned the spit and wiped the wooden tankards inside and out with a discolored cloth that had once
been white. Although the innkeeper's wife had changed her
initial tune when she saw the copper and silver from Morgana's purse, she had still deemed two streak-faced boys as
not fit for the public room and its occupants: two well-to-do
merchants, a priest of the preaching order and a clerk.

The woman bustled in as Morgana mopped up the last bit
of gravy with her crust of coarse-grained bread. "One of
you may share a bed with the merchants and the other will
have to stay the night in the kitchen with Audre and Hayes.
You may place your pallet under or upon the table, it is all
one to me."

Morgana was taken aback. "We will share a room."

"There is only one to share, and several travelers to share
it with."

"Then, with your permission, we shall both sleep here
instead."

"Oh," the woman bristled, "and leave two healthy young
men alone here with Audre and only that poor half-wit to
guard her virtue? No, that you shall not!"

Morgana caught the pleading in Bronwen's eye. "You
may stay here by the kitchen fire. I shall go upstairs." She

stilled her maid's protest with a gentle touch on her sleeve. She could fend for herself among the others, but Bronwen would be safer here. The half-wit was gentle and as sleepy as Audre. Bronwen would come to no harm with them. Feigning a nonchalance she did not feel, Morgana followed the woman up the crooked stairs to the room built under the slanting eaves.

The sleeping chambers were spartan. One low-pitched room with two large straw mattresses, a place for pallets on the floor, and two homely chamber pots; and to the side a dark storage area, ventilated by a tiny window, which could accommodate one small body in a pinch.

Three weary servants belonging to the merchants were rolled up in their blankets in the far corner. The two merchants and the clerk each claimed their own mattresses but were shouted down by the others. The priest brought out his breviary and read his prayers in a low undertone, ignoring the uproar. By rules governing such matters he was entitled to have one mattress to himself and the others might settle it how they chose.

The innkeeper stated his opinion that the clerk and the merchant should share a mattress, as they were closest in station to one another. The stout merchant shook his rich robes of russet and green and declared his nose told him the clerks had not washed in many a week. The two men argued that their superior education gave them precedence over a mere "successful shopkeeper."

After much talk, the priest put away his book and stepped deftly in. "Come, brothers, such wrangling is unseemly and no doubt you are all weary from your travels." He inclined his head to the wealthy merchant. "If you, sir, will deign to share a mattress with me, I will gladly give up my right to sleep alone in the interests of harmony and brotherly love." The wealthy merchant agreed to share one of the mattresses with the dulcet-toned preacher, leaving the clerk and the other merchant to settle their own problems.

Morgana had no patience with such folly. She had already claimed the storage area for herself. It was drafty but she had her warm cloak, now dry from the heat of the kitchen fire, and she was grateful for the semblance of privacy. Without further ado she curled up on the plank floor and listened to the rain pelting the heavy layers of thatch that covered the roof. Soon the only sound was the gentle snoring of the clerk and the mumbled prayers of the kneeling priest.

It did not take long for the travelers to fall into a sound sleep, lulled by the effects of ale and full stomachs. Only Morgana lay awake. She wondered what was happening at Court. The King was surely in great anger against her. He might banish her from Court, which was just as well. She preferred exile in her own land to an idle life amid the intrigues and assignations. She wondered what Margot de Maurais was thinking. Margot had set many a snare for the bold Sir Ranulf, if current gossip was well-founded. Whether he had ever been caught in them was a matter of much speculation.

Now Morgana had something else to tease her mind while the rain pattered against the small, thick panes. Perhaps Ranulf would disclaim her as his wife and seek an annulment. Abandonment was certainly grounds for one. Or perhaps he had not even left to bring her back in disgrace, and instead was dallying with the buxom half-French Margot. Then her worries would be over. She dwelt on this a while and finally rejected it.

At the moment she would have given every coin in her purse for a good night's rest, but although her body was fatigued her brain was running about in circles. She had laid down a dozen false trails, changed horses and garments, dirtied her face and even adopted a squint and a country accent. It was no use.

No matter how clever she had been, anticipating the outcome of each move like a player with a chessboard, it would all be for naught. She could feel it in her bones, in the gooseflesh that walked up and down her spine, the hair that prickled at her nape. Nearer and nearer her nemesis came, a hoofbeat for each heartbeat that marked the passing seconds. She did not know how she could be so sure. But she was.

Time moved slowly. Once she heard stealthy footsteps on the other side of the barrier and the creak of the door being opened. At last she fell into the deep sleep of physical exhaustion. It was well past midnight when the sound of new arrivals broke the peace. Above the steady drizzle of rain, hooves stamped in the mud of the yard, horses blew and snorted, metal clanked upon metal. Voices spoke, low but commanding. Morgana's insides twisted. Below stairs, a bolt was withdrawn and the door opened with a creak of leather hinges. Next came a tramping of boots upon the wooden staircase. The door burst inward.

"Now we have you!" Desmond entered first. Morgana saw no sign of Ranulf. Flickering torchlight filled the room, sending the shadows scurrying back and forth. The sleepers awoke to instant confusion. A servant grasped his dagger, intending to defend himself and his master, if need be— until he saw the drawn sword in Desmond's hand. The clerk threw off his quilt and arranged his sleep-tangled garments.

"The world has come to a pretty pass when an honest man cannot bide the night without suffering the molestation of strangers and ruffians."

"Aye," his bedmate said, sitting up and rubbing the sleep from his eyes. "Whatever your business is, be about it quickly, for dawn will come all too soon."

Morgana watched them through a chink in the planks, trying to control her trembling. Desmond ignored the man's grumbled complaints and glanced briefly at the three servants shaking in their stockinged feet. He walked to the bundled hump upon the other mattress. He poked it with the tip of his sword.

"I think we have found our quarry."

He gestured to a man-at-arms. The soldier went to the bed and yanked the comforters and quilts from the straw-stuffed mattress. The tall merchant lay unmoving like a tiltyard mannikin tossed down upon the bed. But it was dark glistening blood, not straw, spilled from the gaping cut in his throat. Blood was everywhere, oozing down from the stained quilts to sticky puddles on the floor.

"What evil doings are these?"

Morgana felt ill. The merchant was dead, slaughtered, while she slept a few feet away.

"Murder most foul!" someone cried. "And where is the good priest? He has been murdered also!"

It was immediately discovered that the priest was gone. His servant was also missing, along with the slain merchant's heavy purse and the rings that had decked his fingers. Everyone realized it at the same time, and a babble of overlapping stories assaulted Desmond's ears.

"Not a priest then," he said, "but a thief and murderer posing as a man of the cloth. You are lucky the lot of you were not found with your throats cut, as well!"

The shouting broke out again, accented by the wails and weeping of the slain merchant's servant. Morgana remembered the soft footsteps she had heard, the creaking door. For a moment she was paralyzed by fear, horrified at the terrible turn of events. Shaking off her fear, Morgana concentrated her thoughts on her own survival. While the uproar continued she must use this moment of distraction to find Bronwen and escape. If Desmond would only turn his back she could open the narrow window and escape out onto the roof. It was her last hope.

She uttered a brief but fervent prayer, and it was answered. Desmond turned on cue, ordering the soldier to get all the information, and left the room. Morgana forced the

window open and wriggled partially through, catching at the
hips. For a second despair flooded her to the point of im-
mobility. To get this far only to be discovered. And in such
an undignified position!

With a final tug she was through, collapsing onto the reed
bundles of the roof. The rain felt like cold needles against
her exposed flesh. The surface was more slippery than she
had expected and she used the lines holding the bundles in
place to pull herself along. She crawled forward at snail
speed, barely able to see her way in the darkness. Her hair
hung wet and dank from beneath her cap. She scraped her
knuckles badly on a rock some child had tossed upon the
roof and sucked at them for a moment, rocking back and
forth in pain.

There was no time to lose in feeling sorry for herself. At
the far end there was a tall oak, the last remnant of some
ancient grove. If she could reach a branch, she could swing
herself down noiselessly, make her way to the kitchen and
find Bronwen.

Near the end of the roof was a wide limb, arching above
the eaves a mere two feet or so away. Morgana had climbed
a hundred trees in her childhood. She hoped her skills had
not deserted her. With a quick prayer and a deep breath she
bent her knees and launched herself into space. Her foot
slipped, the branch cracked and she went plummeting down
like a stone.

Her fall was broken by a wide chest and an iron band of
arms that crushed the breath from her. She gasped for air
and struggled and kicked until something cold and metallic
pressed against her throat. Sickening knowledge drained the
blood from her face: she had escaped from Ranulf's men
only to fall into the arms of a murderer—the false priest who
had slit the merchant's throat.

She froze with the realization that her slightest movement could bring bloody death, but her mind roamed free
in that instant, thoughts splitting in a dozen different direc-

tions: *Bronwen*. Whatever would happen to her, alone and friendless? No one would ever know what had happened to them. Their bodies would be buried in the woods or some convenient field, unshriven and unmourned, without even a priest to read the requiem over them. And what would happen to her demesne lands and her loyal tenants and retainers? Would they fall into Lord Lindsey's greedy hands?

The metal pressed hard against her flesh, bruising it, cutting off the breath. She closed her eyes, waiting to feel the nick of the blade as it passed across her throat. Oh, why had she left London? If only Sir Ranulf were here. She was scarcely conscious of the notion but it was there—certain and rueful. Her captor set Morgana firmly down upon her feet without releasing her.

"Well met, wife," a deep and familiar voice said in her ear. "I see that my late arrival has not curbed your habit of slipping away unseen in the early hours."

The grip on her loosened and Morgana swung around within the circle of Ranulf's arms, leaning her suddenly limp body against the solid strength of his. In her relief at discovering she was not about to be murdered by a cutpurse, she clung to him gratefully.

"Oh, thank God and all the Saints that it is you!"

Ranulf's carefully rehearsed speech evaporated on his lips. Instead he found himself cradling his shivering wife with both tenderness and alarm. Her fright was real and she trembled in his embrace until her teeth rattled.

"Can it be one day has wrought so great a change at heart?" he chuckled. "I did not dream to find you so willing, so soon."

"It was terrible, horrible!"

He could barely make out Morgana's words, muffled as they were with her face pressed close against his chest. He let his arms enclose her and she tilted her shocked white face up to his. His anger drained away.

"What is it, sweeting? What has frightened you?"

"Blood. Blood everywhere."

The shouts and wails from inside the hostelry now were the final confirmation that his first reading of the situation was all wrong. Ranulf flushed with chagrin, glad of the covering darkness. He bent to ask an explanation, but the arrival of a man-at-arms made that unnecessary.

"A merchant has been murdered in his bed by a black-guard posing as a priest. We searched the grounds, but he has made good his escape."

Ranulf put Morgana away from him. "I will go inside. Guard your Lady well."

The man nodded, not quite sure whether he was to protect her from harm or prevent her from escaping. The soldier took his duty seriously, standing watch over his mistress like a hound holding a stag at bay. His baleful stare made her nervous, and Morgana felt cold and bereft without the warmth and security of Ranulf's nearness. Her teeth chattered like hail upon a slate roof and she hugged herself to shake off the chill, to no avail.

Ranulf had not gone three strides when he turned back, took off his own warm cloak and spread it over her shoulders. "Wrap yourself in this. And no trickery, mind you." His brows shot together in a straight line. "I am weary and shall have no tolerance for any more of your foolishness."

Morgana nodded. She hadn't heart or strength to tell him that, with a throat-slitting murderer at large, she had no intention of straying from the protection of his courage and good right arm. Thus she was quite relieved when he returned. A watch was set, although the false priest was surely far away by this time, mounted on the dead merchant's fine horse instead of the meek little donkey he had left in its place.

Ranulf took Morgana by the arm. "Come."

She balked. He was leading her, not to the inn, but toward the cow biers and stables. "Where are you taking me?"

"Unless you wish to sleep on a blood-soaked mattress or on the inn floor crowded with my men, you had best come with me. We will sleep on a pile of fresh hay and none the worse for it."

Now the hour of retribution had come, she thought. He had every right before the law to beat her, to chastise her and work his will upon her in any way he desired. She swallowed around the dry lump in her throat. And Bronwen? Where was her shy little maid in all this?

"Where is Bronwen?"

"Sleeping like a dormouse before the kitchen fire," Ranulf assured her, "with my squire guarding the kitchen door. No harm will come to her there."

"And what of me, sir?"

He whirled to face her. "Do you fear me, little wife? Perhaps you have every right to do so." His wide smile shone in the torchlight. "In any event, you shall soon find out."

He marched her across the rain-slicked earth and into the stables. The smell of sweet hay and oats, of horse and leather rose up around them, homey and comforting. Still, Morgana could not keep her knees from knocking together. She stood in the beam of golden light while Ranulf regarded her intently.

Face smudged, knuckles scraped. Quite a transformation, he thought. There was nothing of the arrogant lady who had snubbed him so thoroughly before King and Court, and little of the seductive beauty he had found waiting in his marriage bed. She looked like a bedraggled urchin in her torn boy's clothing, dripping hair plastered close to her head and neck.

The only thing left of the woman he had seen before was a certain defiant courage against all odds. He had witnessed it in Edward's royal banquet hall and again on Tower Hill, and it had touched him deeply. It did so now. The warrior in him could appreciate her valor; and the poet, the part of himself he had buried beneath armor and battle scars, her soul. It burned like a pure white flame before him. But it was Morgana's womanliness that made his arms suddenly ache to hold her.

He pushed the thought away. She'd likely stick a dagger between his ribs, if he made the attempt. His wife had made it defiantly clear that she despised him. Ranulf turned away and removed his cloak, spreading it out over the fresh straw of the nearest empty stall.

"You are near to swooning with fatigue, my lady. Make your bed here and rest well."

Morgana looked at him doubtfully. The torch flickered in the wind and in the shifting light the strong bone structure of his Celtic and Viking heritage was evident—wild, fierce and untamed. He saw her momentary indecision.

"Lady, I have ridden hard and long in search of you. Be assured that my only lust, at the moment, is for an undisturbed night's sleep."

Ranulf smiled and Morgana felt her fears drain away. She discovered she was exhausted now that her burst of alarm had faded. The makeshift bed was as inviting as a feather mattress. "As you will, my lord."

He quenched the torch. The rain had ceased and a silver moon sailed among the clouds. She did not completely trust him, but she lowered herself to Ranulf's cloak and stretched out on her side, hands clasped against her face. The light woolen garment was soft and warm and carried his scent. How odd, she reflected sleepily, that she already recognized it, when she had been near him on so few occasions—she could have picked him out blindfolded from among a hundred men. Dreams edged into her thoughts and she was drifting off to meet them, when harsh reality yanked her back. She tried to sit up and discovered Ranulf had slipped a strip of soft leather around her wrists. He drew the loop shut and she found herself bound to the pole supporting the side of the stall. Her struggles only tightened the knot and she glared at him, outraged.

"By God's Eyes, have you lost your mind? What do you mean by this?"

Ranulf lay down beside her in the straw and propped himself up on one elbow. His eyes glittered dangerously in the half-light and his voice was grim. "It is not wise to cross swords with me, and you had best learn that now."

She could not speak around the catch in her throat. What foolhardiness had caused her to lead this man such a merry dance? He was much larger and stronger than she, a soldier peerless in battle and implacable in enmity. She had played him for a fool and now she would pay the penalty for her actions. His breath touched her face, fanning along her cheek. Morgana had never felt so small and vulnerable, so damnably helpless before. As she stared at him Ranulf suddenly grinned.

"As to my intentions, I have only one: to have a good night's rest. And I shall, if I have to gag you."

Morgana's apprehensions turned to fury. "Unbind me! There is no need for this."

Ranulf rolled over, so all she saw was the bulk of his wide shoulders silhouetted in the light.

Morgana fought her temper and won. "My lord, I cannot sleep like this," she said dulcetly. "Release me. I shall not run away again. I give you my word."

"Oh, aye," Ranulf replied shortly. "Your word of honor."

"Exactly so, my lord."

He leaned back toward her. "Your word, lady, is like a silver sieve—a pretty thing, but holding nothing...as when you vowed to honor and obey me as your sworn lord and husband. Such honor and obedience I can do without."

He lay down again and turned his back to her. Morgana had no reply. She had indeed made those vows, and broken them within hours. That was her chief regret. Her family

prided themselves on their loyalty and honor. She had held
Ranulf up to shame and ridicule. Most men would have
beaten her, at best. But given the chance she would do it all
again. No man would own her. Still, there was no use in fu-
tile argument. She made herself as comfortable as possible
to invite sleep again. In the morning she would reevaluate
her situation.

Ranulf was bone weary but sleep eluded him. Not so his
wife. Despite her anger and the uncomfortable bonds, he
heard her breathing soften and deepen. Within minutes
Morgana was asleep, and it was not much longer before she
had snuggled up to his back, instinctively curling herself
close to the warmth of his body. Ranulf covered her with the
ends of his cloak and sighed, without realizing it. There was
no understanding women.

Damning Edward's matchmaking ways to perdition he
spent the next hour reviewing battle plans in his mind. A
fine way, he thought bitterly, for a man to spend his second
night of marriage. Cold, wet, and with a bride who had
ridden hell-for-leather to avoid lying with him. And still he
wanted her.

Her breath was sweet, her chest rose and fell rhythmi-
cally beneath her boy's tunic. He thought of her breasts, so
warm and firm to his touch, and of how they had filled his
hands. He remembered the softness of her skin, the soft
budding peaks that responded to his touch. The fragrance
of her skin and hair drove him mad with longing. The urge
to waken her with kisses, to peel away the damp clothes and
warm her with the rising heat of his passion was almost
overwhelming. He wanted to see and feel and explore every
inch of her, to taste and suckle, to claim her here and now,
as his right.

He clenched his hands into fists and fought his desire. To
take her here—in a stable among the animals, with the stable boys sleeping nearby—would only confirm her opinion
that he was nothing less than a barbarian. He throbbed with

the need for her, ached with the pressure building within him. When and how had she captured him so securely in the web of her allure? He was under the spell of her blue-green eyes and womanly scent, ensnared by a tangle of rose-gold curls and a spirit as fiery and bright.

Although the night was cool, his face was dewed with sweat. There would be no sleep or rest for him tonight. He turned away and tried to make his thoughts do the same.

Sometime in the night, Morgana roused from her dreams to find her head cradled upon Ranulf's outflung arm, her body nestled intimately against his. She looked up and found her eyes staring into his wide-open ones. She flushed and quickly pulled back, but his steady scrutiny did not waver. She could not tear her gaze away.

"The night is cold and you...you are so warm," she stammered. "You burn as if you have the fever."

His answer came, soft and low. "Lady, I am burning."

His words sent a shiver tingling up her spine. If he reached out to touch her now she did not know what she would do. He drew her like a magnet. Confused by his reply and her own reaction, Morgana turned away from him. Now it was her turn to lie wakeful, while his breathing slowed and deepened as sleep finally overtook him.

Morgana lay awake till dawn crept up in the east, mauve and lilac and liquid silver, pondering this man who was now her husband. There was more to him than she had originally thought, but it was buried beneath a layer as hard as damascene steel. He intrigued her. He alarmed her. And he stirred her, of that there was no doubt. Ranulf made her very aware that she was a woman, and that he was very much a man. He set her smoldering inside, and if she was not careful he would consume her.

Her thoughts echoed his of only a few hours earlier: damn Edward and his matchmaking plans to hell!

Their path wound through forested land and open meadow by turns, heading southwest in the late-afternoon sunshine. Morgana sat tall in her saddle, craning her neck for the first glimpse of the sea and the wide harbor and the small village overshadowed by the towering walls of Castle Griffin.

"Not much farther now," she said to Bronwen, and saw her maid's tired face transformed with joy.

Soon they could shed their grimy boys' clothing for perfumed bathwater and rose petal soap, followed by women's garments that would be soft and blessedly clean. Soon they would see the limestone walls of the castle rising straight up from the rocky promontory as if it had grown from the sheer limestone of the cliffs. It was one of the earliest castles built along the southern Welsh seacoast, and also the most beautiful. Over the generations, the humble motte and bailey had been transformed into a mighty castle sprawling over many acres.

Morgana's heart lifted with every league they covered. Two days ago they had crossed Offa's Dike, the ancient earthwork barrier and ditch that ran 149 miles past rivers and through the deep shadowed forest, separating Britain from the Celtic fastness the English called Wales and the Welsh had named Cymru. Now the territory was achingly familiar. To her right the hills rose, green, then blue, then lavender in the far distance, and overhead the thick white clouds hung, almost unmoving. On the left, very soon, the woods would open to reveal the sparkling ocean and the first faint glimpse of her home.

They had made the rest of their journey with no untoward incident. Morgana seemed resigned to the situation and an uneasy truce had been forged. It would last only as long as their journey did, she vowed silently. He would not win her so easily just because his nearness roused her. It was only loneliness that made it happen, and the need to be held and made love to—Morgana reminded herself of this at least ten times a day.

It was hard to see his strong square hands and not remember how they had clasped her breasts in their palms, to see his wide shoulders and not recall the sculpted muscles of his body, the crisp golden hairs on his rippling chest and between his powerful thighs. She could not help wondering what it would be like to have Ranulf make love to her. Just to think of that moment when his kiss had taken her by surprise sent a shiver through her, making her nipples tighten and her limbs weak. He had a power over her she could not throw off, and she feared it greatly.

Now they were near Castle Griffin and the sea and the tang of salt water and seaweed rode on the breeze. It should have been the overwhelming scent, fresh and clean and biting, but there was something else. Something, that should not have been there. While Morgana tried to identify the substance Ranulf muttered an oath and reined his mount in sharply.

"What is it?" Desmond eyed his cousin.

"Trouble!" Ranulf stretched tall in the stirrups, every tendon taut, every instinct alerted. He spurred his horse forward without elaboration and Desmond followed suit.

The cavalcade galloped down the road, stirring the dust until it dulled the sheen of their armor and blurred the brightness of the sky overhead. They rode with a haste born of Ranulf's urgency and Morgana, riding with Bronwen in the center of the column, exchanged her eagerness at homecoming for a terrible fear.

Unmindful of anything else, Ranulf pushed forward to the crest of the hill, his eyes raking the horizon. He reined up and went still, but with sudden tension in every line of his face and form. The emerald hills rolled down to sharp-angled cliffs that dropped to the meadows and neatly tilled fields. Glass-green water shone beside the strand far below, where waves crashed against the dark rocks, splintering into glistening diamonds of spray and ruffles of white lace foam.

In the distance, beyond the strand, rose the rocky promontory, a dagger of land pointing toward the heart of the sea. Dominating its heights were the curtain wall and crenellated towers of Castle Griffin, glinting in the sun. But it was not the beauty of the scene that caught and held Ranulf's eye. From several places, plumes of dirty smoke rose ominously against the deep blue vault of the sky, and against the nearest castle wall, a siege tower swarmed with men in orange-and-white tunics.

Ranulf turned to Desmond. "Send Ripley and John Forester to scout the area: one to the high ridge; the other all the way round to the far side."

Morgana moved her mount through the press of men until she was at Ranulf's side. He expected screams and hysterics. Instead she went still. Rigid. For a moment he thought she had even stopped breathing. Her face was white, carved from marble, her eyes as glassy-green and deep as the sea. White lines bracketed her mouth and outlined her flaring nostrils. She spoke one word: "Lindsey!"

It sounded like a curse.

Chapter Five

Morgana's hands tightened on the reins. "So, he has learned of my widowhood and lost no time in pressing his ridiculous bastard's claim!"

Her reaction surprised Ranulf. It was anger, not fear, that held her in its grip. Despite her shabby garb she looked a warrior queen—all fiery beauty and blazing courage. A sudden surge of pride swept through him. What a magnificent woman she was! And she was his. He had never felt in such charity with her, or less indignant with the King's high-handed ways.

Morgana's mare snorted and Ranulf put out his hand to soothe the beast. "A Lancastrian?"

"No. Merely an ambitious man, who has bitten off more than he can chew. Castle Griffin has many surprises in store for any would-be conquerors."

Before Ranulf could question her further, warm color flooded back into Morgana's face. "Look!" She pointed toward the castle and smiled triumphantly.

A haze of smoke hung over the ramparts of the barbican wall and the towers of the inner ward, but the individual plumes of smoke could no longer be distinguished. Her tight smile widened. "An arrow had fired the roofs of the worksheds, but my people have already quenched the flames."

She was right, Ranulf saw. If the castle's defenders were well-drilled and organized, the outlook could not be too bleak. But then a mangonel was moved back to reveal a borer working away at the base of the north tower. Already the powerful auger had broken off a considerable amount of stone and masonry. The wall would be breached in three days' time at the maximum. Ranulf turned to point this out to Morgana, but she suddenly nudged her horse and rode to the edge of the wood.

Before he had time to catch up, she reined in again—so abruptly that her horse snorted and reared in alarm. But it was not merely his rider's change of pace that had frightened the beast. Underlying the scent of burning wood and straw and the clean tang of the sea, was the odor of death.

Ranulf brought his mount up beside Morgana's mare and scanned the view. The hillside fell away to more level ground below, revealing a good-sized village with streets neatly laid out around a central green, holding both church and churchyard. Fresh-turned rectangles of earth told a poignant story. It must have been neat and prosperous, Ranulf thought, the houses well kept with borders of flowers in every yard. But now the burned timbers of the roof beams lay inside the rubble of foundations and the flowers had long been trampled into the dirt.

One third of the village lay in ruins. Even the carved double doors of the church showed signs of battering. The air was heavy with the stench of death. Bloated bodies of pigs and dogs, cows and horses and oxen were strewn among the wreckage, misshapen and grotesque, and that was not the final horror. Alongside the church was a row of ancient oaks, and every tree sprouted a grisly burden. A score of bodies dangled from ropes on these living gallows, twisting idly in the stiff sea breeze. They had been dead, he reckoned, three days at most.

Morgana's hands fisted on the reins and her insides coiled into a cold knot. She could not see their individual faces but she knew every man and boy of the village, and her heart bled. Who were they? Powys, the old leather worker and his young apprentices? Dark-browed Lloyd the Blacksmith and his fine, strapping sons? Perhaps even simpleminded Duer, the lad who tended to the rougher chores for poor, crippled Father Kelwyn? There was a coldness moving through her limbs, as if she had plunged into the icy turbulence of the winter sea. When it reached her heart it would be numbed, Morgana hoped, and then this horrible pain and loss would ease. Soon she would be able neither to move nor think.

Ranulf saw the shock creeping from her stunned brain into her tired body. He had seen that same dulled, anguished look upon hundreds of faces when they met the cruel reality of war for the first time. Men staring at the bloody stumps of their arms or legs, not quite believing the testimony of their own eyes. Morgana was in such a state now. She needed something else to fill her mind and blot out this terrible picture, and there was only one antidote he could prescribe to help her through the next uncertain hours: swift plans for rescue and revenge.

He wanted to put his hand over hers and murmur words of sympathy and outrage, but he dared not. White-hot wrath would keep her going through the hours ahead; anything softer might dissolve her inner strength in a flood of tears.

"What shall we do?" she asked him after a pause.

"That depends on the situation." He gave her a wry look. "Even a landless knight can prove his worth, as long as he has his armor, his steed—and his wits about him."

Ranulf was already aware that Castle Griffin was not at full strength, with only twenty bowmen and three score men-at-arms, plus whatever servants there might be inside the walls. He needed to know the enemy's might. He kept his words brusque and controlled.

"Now, who is this attacker, Lindsey, and what is his strength?"

Morgana did not fail him. She took a deep, shuddering breath and answered in a low but measured tone. "He is Bryce, Lord Lindsey. A cousin of sorts to me, born on the wrong side of the blanket, and English and French by blood." Her face showed disdain in every line. "He has great love for power and wealth and none at all for the people. He dines at Lindsey Keep upon gold and silver plate while the honest villeins starve to pay the taxes he levies upon them."

Bryce, Lord Lindsey. Ranulf had heard of him, nothing of it good. He had married a wealthy and very young widow who had a small child by her first marriage, and had taken his poor bride to live in an isolated household ruled by his mistress. The wife had soon died of a broken neck under extremely suspicious circumstances, the child not long after, leaving Lindsey both richer and unencumbered. That was neither here nor there at the moment: what Ranulf needed to know was the enemy's strength.

Morgana was able to supply the answer. "He has forty archers and two hundred foot soldiers, all well armed. Furthermore, he has ten knights with their men sworn to him, including Llewelyn the Bold. He has boasted he can rally three hundred men and more to his standard."

Ranulf frowned. "A formidable opponent indeed. But do not lose heart. Not twenty years ago, a handful of men held Grantley Castle against two hundred knights and men-at-arms. Desmond and I will explore the area. But first you must show us the layout of Castle Griffin and its defenses."

Morgana took courage from his words. At first despair had caught her in its toils, with the scenes of death and destruction. Now hope dawned. Her fate and that of her people might lie in the hands of her unwanted husband. That they were capable hands she did not doubt. He was ready for what lay ahead. There was a light of excitement in his eyes and he showed no fear. Warfare was his way of life in these troubled times. Was he not Edward's Golden Knight?

She ticked off the defenses. "As you have seen, the eastern and southern walls are protected by the sea and the rocks below. On the western side is a precipitous slope and the mere, a salt-water pond of two acres formed from the earthworks of an ancient fort. It has a depth of fifteen feet and is used as a source of fresh fish, in addition to its defensive purpose. The only safe approach an enemy can make is along the neck of land from the north."

Morgana dismounted and took a broken bit of twig and began drawing in the dirt, not even looking to see if the others followed. Ranulf and Desmond joined her, flanking her on either side. She traced a rectangle with circles to indicate towers in each corner and a fifth larger one along the center of one long wall.

"The curtain wall is well fortified, with its own armament room over the gatehouse and a strong portcullis." Next she drew a second rectangle inside the first, again with five towers.

"The castle itself is built around an inner ward, with another portcullis and the main armament room in this inner gate tower. The whole is built of limestone and the flat roofs have been plastered and covered with mortar and roughened tiles to thwart enemy fire."

It was a simple plan, similar to many built in the eleventh and twelfth centuries by the first Edward in his attempts to control the Welsh uprisings, and strong from a defensive standpoint; but Ranulf saw no surprises for Lindsey or any other attacker. He looked at Morgana questioningly. "And . . . ?"

She met his gaze levelly. "The outer ward, between curtain wall and castle wall, is reached by a sloping ramp. Another ramp on the opposite side leads upward to the level of the castle gatehouse. The floor of the outer ward is twelve feet below either wall."

Desmond frowned. "An ill design for getting troops in and out quickly."

Ranulf laughed and cuffed him on the shoulder. "But if my way of thinking is correct, if flooded it would make an excellent moat."

Morgana was grimly satisfied by his quickness. "Aye, my lord. There is a sea gate that can be raised or lowered to let the ocean pour in. And the castle has always been well provisioned for a siege and has its own freshwater wells."

"Then they cannot be starved out easily. But a battering ram or bore properly applied can bring down the strongest walls in time." He pondered a moment. "Has this moat defense ever been used?"

"It has never been needed. No one has ever dared attack Castle Griffin before."

"How many are aware of this floodgate?"

"Besides myself and Rob..." She broke off awkwardly, then continued in a husky voice. "Only... only Sir Dyllis, my castellan, and his wife, Lady Winifred, who oversees the household in my absence, and Owain who is Captain of the Guard."

Ranulf pretended not to notice her momentary slip, but relegated it to a far corner of his mind for future study. He frowned down at the drawing scratched in the dirt at his feet. "And the sally port?"

Morgana struggled with herself. Every castle had a sally port, or postern gate, some larger fortifications, more than one—the hidden entrance and exit known only to the castle lord and his family, the commander of the guards and a few of the most trusted retainers. It served as an escape route for them, or as the way a troop could exit for a flanking attack on an unsuspecting enemy besieger.

To give out the secret to an outsider seemed almost a betrayal; yet Ranulf was her husband, pledged to defend her estates and people with his sword. And his life, if need be. It was just that handing over this carefully guarded secret brought home the reality of her marriage. She had been responsible for Castle Griffin for many years; it was difficult surrendering away her power to a man who was almost a stranger.

Ranulf's mouth thinned to a hard line. He knew exactly what doubts and conflicts were racing through Morgana's mind, and was ill pleased. No one had ever questioned his honor and lived to make the mistake twice. His gaze locked with hers, darkly blue, burning with resentment and command. She was the first to look away. With the twig she pointed to two places.

"Here and here. The one on the west wall is hidden beside the lady chapel, in the angle of the wall. The other is from the base of the west tower. A water route. But it can only be used at high tide, and even then it is treacherous."

She kept her eyes lowered, but Ranulf thought he saw something in her face that flickered across her finely chiseled features and was gone. She was holding information back. He was sure of it.

"I will not lead my men into this situation blindfolded. If there is aught else I need to know, you must tell me."

Morgana was startled by his shrewdness, but managed to recover quickly. She rose and moved toward her horse. "There is nothing else you need to know."

He stood and followed her. Before Morgana was aware Ranulf clamped his hands on her shoulders and swung her to face him. The lines of his face were taut and there was danger lurking in his eyes.

"Your mouth says one thing and your eyes another. Swear you mean no treachery, my lady. Swear on your eternal soul!"

She tried to pull away but could not. His hands were clamped painfully against her skin. There would be bruises there later, but Morgana was too angry to care.

"Do you dare to doubt the word of a lady? Is honor so foreign to someone raised in your outlandish isles? I would never jeopardize the lives and futures of those who are pledged to me or under my protection!''

His grip tightened and his fury matched hers. ''There is more honor in the meanest peasant of the Outward Isles than can be found in the whole of this benighted island!''

He leaned down close to her, his face a terrible mask of anger that made her heart skitter and jump within the cage of her ribs. How had she ever taken comfort in sleeping by his side?

''Furthermore,'' he said in acid tones, ''you have already shown that you wish to rid yourself of me. No doubt you hope to see your castle rescued and my broken corpse lying at your feet when all is done. But be warned, for I shall be alert to any tricks you might desire to play me. And I swear by God's Blood that I will pay them back tenfold until you beg for mercy.''

He let her go so suddenly that Morgana almost fell. She clung to her horse's stirrup to keep erect. Her brief truce with Ranulf had been shattered by their mutual distrust, and Morgana vowed she would never be lulled again. Robin, Lindsey, Edward and Ranulf. They were all alike.

A woman and her belongings were convenient pawns in their games of power, but by the Holy Rood, she was sick to death of them all. Somehow, some way, she would regain control over her own properties and estates and free herself from the greedy webs they had spun about her. And the first to realize it would be her dear, dear husband.

Desmond strode over to them. ''Ripley is back from reconnoitering the hillside,'' he reported. ''They have brought in the weapons for a siege: a ram, two augers and a trebuchet. And they are trying to tear a hole in the bank of the mere to drain its waters.''

Ranulf frowned. ''We will have to make our plans quickly and execute them with all dispatch.'' He shielded his eyes with his hand.

"What is that jumble of rocks on the high ridge?" he asked abruptly.

Morgana looked up. Sunlight warmed the huge blocks of a stone wall on the jutting cliff high above the devastated village. A few rooftops and the spire of a church were just visible through a screen of trees.

"That is the monastery of St. Tristan, based on the old order from Ireland. It is not extensive, being a place of retreat and contemplation."

"Will they help us?"

"If Lindsey's mercenaries have not driven them away."

Ranulf rubbed his strong chin thoughtfully. "Good. I have a plan."

They made their way quietly through the woodland, with scouts to the fore and rear. Long shadows streaked the hills and cliffs, providing excellent cover. The sun was low over the western ocean, turning the water to blood, and the wind keen, when they at last reached the Monastery of St. Tristan. Morgana and Bronwen had pulled their cloaks over their heads and huddled inside them in the shelter of a huge oak, while Ranulf and his men sought entry.

After a short interval, a thin and querulous voice came in response to their rapping—the vowels and consonants slurred and musical.

"Open your gates to honest travelers seeking sanctuary," Cerdic, one of the men-at-arms, called out.

The friar peered out suspiciously through the peephole set in the heavy oak door and repeated his question in Welsh Gaelic. Cerdic, a wiry man with distinctive taffy-brown eyes, scowled and beat on the wooden planks of the reinforced gate with his sword hilt. "I do not speak your heathen tongue. Open up, I say!"

"Leave be, Cerdic." Ranulf dismounted and strode to the gate, speaking in similar sounds to those the monk had used. The liquid syllables of Ranulf's Irish Gaelic reassured the old man, and he slid back the two long bolts that barred the gate and bid them enter in halting England. There was a grinding of metal upon metal, then the groan and creak of rusting hinges as the oak door swung clumsily inward.

Ranulf came first, leading his horse, and the others rode in after him. Approaching twilight and the overhanging trees sent pools of shadow flowing like ink across the cracked pavement. It was evident that the monastery had fallen upon hard times. The small courtyard and the buildings were in disrepair. Hens scratched in the overrun gardens and outside the chapel door, and the lawn was thick with brambles and weeds. The fish pond was clear and well stocked, however, and the friar's robe was clean, and well mended if threadbare.

"What has happened here?" Morgana was wrapped in her cloak against the evening chill, but as she looked about in surprise it slipped from her hair. The friar's sharp eyes were immediately upon her. He cleared his throat and spoke up in accents as rusted as the gate hinges.

"Women! Ye did not say there were women among ye. No women are allowed inside these gates." He waved his hands at her as if trying to scatter a flock of pigeons. "Off! Off with ye."

She did not know whether to laugh or be dismayed. "Friar, do you not know me in these rough garments? It is I, Lady Morgana. And I have visited with you many a time and heard mass in the lady chapel."

He hobbled closer and squinted at her in the failing light. "By God's Grace, so it is. And what be ye doing in this company o' ruffians, my lady?"

She laughed, a mellow sound that bounced back from the stone walls and paving. Ranulf realized he had never heard her laugh before. It was an enchanting sound, mirthful and bell-like.

"Good Friar," she said, "I have come home, bringing my maid and my husband with me."

The old man crossed himself nimbly. "Praise be. We had heard rumors that your lord had met with ill fate at the King's Court. You are well come, Lord and Lady Hartley."

In the silence that followed the friar's words echoed and re-echoed like the clash of cymbals. Ranulf flinched inwardly, but gave no outward sign. His horse whickered and tossed its head uneasily, breaking the spell. The mistake was a natural one: although tales of Hartley's treason and imprisonment had long reached the Welsh Marches, word of Morgana's widowhood and remarriage had not traveled so far. Ranulf stepped forward and took command.

"I regret to inform you that rumor is proved true in this case. Lord Robert Hartley was beheaded for treason against the crown. I am Sir Ranulf, called by some The Dane. Lady Morgana is now my wife and under my protection."

The words fell like flakes of flint from Ranulf's lips, and he himself seemed carved from granite, harsh, cold and unmovable. The friar bobbed his head. "Just so, my lord. God's blessing be on you both."

The last light was fading and someone had lit a lamp just inside the chapel door, so that the dim glow outlined his profile eerily. There was no softness in his face, only a forbidding and unyielding austerity. Morgana, unable to tear her gaze away from the stern lines of Ranulf's profile, unable to shield herself from the stinging lash of his words, clenched her hands until her fingers ached. Did he truly hate her so much? And was it because of her actions, or because he loathed the thought of her as his wife?

From the first she had known her new husband was displeased with Edward's high-handed matchmaking; but she fully expected that the knowledge of her wealth and estate would rapidly reconcile him to his fate. After all, the handsome young Earl of Dentlough had happily married a wife old enough to be his grandmother for the sake of her gold and lucrative lands . . . just as Robin had married her. A sip of honey to make the tonic more palatable.

Another idea intruded, disturbing and unwelcome. He had made no bones that she was not the type of female he admired. Was there another woman he would rather have wed? Someone enshrined in the heart that beat so strong and steadily in his wide chest? Morgana had not failed to notice the envious and spiteful looks Margot de Maurais had sent her way at the wedding feast. Robin had married her for her possessions, loving another woman all the while. Was Ranulf's case the same?

She forced her mind away from this dampening train of thought. The friar had been joined by an elderly monk and one of the lay brothers who shuffled out from the chapel. The situation here was much worse than had first appeared. While not a major religious house, St. Tristan's had been founded by Morgana's great-granduncle, and was noted for the beauty of the illuminated manuscripts created by its brothers. Small and orderly, it had been fairly prosperous until looters, most likely from Lindsey's army, had ransacked the hallowed premises. Morgana was aghast.

"Great evil has been done!"

"Aye," the monk said mournfully, "we came upon evil times. Lord Lindsey's mercenaries fell upon us like wolves, seeking gold and jeweled treasures. Alas, we are pledged to poverty and had naught of value but the silver-gilt chalice and ciborium used for the Lord's Day and special Feast Days. They took those, but in their anger at finding nothing more, destroyed whatever else they could."

"You are lucky to have escaped with your lives," Ranulf said.

The three clerics crossed themselves. "Few of us did. Father Kelvin died inside his village church of apoplexy. Many of our own numbers fled into the hills to avoid the slaughter." The friar shook his snowy head. "Only a handful returned. 'Twas bitter, bitter cold."

Ranulf smote his thigh with his palm. "By the Blood of the Martyrs! I cannot restore life to your fallen brothers, but this I swear: when the castle has been regained, those responsible shall be tracked down and made to pay the price of their crimes, and you shall receive aid in restoring your buildings to their former state. I, myself, shall provide a new gold chalice and ciborium to celebrate the mass.''

A chorus of praise to God and thanks to the new lord of the castle rose from the monks and the lay brother, but Bronwen raised her brows slightly. On the whole she liked Sir Ranulf well enough—although she was much less sure of his conceited cousin; but one moment he joked of being landless, and the next was acting as if he were born to the velvet and ermine. It seemed a grave misjudgment on his part: a man should be certain of his wealth before distributing it so wholeheartedly to the less fortunate.

She looked to see how her mistress took her husband's announcement. Morgana's face was pale, and as blank and impassive as that of a marble statue. Bronwen was not fooled. It was the deceptively composed look she wore when extreme anger rendered her speechless.

Desmond was fiercely loyal to Ranulf and would have given his life for him. It was painful to see his cousin treated so shabbily by this haughty wench, held up to public ridicule by her scandalous behavior. It was even more painful to see him falling day by day under her spell. Well, if Ranulf would not look to his back, Desmond would protect it for him. He would keep close watch on the Lady Morgana.

While the Orkney knight thought his dark thoughts, Morgana was busy with her own. Ranulf's speech had infuriated her. *Fine promises from my poor, landless husband. And how does he expect to pay for his grand gesture? With gold from my coffers or wrested from my lands? Taxed from my people?* Years of training came to her aid, and Morgana was able to mask her emotions; but not before Desmond had seen the spark of fury in her eyes. *When we are alone,* she swore silently, *we shall have this matter out, my dear lord and husband.*

Desmond felt her anger as if it were his own. Yes, he would watch her closely, for she meant Ranulf no good.

Meanwhile Ranulf accepted the thanks of the monks with a good deal of embarrassment and hastily changed the subject. "And now, good brothers, if you will provide us with beds for the night you shall have our gratitude, for we are weary."

The older friar—Ewen, by name—wrung his hands in distress. "Ah, my lord, that puts us in a quandary. We have beds aplenty; however, it is against the rules of our order that any woman remain in these precincts between sunset and sundown."

"There are times when rules must be bent or broken," Morgana said persuasively. "You cannot expect us to sleep in the woods."

Before Brother Ewen could reply, Ranulf took charge. "The higher laws of God take precedence over the laws of man, no matter how saintly. I claim the right of sanctuary in your chapel for myself, the Lady Morgana and her maid-in-waiting."

The clerics readily agreed to this solution and went off with several of the soldiers to fetch oil lamps, blankets and sleeping pallets, while Ranulf took the women to the chapel. A lamp of ruby glass hung near the altar, casting jewels of light upon the gilded altar.

Morgana remembered the small stone building, with narrow, pointed windows glazed with stained glass, from childhood visits with her grandmother. Then, as now, there had been no chairs or pews, only the dressed stone flags stretching from door to altar. But on those occasions, ranks of the faithful had filled the nave with warmth and color. Now the space was open and empty, the floor cold and bare, the vaulted ceiling deep in shadow.

It did not bode well for a comfortable night, she thought, but it was a vast improvement over the flea-ridden farmhouse where they had sheltered the night before. At least she would not have to worry that some thief would slit her throat while she slept, as had befallen the hapless merchant at the inn. She could put her safety and Bronwen's in Ranulf's capable hands. But it was not the quality of their shelter that knotted her brow or put smoldering fire into her eyes.

Ranulf frowned down at her. "You are ready to burst with words unsaid. You may speak your mind freely."

"How generous of you, my lord," she replied hotly. "But then you have already displayed your generosity by vowing to present a new gold chalice and ciborium to the monastery!"

"I see that I have erred somehow in making that promise. I did not mean to offend any local custom in doing so."

She had the grace to blush. "You have said and done all that is proper—made the same vows and promises that I would have pledged myself—had you not forestalled me!"

Ranulf glowered at her. There seemed to be some obscure point of honor here beyond his ken. Neither one noted Desmond standing nearby in the shadows. "Kindly explain what I have done to earn your ire."

"The patronage of the monastery is *my* right and *my* responsibility, and has been since the death of my father. Our marriage is mere days old, a marriage on paper only, but already you are usurping my authority, relegating me to the role of powerless consort. I will not stand meekly by!"

Surprisingly there was now a gleam of amusement in his eye. "It seems you have two varying complaints against me, my lady. I cannot take back my promise to the monastery, as well you know."

The gleam grew to a decided twinkle. "But as to the lack of consummation of our marriage, that is something I plan to deal with at the first opportunity."

His gaze swept over her face, then slowly and thoroughly surveyed the curves of her slender body beneath the boy's raiment. He watched the blush creep up over her cheeks.

"The very earliest opportunity, my dear wife. I only regret that matters of utmost urgency make it impossible to set the final seal on our contract now, for I swear by St. George that I am full ready!"

There was something in his voice and the sudden light in his eyes that made her body grow weak. So weak that, for just a few seconds, she swayed toward him and her breath came a bit fast. The urge to surrender her cares, to lose her concerns in the strength of his arms and the might of his body was suddenly almost overpowering. He would be a masterful lover, sure and direct, giving and taking pleasure equally and with much enjoyment. Only iron discipline kept her from giving her feelings away.

Morgana stepped away from him quickly and spoke in wintry tones. "This is no time for such nonsense. There are matters of much greater importance at hand."

"Aye, there are." Ranulf turned away from her angrily. For an instant, she had softened toward him, he was sure of it. And then she had remembered that he was only a knight and she was a great lady. Their difference in birth and status lay between them like an icy river and she would do nothing to bridge the gap.

Lamplight outlined his face in black and red. His chin and jaw were determined, his eyes dark and distant. "If only there were some other way of gaining admittance to the castle!"

Morgana saw that he had already forgotten her, as the warrior in him superseded the angry husband. She pushed away her sudden sense of disappointment. "There might be another way," she said quietly. "A dangerous way. From the mere."

She had his full attention now. "There was once a tunnel beneath the walls to the north side. It ended at a grate fastened to the rock and well hidden from view. But in my grandfather's time the sea rose, covering the grate and making it useless for escape. Part of the tunnel is flooded."

"But it is a way in. If I can find this grate and this tunnel . . ."

Morgana put out her hands in protest. "It is a foolhardy scheme. If you fail, you will die."

He gave her a long, hard stare. "Then, madame, you will be a widow once more, and may choose a husband more to your liking. But in that case, let us have a softer parting."

He pulled her into his arms, purposely forcing her body against the length of his. "Kiss me, Morgana."

Her lips parted slightly as his mouth came down on hers. The pressure was soft at first, tentative and exploring. She trembled in his arms. His tongue touched her lower lip, outlining it so sweetly she sighed. In that instant his kiss became hard and fierce, tasting, probing, demanding surrender. She clung to him, drawing strength from his nearness and felt the deep pull of passion in her loins. It grew until she was lost in it and there was nothing but the power of his arms about her, the heat of the moment and the naked hunger for more.

Her body strained against him, wishing away the garments and armor that separated her flesh from his. She wanted to feel his skin against hers with nothing in between. She met him kiss for kiss, fire for fire. When he lifted his mouth from hers Morgana was dazed and shaken.

Ranulf held her chin in his hand, his eyes midnight dark and burning with intensity. "If I should die, Morgana, remember this—and what might have been between us."

"Don't go!" She didn't want the moment to end. And she didn't want him to risk his life.

He cursed softly. "Do you know what you do to me when you gaze at me so? If we were anywhere else—*anywhere!*—I would take you here and now."

Abruptly he swung away. Morgana pressed her fingers to her bruised lips, still warm from his fervid kisses. She had been right to fear him. He could rouse her with a look or a touch. She had never wanted a man in the way that she wanted him. She had never been so willing to surrender herself. And by morning he might be dead. She closed her eyes and leaned back against the wall for support.

Ranulf went out into the court, where Bronwen stood a few feet away. His mind was still on Morgana, on the softness of her mouth and the way she had clung to him. *"Don't go!"* The words echoed in his head. He had never wanted so much to stay or damned so long and hard the call of duty.

Bronwen saw his frown and smiled shyly. "Sir Desmond says we are not to fear, that you will find a way to bring us safely home."

He smiled confidently. "Tomorrow you shall sleep beneath the roofs of Castle Griffin. But first we shall see how badly this Lindsey covets it for himself."

Desmond came forward. "It is not only the castle Lord Lindsey desires, but my Lady Morgana. Or so this maid tells me."

He did not see the look of hurt betrayal Bronwen sent his way. "Aye," Desmond continued. "Lindsey went into a fury when he learned she had been married to my Lord Hartley. I doubt he will take her remarriage to you in any better light."

Ranulf swung back to Bronwen. "Is this true? He aspired to her hand himself?"

"Aye. At one time he courted her. They were pledged to one another in their cradles, so he claims," she continued. "And that they were handfasted, before she was wed to my Lord Hartley—may God rest his soul."

Handfasted? Jealousy was rising inside Ranulf like a black tide. The custom was still honored in the Orkneys where he had been raised: a youth and maid in love clasped hands through a hole in an ancient betrothal stone and were then bound to each other for a year. Most people considered handfasting to have all the legality of a marriage before a priest—with all the benefits and privileges attached to such a union. Suddenly he wanted Morgana with a ferocity he had never known before. By all that was Holy he had taken a spitfire to wed, but she gave a man something to live for!

Ranulf bade Bronwen goodnight and took up his watch outside the chapel in a thoughtful mood. For the first time he wondered if Morgana would prefer throwing her lot in with Lindsey to being the wife of a simple knight. Well, he would have his answer soon after dawn when he discovered whether or not a flooded tunnel really waited for him in the dark waters of the mere.

Long before the first rays of morning sun reached across the sea to light the crenellated walls and towers of Castle Griffin, the army camped below was up and stirring. It was an orderly and disciplined commotion with men and horses moving through the preset patterns of many campaigns, centered around the orange-and-white-striped command tent. But as Lindsey's soldiers arrived to man the siege machines and the archers took up their positions to renew the assault, three men on horseback came along the coast road. The lookouts gave warning, and all activity ceased.

The sea was calm and mile-long scallops of molten gold and copper foamed and lapped against the rocks and along the strand, providing a backdrop for the newcomers. They advanced slowly, hampered by their aged and bony steeds.

Lord Lindsey, a lean man with pale olive skin, galloped to the perimeter of the camp, scattering soldiers to either side. Although his forces fought bravely under his command, his nature was cautious where his own skin was concerned. He saw no reason to soil his hands or endanger his life when others would do so for pay, but the brothers of St. Tristan were no threat. His gray eyes were keen and speculative beneath a cap of smooth dark hair as he reined in.

"Let them approach."

The sentries lowered their swords but stood alert and ready, although the chance of misadventure seemed low: the

lead rider carried a bronze crucifix high in his outstretched
hand, and all three were clothed in the threadbare habits of
St. Tristan's monastery. One soldier grinned outright at their
raw-boned, elderly mounts, and Lindsey's mouth was wry
and cynical as the monks drew near. Did these mystic fools
hope to sway him from his course with prayers or exhorta-
tions?

To show his courage and disdain for such soft tactics he
rode out to meet them, his helm held in the crook of his arm.
He raised his sword in mock salute and the wiry lead monk
made a sign of the cross in the air before him.

"What haste, good brothers! Is it some dire need that
impels you from your morning devotions?"

The face of the spokesman was shadowed by his cowl, but
his distinctive taffy-brown eyes were humble and guileless.
"Peace be with you, my lord. We come on urgent business."

"Weevils in the flour, perhaps? Or have you sighted an
ominous ship from your clifftop aerie? Banish your fears,
for the viking raids are things of the distant past."

The monk removed a small roll of parchment from his
capacious sleeve. "We come bearing a message to the castellan from Lady Morgana."

Lindsey tensed. "What nonsense is this? The lady is at
Court."

"Nay, my lord." He pointed a work-worn hand to the
clifftops that rose behind the ravaged village and every eye
in the camp followed the gesture.

A woman waited on horseback, her posture regal, red-
gold hair cascading down her back like a brilliant veil. She
was accompanied by four armed men and from a standard
beside her fluttered the blue and white personal pennon of
Lady Morgana, heiress of Castle Griffin. A murmur went
through the camp like the roar of an incoming tide.

Lindsey had excellent distance vision. Well he knew the
tilt of that proud head and that unique rose-gold hair.

Morgana! There could be no doubt of it. While a dozen plans and counterplans spun around in his wily brain he snatched the parchment from the monk and, breaking the seal, unrolled it. The brown-eyed monk watched impassively as the knight scanned the lines of graceful script and a succession of emotions flitted over his swarthy cheeks. Surprise, disbelief, and then a wary eagerness. The Lady Morgana was ordering her castle to surrender.

But why? "To spare further bloodshed in a cause we cannot win," the message said. It was true that a widow far from the protection of the King was at the mercy of any man strong enough to conquer her estates and hold them. And once he controlled her lands, it would be no time at all until he controlled Morgana, as well. Lindsey was convinced that once he wed her—either with her consent or against her will—Edward would accept his renewed pledges of loyalty and be quite content to let the matter rest. It had happened time and again through history: a loyal ally was forgiven his impetuosity and costly warfare averted.

But what tipped Lindsey's final decision was the memory of the one autumn when he had gone courting a certain red-haired lady of sixteen summers. With her parents away, it was no difficult task to persuade the seneschal that his visits would be countenanced by the Master. Had his grandfather and Lady Morgana's grandfather not been cousins? And had he not been a guest within the splendid walls of Castle Griffin innumerable times in the past?

Once inside, Lindsey had wooed his former playmate, the lovely, ripening Lady Morgana, not just for the wealth of her estates but for the sake of her wit and beauty and the fire in her flashing blue-green eyes. He had kept the fire in his loins banked while they walked within the gardens or sang to his lute-playing in the courtyard. And after every encounter he had found some willing kitchen maid to fondle and slake his thirst.

As for the naive and innocent Morgana, he had kissed her but once, keeping his lust kindled most tantalizingly. Once she was his, there would be time for more. The rose garden had been fragrant in the twilight and her body soft and pliant, bending to his as they embraced beneath the rose arbor. The thrill of impending victory had filled him with elation.

It had been going so well—until her father's abrupt arrival had broken the brief spell, and a few days after she had been taken to London. Two months later she had been wed to Robert, Lord Hartley. Lindsey had been prey to bitter jealousy as he watched the destruction of all his grandiose schemes. But now, he thought with a flare of excitement, the wheel had come full circle.

In the years since those days he had fought and gambled and pressured and connived, consolidating his might and his holdings. The poor and reckless young knight was now a man of wealth and power along the southern coast, a man to be courted and feared. Meanwhile Morgana had returned to her castle, a traitor's widow sent from the Court in disgrace. She would be so grateful to him. He could envision it all.

Lindsey smiled unpleasantly. The two things he wanted were within his grasp. Before the sun was much higher, he would be in full possession of the castle, home of the proud Griffins who had disdained his suit and sent him packing. The once-penniless relation would be master of Castle Griffin at last.

He had planned long and hard for this day, and when the walls fell he had further plans to avenge the old slight and atone for the old humiliation. Once he held the castle, it was only a matter of time until he possessed the Lady Morgana, as well. That too, he had carefully planned. He would fling her over his shoulder and carry her up the stairs to the old lord's chambers. He would even the score by taking her in her father's bed. And he knew exactly how he would tame and enslave her with his lovemaking, step by step. Lindsey looked up to where she waited on the heights, and his smile grew.

Soon, my lovely, soon.

Chapter Six

The die is cast."

Morgana heard the hoarse whisper of one of her guards, but made no reply. Placing her hand over Bronwen's white knuckles she gave a reassuring squeeze and her maid returned a tremulous smile. For all Morgana's calm exterior, her insides were in turmoil. It was taking every ounce of energy she had to appear totally poised and in control, while near panic sent her blood coursing through her veins like a river in spate. It was hard to wait with seeming patience when her mind was seething; but soon—too soon—her turn would come.

Nervously she pleated her white damask brocade gown between her fingers. It had been unearthed among various items in the monastery storehouse, a donation from her own grandmother some sixty years before. Surely that lady, for whom Morgana had been named, had intended the gold-shot cloth to be made into vestments for one of the altars; but the gown and a cloak of fine emerald wool lined with gold satin had been packed away in a cedar-lined chest and forgotten.

While the garments were in the old style, they suited Morgana and she felt they conveyed the necessary air of ancient lineage and authority that she must project when it came time to play her own part in Ranulf's scheme. Certainly they were more suitable than the soiled and tattered scullery boy's tunic and hose she had worn since leaving court.

Far below the sea sparkled, the stone of Castle Griffin glinted and Lindsey's army prepared to renew their assault. Morgana's hands tightened on the reins. If only Ranulf were beside her she would not feel quite so forlorn. The world seemed empty without him. For all she did not want him as her husband, there was something reassuring about his splendid height and strength and the way he took command of a situation.

Talons of fear clutched her. His plan was so bold, so dangerous! Morgana's grandfather's father had enlarged and added to the small fortification, giving Castle Griffin its present shape and area. Those were perilous times and her ancestor had been an engineer and architect of sorts, riddling the place with hidden rooms, secret stairways and escape routes leading to God knew where. There was a hidden strong room inside the older section of the keep, and Morgana's father had told her of the tunnel and the submerged grate.

Ranulf had left long before sunrise, intending to discover this grate and find his way inside the castle unseen by Lindsey or his men. Everything hinged upon his success, but Morgana was not sanguine. Perhaps the grate was rusted shut. Perhaps it had never really existed.

She could only wait and try not to think. But she was having little success. Her thoughts were firmly fixed on her husband.

"He is gone so long!" she cried beneath her breath. "Surely it should not take this long?"

"Patience, Lady, such matters have no measure," the soldier beside her cautioned.

Morgana folded her hands as if in prayer but gripped them so tightly her knuckles were white. She had given Ranulf her solemn oath that she would follow his plans without deviation, no matter what happened. And at her urging, he had promised to raise a signal to reassure her if his dangerous plan succeeded. Her grandfather's star-and-dragon pennant was to be hung from the eastern tower. But the appointed hour was long past and the sun was rising higher in the dazzling sky and still there was no signal.

She stared fixedly at the two-acre mere, gleaming like a brightly polished mirror. Nothing disturbed its shining silver surface. Not a wave or a ripple. Below she watched Lindsey turn back toward the castle, the three monks trailing meekly behind, and still the ramparts of the east tower remained bare.

As she waited, inwardly agonizing, outwardly serene, the sunny scene before her was blotted out by another. Dim, green, murky. She saw metal latticework covered with brown algae, a man's square, bronzed hands grasping at it urgently. Futilely. For even as she watched, that desperate grip slackened, loosened. Let go.

Morgana felt as if her lungs would burst from lack of air as the strange vision darkened and faded away. Once again, Castle Griffin was silhouetted against the sky and shimmering sea. Sunlight beat down upon her, but a creeping numbness began in her midsection, cold as lead and equally heavy. She did not question what had just happened, although she had hoped to escape the bitter gift. It was too late. She had inherited The Seeing, her grandmother's strange talent, and it had taken the trauma of this moment to bring it out.

Her heart cracked and splintered within her chest. The plan had failed—and Ranulf was dead.

Morgana wished that Desmond had stayed with her little group, but he had gone off on some mysterious errand in the hour just before dawn. Her thoughts were torn between fear for those under her protection and unsorted but painful feelings where Ranulf was concerned: she had been widowed again, before she had even become a wife. He had lost his life in the attempt to outwit Lindsey and rescue her castle. And if not for her angry flight, he would never have been in Wales in the first place without a full complement of his men. The guilt weighted her soul like a pall of lead.

Too late she regretted her heated words to Ranulf in the shadows of the chapel. She had sent him away with them ringing in his ears, and he had gone to his death thinking her a shrew. He had never had a chance to know the person that she really was. Nor she him.

The guilt pressed more heavily, and with it a sense of loss that she could not quite face and examine this soon. Despite the nightmare web of shock and anxiety that held her, Morgana kept her head high. She would carry out Ranulf's instructions to the letter. There was nothing left to do but watch the drama unfolding before her.

The three monks rode through the ranks of Lindsey's soldiers, carrying her signet seal and the message of surrender to her castle. The drawbridge was lowered and a lone horseman came out to meet them. Lindsey, not anxious to endanger his own skin, took up a position on a hillock in the distance, along with several of his knights.

The horseman from the castle took the seal and parchment and went back inside. Morgana waited, heart hammering, for the next step.

Not five minutes later the rider came out again, and soon a courier was on his way through the fearsome ranks of the hostile army. At a sign from Lindsey ten mounted men flanked the rider and set their pace to his. He rode stiffly toward the cliffs, as if he was not used to the saddle, and as the cavalcade drew closer a single word escaped Bronwen's lips: "Daffyd!"

Morgana saw that her maid was correct and was angry. She could not believe her castellan would place her young harper's life at risk. Daffyd was a musician, after all, not a warrior—and very young for his not-quite-sixteen summers. Her next emotion was one of gratitude for the youth's courage in volunteering for such a mission. By the time they had picked their way up the trail to the clifftop she was able to greet her harper with the warmth his courage deserved.

"I see," she said, turning to Lindsey's men, "that it takes ten of your lord's English lackeys to guard one Welsh harper who has scarce outdistanced his boyhood. I wonder how many more would be required for a man fully trained to arms."

The English soldiers were taken aback, except for the burly sergeant leading them. "You are mistaken, lady. 'Tis not guards for the young lad we are, but rather an escort to honor yourself and see you safely to the castle."

Daffyd dismounted and knelt in the dust. His mellow, dark eyes shone with admiration at her daring and distress at the message he must deliver. "I bring you greetings from Sir Dyllis, my lady, and the news that, for fear of trickery, he will not surrender the castle unless he hears the orders to do so from your own lips."

Morgana lifted her chin proudly. "Then let us be on our way."

As they started off, she sent Bronwen a brave smile and said a silent prayer: *Jesu, grant us strength for what is next to come!* Afterward she could never quite recall the details of the journey down the cliff side and along the coast road. It seemed that one moment she was with Bronwen and Daffyd and the joint escort on the heights above the encampment, the next riding over the familiar drawbridge to her childhood home with the three monks following behind. The thick wooden planks rumbled beneath the iron-shod hooves and the heavy suspension chains creaked beneath the weight of horses and armored men. On either side, the surface of the moat shone and sparkled in the sunshine.

Morgana's hands were damp upon the reins. Could she really go through with it? As they reached the portcullis, Sir Dyllis, her castellan, came forward to greet her. Removing his cap to reveal his shiny bald dome, he dismounted and knelt before her.

"Ah, Lady Morgana, 'tis a sad day that we meet so."

"You have defended my castle as well as any man could, in the circumstances. Arise, Sir Dyllis, and lead us in, that we may conclude this sorry business."

She glanced back on the double line of horsemen and foot soldiers that trailed behind her. "As you can see, I have brought a goodly company with me."

To the tolling of St. Tristan's bells, the mounted cavalcade rode beneath the open portcullis. Sir Dyllis and Morgana led the way, with Bronwen and Daffyd close behind. Ahead stretched the descending ramp into the open space behind the first curtain wall, and beyond that, at twenty yards' distance, the ascending ramp leading to the second portcullis in the inner curtain wall. They seemed to be heading straight toward it, but once inside the first four riders swerved sharply, Sir Dyllis and Morgana to the left, Bronwen and Daffyd to the right upon narrow ledges. Wooden gates swung to behind them, compelling those following to proceed downward along the descending ramp. There was nowhere else they could go.

The bars of the second portcullis thundered down, blocking entrance to the inner bailey, and from behind came shouts and curses and a press of cavalry, propelling the now disorganized troops into the deep trough between the ramps. Morgana realized some unknown force was driving Lindsey's men from behind. Simultaneously there was a hissing sound, growing to a roar from the left. Without warning, a wall of turbid water came toward them in a foaming, rushing torrent.

Horses neighed and bucked in their panic as men and beasts were engulfed in the surging flood. The weight and force of the water was enough to send most of them tumbling into the swirling witch's brew. The scream of frightened animals covered the hoarse shouts of the soldiers as their heavy armor pulled them beneath the surface.

Morgana's mare rolled its eyes and tossed its head in fear, but she kept it under firm control. Behind them echoed the clash of sword on shield, and the screaming death throes of the beasts. With Sir Dyllis leading, Morgana picked her way along the spray-splashed ledge, always aware of the danger. The shod hooves might slip on such unsure footing, a mistake by the rider or the beast would send them skittering sideways into the flood. Or the defenders might have trouble closing the water gate. She glanced sideways uneasily. How much farther would it come up before leveling off?

Meanwhile Bronwen and Daffyd had gone in the opposite direction and Morgana could not help wondering if any or all of them would reach their destination. As it was, it took them an hour to reach the far side of the castle and the camouflaged opening. They would have gone past it, if not for the narrow wooden plank bridge that spanned the still roiling waters. At least the level was no longer rising.

Again, Sir Dyllis led the way, testing the solidity of the makeshift bridge before allowing Morgana to follow. Once certain it would bear their weight, he waved her on before him and stayed upon the ledge to guard their rear. He knew at least two horsemen had broken through the wooden gate and were following them, just out of sight around the bend. When Morgana was halfway across, their pursuers came into view and the castellan shouted for her to go on. A huge stone section of wall on the far side of the bridge pivoted open, leaving a dark yawning gap with just a glimpse of sunlight beyond.

As her mare covered the last few feet she looked back over her shoulder. Sir Dyllis's sword swung in a long arc and the knight nearest him reined his horse back. It was a fatal error. He careened into his companion and both animals slipped, stumbled, and fell, vanishing beneath the rushing waters.

Riding into the recess in the wall, Morgana's eyes took a moment to adjust to the light. Hands reached out to lead her mare into the sunshine, while figures moved past her to assist Sir Dyllis. She was so slack with relief she almost fell, but a pair of well-muscled arms reached out to steady her and pluck her from the saddle.

Caught safe and secure in an iron grip, her face tightly pressed against a wide chest, she was carried like a newborn babe into the bright light of the inner bailey. Her rescuer set her down and for the first time she realized who it was that held her.

Disbelieving the evidence of her own eyes, Morgana stood gaping at him. "My lord Ranulf!"

His armor was removed and she wondered if he were a specter raised up by her own guilt. The past twenty-four hours had been so strange she would not have been at all surprised to discover that was the case. But this was no ghost: he was solid and warm and intensely alive. It was such a shock after the anxiety of the past hours that her face blanched and her tongue was wooden.

"But . . . I thought you were surely dead!"

Her surprise and the sudden whirling of her disordered emotions left her unable to continue. She had been so positive he had perished in the mere that she could only gaze at him and shake her head numbly.

He looked back at her in silence, seeing only the stunned expression in her lovely eyes and misinterpreting her pallor. Anger burned like a fire in his chest. He had risked the lives of his men in her own desperate cause, and instead of receiving words of gratitude from her lips she could only stammer and exclaim her disappointment that he still lived. There was nothing he could do to win this haughty beauty to his side. His face twisted into a hard, cynical mask.

"My apologies, lady, for causing the acute chagrin you are suffering. I have no doubt my survival wreaks havoc with your plans for a second widowhood." He stepped away, his face grim. "Do not despair. The fighting is not yet over, and perhaps your hopes may still be realized. As it was, I nearly perished in the mere when at first I could not force the rusted grate."

Morgana took in a sharp breath. So her vision had been a true one, showing her Ranulf's terrible danger as clearly as if she had been at his side.

Ranulf did not see her reaction, but turned and began shouting orders to his men. "The castle is secure. Remove the bodies from the inner moat and strip them of weapons. There will be no looting of personal effects. Any man caught looting will have his hand struck off. When that is done, load the corpses onto carts. When the all clear is sounded, lay them out in the field to the north of the promontory."

"Aye, Sir Ranulf." They hastened to carry out his commands.

Morgana was angered by his threat to her men, but more so by the callous disposal of the fallen enemy troops. Her everready tongue took charge: "What right have you to issue such commands? And do you mean to deny Christian burial to the dead?"

In answer, Ranulf whirled around and pulled open his doublet to expose his deeply bronzed chest. "This gives me the right, lady, as well as the vows we exchanged as man and wife!"

A gaping wound across the lower left side of his ribs was packed with wicks of cloth stained with his blood. Morgana's gasp was drowned out by his savage tone as he refastened his garment.

"As to the dead, to leave them where they fell would invite pestilence, and the men are too weary and wounded to play sexton to those who would have murdered them at Lindsey's bidding. Furthermore, I wish to make it clear that we hold no prisoners within our walls who might aid another attempt to assault us from without."

Ranulf hailed the first man at hand. "Escort Lady Morgana to the keep and see that she remains there. By force, if necessary."

He swung around and walked away, calling out to one of the sargeants-at-arms as he went. Morgana knew Ranulf's decisions were sound and that she owed him a profound apology. It was only reaction to the circumstances and her inexperience with the aftermath of warfare that had made her blurt out such nonsense. She held her hands out imploringly.

"Sir Ranulf, wait!"

He paused in midstride and glanced back over his shoulder with a withering look. "Madam, I have the business of defense to conduct here. It were best that you take shelter in the keep and busy yourself in housewifery—and leave military matters in more capable hands."

While Morgana's face burned with embarrassment before the assembled men, who had heard every word of the exchange, Ranulf strode angrily away. She gritted her teeth and followed.

"He led her into the fair green wood,
O! sing the birds in every tree.
And pledged his heart and sword and word,
And she loved him all willingly.
O! sing the birds so sweetly..."

The strains of Daffyd's harp filled the torch-lit hall, soothing those who had fought and won the day's battle. To repel the damp of the thick stone walls, fires leaped and danced in the two massive hearths, each large enough to roast an ox whole over a burning tree trunk. The mood was relieved and festive.

The enemy was routed, with nearly half their number slain, and Castle Griffin, with no fatalities among its ranks, rejoiced with quantities of ale and good food: great roasts of veal and loins of beef, stuffed flounder and eels in wine sauce, leek and turnip pies, stewed salt venison and the favored mixtures of hard-boiled eggs with onions and cream, flavored with garlic, dittany and pepper.

There was little talking among the lower tables as the men and women ate from their trenchers of thick-sliced bread, but at the head table the plate was of silver and gold. Sir Dyllis—who had suffered only minor injuries—sat at the head table beside Ranulf, in recognition of his fine defense as castellan.

Arvil, Morgana's seneschal, signaled for the servers to bring in the next course of well-larded duckling and roast crane. He was a bluff and genial man of common stock, unlike most men of his position in aristocratic English domiciles, but he performed his tasks and oversaw the household with efficiency a duke might envy. Sir Dyllis accepted a helping of crisp duckling and continued his one-sided conversation with Ranulf as he relived again the battle that had won the day.

"Aye, my lord, you did surprise Lindsey's men in your clever trap—and myself, as well."

Ranulf nodded, and signaled to a page to bring fresh tankards of ale and refill the goblets of wine as the castellan rehashed the stirring events. The new master of the castle was richly dressed in a tight-fitting jacket of satin as deep a blue as his eyes over a doublet of white silk, and a heavy gold-link chain shone in the torchlight. He looked every inch the lord.

Morgana sent him occasional glances from beneath her lowered lids. The man who had kissed her so ruthlessly in the chapel at St. Tristan's had nothing in common with the man dominating the high table. The first had looked at her with heat and longing; this other man, who wore his face and form, was cold and hard as granite. He had not spoken a single word to her all evening. He truly believed she had wanted his death, and Morgana was too angry and proud to disabuse him of the notion.

Ranulf was equally angry, and his wrath had been for hours. He was good enough to save his haughty wife from cutthroats or greedy besiegers. Good enough to dive beneath the dark waters of the mere and fight for life, to force his way inside the castle and rally her people. But not good enough to be her husband. Rigid control kept him from giving away the fact that she was the center of his thoughts. From time to time his arm brushed hers and both quickly drew apart, as if burned. There was no way to avoid hearing her voice and smelling the wonderful combination of flower and spice and woman that was her scent. Her nearness tormented him.

Ranulf listened with half an ear to the conversation and contributed his own answers by rote. From time to time Sir Dyllis passed a hand over his bald head—as if assuring himself that it still remained safely upon his shoulders.

"Aye, Sir Ranulf, I thought your ruse was only to bring Lady Morgana safe within the walls until our allies could send support. When your troops came up behind Lindsey's men, forcing them into the flood and blocking their retreat, I could scarce credit my eyes. Sixty men to the rescue, when I thought we had but six more to rally to us!"

Desmond set down his tankard. "A wise commander always holds something in reserve. Before we left the Court, Sir Ranulf mustered the rest of his men to arm and follow our party with all due speed. They were never more than a day's forced march behind us."

"Ah. Lindsey was sore surprised by that, I'll warrant!"

"Yes," Ranulf said in a lowered tone. "And soon we'll have another unpleasant surprise in store when we ride on Lindsey Keep. But first we must put our own affairs in order here. He is in no position to attack again, and when he least expects it...."

The conversation had been going on in this way for the past hour while course after course was served for the triumphal feast; but the two most involved sat like stone statues through the greater of it, speaking to each other only when necessity dictated. Ranulf was in a good deal of pain from his injured side, but he had trained his warrior's body to ignore it as much as possible. The strong ale helped.

At his side, Morgana looked every inch a pampered lady, dressed in a high-waisted gown of amber silk with a necklace of citrine and topaz adorning her white bosom. No one would have recognized her as the weary youth who had ridden to the monastery gates the previous day. Even Ranulf, who tried to remain aloof, could not help admitting to himself that she was as alluring as she was aggravating. Damn her!

She picked at her morsel of capon, slivering the succulent flesh from the bones, but very little had gone into her mouth. Anger still bubbled deep inside her, and injured pride lodged in her throat like a bone. She had expected her people to be leery of Ranulf, but he had earned their respect. In fact, they admired him readily. And that rankled.

She had expected to clash with Ranulf over the question of authority at some time, but certainly not immediately after the battle, and with half her retainers for witnesses. The memory stung.

Before her eyes, blotting out the banner-hung great hall, the battered soldiers and relieved retainers, she saw Ranulf snapping orders to Owain, her Captain of the Guard. In that moment she had felt her authority and lifelong status as heiress of the castle being wrested from her hands. It was not right. She had been raised like a son, trained from birth to look after her people wisely and justly. Now, because she was a woman, a stranger had come in to take it all away from her. It was unfair, unjust.

Even so many hours later, her humiliation was still fresh and raw. It did not help matters to realize that Ranulf's orders had been sound, once she understood his reasoning. Taking a deep breath, she turned to offer some polite comment to Lady Wyn, her castellan's plump and kindly wife, only to discover that dame dozing contentedly over her cup. Morgana sighed. Would this night never end?

Snatches of conversation rumbled beneath the lyrical strains of Daffyd's song, but from time to time he sent a piercing glance toward the head table. And when he looked at Morgana, his eyes softened: it was to her he sang of gallant deeds and undying love, and every note plucked from his instrument was a message from his heart. Today, seeing her courage and spirit, the young boy's loyalty had deepened into something more.

"I sigh for you, lady,
I would die for you, lady..."

The lady of his dreams was completely unaware of his barely disguised devotion. She had a more immediate problem: her husband. Ranulf was pointedly ignoring her, and there was talk among the observers. He was ready enough to converse with Desmond and Owain and Sir Dyllis. He had made many a toast to their bravery and seemed as fit and hale as any of them. But over and over the past several minutes he had fallen silent—his brows drawn together in a fierce scowl that Morgana could no longer, in all good conscience, ignore.

She was sure his wound pained him greatly. It provided an excellent opportunity to show wifely compassion, while giving her a reasonable excuse to withdraw. "You suffer from your injury, my lord. I will retire to my chambers and prepare you a stronger herbal draught and have it brought to you."

She started to rise, but he caught her arm in a powerful grip just above the elbow and forced Morgana back into her chair. He leaned toward her so his voice carried to no other ears.

"Sulk and glower all you wish, but you shall stay and play your part as mistress of the castle."

"There is no need to use brutal tactics," she snapped. "If you wish me to remain in the hall, you have only to say so."

"Yes," he retorted beneath his breath. "Just as you have respected my wishes and obeyed my commands all along. You shall bear my company tonight until I give you leave to go."

"I did not know, my lord, that you were so desirous of my company. Indeed, nothing in your demeanor has ever given me cause to suspect it."

"I find no more pleasure in your companionship this eve than do you in mine. But you will follow my lead and present at least an appearance of enjoyment. I cannot command this castle if I cannot command proper behavior from my wife."

He let go her arm, thinking the matter settled. Morgana smiled with an arctic air that belied her heated blood. "I see you have been laboring under a misapprehension, Sir Ranulf. You must learn, my lord—and soon—that I rule this castle, and that no man rules me!"

Before he could respond she rose with such haste she overturned her chair. The thud of the brass-studded wood rang out clearly, for Daffyd had stilled his strings a moment earlier. Every eye in the hall, at least of those who had not imbibed too deeply, was focused on the head table in time to see Ranulf glower at his retreating wife. As for Morgana, she did not look back at all, but fled to the staircase leading to her chambers, knowing he would not submit to the indignity of following her.

Ranulf watched her go in a black rage compounded by utter frustration. Damn the woman for the Welsh witch she was! No matter what he did or said, she took instant offense. It seemed he would have to find some other means of winning her over and extracting the obedience that was a husband's due.

Desmond watched her dramatic exit and frowned indignantly across the sprawled chair. "By the Holy Sepulcher!" he growled. "You have risked your life a hundred times today to save her lands and she shows you no courtesy. For all the lady's fine estates, Edward has not been kind. He has shackled you to a troublesome, headstrong spitfire, when you might have taken your pick of a dozen Court beauties."

In spite of his wrath and the overwhelming desire to close his strong fingers around his wife's neck, it was then that Ranulf realized the desperateness of his situation. He did not want his pick of a dozen spoiled Court beauties.

He wanted only her. Morgana. The wife who scorned him.

It was like a blow to the head, stunning in its impact. He fought the urge to march up the stairs after her and demand his rights as husband. Right of law, the regulations of the Church and sheer force were all on his side. The thought was tempting. So tempting, he felt the heat in his loins set his blood aflame with desire. But he would likely win the battle, only to lose the war.

While this marriage was not of his own devising, there was no need for them to struggle through it like two armed foes. Perhaps he had been going about this business all wrong. There might be a much easier way to tame his maddening, yet bewitching, wife. There was no denying that she had been roused by his kisses in the chapel only last night. She had begged him not to leave. He wished he had thrown her over his shoulder, carried her out beyond the monastery walls and made her his, in the cool beauty of the moonlight.

A sudden optimism rose within him: sweet, honeyed words could work magic between a man and a woman. With Morgana's own passionate nature on his side, matters were not beyond mending. It was well known that all women were soft in their hearts, and that those soft hearts ruled in place of their heads. He would set about wooing his reluctant wife, and in short order harmony would be restored.

Forgetting his weariness and the throbbing of his wound, he stood up abruptly, almost spilling his wine cup. There were dark lights dancing in the depths of his eyes and determination in the set of his firm mouth.

"I will bid you goodnight, gentlemen. It is long past the time to seek my bed—and my bride."

Morgana's chamber was the one traditionally belonging to the lord and lady of the castle. It was a luxurious apartment, twenty feet wide by fifty feet long, with tall, arched windows on two sides and a massive fireplace. Flames burned brightly on the stone hearth, illuminating the huge canopied bed with its velvet hangings, and the table and chairs along one wall. A large carved cupboard dominated a third wall.

This was Morgana's private sanctuary. Here she could retreat from her duties as chatelaine of Castle Griffin and relax. The plaited rush mats were covered with fine carpet, and tapestries hung over the stone walls to keep out the chill. A new cushioned settle in one window embrasure, two high-backed chairs, several chests of ancient vintage and a low table from France, made to hold a lady's creams and lotions, completed the furnishings. The room across the wide corridor, where she had directed Ranulf's things to be taken, was smaller but also handsomely furnished. Once it had been her own.

Morgana kissed Bronwen, who had followed her from the hall, and sent her on to bed; but Elva, her old nurse, stood her ground and refused to leave. "Sir Ranulf was greatly angered, my lady," she said in her high, fluting voice. "I will stay with you yet a while."

"There is no need. I do not fear him," Morgana replied, and realized it was a lie. "He will not harm me," she added, and realized it was the truth.

Her perceptions of her new husband were as conflicting as her feelings regarding him. She knew she was in no physical danger from Ranulf, yet he *was* a threat to her and to her peace of mind in ways she did not fully understand.

Elva still hesitated, unwilling to leave her charge to the whims of an angry bridegroom. "'Tis easier to catch a bee with honey than with vinegar. An infusion of rosemary leaves and chamomile in wine is said to sweeten the disposition of a truculent husband, and cause him to love his wife full well."

"Sir Ranulf's disposition does not affect me, and I have neither wish nor need to engage his affections!"

The old woman tried to hide her smile at the heat in Morgana's voice. A woman who did not care would not become so proud and angry, therefore the falling out between the master and mistress was nothing more than a lover's quarrel, after all. But she still thought the rosemary and chamomile drink would smooth the way to a swift reconciliation.

When her waiting women were gone, Morgana sat on the small stool upholstered in velvet and pushed her heavy mass of hair away from her face. Despite the circumstances it was good to be home and in her own chambers. Everything in the room had special memories: the carved chest from the Low Countries her mother had given her for a dower chest, the richly hued Flemish tapestry from the old solar, the iron candle stands that had graced the great hall in her childhood years, the massive bed that had been her parents' and in which she herself had been born. Yes, it was good to be home.

With clever fingers she began to plait the silken tresses into a fat braid to lie over one shoulder, as the chamber door opened again. Thinking Bronwen or Elva had forgotten something, she continued her task until she heard the sound of the bar sliding home into its metal socket.

Morgana jumped to her feet, forgetting about her hair, which fanned out behind her in a shining cloud. Ranulf stood with his back to the bolted door, and she knew the moment of confrontation had come. Even with dark shadows of pain and fatigue beneath his eyes, he looked strong and vital, and more than a little dangerous. "We have unfinished business, madam."

He stripped off his doublet and shirt, revealing a fresh cloth bound over his wound, several severe bruises and a wealth of lean and rippling muscle. Now Morgana regretted dismissing her ladies with such blithe nonchalance. If only she had asked Bronwen to spend the night on a pallet beside her bed!

She drew herself up haughtily. "These are my sleeping chambers, my lord. The servants have prepared the one across the hall for you—as no doubt you have forgotten."

Ranulf came toward her purposefully, all his good intentions fled. Could she never once open her lovely mouth without baiting him in some way? "It would be wiser, lady, if in future you confine your temper tantrums to more private quarters and do not display your unseemly behavior before the entire hall."

Instantly Morgana's temper exploded. "I will not have you treat me as if I am of no account! I am the lady of this castle and used to seeing to the disposition of its wealth and welfare. I will not be relegated to the role of mute and dependent wife!"

Blue flames flickered in the depths of Ranulf's eyes. "And *I* will not be relegated to the role of mere consort. If I am not the master of the castle, if I have not the authority due me, then discipline will suffer and discontent will follow. Then we shall be ripe to fall into enemy hands on the next assault."

His unassailable logic acted like a bucket of ice water on Morgana's heated emotions. Ranulf was right again and she knew it. That did not make the fact any more palatable.

He saw the change in her face and smiled. "We can do better than this, wife. Let us forget for a moment that you are mistress here, and remember only that we are husband and wife. Alone together."

The timbre of his voice was low and vibrant, rousing memories of his touch. She paced to the window and looked out, unaware of how the soft illumination outlined her figure through the thin chemise. Ranulf's hasty temper was vanquished by the sudden remembrance that he had come here to woo, not fight. She was graceful in every movement, and the breeze through the open window molded the thin cloth about her figure. Need rose in him, but he waited, drinking in her beauty.

Morgana let the calmness of the night seep into her spirit. Moonlight iced the castle walls and latticed the restless sea. They had come through a perilous day together, and without Ranulf's cool daring and brilliant scheme, death and destruction would have followed. Perhaps a truce was indicated. Without turning her head, she spoke.

"Very well. We shall accept the formal oaths of fealty together. But you must understand that my people's great allegiance is first to my line, and thence to me. I cannot compel them to give the same degree of loyalty to you, who are a stranger to them."

Strong hands clamped down on her shoulders and she jumped, startled almost out of her wits. She had not heard Ranulf move; indeed, would not have guessed a man of his stature and muscular build could step so softly. Holding herself rigid, she kept her gaze on the night landscape far below.

Somehow, when he was so close to her, her brain stopped functioning in its normal and proper manner. She became witless and speechless. But there was nothing wrong with her female reactions, for they were markedly evident. She dared not let him know how much his nearness unnerved her, how the heat of his hands was burning through the fabric of her chemise.

He roused her with his closeness until her limbs trembled, her breasts strained against her bodice and heat spread out from a point below her waist to engulf her entire body. Suddenly she realized he was speaking to her, but had no idea of what he had just said. Ranulf swung her around to face him and her eyes were wide and dark in the half-light.

"That is an essential step in building unity," he said in a deep, low tone next to her ear. "And you must set the pace for your people in other significant ways if I am to win them to me. As I fully intend to do."

"And how do you propose that I bring this about?" There was a soft catch in Morgana's voice and her cheeks were hot.

"By example. You must show them that you accept me. As your lord. As your husband." His grip tightened, his powerful fingers kneading the tension from her shoulders.

There was no way she could mistake his meaning. Morgana was unable to meet his eyes. She looked away. Ranulf pressed closer, one big hand slipping down to rest at the curve of her waist. She was unable to move, to breathe. It was not Ranulf she feared now, but her own reactions. If his mere touch could render her so helpless, what would anything more do to her? Would she lose her sense of self, subordinate her will to him in all things?

Ranulf smiled down at Morgana, trailing one finger along the line of her jaw to a sensitive place near her ear. That smile did strange things to her insides. He touched his lips to her temple.

"Let us to bed, wife. It is time we grew to know one another within the bonds of marriage."

His breath touched her face, light and tingling against her skin and she found herself grasping at straws. "But... your...your wound, my lord."

"A mere scratch." He replied, lowering his head until his mouth was only a whisper away from hers.

"Perhaps I should re-dress it for you. I have a salve of my own making that hastens healing." Morgana was thinking fast now. "The salve and...and several days' rest are what you require. I...I would not wish you to come to any harm."

Ranulf's smile went crooked. "You would have been pleased enough had I perished in the mere, as well we both know. Do you think to make me forget how you ran from Court rather than share a marriage bed with me? But I remember how you felt in my arms last night, how your mouth softened and opened for my kisses."

His hand curved along her waist, rising to cup her breast in his firm palm. She shuddered and took a deep gasp of air as his hand closed around it possessively. "It is time we put the past behind us, Morgana, and live here and now."

He was so close she could feel the steady thrum of his heartbeat. She was only vaguely aware of the cold stone of the window embrasure against her back. Everything had faded into the background except for Ranulf's disturbing presence and more disturbing words.

He bent his head nearer. "We can neither of us run from our fate, lady. It is time to face it. Here. And now."

Ranulf's callused fingers stroked her cheek once and paused, cradling it against his palm. The gentle touch wove a spell of sudden intimacy about them. His breath was coming more quickly now, and so was hers. When he spoke, his voice was low and so deep it seemed to reverberate through her body.

"It is time, Morgana, that our marriage vows were proved by deed, as they have been by the spoken and the written word."

Seeing the flush that stained her cheeks and feeling the faint tremor that went through her body, he knew she was not as indifferent as she pretended. Desire rioted through his veins. His mouth came down upon hers hungrily. He stifled her protests with his kisses as his hands moved over her breasts, quickening her breath with every touch. Her scent and the warmth of her body intoxicated him. He gave in to the need coursing through him.

Sweeping her up into his arms he carried her toward the massive bed with its rich hangings, pausing only briefly to blow out the tall candle that burned beside it. A curl of blue smoke rose from the snuffed wick, filling the air with its pungent aroma. Now there was only moonlight and firelight to paint their bodies silver and gold.

A sweet languor filled Morgana. For so long she had been alone and thrown upon her own strength and resources. But now, for the first time in many years, she could lean upon someone else, let someone else be strong. At least for the moment. Her arm curled about his shoulder and she closed her eyes. Her fingers touched the warm solid muscles of his neck and wove themselves through his hair. She felt its texture and the way it curled at the nape as her fingertips moved lightly, exploring and memorizing as they went.

Without speaking, he placed her on the mattress, then removed the rest of his clothing. The mattress dipped beneath his weight and he reached out for her. There was only the flickering of the firelight through her eyelids, the deep silence, and a man and a woman. Then his lips, warm and soft, grazed her temple and left a line of fire along the side of her throat and down to the hollow at the base of it. Time stood still while her breath mingled with his.

She felt his hands pulling her chemise up to her hips, stopping to explore the silken softness of her thighs, and sighed with pleasure. She was torn between the need to stay whole and separate, and the need to join and merge. The decision was taken away from her conscious effort by the sensations of Ranulf's warm mouth skimming downward toward her breast and his fingers sliding upward between her thighs. Her own desires—the longing to be held and touched, the flaring urgency of her own passion—took over. She was as eager as he for the joining.

Now it was her hands that reached out to him, her fingers that twined in his hair, guiding his lips toward her breast. Her arms that strained to mold the hard planes of his scarred warrior's body against the feminine softness of hers, until his heart hammered inside his bruised ribs and his breath came in ragged bursts. When he straddled her and clasped her she raised her hips to meet him, and when he entered she cried out in pleasure. In victory and surrender.

His lovemaking was fierce and direct, as she knew it would be, answering something wild and untamed that rose like a fountain of light within her, showering sparks against her closed lids. She drew him closer, wanting to share the sensation. And when he arched and called her name out hoarsely, she was caught up again in a need as intense and potent as his own. The moment spun out a vortex of color and sensation that left her spent and gasping in his arms.

Much later, when he lay sleeping with his left arm and leg flung across her possessively, protectively, she was still awake, watching the glowing embers in the fireplace. Her fingertips stroked his bare skin, reveling in his sinewy strength, the corded muscles of his neck and shoulders and arms. Had he felt the same thing she had? That rapt sense of merging that was beyond anything she had ever known or dreamed of?

Her body was replete, content. Sated. Somehow his love-making had stirred her as Robin's calculated touch had never done. Perhaps because Robin had made it all a game of showing her how skillful a lover he was, proving that he could rouse her against her will even while his thoughts dwelt on his latest mistress. That had wounded her terribly.

In time, the emotional scars had thickened and she had learned to take what she could and give as little as he had.

But Ranulf had made love to *her*, wanting *her*. And that had created an emotional whirlwind that had caught her up before she had realized what was happening. Ranulf's love-making had been honest and direct, and wholly consuming. And in some ways, terrifying. The way he made her feel, the way her wits tangled and her bones melted at his nearness, his touch—at those moments he might persuade her that night was day or that snow fell in the summer's heat. She could lose herself, her very identity could be subordinated to his own, to his aims and needs and goals. She would have no defenses against it. Or him. That could be a powerful weapon in his hands. There was only one way to save herself.

She must never let him know.

Chapter Seven

"Good morning, my lady. I've brought you ale and bread and cheese, and the scullery maid will be up with some warm water."

Old Elva's voice, light and frail and incredibly dear. Morgana turned over lazily and yawned, suspended in that mellow state between a healthy night's sleep and a gentle awakening. She was only half aware of the chamber door opening and shutting again, softly.

It was wonderful to be home, to smell the familiar fragrance of her own special mixture of sweet herbs scattered over the woven rush mats and fine-piled carpets of her bedchamber. How luxurious the deep feather bed felt after so many days of travel and...

Suddenly she was startled fully awake by thoughts of the previous night. Of Ranulf. Her eyes blinked open. With mingled regret and relief, she realized she was alone. It would make their next meeting easier in some ways but more difficult in others. At least, she thought, it would be easier to maintain a careful distance if their first encounter of the day took place in a public setting. Morgana could not let Ranulf's lovemaking cloud her judgement. She must make clear that the castle and its inhabitants fell under her jurisdiction, that whatever occurred between them within the marriage bed had no bearing on anything else. But her heartbeat accelerated, remembering.

An hour later, by St. Tristan's bells, Morgana put her resolution to the test. Breaking her fast with bread, cheese and ale, she bathed and put on a gown of white kendal with deep, scalloped sleeves over her kirtle of fine white linen. The hem, sleeve edges and low square of the neckline were trimmed with embroidered sapphire ribbons that matched her daintily pointed slippers.

Instead of a more modern collar necklace, such as she would have worn at Court, Morgana chose an intricately worked torque of thin gold leaves. They caught the light as they trembled on their fine wire stalks, weightless as down and capturing the sunlight with rare brilliance. This was the ancient necklace of extraordinary Celtic workmanship, handed down for generations to the heirs of Castle Griffin. Its worth was in more than the value of the gold or the skill of the craftsman, for it symbolized for the people Morgana's invested power and authority.

Bronwen, too, was dressed splendidly in her best gown of apple green velvet corded with canary silk, and an inch-wide collar of gold inlaid with cabochons of apple green chrysoprase.

"My lady," Bronwen said rapturously, as she prepared to place a gauze-veiled headdress upon her mistress's hair. "You look so beautiful that Sir Ranulf will be dazzled."

And indeed Morgana did look particularly beautiful in the warm morning light. Her eyes sparkled, her cheeks glowed and her skin had a soft, rose-petal flush that deepened whenever her thoughts strayed to her night in Ranulf's arms. But now she must think of other things and put her own inner turmoil aside. She waved away the headpiece.

"No, not the hennin today. I want my pearl fillet and the matching net."

While at Court she wore the sometimes extravagant headdresses that fashion required, but in the country she usually confined her hair to a simple snood or coiled it over her ears and pinned a sheer veil over it. Today she meant to visually establish her role as the heiress and mistress of Castle Griffin before Ranulf and his men. This first impression would be crucial to her success.

Bronwen unlocked a metal-banded coffer and took out a simple gold and pearl circlet centered with a large cabochon sapphire and placed it on Morgana's head. Next she caught the heavy rose-gold tresses in a gold net studded with small pearls and sapphires that fell long behind her shoulders.

"Ah, how beautiful you are, my lady!"

Bronwen was not flattering her mistress. Morgana looked every inch the princess she would have been if history had gone differently. Her great-grandfather had been a Celtic prince of Cymru who had fought vainly against English domination and, in battle, had effected deeds of such chivalry that he had won the respect and admiration of the English King.

In recognition of Owain ap Griffin's extraordinary bravery and fairness—and to prevent further uprisings among his Welsh partisans—her grandfather had been "pardoned" for protecting his own country and people, given a noble English wife and allowed to keep his estates; but he was Cymric to the core, and saw to it that his son and grandson married Welsh women to dilute the blood of the conquering English.

Morgana could not betray her heritage by meekly turning over her birthright to a man she scarcely knew. Under English law, a wife could defend her husband's domain in times of war or danger—but those same laws transferred a wife's wealth and estates to her husband. They became his, and she, merely another possession. That same husband could imprison or abuse his wife, insult her by sleeping with the serving wenches or bringing home a mistress, and she would have no recourse except murder or death by natural causes. But Morgana's situation was different: the castle and chief estates could pass along the female line, and it was only through her children that it could be inherited. If she died, without direct heirs, Castle Griffin would pass, not to Ranulf, but to her closest kin.

This gave her an immeasurably better position. By her carriage, appearance and demeanor, she must at all times project that same authority, justice and leadership that her people looked to. Ranulf and his men would learn that she ruled here. Alone.

After a moment's hesitation, Morgana rejected the gold-hilted dagger inlaid with rubies that Ranulf had given her as one of his marriage gifts. Instead she tucked her old dagger with the cabochon sapphire in the hilt into the gilt leather sheath attached to her gold link belt. Armed with her dignity and the resolve that no man should conquer her so easily, she descended to the great hall, accompanied by Bronwen.

A large room that had once served as the old hall had been converted to an infirmary. A score of men lay on the straw mattresses recovering from their wounds and Lady Winifred reported cheerily that none seemed to be in any danger, although they had amputated two fingers from one of the soldiers earlier. As Morgana went from pallet to pallet with Lady Winifred and Bronwen, offering words of comfort, she found that Ranulf had been there before her.

"Aye, my lady," the castellan's wife told her, "Sir Ranulf came to check the progress of each man before breaking his fast. Quite knowledgeable about the care of wounds and such, he is. He was closeted with Sir Dyllis in the armament room earlier, but I believe he is watching the sword practice now."

Morgana made her rounds, but Lady Winifred and Elva had things well in hand, overseeing the care of the men with the help of Cerdic and some others. She was surprised to find that Bronwen was rather silent and stayed on the periphery, for her maid was much interested in the healing arts. Was she avoiding one of Ranulf's men? As chatelaine, the welfare of every person within Castle Griffin's walls was Morgana's responsibility and she made a mental note to look into the matter further: no matter how much reliance Ranulf put in his men, she would not have them harassing her women. Perhaps she should make this clear to her husband now, and nip the potential problem in the bud. Leaving Bronwen to prepare bandages for Elva, she went out to the inner ward in search of her husband.

Overhead terns arced in the cloudless blue sky and the sun baked its warmth into the ancient stones. As she approached the area set aside for arms practice, she heard the clash and ring of steel on steel. She expected to find Ranulf in the yard overseeing the training, but certainly not actively taking part. Her expectations were wide of the mark.

Flashing in the morning light, the blade of Ranulf's sword carved shining swaths through the air and rang against the rim of his opponent's shield. No matter that their swords were blunted, their bodies heavily padded against the blows—this was a hard and hazardous contest and neither man held back.

For a fraction of an instant, Morgana took great pleasure in observing the masterful way Ranulf handled himself and his weapon, the quick thrust, the strong parry that were inexorably backing his adversary into the angle where two walls met. But a closer look showed he was beginning to tire visibly and the strain was etched deeper in every line of his face. Morgana ran down the steps into the yard.

"Stop! Put up your swords! My lord Ranulf, what in God's name do you mean by such foolishness?"

They could not hear her over their heavy breathing and the rending clash of metal on metal. Morgana moved in closer behind Ranulf, and a mighty swing brought the sword whistling through the air. She felt the turbulence of its passing flutter the hair near her neck and then Ranulf

pushed her aside with a painful nudge of his shoulder and
sent her sprawling against the wall.

Instantly Ranulf dropped his arms and whirled toward
her angrily. The other man's reactions were not so quick. He
followed through with his blow and was unable to stop in
time. The flat of his blade caught Ranulf in the shoulder and
sent him heavily to the ground.

He was stunned but even before his head cleared Ranulf's
mighty roar filled the little courtyard. "By St. George and
the Dragon, what cause have you to interfere in man's
work?" He rolled to his knees and used his sword as a lever
to pry himself upright. Morgana was trembling with reaction from the near miss but was painfully aware that
Ranulf's left arm hung at his side, near useless from the
bruising blow it had taken.

"My lord, I fear your wound has opened under the press
of the swordplay, and now you have sustained another injury. Let me take you within."

"No, by God! 'Tis you should be within the walls tending to your woman's work, and not rushing about where you
have no business to be!"

He rubbed his arm, trying to restore the circulation.
Morgana could see the dark shadows of exhaustion beneath his eyes, the white pain lines around his mouth. She
was so agitated that she hardly heard his words, and she
started forward to help him before their meaning sank in.

"You overspeak yourself," she said haughtily. "I have the
right and obligation to know what is happening anywhere
within these walls."

Ranulf waved her away roughly. "Leave military matters
to those who are skilled in them, madam, and return to your
embroidery and housewifely concerns!"

Her temper flared, but Morgana controlled it. How dare
he! To treat her as his lady love by night, and like a scullery
maid by day! Well, she would not let his rough tongue re-
duce her to a shrew in front of the others. "I shall not leave

until you agree to come with me, so I may examine and re-dress your wound."

He would have argued further, but where Ranulf had been ruddy-faced before, he suddenly went pale and beads of sweat stood out upon his upper lip and brow. "John Potter, give me your arm," he said gruffly, and let his companion assist him across the yard. Blood stained his doublet and dripped down his sleeve.

Lifting her skirts, Morgana ran on ahead and instructed another man to assist John Potter in bringing their master inside. She raced through the hall, giving orders as she went, and up the stairs to her own chamber. By the time they half carried Ranulf up to the room, she had needles, heavy waxed thread and strips of clean cloth at the bedside, as well as a variety of herbs and unguents.

They placed Ranulf on the bed and quickly stripped him of his clothes at her bidding. The linen bandage bound over his ribs was soaked with scarlet and new runnels of blood dripped from beneath it. He was conscious but weak from rapid loss of blood, which scarcely hindered his ability to curse low and fluently. As long as he could do so, Morgana was not too frightened; but when his flow of words ended abruptly with a hiss of pain and she saw him go gray with it, a cold fist closed around her internal organs and squeezed her own breath from her lungs.

"Do not try to speak," she commanded urgently. "I will have the bleeding stopped in no time."

Bronwen entered with the container of hot water Morgana had requested, almost dropping her burden when she saw her master's pallid face.

"Oh, my lady, he is dying!"

"Nonsense! Put the basin down on the chest, Bronwen, and hold your tongue."

"Yes, my lady. Shall I fetch Elva, my lady?"

"Yes. And Lady Winifred, too." Morgana was already at work and concentrating on the task at hand. Ranulf's skin was slick with sweat, his breathing rapid and shallow as she removed the bloodstained pad that had been bound over the injury site. The edges of the wound had pulled apart and beneath the welling blood she saw the exposed muscle. Some of the tension went from her body. Although bruised and discolored, his skin appeared healthy with no sign of infection. Ranulf was strong and hale and in time he would recover from the blood loss.

"I shall sew the edges together tightly and apply a special poultice to keep the wound clean and sweet. A few days' rest are all he needs to recover completely."

"The wound must be cauterized," a sharp voice said behind her.

Morgana looked over her shoulder, to see Desmond's frowning visage. "There is no need, and cautery would form scars that might not knit properly. My poultice will suffice, as you shall see, Sir Desmond."

"It had better!"

He watched until Morgana had packed Ranulf's side with an absorbable paste and stitched the raw edges of skin back together, then helped her force a sleeping draught between the patient's pale lips. There was a long purple bruise forming on Ranulf's left shoulder, but she was glad to see the circulation in his arm and hand were normal. No great damage had occurred. When his breathing softened and he slipped into welcome sleep, the others left the room—except for Bronwen and Desmond. He stood at his cousin's side like an angry avenging angel until reassured by Ranulf's returning color. He then left, pausing briefly on the threshold.

"If anything should happen to Ranulf, lady, I will hold you greatly responsible."

"You cannot blame me for his actions. Had he not been so foolish he would not have opened his wound again."

"You forget I witnessed the incident. It was when he twisted so suddenly to save your life that he caused the damage."

"Your accusation is ridiculous," she said impatiently.

Desmond sent her a disgusted look. "Let your mirror be the judge of that." Then he was gone.

"Your hair!" Bronwen cried out softly.

Morgana rose and went to her mirror, not understanding at first. Her hair seemed to have escaped its confines, falling in shining waves down her back. And then she noticed her jeweled netting was sliced neatly through on the right and a lock of her hair was cut off level with her collarbone. Another inch closer and her throat would have been sliced open. Ranulf's quick action had saved her life. And if Desmond's observation was correct, saving her was what had endangered his own.

She sent Bronwen back to the hall and sat on a low stool beside the bed to keep vigil, alone with Ranulf's sleeping form and her own bleak thoughts. From the start she had been proud, hasty and far too ready to treat her unwanted husband as an encroaching peasant.

In return, he had demonstrated daring, ability and great courage in his public role—and in their private dealings he had shown generosity and restraint until the previous evening. Last night, lying in his strong arms, she had learned another facet of the complicated man she had wed. He had shown a tenderness that was both unsuspected and remarkable in a man of such deep all-consuming passions.

She touched his cheek with her finger, feeling the heat of his skin, the hard, sculpted line of his jaw. Morgana could not help wondering who this man she had married really was and what he truly wanted from her—and what the future held for them.

Three days later, Morgana stood upon the ramparts and surveyed her domain. Things were returning to their normal state. Those villagers who had survived and fled Lindsey's army straggled back to their homes from hiding places among the cliffs and woods. Thin and hollow-eyed, they set about their daily routine as if death and disaster had not intervened. Cattle grazed on the slopes, men and women tended the fields not trampled by the troops and children dug for clams along the shore, shouting and calling to each other.

The fishermen who lived along the strand returned again with their boats on each evening's tide, nets straining with the bounty of the sea. Life resumed its familiar routine. In the shadow of a tree or behind the cow byre, young lovers met to steal a kiss or even a hasty tumble. There was something about those happy, furtive figures that made Morgana ache inside, with a restlessness she could neither name nor conquer.

A small figure on horseback, accompanied by a man-at-arms, trotted down the lane from the village and Morgana had no trouble recognizing Bronwen in her blue cloak. It was a surprise, however, to recognize her escort as the red-haired Desmond of Orkney. For one thing, he scarce left Ranulf's side except to attend to military matters; for another, he had made abundantly clear his dislike of Morgana and all she stood for. Apparently that dislike, rooted in anger at her treatment of his cousin, did not extend to Bronwen. She would have to keep her eye on him. Bronwen was innocent and inexperienced, and ripe to fall for a dashing young knight.

Morgana had sent her maid to obtain a salve of rare restorative properties from an old woman known for her wisdom in herbal lore. She would mix it with an infusion of her own making and apply it to Ranulf's side to facilitate the healing process. His wound was not responding as rapidly as it should have, most likely because he refused to "lie abed like a puling infant."

Leaving the windy parapet, she went down the winding stairs to the lower level and into the great hall, where her red-and-gold griffin banner hung side by side with Ranulf's blue-and-white dragon-prow pennant. A small army of servants swarmed over the plaited rush mats that covered the stone flags of the floor. A young boy polished one of the tall, twisted candle holders flanking the open doorway and old Elva herself burnished two rare and valuable silver chargers in a bright window embrasure. Morgana surveyed them with satisfaction. All would be in readiness for the afternoon's great event.

"Place that before the dais, and the other just below," Lady Winifred called out to the two servants carrying carpets purchased by Morgana's ancestors during the Crusades. Sweet herbs had been scattered about, the long tables pushed against the side walls and the canopy of state erected over the dais where Morgana would sit: today she would receive the oaths of allegiance from her retainers and the people of the castle and its environs, and settle any disputes or grievances.

The head table had also been pushed back on the low dais and Lady Winifred bustled about, directing two men as they carried Ranulf's heavy chair back and brought Morgana's heavy chair out to the center of the platform.

"No," a deep voice said with firm authority. "Bring both chairs forward."

Morgana spun around to see Ranulf descending the last few steps. He moved rather stiffly but with his usual commanding presence, which was enhanced by the gem-studded chaplet upon his head. Lady Winifred sighed aloud. "So handsome," she murmured. "A prince among men."

Morgana had to agree. A stranger wandering in might easily mistake her husband for the King. Ranulf was dressed with simple elegance in a doublet of sapphire silk embroidered on the breast with his own insignia. A chain of massive gold and silver sunbursts, another gift of the King, hung around his neck and a square-cut emerald gleamed with cold fire on the index finger of his right hand. Neither the fine fabrics nor blaze of jewelry could hide the strong muscles and sinew beneath or give an observer the slightest doubt that he was a warrior through and through.

Without hesitation, the servants brought his chair to the front of the dais, also, and Lady Winifred came forward, beaming. "Sir Ranulf, I am gladdened to see you up and about. Indeed, I did not think you would leave your bed this sennight, although you were in my prayers at Mass this morning."

"I thank you, Lady Winifred, for your good nature as well as your kindly prayers."

He returned her greeting courteously, and with a smile that made the older woman's face go pink with pleasure. Ranulf had lost weight since the battle, which only served to highlight his handsome, hawk-like features; still he could not hide from Morgana's keen sight the effort the exertion had cost him.

She narrowed her eyes. "I left strict instructions with Cerdic that you were to rest today. You are in no condition to be out of bed, my lord."

"Is that why you have tried to keep me an invalid? How solicitous of you, my dear wife."

His eyes were hard and cynical and she looked in vain for any sign of the tenderness he had shown only a few nights past. She swallowed her disappointment. "I do not understand your meaning."

Now his mouth twisted in a hard line. "No doubt I have spoiled your plans by rising before you could officiate alone at the oath-taking today; however Cerdic is not one of your underlings, but a soldier under military command. He takes his orders from me."

"Then let him accept the responsibility for your relapse. Which I am sure is not far ahead of you! As to today's ceremony, you will of course participate now that you are able."

"Of that, I have every intention." He bowed mockingly and went out.

Privately, Morgana doubted he would make it through the morning without collapsing, but as the day wore on Ranulf proved her wrong. The hall was thronged with people, a shifting mass of color and sound as a steady stream came forward to pledge their loyalty and force of arms to the lady and lord of the castle.

Ranulf's amazing stamina astonished Morgana. It seemed her husband was made of iron or some other durable substance. Or perhaps, she thought, it was his pigheadedness that kept him going—for during the oaths of fealty he did his part as regally as any monarch, extending his hand for the ritual kiss and making all the proper responses. Only Morgana, and perhaps Desmond, realized his hands grasped the arms of his carved chair more for support than effect, and that the gravity of his face was the result of pain and not merely the solemnity of the occasion.

Morgana could not help glancing at him from time to time, wondering how much longer he could maintain his strength. And she could not help remembering how his face had looked in the firelight that one night as he held her, the warmth of his lips upon hers, the touch of his hands upon her skin. Hurriedly she brushed the memories away and attended to the business at hand. Now the second part of the day's events would begin with the presenting of legal differences and grievances to be weighed and judged by the lord and lady of the Castle Griffin.

The bailiff presented the first case, a dispute between a poor village woman who, in early spring, had sold a milk cow to a prosperous miller from the next valley. The cow had subsequently died and the miller wanted his money and barter goods back.

Morgana had dealt with many like situations in the past. She addressed the man: "The widow Gleyn vows the cow was in good health at the time of the exchange and that the beast did not fall ill for three weeks after that. Is this true?"

The miller admitted the truth of it. "Then," Morgana ruled, "you both agree that the animal was fit at purchase and for many days afterward. This widow acted in good faith and cannot be held responsible for the death of your cow."

The woman was overjoyed to be vindicated and the miller accepted the decision resignedly. He had known his case was not very strong but felt it would have been foolish not to at least try and recoup his loss.

The next issues dealt with boundary disputes, a garden raided by pigs and an unpaid bride fee, all of which Morgana dispatched efficiently. She noticed that Ranulf seemed surprised at her ability to quickly sum up a situation and hand down a just decision. Did he think her incapable of conducting her own business? This was what she had been trained for from birth.

The next matter was something quite different, and she saw a chance to even the score. A Welsh archer named Meredith challenged the claim of an English soldier to ownership of a great sword and other weapons stripped from an enemy corpse. The Welshman's arrow had pierced the enemy knight's mail and knocked him from his mount, but it was the axe of the Englishman that had actually delivered the coup de grace. Now each man claimed the spoils for himself.

Morgana was caught on the horns of a sharp dilemma, for only a Solomon could render a judgment that would not split the castle forces into two opposing factions. She saw a golden opportunity to drop this hot coal in Ranulf's lap. Not only would she escape unscathed, but he would quickly learn that her duties, which he was so anxious to assume, were not always pleasant ones.

She turned to Ranulf and favored him with her sweetest smile. "My lord," she said dulcetly, "perhaps you would wish to render judgment in this matter."

Ranulf sent her a long, assessing look, but his reply was as bland as milk. "Madam, the incident involves your man and occurred upon your demesne lands. I would not trespass on your authority."

It was the perfect answer and her followers murmured their approval. Morgana sprang her trap. "Ah, sire, but I most sincerely beseech you to accept the role of adjudicator, as the dispute occurred during military action and *your* experience in such matters far outweighs mine."

The words were hardly out of her mouth when she saw Ranulf's look of triumph and realized her great error: he had turned the tables on her. Before her knights and squires and all the rest she had openly—if unintentionally—acknowledged her husband's position to be equal to her own. Furthermore, she had conceded his superiority in affairs concerning the defense and protection of her people and estates. Morgana ground her teeth in frustration.

The faintest suspicion of a smile lifted the corners of Ranulf's mouth and the tiny lines of strain around his eyes were momentarily eased. "Your confidence shall not be disgraced, my lady." He nodded to the bailiff. "Bring forward the items in question."

The man brought out a long, damascened sword with a gilded hilt enclosing a polished chrysoberyl, a short sword of plain workmanship and a thin but deadly looking dagger with an orange carbuncle set into the hilt. Ranulf quickly assessed their worth. "Is there any man here who can attest to the nature and severity of the wounds suffered by the late owner of these implements?"

"Aye, my lord." Desmond stepped forward, his ruddy hair gleaming in the sunlight. "'Twas the axe that dispatched the man, although given enough time the arrow would have accomplished the same end. Later, as we cleared the battlefield, both men arrived on the scene together.''

''Very well.'' Ranulf eyed each of the claimants in turn with his piercing blue eyes. ''The matter is quite clear. In a melee or pitched battle, a man needs a long sword to properly fight and defend himself, while such a weapon would prove ineffectual and dangerous at close quarters. On the other hand, a small sword or dagger could prove ineffective in the field yet save the day and its owner's life upon the ramparts.''

A hush had fallen over the assemblage. There was not one whisper, one cough or careless footstep to break the spell of Ranulf's judgment. He rose and stood at the edge of the dais commandingly.

''Hear my decision. By custom of war, you are each entitled to the spoils. Therefore, let each man be given the weapon most likely to save his life in battle. To the archer I award the short sword and dagger, which his clever marksmanship have earned him. To the soldier I grant the long sword. May you each use your weapons well and may they protect you in peace and in war.''

Morgana was surprised yet pleased at Ranulf's deftness in averting ill feeling. The archer and the soldier showed no signs of displeasure with the decree. While she had meant to hand him a stinging nettle, she was mistress of the castle as well as wife, and relieved that harmony had been preserved. But the cynical look he directed at her now let Morgana know he had been aware of her motives. Their shaky relationship had lost some of the solid footing gained with the defeat of Lindsey's forces and their night together as husband and wife.

Only later did she realize that she had lost something else. It appeared that Ranulf had managed to usurp some of her authority. The servants, as well as the soldiers, turned to him for advice and questions as they had previously turned to her. Strange, for her people had never given the same acknowledgment and ready obedience to Robin, although they had known him far longer. Perhaps they were tired of "petticoat rule," as Robin had once called it. Yet it seemed to be something more. In the space of days, Ranulf had carved himself a role within the precincts of Castle Griffin.

Morgana felt a bitter sense of hurt and abandonment when she saw how her men accepted him. Soon they would turn to her husband for any and all decisions, and her sphere would shrink to the sickroom, the stillroom and the storeroom. Not a happy outcome, from her point of view, and she was determined to fight such a fate.

After the formal audience was over, Elva urged Ranulf to retire to his chambers so she might repack his wound with fresh lint. Morgana saw her old nurse was tired. "Do you rest a while, Elva. I shall dress the wound with a special salve I mean to prepare, for Bronwen returned earlier with the necessary ingredients."

She bowed to Ranulf. "Come, my lord, and I shall put a soothing poultice on your injury and pour you a refreshing draught of wine and herbs." Ranulf seemed on the point of refusing. Morgana lowered her voice to a whisper. "There will be great feasting tonight and you must maintain your strength before the others."

"As you wish, my lady."

He mounted the steps with her and she noted how rigidly he held his body. Was he angry with her, or did he fear her ministrations would not be as gentle as Elva's? She pushed the door to her chamber open and they went in. Sunlight spilled through the windows, making the colors of the tapestry glow like jewels. While Ranulf stood by the bed, one hand gripping the heavy post, Morgana brought out her materials and began to mix them into the paste she had prepared earlier. Adding extract of primrose and cinquefoil to her concoction, she stirred the liquid into the salve.

"There. It is ready." Turning toward the bed, she offered words of reassurance. "Have no fear, I will not cause you undue pain."

Ranulf did not answer. He lay collapsed upon the bed, white-faced with pain and exhaustion. She ran to his side in alarm. His pulse was strong but tumultuous, and drops of water stood out like crystal beads along his wide forehead.

"It is only the pain," he said between clenched teeth. "It will ease if I remain still."

Morgana hurriedly prepared him a cup of wine laced with poppy juice, and cradled his head against her breast while he drank the bitter draught. Then she helped him settle back against the cushions of the bed. Within a few minutes his breathing came easier and his rapid pulse lowered; but his pallor concerned her. It was a wonder he had been able to hide his true condition throughout the long and tiring ceremony. For the first time Morgana appreciated the willpower and discipline that gave him such tremendous inner strength.

It would not do to leave him until she was sure of his comfort. Morgana sat beside him on the bed, contemplating this stubborn man who was her husband. Earlier he had proved his courage and physical prowess in danger, and today he had shown that he had a keen wit, as well—coupled with integrity, a sense of justice and the ability to command loyalty from his troops. An excellent combination of abilities for the security of her estates—and a dangerous combination where her own foolish heart was concerned.

Careful not to disturb him, she blotted the beads of sweat from his face. Of their own volition, her fingers stroked the thin white line of scar that bisected his left eyebrow. Quickly she removed her hand as if the touch of his skin had burned her. She was drawn to him, attracted to his strength and warmth like a moth to a candle flame. Again the fear welled up in her.

Robin had hurt and humiliated her with his scandals and infidelity, but he had never conquered her, never driven her to her knees. She had survived that tragic marriage with her heart intact, for he had never touched her deepest emotions. They had been insulated from pain by exchanging suspicion for trust, endurance for hope, indifference for love.

Ranulf was as different from Robin as fire from ice, but that made him even more hazardous to her peace of mind. Morgana knew he had married her for her wealth and position. Such marriages were expected for a woman of her station. And it was imperative that she remember, at all times, that romantic love was merely the stuff of ballads. She must not allow her gratitude and growing regard for him to blossom into something more. It could destroy her.

Leaning down, she listened to his soft breathing. He would awaken from this slumber refreshed and...his mouth, she thought, is the most beautiful mouth.... A wave of tenderness swept through her, followed by such intense longing it frightened her. She touched a finger to his lips. A word from them could bring her anger to full fire and turn her to a shrew; a kiss from them and she became a fool, giddy with delight. Morgana frowned down at him. What sorcery had he woven, to beguile her so? Anger was a good antidote and she tried a dose.

"If you had not been so imprudent as to rise from your sickbed," she chided softly, "you would not be in such a sorry state now. I sincerely wish you would use half the brains the Good Lord gave to you."

Ranulf's eyes opened, drowsy and dark as the midnight sea, and his mouth curved in a slight smile. "And I sincerely wish, my sweet wife," he whispered, "that your tongue were even half as gentle as your hands."

He took the sting from his words by grasping one of Morgana's hands in his and bringing it up to his lips. He did not release it again until slumber truly claimed him. Morgana stayed at his side awhile, at war with herself and her fate. Long after she left him sleeping, with Elva to keep watch, Morgana went about her own duties, still feeling the warm imprint of that kiss tingling along her fingers.

She went up to a room high in the west tower that had been her favorite retreat in childhood and later, a place of refuge when she was troubled. This had been her grandmother's room and even now it carried the faint familiar scent of her. How Morgana had loved her wise and gentle grandmother—just thinking of her namesake brought a feeling of security, of being loved and cherished.

Whenever she was at the castle, she always cleaned and dusted the few items of furniture herself. They were quite modest. There was a small platform, still hung with curtains of red brocade, and an old mattress stuffed with wool and covered with a matching throw. Beside it stood a deep chest some seven feet in length, and opposite was another carved with intricate intertwining scrolls. This second chest was smaller and quite ancient. It had come from across the Irish Sea with a long-dead ancestor and held her late grandfather's most prized possessions.

Kneeling beside it, Morgana unlocked the iron clasp and lifted the heavy lid. Inside, protected by folds of green brocade, was a bulky object wrapped in yellowed silk. She withdrew it carefully and pulled off the fabric to reveal a splendid harp of gilded and inlaid wood, carved with scrolls and whorls that had neither beginning nor end. It had been in Morgana's family for generations, its history buried in the very mists of time. Legend said it had been made by the mighty Merlin himself, and that Castle Griffin and its heirs would endure as long as the harp remained in the possession of its descendants.

Although Morgana was skilled upon such instruments, she could not play this one, for it was much larger than the usual bard's lap harp. It had been made for the hands of a giant of a man and was beyond her female strength. Her grandfather had been the last man to play it, but Morgana kept it carefully preserved and in perfect readiness. Despite her Christian upbringing, deep inside her Celtic soul Morgana truly believed the safety of Castle Griffin was magically entwined with the safety of the harp. It was her sworn duty to protect and guard it.

She rewrapped the instrument and placed it within the chest but did not lock it just yet. The strings had sounded flat when she tried to pluck them. Perhaps it was time to have it restrung.

Usually just entering the room brought a sense of peace and tranquility to Morgana, but today she was tense and restless. Crossing to the window she knelt on the cushioned seat to open the casement, and folded her arms on the cold stone sill. A sea of rippled green silk stretched out to the bright horizon and gulls wheeled and called to one another. Morgana took no notice. Her eyes were fixed on some nebulous internal landscape where the horizon was dim and far away. Suddenly she was afraid. Love carried with it such a terrible threat of loss. Her thoughts turned to Ranulf and she knew he was the source of her inner turmoil.

"Please," she whispered desperately. "Please don't let me love him."

But though she could not admit the fact, even in the hidden corners of her mind, it was already too late.

Chapter Eight

Far below, the restless night sea threw dark waves against the solid rock, spattering it with showers of diamonds. Wrapped in a cloak of wool lined with miniver, Morgana stood high on the uppermost parapet while her hair streamed in the gusting wind. She did not subscribe to the theory that the night air carried evil humors, and loved to fall asleep with the tang of the sea blowing in to the muted roar of the surf.

Her husband was still in the hall with the men, but she had retired to her chamber earlier—only to find herself unable to sleep. So many changes in so little time. It would take some adjusting to become used to them all.

Especially to her new husband. What did she really know of Ranulf except his prowess in battle...and in bed? She knew little of his background and less of his character, and her emotions and thoughts were a constant jumbled confusion. Heavy footsteps came along the battlement, startling Morgana. She was not dressed properly for public view, and she shifted into the shadow of the tower.

"...and a right proper little hellcat," Perry was saying, "but the Lady Morgana seems in a way to be tamed now."

"Yes," Desmond replied. "Ranulf is cunning and has laid careful siege to her, aping the part of amorous suitor. He will soon have her meek as a mouse and ready to accede to his every wish. Then he will truly be Lord of Castle Griffin.''

Twenty years ago, Elva had warned her mistress that those who eavesdropped heard no good of themselves or others, but Morgana was not prepared for the way Desmond's words hit her. She was angry and shaken and sickened all at once. How dare they discuss her as if she were a common serving wench! Where was their chivalry and honor?

But that was not the source of her indignation. It went much deeper. Was what they were saying true? Were all Ranulf's tender caresses and passionate lovemaking nothing more than an act to win her foolish heart—and thereby control of her possessions?

Memory came to the rescue and eased the pain in the pit of her stomach. Ranulf was not a guileful man, seducing women for power and gain. He was too open and plain speaking to pull the wool over her eyes by such knave's trickery. She wrapped the cloak about her and proceeded toward the door in case Desmond and the squire returned, and her heart felt appreciably lighter.

But she had been used before and her emotions were protected by only a thin shell. Morgana might convince herself to ignore what she had overheard, but the dark seeds of doubt had been planted.

In her chamber that night, long after she should have been asleep, she lay staring at the patterns of moonlight that moved and shifted with the swiftly scudding clouds beyond her open window. Suddenly she heard the sound she had been listening for, half in hope and half in dread. The sound of Ranulf's footsteps.

They went past the chamber that had originally been prepared for him, at her orders, and stopped outside her door. Morgana froze. What would she do if he came in? What *should* she do?

If she could have one wish, it would be for tender love to bind them one to another. Since she had no way of making that wish come true, she feared greatly to make herself vulnerable to him. Ranulf could not hurt her if she kept an emotional distance between them—but she did not trust herself to maintain that distance when he was near.

She desperately wanted more time to think it over. Another night in his arms and she would only be caught more firmly in his spell; yet she longed for the strength of his arms about her, the warmth and urgency of his body pressed against hers, the touch of his mouth against her breast.

The decision was taken from her. The door opened partway. There was no light, only the smoky fragrance of a snuffed candlewick. She closed her eyes and listened for his tread but heard only a faint rustle that might have been the breeze through the open window. Then he was beside the bed. She recognized his own particular scent. Leather and ale and horse and man, and a spice that might be cinnamon.

She lay unmoving, expecting to hear the sounds of his undressing and feel the weight of his body sinking into the bed. Instead there was only a gossamer touch along her temple as his knuckles smoothed her hair. Morgana kept her breathing soft and regular although her heart was racing, and waited to discover his intentions. Let him be the one to make the first move, let him make himself as open to her as she was to him. Then, and then only, could she give her heart freely and without fear. The wait stretched out interminably. Then she heard it. The sound of her door closing. He was gone.

First she cursed her own foolishness, then she cursed him. Morgana wept into her pillow in sorrow and frustration until it was wet. And at last she dreamed. She was amidst great riches and luxury but was dying of a profound thirst. A silver goblet was offered to her. It would slake the terrible thirst that wracked her, but she pushed it away weeping, knowing it was poisoned.

"Oh, my lady!" Elva came scurrying up, her wrinkled face pink with agitation. "I went to bring Sir Ranulf the broth you ordered, but he is not in his bed. Indeed, he is nowhere to be found!"

"He is not with Sir Dyllis?"

"No, my lady. Sir Dyllis has not seen him this day."

Morgana shook her head in exasperation. Ranulf refused to stay at rest—and only she knew what the effort cost him. Although he eschewed sword practice for the time being, he kept up normal activities and appeared to be in no distress. Perhaps once a day, when the effort of keeping up the pretense became too much, he would accept one of her medicinal draughts, but he would not rest and let nature aid his healing.

"Sir Ranulf is too impatient for his own good. The flesh around his wound is red and inflamed, although I changed the dressing and applied more of the unguent this morning."

Elva looked worried. "If only we had some crushed dragon leaf. That is the only cure we lack, but it has been many years since it bloomed along the cliffs. Perhaps the village woman might have some among her store for the master."

"I will send Bronwen to the village again in the morning with one of the men-at-arms. Meanwhile, I am at my wit's end: he is either down in the tiltyard or up on the battlements, visiting the stables or the mews when he should be taking his ease. Was there ever such a hardheaded man?"

"Ah, but such a magnificent one. Such knightly bearing." Elva's withered face grew pinker. "And so handsome."

"I see he has won even you over."

The old woman smiled widely, showing her fine set of teeth. "In my youth I always had a soft spot for a gallant handsome lad. 'Tis hard to change the habits of a lifetime, my lady."

Morgana was less than pleased. It seemed that Ranulf had cast a spell over every man and woman within the walls. Was she the only one who saw his stubbornness and overbearing ways? The way he encroached, bypassing Sir Dyllis's authority and summarily taking over duties that had belonged to the castellan for the past ten years? Wheedling loyalty from her servants with his calculatedly winning ways, ordering them about and setting everything on end?

"Do not be concerned, Dame Elva, but retire to the solar as I know you like to do on these fine, mellow days. I shall go in search of Sir Ranulf myself."

A sly twinkle came into the older woman's eyes. "Aye, perhaps that would be best. Surely a new bride will have more influence upon her husband and you may urge him to his bed."

Firm steps sounded on the stairs behind them. "A moment ago you were concerned for my health, Dame Elva, and now you wish me to exert myself! Although I must say I prefer your newer remedy."

Ranulf bowed to the ladies from the landing just above. He was dressed for riding in a doublet of azure linen, with sleeves slashed to show the dark blue lining and white linen shirt beneath. With every step he descended, the leather buskins folded down at the top and showed his muscular legs to great advantage. Morgana could not help but concede that he looked incredibly handsome and virile.

He finished his descent and held his hand out to Morgana, favoring her with a meaningful look. "Come, wife, and we shall follow this good woman's advice. I have a sudden great longing for my bed."

Morgana's tongue turned to a lump of lead and she felt her cheeks grow hot and flushed. She was angered as much by her reaction as by her inability to control it. And there was no need for him to smile at her predicament.

Seeing her master's laughing eyes and her mistress's blushes, Elva chuckled. "I see that I am not needed here." She bobbed a curtsy and disappeared beneath an archway leading to the linen-storage room.

Morgana turned and would have taken her leave, also, but Ranulf stopped her with a hand to her arm. Instantly a current of sensation shot up her limb, swift and shocking as a lightning bolt. He took advantage of the moment. He drew her back against his chest and she felt his warm breath against the side of her neck as his arms went about her waist.

"My lord," she protested softly, but his lips were pressing persuasively against her temple, the side of her throat and along the bit of white shoulder exposed by the wide neckline of her dress. Her knees turned to jelly, as did her brain. Morgana could not think. All the fine resolutions of the morning evaporated in the face of the wild yearning that enveloped her. She had spent the long hours of the night wishing she had not feigned sleep, imagining the wonder of being in his arms again. The reality was far more overwhelming.

Slowly Ranulf turned her to face him. He was not laughing now as his mouth touched hers with swift possessiveness, savoring her taste, her scent. His embrace tightened and his mouth explored her lips until she sighed and opened them to him. The rest of the world ceased to exist. Ranulf's strong hands smoothed the fabric covering her back with long strokes and his fingertips remembered the way her bare skin had felt beneath them. Warm. Velvety. Seductive.

The kiss deepened, as did the spell that held them both ensnared. He felt her tremble beneath his touch and knew she ached with the same desire that wracked his own body. It inflamed him all the more. The male need to conquer, to possess the object of his desire took over. "Morgana..."

Her hands against his chest. "No. Someone will come upon us," she murmured, trying to marshal the last of her fast-fading willpower.

"Hush..." Drawing her into a shadowy alcove half covered by an arras, Ranulf continued his sensual assault of kisses and caresses. His hand now covered her breast, cupping it in his large palm as his thumb drew tingling circles around its peak. Even through the fabric she could feel the heat of his hand, and her body arched instinctively toward him. He tugged the edge of the neckline down and down until somewhere a seam gave. The stitches parted with a faint popping of linen threads. His strong fingers found the chemise she wore beneath and worked the garment down and away to expose one rose-tipped breast. Where his hand explored, his mouth followed, lips trailing over her skin until they parted and claimed the rosy summit. Morgana felt an ache in her loins followed by a swift rush of desire so intense she felt faint.

His lips moved over the cleft between her breasts and up to the base of her throat. He was filled with a lover's exaltation. "I knew I could win you to me, Morgana. You are mine. Mine!"

She opened her eyes in surprise and she saw his face. It was filled with a keen possessiveness and something more—the victor's elation, a conqueror's triumph. The memory of Desmond's words came back like the blow of a battle-ax and her ardor vanished like a puff of smoke, leaving a sick feeling in its place. Ranulf was no different than Robin or Bryce Lindsey, and no less false.

They had all pretended to want her for herself, yet each had tried to use her to further his own ambitions. Only the means had been different. Robin, by marriage first and then by mockery and neglect; Lindsey, by personal charm and physical force. And now Ranulf had done the same, using her attraction to him and her loneliness to conquer and subdue her. She felt betrayed and shamed.

At that moment a plump white hand drew the arras back and Lady Winifred stared at them in confusion. She took in Ranulf's flushed face and Morgana's torn bodice and her own face was red as a pomegranate.

"My lord! My lady! A thousand pardons," she gasped. "I heard someone...I never thought...I mean...oh, dear!"

She dropped the curtain, but not before Morgana saw Daffyd, her harper, less than ten feet away. He was white with shock. The arras fell back in place, leaving Ranulf and Morgana half in shadow. The only sound was their quick breathing and the scuffle of Lady Winifred's slippers as she hurried away.

Morgana's overwhelming emotions held her immobilized, and Ranulf recovered first. He gave a low chuckle and reached out to pull her close. "Perhaps, in future, we should retire to the privacy of our own chambers for such dalliance."

She pushed him away so unexpectedly Ranulf was caught off balance and fetched up against the wall. "Perhaps, in future, you will remember that I am your lady wife and not a hapless serving wench to be tumbled against her will in some convenient corner."

At once, Ranulf's face was wiped clean of all expression. "You did not flinch from my touch two nights ago. Have I said or done aught to offend you?"

Morgana was furious with him for reminding her, and equally angry with herself for her weakness. She must not let him know how close she had come to falling into his trap. Tears were just a moment away.

"Would it matter if you had? There is no use to make a sham display of affections. I am fully aware, as are you, that this is no love match between us."

If she hoped for him to contradict her, she was sadly disappointed. His face altered subtly until it looked alien and reft of all humanity—as blank and cold as a stone effigy. His voice, when he spoke, was controlled, and as clear and icy as a mountain stream.

"I did not guess your wifely duties were so onerous to you, madam. Be sure, I will not distress you further with my presence."

He turned on his heel and stalked away. Morgana was alarmed at his reaction and the width of the chasm that yawned between them. Her pride and hurt had led her to say more than she had wished, and with greater heat. She had meant to keep him at arm's length, not drive him away. And that was just what she'd done. She must not let him leave without attempting to mend the breach. As Ranulf crossed the long gallery she followed hesitantly. He held his left arm stiffly to his side and she grasped at the handy means of effecting a minor truce.

"My lord, you forget. Your wound wants fresh dressing and an application of my special unguent."

Ranulf paused under the archway to a connecting hall, his face grim. "You need not concern yourself. Dame Elva will tend to it."

"As your wife, it is my duty..."

"Then I absolve you of it. From this day on I will not importune you for even the *least* of your wifely duties."

There was something in his voice she had never heard before. A chill detachment so profound that a wintry draft crept down her neck and spine and through her body until Morgana thought she would never be warm again. It was as if, to Ranulf, she no longer existed.

While she stood frozen to the spot, he stalked away and vanished down the connecting corridor, almost shaking with the effort to control his fury. *By the Cross, what had he ever done to be cursed with such a wife?* She changed like the wind, warm and caressing when it suited her ends, cold as an ice storm when it did not. Well, she would learn that he would not play stud to her mare in heat in private, only to be dismissed publicly as if he were some lackey, when she cooled off! Pulling the heavy emerald and gold ring from his left hand, he thrust open the door to Morgana's chamber and went in.

After discharging several duties, Morgana went to exchange her slippers for footwear more appropriate to the stables. She paused before opening the door, wondering if Ranulf was within. Taking a deep breath she lifted her chin and pushed the door open. The room was empty, but either her husband or his agent had been there in her absence. Every item belonging to Ranulf had been removed. Even the candlestick that had come from his room.

On the chest beside the bed, something glittered in the late afternoon light. She picked it up and held it in her palm. A thick gold ring set with an emerald. Her wedding gift to Ranulf. She understood his message. His repudiation of her was complete, his intentions quite clear: they were to be husband and wife in name only. She could live her life just as she had before their marriage. That was what she had originally wanted. Wasn't it?

Then why did she feel so low and melancholy?

Morgana stared blindly ahead and tried to think of what to do next. By now the news that the new lord had moved from his lady's chamber would be all over the castle, the gossip of their rift common knowledge. She must confound the tattlemongers by pretending that nothing untoward had happened, smile and nod and take interest in her duties, when all she wanted to do was throw herself down upon the bed and weep until her tears ran dry. It was only her mortification at wagging tongues and prying eyes that made her feel so miserable.

She smarted under the knowledge that speculations about his repudiation of her would already be spreading. At least Ranulf was gentleman enough not to be publicly discourteous to her, but that was very small consolation; over time their estrangement would become obvious to all. And insurmountable. She also knew that bickering between her supporters and Ranulf's could divide her house, corrode loyalties and discipline, and leave it ripe to fall into an enemy's hands. Why could Edward not have left her to make her own choice of husband?

Wiping her suddenly moist eyes with an embroidered handkerchief, she made her plans. She would persist in her daily routine and tonight at the high table she would be attentive and cordial and show an unruffled face to the assemblage. That would confound the gossipers. Morgana bathed her eyes with witch hazel to remove any trace of puffiness and went off on her mission to confer with Dal, her stable master.

The stables occupied their own enormous yard along the north wall of the ward and Morgana felt remiss in not having visited them sooner. It was one of her duties, and one she enjoyed particularly. Riding was one of her passions and Dal had been a childhood hero. He ran the stables with an iron hand, but was kind as well as firm, and communicated silently with the horses in his own mysterious way. He knew their thoughts and needs as readily as he did his own, and that made him invaluable as horse master.

A freckled stable boy came by, leading a palfrey. Spying his mistress, he made a bow and touched his forelock. "Good day to you, young Tris. Where may I find Dal?"

"In the harness room, my lady."

Morgana turned her steps in that direction and found Dal checking to see if the leather straps had been oiled to his specifications. She rapped softly on the doorjamb and the lanky man looked up, frowning. His weathered face crinkled with pleasure when he saw his mistress. He had been a friend of her late father, a widower who had fought at his side against the English. And for love of his friend and master, Dal had bestowed his manor house upon his eldest son and taken on new responsibilities at Castle Griffin. His loyalty now was wholly to Morgana.

"God's blessing on you, my lady. 'Tis good that you are back home where you belong once again."

"And God's blessing on you also, Dal. And I am happier to be here than I ever thought possible."

"Well then, all's right with the world." He had known the Lady Morgana all her life and his sinewy hands had placed her on the back of her first pony. His keen blue eyes took note of the almost invisible lines of strain around her eyes, but he was warned from comment by the stubborn set of her mouth. How well he knew that expression!

Morgana grew uncomfortable under his kindly scrutiny, and hastened to turn the conversation from personal observations to the matter at hand. "You must think me remiss in not seeing to the stables sooner."

Dal seemed taken aback. He looked at a spot somewhere to the left of her and chose his words carefully. "Nay, why should I think so when Sir Ranulf made rounds yesterday and left full instructions with me?"

Morgana stiffened. "Orders?"

"Yes, my lady. Och, he was full of them. New stalls along the far side and English-type harness for the destriers. And we're to try at breeding that bay mare you are so fond of with the big chestnut stallion, when the time comes. Wouldn't have thought of it myself. Ah, Sir Ranulf has many a surprise up his sleeve, I don't doubt."

"Nor I!" She could scarcely believe Ranulf's arrogance. Breeding her dainty mare to that monstrous stallion! It would kill the poor creature for sure. How dare he?

She made a quick decision, one she was sure she would later regret.

"Unfortunately, the mare is neither Sir Ranulf's nor mine to give: during the seige I made a vow that I would bequeath her to the abbot of the monastery if we were favored with the victory. You will see to it once the monastery is back to order, of course."

"Aye, my lady." Whatever thoughts were circling through his head, Dal hid them well.

Morgana thanked the marshal and retraced her way through the yard and courts to the great hall, with a pang of sorrow for the prospective loss of her mare and a lesser one for the lie she had manufactured on the spot. Her mood was no better when she entered the main hall and received covert looks from a manservant trimming candlewicks and a wench carrying fresh linens to the infirmary. There was little that remained private within a castle's walls.

Next, Morgana discovered Ranulf had countermanded her orders concerning Desmond's accommodations. She had arranged to quarter him in a quite adequate room used for guests, but her husband had set his cousin up in chambers identical to those shared by Sir Dyllis and Lady Winifred.

Perhaps, she thought angrily, Ranulf did not understand the rules governing hospitality and status, and their ramifications—or perhaps he was too arrogant to care. Regardless of her husband's intention, Desmond's preferential treatment would be looked upon as a slight to the aging castellan's status and authority; and already rumors drifted about that Desmond would be appointed in his place.

By the Saints, but the red-haired knight encroached everywhere, presuming on his cousinship to Ranulf. He was always poking his nose into business that was none of his, and his growing interest in Bronwen had not escaped Morgana's keen eyes. Did he, like Ranulf, think everything at hand was his for the taking? If so, he would be in for a shock. She would see that Bronwen was never alone where Desmond could have private speech with her or try to press his advantage!

She found Lady Winifred in the chapel arranging a fresh bouquet of flowers before a carved and painted statue of the Virgin. The castellan's wife smiled when she saw her mistress, and dropped a curtsy. From Lady Winifred's sunny

face Morgana felt sure she did not know of Desmond's rise
in status and hadn't heard the rumors: such was not the
case.

"Ah, Lady Morgana, I was offering a prayer of thanks.
Since your return, things go on so well here! I cannot tell
you in what good spirits my dear old Dyllis is these days,
with Sir Ranulf and now Sir Desmond to lift some of the
cares from his shoulders. He is no longer young, you know,
although to me he is still the handsome knight I gave my
heart to one midsummer's eve so long ago."

Morgana was taken aback. She had expected tears or re-
criminations, not joyous appreciation. "If it eases his burden of responsibility and Sir Dyllis is well pleased, then I
have nothing to argue against it. But be assured that he will
not be displaced as castellan of Castle Griffin."

Lady Winifred beamed. "Aye. So Sir Ranulf pledged."

Morgana smiled a bit stiffly. It was evident to her that her
husband meant to wrest the reins of power from her hands
without delay.

Meanwhile Ranulf was learning the complete layout of
the castle, with its winding stairs, towers and turrets, dungeons and storage chambers and multitude of interconnect-
ing rooms. Castle Griffin had grown from a simple ancient
motte and bailey to an enormous fortress of considerable
complexity. Unfortunately the builders of various generations had followed no single plan, and there were dead ends,
blind alleys, unused courts and tunnels, and galleries and
warrens leading in all directions.

"'Tis like a madman's maze," he said to Sir Dyllis.

"Aye. It took me many months to learn my way about
handily."

Ranulf frowned. "And there are no maps or building
plans of the whole?"

"No, my lord. Nor even of all the parts. There are few
plans from the early days, but nothing after that until the
last century when better records have been kept."

"Well, then, we must assemble what we have and assign men to mark and measure what we lack. Send a message to the good friars, and inquire if one of their number would be willing to come to stay at the castle and prepare a detailed map for us. There would be fair recompense for the task."

Ranulf put his hand on his companion's shoulder. "You, of course, shall oversee the work. Obtain whatever you need to complete it, in my name."

Sir Dyllis was gratified by the trust the new lord placed in him, and, in fact, to have such a scheme carried out had long been a wish of his. Fortunately, Lady Morgana's bridegroom had a quick grasp of what needed to be done and the authority to carry it out, where a mere castellan had not. He smiled and tugged at his beard. Surely this marriage was a boon to all concerned.

Not everyone was of a like mind. Daffyd sat on the steps outside the hall, replacing a harp string. The sun shone brightly but his mood was dark as he brooded over what he'd seen earlier behind the arras in the gallery. Although Lady Morgana put on a brave face before the company, she had shown her true feelings of revulsion for her husband in that frozen instant of time.

For the first time in his life, Daffyd rued the fact that his birth gift from the Old Ones was a talent for music and song, instead of might and brawn. If only he were older and better versed in arms, that he might rescue her from a husband she so plainly despised! He would carry her off over his saddlebow to some isolated tower where he would worship her and spend the days singing paeans to her eyes, her lips, her graceful figure. He was much too chivalrous to let his mind dwell on the nights.

As for Sir Ranulf, whom he had earlier envisioned in the light of a hero, he was nothing but an uncouth, unchivalrous barbarian. But then what could one expect of a man whose heritage came partially of bloody viking stock? Ah, if only he could meet Sir Ranulf alone, if only he had the...

A shadow fell across him and his wish was granted. Daffyd flushed and started but Ranulf gestured for him to remain seated. "Do not rise on my account. Go on with your playing."

But the harper's fingers struck a false note as he looked at his new master in awe. He had never been so close to Sir Ranulf before, and this worm's eye view was quite daunting: the new lord's padded doublet of red leather accentuated his great width of chest and the dark hose and thigh-high buskins showed the powerful muscles of his legs. Even more intimidating was the aura of power and determination that radiated from the man. He would make a formidable foe.

At the same time Ranulf assessed the harper: the youth's face was as reflective of his thoughts as a pond was of the sky. Here was yet another one filled with doubts and needing to be won over. Well, lads were inclined to chivalrous fantasies, especially where beautiful ladies of rank were concerned. And Morgana was both.

"I have broken your concentration," he said, "and for that I am sorry. There are three things that should never be disturbed: a babe at sleep, a musician at work—and lovers at dalliance."

Daffyd's face went a brighter scarlet with embarrassment. He had been sure that his presence in the gallery had gone unnoticed.

"Play on." Ranulf leaned against the wall and watched interestedly as the youth tightened the peg and strummed the strings. A ripple of bright notes sang out, the pitch clear and true, and the harper plucked out the strains of a poignant ballad.

"You are blessed among men, young Daffyd," Ranulf said quietly, when the strings were stilled. "Music that soothes the aching heart or lifts the sunken spirits is worth more than gold. With whom did you study, that you are so skillful so young?"

Another wave of color bathed Daffyd's face at the compliment. "I was taught by the old master, my lady's grandfather, who died but six years ago, God grant him rest." He looked away in embarrassment. "I was a sickly child and much inclined to melancholy. Since I could not be at swordplay with the other lads and I was ever fond of singing, he taught me of his own goodness."

There was a wistful note to his voice, and Ranulf guessed its cause. "You have overcome your earlier trials, it seems, for you are sound of wind and limb now. Is your arm as strong with a sword as a song?"

Daffyd hung his head. He hoped the ground would open up and swallow him, but no miracle intervened to spare his humiliation. "Alas, I am more learned at music than at arms. Having had no lessons in that art, I have no skill."

"Do you wish to learn?"

"Aye, but none will teach me, for fear of causing a harper injury." The boy looked morosely down at his hands. Music was his life, but a man needed to know how to defend himself and others.

Ranulf sat on the step next to him. "Let us make a trade, then."

His finger touched the smooth wood of the harp lightly. "Once I had some little skill at music, but I have grown rusty over the years, like a sword left untended in the sea air. If you will agree to refresh my abilities with the harp, I shall contract to teach you the use of weapons. And I shall engage not to harm you or endanger your skills."

The boy's opinion of his new lord shifted radically once more. Hope shone briefly in Daffyd's eyes, then flickered out. "I have not the bulk and strength of a soldier."

"Do you give up so easily? Cerdic will show you exercises to strengthen your legs and back, as well as your arms and shoulders. And many an excellent swordsman is built lean as a hound and therefore able to dance more nimbly around a larger foe."

"Truly?" Daffyd was elated by Ranulf's words, yet torn in his loyalties. After a brief struggle he convinced himself it was in Lady Morgana's best interest if he learned some skill at arms. "I thank you most humbly, Sir Ranulf, for your great kindness."

The capitulation was easier than Ranulf had expected. He smiled and put his foot up on the bench. "If you wish to thank me, tell me this: is there another harp in this castle?"

"Aye, more than one. But I will tell you where you may find the finest one of all."

Morgana and Lady Winifred made a final tour of the huge kitchen area. A bevy of industrious servants were hard at work and the air was filled with tantalizing fragrances: the yeasty aroma of freshly baked bread, roasting meats and sweet, simmering fruit.

Under the directions of the cooks, several maids were stirring copper cauldrons of chopped fruit, and a scullery lad sat on a three-legged stool beside one of the hearths, turning capons on a spit. Over another fire, fat from a huge joint of meat dripped and sizzled into the flames below, and an undercook added diced leeks and sage to boiled pheasant meat and rolled the mixture up in pastry for baking.

Morgana noted that all was clean and in good order. "Despite the siege, Lady Winifred, you have kept my house well and I commend you for it most highly. Let us repair now to the solar for a rest over some wine and sweetmeats."

"Thank you, Lady Morgana, I would indeed like to join you." Here the castellan's wife smiled indulgently. "However, I did promised Sir Ranulf to prepare with my own hands a special dish I discovered recently: a pie of roast goose stewed with figs, apples and onions in a sauce of brandy and butter, the whole spiced with juniper berries. 'Tis fit for angels, my old Dyllis tells me, and you shall see for yourself tonight."

Glancing around one last time, Morgana realized something missing. "Was there not to be a roast loin of pork?"

"Aye, my lady," the chief cook said, wiping her hands upon her apron. "I did send for a nice pig to be slaughtered, but the master said he was hungered right well for veal with pepper sauce, so we had the calf instead."

"Then we shall have the pork tomorrow," Morgana said, and turned away. All morning her mouth had watered for roast loin of pork, but even here in the kitchens Ranulf's influence had penetrated.

As she left the kitchens, her anger at her husband was simmering and bubbling like the jam in the great cauldrons. Lady Winifred was going to prepare a dish for Ranulf with her own plump white hands. What power did the man have over people, that he could sway their loyalties to him so effortlessly? He was setting the castle and all its inhabitants on their ears and they only smiled the wider.

Soon, she thought wrathfully, *he shall busy himself from the highest tower to the lowest dungeon. I shall be nothing more than a guest in my own castle, my orders ignored or countermanded, my presence suffered only because the castle is my inheritance and protected by law.*

She made her way to the ladies' solar with no plan in mind other than to take what little comfort she could in feelings of outraged pride and ill usage. By accident of birth, she had been stripped of many of her rights at marriage: Ranulf, a stranger to these lands and people was made master of Castle Griffin and its inhabitants. Including Morgana. He could abuse her, waste her resources and beggar her people while she stood helplessly by. Well, the Law, the King and the Church might be satisfied with such arrangements, but By All the Saints, she was not!

If Ranulf meant to play fast and loose with her inheritance he would be greatly surprised, for she would fight him tooth and nail. Peace might reign throughout the countryside since Lindsey had been vanquished, but there would be war within the castle.

The decision loosened the tension that had been building inside Morgana, and in her growing anger she no longer felt helpless and outflanked. Let Ranulf claim victory in these minor domestic skirmishes, she would win out in the end. When she passed two serving men moving a screen from the small reception room into the great hall she did not even stop to inquire who had given the command; and by the time she reached the solar her mood was determined and optimistic. All her Celtic blood was stirred and ready for the battle of wills.

The room was empty, unusual at this time of day, but Lady Winifred was down in the kitchen and Bronwen and Elva were taking the air in the rose garden. Morgana sat down on her cushioned chair and leaned her head against the high back, smiling grimly as she laid her plans. From the open window drifted a gull's harsh cry, fading with distance. But there was another sound, also. Faint, discordant.

She sat up straight and listened intently. Although a dozen years and more had passed since last she heard it she recognized it at once. There it was again. She jumped up and followed. It came from above, in the east tower, from the room her grandparents had shared.

Along the silent gallery and up the winding stairs she went, over treads worn concave by generations of feet. The tone echoed and vibrated softly on the air, the mere ghost of a sound now. Morgana paused before the chamber door. Would she find the spirit of her grandfather inside, the restless shade of brave and gallant Owain ap Griffin? Or merely a mouse or squirrel rolling a scrap of metal across the dusty floor?

She pushed the door open. No ghost lurked inside, only Ranulf. He sat at his ease in the window seat, his battle-scarred and callused hands holding an ancient harp that was the symbolic heart of Castle Griffin. But it was not of this that she was thinking at the moment, only that the privacy of her sanctuary and her most cherished and sacred heirloom had been violated.

Morgana was so blinded by anger she could not see how pale Ranulf was beneath his sun and windburned skin, or the gentle reverence of his big hands as they cradled the harp. She hurled herself at him, snatching the harp from his arms with all the strength of a Fury.

"How dare you? You have no right, no right at all. This is an instrument of music and mystical power, not a toy to be defiled by a warrior's bloody hands!"

Tenderly she wrapped the instrument in the length of yellowed silk spread out upon the bed. Ranulf watched her in silence. Turning her back to him, Morgana replaced the harp with great care in the carved chest beside the bed. Next she withdrew a long key from among her chain of others and locked it. The air in the room seemed infinitely colder. When she rose, he stood facing her, his eyes diamond hard. Her own were the cold blue-green of glacial ice.

"You are never to set foot in this chamber again. Never! As Master you have taken over every other room in the castle, but this—this, at least—you will leave to me."

"It seems, madam, that you find me unsatisfactory in every way but one. Perhaps you would have found Lindsey's rough suit more to your liking."

She lifted her chin and uttered the fatal words defiantly. "Perhaps I would have at that, my lord. But then you would not have my estates and wealth to plump you up with such arrogance."

For an instant she thought he was going to strike her, and it took a massive effort of will to keep from flinching. Their eyes locked in a deadly duel of wills. It was Ranulf who broke the silence.

"Be assured, lady, that I covet neither your possessions nor your person. As to this marriage, it has become the very bane of my existence! As soon as possible I will return to London and petition the Archbishop for an annulment."

The door shut behind him and he was gone.

Chapter Nine

"Good day to you, Owain."

"And to you, my lady." The Captain of the Guard saluted Morgana as she descended a stairway leading from the north tower to a series of walled courtyards, mostly unused. This route cut both time and steps back to the massive central tower housing the hall and main apartments.

Inspecting the household from top to bottom was hard on the feet, when the household spread over several acres and several floors. Lady Winifred's efficiency had kept very good order inside and Sir Dyllis had done the same without, but Morgana would have considered herself a lazy mistress had she not made a complete survey. But now, for an hour or two, she was at leisure.

With the sun so bright and warm it seemed a shame to hurry inside the thick stone walls. Morgana followed a covered passage and went down a second stairway toward a maze of unused storerooms and empty barracks, which dated to the original castle three hundred years before. It led to a small, protected court where she had often gone in childhood days, but not at all in recent years on her brief visits to Wales with Robin.

There it was, just as she remembered it. The little bench was still at right angles to an arched opening cut in the wall, and through the gap the sea shone deep green and blue, sparkling like a royal ransom of sapphires and emeralds.

When she was only seven, her favorite pet—a parti-colored cat—had died of old age and good living, and she had buried it here. One of the masons had carved the paving stone with the image of a sleeping cat to ease her sorrow. Other memories choked her with sudden tears. This is where she had sought refuge time and again, her solitary retreat from the pain of losing, first her grandparents and then her father. She had never known her mother, who had died of milk leg soon after giving birth to her only child.

It seemed fitting to be in this place of solace again. As mistress of Castle Griffin she had a hundred tasks to perform, but not one of them kept her so busy that she was able to blot out the repercussions of her acrimonious scenes with Ranulf. Of late she was too quick to speak or act, too near to anger or tears. She did not understand the cause but she was restless and increasingly unhappy, though she blamed Ranulf she feared the root of the problem lay deep within herself.

Taking a seat on the low bench, she cupped her chin in her hand and watched the waves tumble and roll. Minutes slipped by, uncounted. She was scarcely aware of the music when it began so low and distant. Then the wind shifted and she realized it was quite near. Daffyd was close at hand and playing softly, dreamily and his song, she thought, was slow and incredibly sad. She rose like a sleepwalker, following the poignant notes. Music always had the power to lift her spirits, soothe her troubled soul.

The sound of his harp drifted along the passage, each note as pure and clear as water from a mountain stream. The melody suddenly skipped and danced, changing from low ballad to a murmuring lullaby, then swelling into a rousing chanson, skipping from tune to tune like a butterfly fluttering from flower to lovely flower.

Morgana traced the sound to an outlook on the lower ramparts, and went up again. At the sound of her footsteps the music stopped, the strings abruptly stilled.

"Pray play on, Daffyd," she called out encouragingly. "You have waxed proficient in my absence and are as accomplished as any musician at Court."

Reaching the outlook, she stepped inside the high, machicolated walls and stopped short. Ranulf sat on the wooden bench in the golden sunlight, Daffyd's stilled harp in his hands. From the way he held it, she knew to look no farther for the harper whose music had drawn her.

She was startled and dismayed, and Ranulf read both emotions in her expression and the posture of her body. One moment she was relaxed and gay and eager, laughing and so very beautiful. The next stiff and stilted and pale, looking as if she wished to be anywhere in the world but here with him.

"I hope, if I have disturbed you..." he began formally and Morgana spoke in a breathless rush at the same time. "I did not mean to intrude..."

Both fell silent—Morgana because of embarrassment at her terrible tirade a few hours earlier and shame at her wrongful conclusion; because he looked so fierce and handsome with the sun glinting on his hair and skin, a golden god of the pagan Norsemen or the wild Celts. And because his face was so pensive and grave, it wrung her heart. She had wounded him deeply and he looked at her impersonally now, as if she were little more than a stranger.

She gestured toward the harp. "I did not know or expect... How... foolish you must think me. And... and a shrew into the bargain."

Ranulf rose. "The right was yours, lady. I did not mean to trespass or upset you by meddling among your private possessions. Be sure I will not make that mistake again."

He prepared to leave and she wanted to prevent it. "You play with all a trained musician's skill."

"In Ireland I was schooled to be a bard from my youth. I was born a musician; necessity made me a warrior."

Her sense of shame was overpowering. How could she make amends? "I beg your forgiveness for my sharp tongue, my lord. And I would be pleased to hear the Harp of the Griffins sing in your hands. I will have it restrung for you."

Ranulf hid his surprise. She was as changeable as the sea, it seemed, rough and dangerous one day and calm and playful the next. From the very beginning she had kept him off balance with her fits and starts. It no longer made any difference. He would not play her game.

"There is no need. If the weather holds I will depart for London with my men in three days' time."

Swallowing her disappointment, Morgana tried to smile brightly. "And how long will you be away, my lord?"

Another pause, heart-stoppingly long to Morgana, and even before he answered she knew she had already lost him.

"I thought you understood, lady. I go to petition the Archbishop to begin preparations for an annulment of our marriage. When I go, you will have seen the last of me."

He left then, but Morgana stood at the wall staring out to sea with eyes blinded by tears.

By late afternoon, it was apparent that Ranulf was in no shape to even make plans for a journey to London; he was increasingly feverish, but kept to his chambers only because of Desmond's threat to lock him in if necessary.

Morgana was unaware of the problem until the following morning. Desmond accosted her in the stillroom where she was teaching Bronwen how to make a soothing lotion of rosewater, witch hazel, pounded lily root and clarified mutton fat for Lady Winifred's chapped hands.

"Just a drop more of the witch hazel, Bronwen."

"Like this, my lady?"

"Exactly so. I believe you have a natural talent for preparing medicines."

The girl's pleasure at the compliment was cut short by Desmond's arrival. He blocked the doorway, his fox-colored hair bright as polished copper in the light from the windows, his face hard and suspicious. They looked up from their work in surprise and Bronwen shrank back behind her mistress, her face becomingly flushed.

"You are far from your usual haunts, Sir Desmond," Morgana said acerbically when he offered no greeting. "Are you in need of a medicament—a strong physic, perhaps, to ease your choler?"

"Your potions and unguents may please your tiring women, but they satisfy me not."

She set down the pestle she was using to grind the lily bulb. "As you can see, I am busy and have no time for riddles."

"Then let me say it straightly: my cousin, your husband, fares no better for all your salves and medicines. He burns with fever and, so Cerdic tells me, raved and rambled insensibly for a goodly part of the night."

"Why was I not told of this?"

He slouched insolently against the door frame. "Can you not guess? There are those who think your remedies are shams, as impotent as a eunuch."

Morgana was shocked. "My balms and elixirs are much in demand. Why would I be the subject of such slander?"

Desmond's mouth turned up cynically. "It is common knowledge, lady, that you love your husband not. You have publicly berated him like a fishwife on more than one occasion and barred him from your bed."

"That is untrue!"

He came inside and walked beside the shelves filled with pots and jars of simples and syrups, roots and restoratives, tinctures, ointments, liniments; cordials, elixirs; cathartics and emetics; leaves and flowers and berries. "Aloe, borage, capsicum, dock. Horehound, henbane, balsam and rue." He scanned the rows. Hundreds of others, marked and ranged in alphabetical order.

Desmond swung back to Morgana impatiently. "Among your herbs and oils and powders there must be some concoction to ease Sir Ranulf's ailment and produce a cure."

Morgana's spine was stiff with dislike and hauteur. The Orkneyman made no bones that he thought her a harpy, and she returned his sentiments in kind. "I have no doubt that he will soon be restored to health."

Desmond nodded grimly. "I am sure you will be able to effect a cure, knowing that your own health depends upon it."

She quelled the urge to heave a heavy clay pot at his head as he withdrew. "Threats and accusations from an arrogant and landless knight! Insolent knave. I have no liking for him at all, and will be glad to see the last of him when he returns to Court."

But Bronwen was silent and averted her face. Desmond both frightened and intrigued her. She was of a more placid nature and found his mercurial moods as fascinating as his warm but infrequent smile. Elva had said there was naught amiss with his disposition that a pretty maid could not cure with a kiss or two.

Morgana was unaware of Bronwen's attraction to Ranulf's cousin. She pounded a bit more of the root with great energy, pretending it was Desmond being ground to bits between mortar and pestle. She put her things aside and glanced at the leaves steeping in boiling water in a container of glazed pottery: a decoction of willow and feverfew, mixed with a few drops of syrup of poppies and a few needles from a certain species of evergreen tree.

"The febrifuge is ready."

"Shall I take it directly to my lord?"

"Thank you, I shall take it to Sir Ranulf myself, that I might examine his wound while I am there." She was furious at not being told of Ranulf's worsening.

Morgana pictured his body, so strong and muscular. Only much-dreaded infection could account for his fever and failure to heal. It was frightening to imagine his vigor and vitality drained by evil humors, but she was sure his strength would soon be restored. By then he might have forgiven her angry words. It might even be possible that they could begin anew, learning to know one another better. It was not well for husband and wife to be estranged. She had learned that bitter lesson once before.

Carefully she poured the liquid from the steeped leaves and decanted it into a silver goblet. She hesitated and checked the jars and pots in the narrow cupboard and her hand reached behind them.

"Perhaps just a sprinkle of this . . ." she murmured to herself.

Bronwen was so intent on her own task she had not been paying attention, but she looked up wondering what other preparation her mistress would add to enhance her decoction. Cherry bark was used in some nostrums, she knew. But it was not the lidded jar of cherry bark that Morgana held. It was the tiny unlabeled glass vial from the back of the cupboard, and Bronwen was acquainted with its contents: Elva had said it was a love potion, to inspire passion between the one who served it and the one who drank it.

She knew something else about the love elixir. Whatever powers the pale lavender liquor might once have had, they were no longer effective. Bronwen knew, because she had tried them one summer past on Daffyd, and to this very day he was scarcely aware of her existence. Fortunately her brief interest in him had flickered out and had never been rekindled.

Bronwen wanted to tell Morgana of her own experiment, but decided to hold her tongue. She did not want her mistress to know of her foolishness or that she had raided the stillroom without permission—a fact which would land one of the kitchen maids in serious trouble. It was too bad the elixir had lost its potency. If Sir Ranulf returned to Court, as Desmond had hinted, he would also go. The thought made her feel bleak. She had never known a man like him. But if Sir Ranulf was deep in love with his lady, he would stay on—and Desmond with him. Bronwen frowned thoughtfully.

Carefully Morgana replaced the vial and stirred the drink with a glass rod. "There. That will do quite well. I will go to Sir Ranulf now, and you may come to assist me when you have finished."

Bronwen bent her head and measured out a spoonful of the lily root. "Would you like me to seek out the old woman in the village again? There might be some other rare herb among her stores that could be of use to you."

"Yes, that is a wise idea. Or she may recollect a remedy unknown to me." She reached for the purse that hung inside her pocket and took out a coin. "Take this for payment. And pray do not go alone. Take one of the men for escort."

Bronwen slipped the coin into her pocket. "Of course, my lady."

Morgana was so intent on preparing the decoction for Ranulf that she didn't see the self-conscious expression that crossed her little maid's face or the rosy blush that crept up her cheeks.

A short time later she made her way to her husband's chamber with a cup of clear green liquid. Cerdic answered her knock. "'Tis well that you've come, my lady. He worsens before my eyes."

He stepped back to let her in and she spotted Desmond pacing back and forth by the closed and shuttered window. A brazier of coals burned merrily in the center of the room. The chamber was like a furnace, the air stifling.

Halfway across the room Morgana stopped, her heart wrung with pity. Desmond's talk of fever had not prepared her for this.

Ranulf lay on his back in the great bed, the sheet up to his waist. His massive chest rose and fell too quickly with every shallow breath, his cheeks were hollow and his eyes closed and sunken deeply in their sockets. As she watched, his head thrashed from side to side and he groaned, a heartrending sound that sent shivers of fear up the backs of her arms. She hurried toward him and placed one hand on his forehead. Hot as a hearthstone, dry as a bundle of leaves.

"My lord, you burn with fever!" He did not seem to hear. She knelt beside him and clasped his hand in hers.

Desmond moved out of the shadows. "Enact no sickroom tragedies, madam. Your feelings are well known to all us."

Cerdic came to her side. Seeing that Morgana's concern was genuine even if Desmond did not, he spoke soothingly. "He does not hear you, my lady. He is drifting in nightmares, I fear."

His kindness braced her and she took charge. "Assist him to a sitting position and I will endeavor to pour this liquid down his throat."

While the man-at-arms complied, she addressed the other bystander. "If you would make yourself useful, Sir Desmond, kindly open the casement to let the cool air in and then bank the fire down with ashes."

"What, would you have him suffer a lung inflammation, too?"

Now she lost her temper. "I have agreed that military matters fall under my husband's jurisdiction and yours. But leave to me the command of the sickroom if you wish to save him from his fever."

After a stubborn moment and an exchange of glances with Cerdic, Desmond did as he was bidden. Cerdic lifted Ranulf into a semi-sitting position against the cushions of the bed and Morgana put the cup to his lips. He twisted his head from side to side and flung his arm out wildly. She ducked in time, but the soldier did not. There was the snap of bone on bone and Cerdic went sprawling, an angry red weal rising along his jaw.

Desmond pulled him to his feet and tried to aid Morgana, and this time he was the one in danger as Ranulf mumbled and flailed his arms. Morgana leaned forward to soothe her agitated patient.

"No, my lady..." Cerdic began, but stopped in wonder. As soon as Morgana's hand smoothed his cheek, Ranulf quieted. She spoke to him in low tones, stroking his face all the while and his combativeness vanished.

"Hush, hush now. We mean you no harm. Only drink, my lord, and your pain will be eased."

When Desmond lifted his head, Ranulf did not lash out, and when Morgana put the cup to his lips again he let her dribble a few drops into him. She repeated the action until the liquid was gone and nodded.

"He will sleep. And when he awakens, God willing, his fever will abate."

Desmond placed him back upon the pillows with a gentleness Morgana would not have expected from him. When Ranulf's breathing deepened, Cerdic helped her remove the bandages wound around her husband's chest. She gasped in dismay. The wound, so clean and pink about the edges before, now oozed purulent drainage.

"This is the cause of his delirium. It must be drained and cauterized before the flesh becomes morbid."

After a pregnant pause, Desmond removed the long dagger from the sheath on his belt and thrust it into the fire. His face was haggard with worry, and for the first time Morgana saw the resemblance between the two men. It would have pleased her more to see Desmond in the bed and Ranulf on his feet, but she brushed the unworthy thought from her mind and set to work.

Ranulf slept through her ministrations, but the touch of Desmond's red-hot dagger to his side brought forth a bloodcurdling cry that made their ears ring; and afterward,

Morgana did not know if the cry had come from Ranulf or herself. When it was over, she washed her hands and threw the soiled bandages in the fire.

"Thank you both for your assistance. He will rest now for some hours, and Cerdic, you must rest also. I will send a trusted servant to take over the vigil."

"No, by God's Toes, that you will not!" Desmond strode forward and grabbed her by the shoulders.

"Think, woman: the danger from beyond the walls is not over. We must keep his condition secret or the morale of the men will plummet to the depths. And if your enemy, Lindsey, learns of this he might find cause to assemble a new army and attack. No one must know, not even the chaplain unless . . . unless death is imminent."

Morgana mulled it over. "Your point is well taken. I will exchange watches with Cerdic that he may sleep awhile, and we will switch off in shifts until the fever breaks."

She smiled at Cerdic. "Before you retire, I have one more task for you. I have asked the lady, Bronwen, to fetch me more medicines from the herb woman in the village. I left her in the stillroom and if she has not departed yet urge her to do so with all good speed."

Desmond took a step toward the door. "There is no need to keep this good man from his rest. I will speak to the lady myself and accompany her to the village if need be."

The door closed behind him and Cerdic refused to leave. He lay down upon a cot by the bed so he might be near at hand if Morgana needed him, and she took the upholstered stool beside Ranulf. How still he lay! His former agitation had been difficult to witness, but now it was more unnerving to see him thus. For the first time, it occurred to her that he might die.

She touched his forehead. "You must be well again," she whispered fiercely. "I will not let you die. I will not!"

Ranulf stirred. She thought he was trying to speak, but could not make sense of his low mumbling. A crisis of fe-

ver was coming upon him and she was sick with fear. There
was nothing to do now but wait. And pray. Morgana knelt
by the side of the bed and said her *Aves* as he grew more
flushed. His skin was so hot she could barely touch it. Suddenly he opened his glazed eyes for the span of a heartbeat.

"Morgana..." he said hoarsely, and reached for her
hand, clasping it firmly within his own. Ranulf drifted back
into demon dreams caused by his dangerously elevated body
temperature. Her fingers grew numb from his grasp, but she
made no attempt to withdraw them.

Time passed and beads of sweat broke out on his brow
while the kneeling Morgana prayed.

Bronwen looked at the sky as one big drop of rain splattered on the veil covering her head. The thick gray clouds
had turned darker and dirtier and the wind was gusting from
the north. It was going to pour before she reached the old
woman's place and she wished she had brought a woolen
cloak instead of the one she was wearing. The yellow satin
lined with linen was flattering and did much for her girlish
vanity; however, it would do nothing at all to keep out the
chill or the wet.

She glanced at her companion, wishing it had been anyone but Desmond of Orkney. He had not said one word to
her since they'd left the castle, and the scowl on his face was
as black as the clouds overhead. He always made Bronwen
feel awkward and tongue-tied and today even more so. She
was determined to act the lady and not be put out of
countenance. But what *was* there to talk about? They had
very little in common.

"The Lady Morgana is highly skilled in the healing arts,"
Bronwen offered. "More so than many women twice her
age. She will have Sir Ranulf restored in a twinkling."

"Let us hope, for her sake, that it is so."

"Do you doubt my word?"

"No. I only doubt the lady's intentions."

There was nothing to say in reply to such impertinence, and Bronwen fell silent. Let Sir Desmond see that he had stepped over the bounds of what was proper.

The rain came pelting down all at once, cold and hard and stinging. Bronwen kept her head high as they picked their way along the quickly muddied road, although her loose hair was plastered to her head and back and her gown in a fair way to becoming soaked. The wind snatched at her gauzy veil and tore it completely away.

Her horse stumbled and Desmond grasped the bridle, leading her palfrey into the lee of an enormous rock. At least with the wind cut off it was warmer, but Bronwen's teeth were chattering uncontrollably. Shivering, and with water streaming down her in all directions, she fought and lost the urge to burst into tears.

Desmond dismounted and held out his arms for her to do likewise. "Foolish chit, to go out so ill prepared," he grumbled, but his voice was softer than she had ever heard it. He pulled her under the overhang of the rock and removed his cloak of finely woven wool. Although light in weight, it was warm and the fibers wicked the wetness away from her body. Her shivering stopped. She felt bedraggled and embarrassed and could not meet his eyes. Perching on a rock she stared fixedly at the misty gray landscape.

Desmond had little experience with young and innocent girls: he assumed she was angry because of his remark about her mistress. The rain hissed and spattered and pinged against the rock like hailstones. It seemed as if they would be stuck in this makeshift shelter for a while. He glanced at Bronwen's dainty back. *Such a small lass to be so aloof and haughty,* he thought. *I suppose my sharp tongue has offended her sense of propriety.*

He cleared his throat. "You are very loyal to your mistress."

Bronwen did not turn her head. "Lady Morgana is the best mistress anyone could hope to serve. I was left to her wardship when my father died, and she has stood in the place of sister, mother and guardian since that sorrowful day. She is wise, just, fair and generous.''

''High praise indeed!'' He mulled this over while the downpour continued.

The conversation languished and both parties were relieved when the pounding rain changed to a soft drizzle. Desmond helped her to mount but did not ask for his cloak back, and Bronwen was unsure if she should offer to return it. It was warm and quite cozy. And it smelled like him. A rather nice smell, she decided, and urged her horse into an injudicious trot to hide her blushes.

Her horse stumbled in the rutted road as he caught up with her. ''Less haste and more caution,'' Desmond said caustically, ''or you will go head over heels into the mud.''

Bronwen was chagrined. She found Sir Desmond both frightening and attractive. He had a temper that matched his fiery hair, but she had heard no ill of him. He was not as well liked as Sir Ranulf, but she discerned a good heart beneath the Orkneyman's rough exterior. Of course he had not noticed her, dismissing her as a mere girl. Perhaps if he stayed on, he might begin to notice that she was really quite grown-up.

But if Sir Ranulf returned to Court, as was whispered, there would be no chance of that. Oh, if only Lady Morgana and her husband could settle their private differences, how comfortable everyone could be! Bronwen, inexperienced in the eyes of the world, was sure of one thing: Sir Ranulf and Lady Morgana were made for each other. If only they could see it as clearly as she could! Lost in thought, she was surprised to discover they had reached their destination.

The old crone lived in a tumbledown house, just outside the village. Desmond helped Bronwen alight before the door. ''Will you come?'' she asked doubtfully.

"Not I! 'Tis said the woman practices secret arts, for all you claim she is a healer. I'll have no truck with such."

The door swung inward and Bronwen ducked inside the opening without looking back. The house was dim and the low ceiling black with soot from the flickering cook fire. It consisted of one room of moderate size which served as kitchen, bedroom, parlor and goat pen. An animal sauntered up to Bronwen and butted her leg gently.

"Don't ye mind my horned friend, now. He'll not harm ye."

The voice came from a dark corner and when her eyes adjusted Bronwen spied a tiny woman, no bigger than a child, with eyes as wide and seemingly as guileless. She was seated on a rudely made stool.

"Ah, 'tis ye again, from the castle. Come close to the fire and warm yer bones," she invited, "and tell me why ye've come in such a downpour."

Bronwen edged closer. She was frightened of the old woman, as much by the large hairy mole on the wizened cheek as by her reputation.

"Ye've brought a man wi' ye. Be he yer lover?"

"No!" Bronwen's cheeks bloomed with bright color.

"Ah, then ye wish he was, don't ye! And who can blame a young girl for giving her heart to one as handsome as that."

Bronwen was too embarrassed to reply. The old woman broke into a cackle of laughter that changed to a hacking cough. "Ah, this damp will be the death o' me." She rose and indicated the stool. "Sit yerself down, child."

Gathering her courage, Bronwen demurred and hastily explained her errand. "My lady is hopeful that you may have a further remedy to heal her lord's injury."

The childlike eyes grew keen. "'Tis a grievous wound if the balm I give ye afore has not healed your master. I have nothing more to offer ye."

Bronwen reached into her pocket and pulled out a coin. "This may encourage your memory."

Instantly the wrinkled paw shot out to snatch it from her grasp. "There is one receipt I recollect now, but t'will take a mite o' time to mix it properly."

"I will help you."

"No, child. I must do it alone. Get ye out into the garden with yer young man, for the sun is coming out again." She waved her visitor toward the door. "Take ye a walk in my garden with yer swain."

When Bronwen stepped out, she almost jumped out of her skin as Desmond loomed over her. He darkened to the roots of his ruddy hair. "I did not like to leave you alone with the old woman unless I was within earshot."

It was Bronwen's turn to blush, when she realized he had overheard every word. *"Be he yer lover?... Ah, but ye wish he was, don't ye!"* Turning away she pretended to examine some of the plants growing in the cottage garden. No matter where she went, Desmond was only a step in back of her.

Behind the cottage was a fine little copse and inside the trees they found a semicircle of low gray stones, one with a circle scratched upon its side that looked for all the world like a wise and knowing eye. Although Bronwen was superstitious, she was not frightened, for the place had an air of peace and tranquility. Or perhaps it was only Desmond's sturdy presence that banished her fear. But he also responded to the atmosphere and was soon telling tales of his youth, of how Ranulf had saved his life and avenged his father's death.

Bronwen read between the lines and saw that behind Desmond's stony facade there was a wealth of warmth and deeply felt emotion. His history, told haltingly, revealed a harsh life that he seemed to take for granted and her soft heart, already disposed to favor him, opened like a flower. His loneliness invoked the nurturing qualities of her personality, and her ready affection responded to his unspoken need. Somehow, between one word and the next, the sentiment he roused in her became something real and true and Bronwen realized that she cared deeply for this hard-edged, thorny knight. He was not the prince she had dreamed of, but he was the man she loved.

After a bit Desmond fell silent, but there was no awkwardness between them. Their unspoken companionship ended abruptly when the crone came to the doorstep and motioned to Bronwen. The young girl rose, sorry the interlude was over and wondering if Desmond would ever return her feelings. Dazzled by her new discovery, she took the sealed clay pot the woman handed her.

"Ye must follow my instructions faithfully. Add this to the balm I gave ye t'other day until it forms a jelly to apply to the wound. It should be put on the injured part four times between sunrise and sunrise."

Bronwen hesitated. Another opportunity might not arise. "I...uh...there is something else I require..."

The old woman smiled widely, exposing her toothless gums. "Ah, I can guess at what ye want. Ye've a wish to cast a love spell on some likely fellow. Mayhap the flame-haired knight escorting ye, eh?"

Blushes covered Bronwen's cheeks. "'Tis not...not for myself, you understand. And I can pay you for it." She took a small bag of silk and netting from the bodice of her dress and removed another coin. Again the age-withered hand came out, palm up.

"Ye've come to the right place, child. I know exactly what ye require."

She broke off to look around, and retrieved a small vial from the wobbly table just inside the door. The cracked voice lowered. "This vial will achieve everything ye wish. 'Twill make any man fall in love with ye whether he will or no. Even the King himself."

Bronwen's eyes grew wide in fear and wonder. "And there is nothing harmful in it?"

"It be safe as mother's milk. Put it in his cup with fresh ale or wine, and within three days he will be mad for ye."

She pressed the small vial into Bronwen's hand so quickly Desmond did not see it, and leaned forward to whisper in the girl's ear.

"Ye'll be a wife by Christmastide. I saw a vision of it clear as anything when I glanced into the bowl of water on the table."

Bronwen slipped the clay pot into her pocket, but the tiny vial with the love potion she placed in the purse she carried within her bodice. Desmond lifted her into the saddle as though she weighed no more than thistle-down.

They left the cottage and as they neared the castle the stiffness returned between them. Desmond turned his eyes away from Bronwen's glowing little face and reminded himself that she was as high above him in station as Lady Morgana was above Ranulf—and that unlikely marriage had brought no happiness to either party.

Bronwen was happy enough to ride beside him and paid no heed to Desmond's silence. *A bride by Christmastide!* But now, away from the old crone, she lost her taste for magic potions and spells. There was little chance of administering it to Desmond, in any case, and she might well lose her nerve even if the opportunity arose. But it was just as well to keep it close to hand.

By the time Desmond and Bronwen returned, Morgana was at her wit's end. Ranulf alternated between periods of stupor, where he lay like a dead man, and others of frenzied thrashing, when it took all her strength and Cerdic's, too, to keep him from flinging himself from the bed in the violence of his efforts. He knew no one, and even when his eyes were opened they seemed wild and sightless. As the dreary afternoon faded into gloomy-shrouded evening, his reckless flailing grew worse.

"Lie easy, my lord," Morgana pleaded, attempting to push him back against the pillows.

He swung his arms and one of his outflung fists caught Morgana high on the cheekbone. She went flying backwards, and if Cerdic had not caught her she would have suffered worse injury. As it was in mere minutes her eye was bruised and swollen half shut. Fortunately Ranulf fell into one of his deep swoons almost immediately.

"My lady, you have taken a heavy blow," Cerdic said. "I fear you may have suffered a broken bone."

Morgana probed the lump along her cheekbone gently and winced. "'Tis only the flesh that is injured, God be praised. We must restrain him somehow. A sheet or strap, padded and tied across his chest, might suffice."

The soldier found a long piece of leather and wound cloth around the center, then tied it across Ranulf and to either side of the bed frame. When he finished, he handed Morgana a dagger with a large polished bloodstone in the hilt. "Lay this upon your eye, my lady, and it will draw the swelling out."

There was a discreet knock at the door and Cerdic opened it to admit Desmond. The Orkneyman entered to the sight of Morgana with a battered face, holding up a dagger and his cousin strapped to the bed. "What murderous mischief is this?"

Morgana turned. "Would you have him fling himself through the window opening or dash his brain out upon the floor in his delirium?"

"He is quiet as a corpse." Desmond strode to the bed and looked down.

It was then that Morgana realized Bronwen had come in the chamber, also. "Have you brought what I required?"

"Aye." Bronwen handed her the clay pot. "Four times a day between sunrise and sunrise, applied to the wound."

"Thank Heaven and all the Saints. We had best apply it quickly, while he sleeps, for he is like a raving madman at intervals."

As they redressed his wound with the new ointment, Bronwen saw how gentle Morgana's fingers were whenever they touched Ranulf, and recognized the worry and tenderness in her face. There might be a better use for the love potion she carried. That night she fell asleep wondering how she might administer it to my lady's husband.

By morning she had put it out of her mind. There was good news from her mistress. Sir Ranulf had gone from delirium to a deep and dreamless sleep. All through the day and ensuing night, Morgana kept vigil at his side along with Cerdic and Desmond. Only twice did she leave the room for any length of time; once to bathe and refresh herself and another to make another batch of ointment. From time to time weariness overcame her and she dozed in the high-backed chair, but the slightest sound wakened her immediately.

Toward dawn of the second day Ranulf's breathing became labored again, and she began to truly despair. Was this how it was to end—an ill-starred marriage, beginning with anger and suspicion and ending in anger, suspicion and death? And for her folly and pride, she was punished now with the knowledge that she had misjudged her husband.

Rain dashed against the windowpanes, the weather matching her gray and gloomy spirits as she thought of her arranged marriage to Ranulf. Their union had been no more to his taste than to hers, but while she had rebelled against it he had tried to be a husband to her, fulfilling his duties well. Defending her castle and people, he had given everything in the attempt—perhaps even his very life.

Morgana bowed her head and hid her eyes behind her hand. Desmond would scorn her tears. He did not understand that now, when it might be too late, she was faced with the knowledge that her heart was no longer wholly hers. If she could have turned time backward, how differently she would have done things! And if the Good Lord gave her another chance, she would prove it.

She leaned her head back against the chair wearily, too apprehensive to sleep, too numb to think. She had long run out of prayers and petitions. There was nothing to do but wait. Suddenly there was a great sigh from the immobile figure on the bed and her eyes flew open in fear.

Ranulf's face, so flushed before, was pale as wax, the bones standing out starkly. Desmond leaned over the big bed and his eyes glistened with unshed tears.

"Is he...?" She was unable to move, her limbs turned to heavy leaden weights.

Desmond looked up, blinking to clear his vision. He seemed to have forgotten she was there. "The fever is broken. The crisis has passed."

Morgana rose so suddenly she was overcome by dizziness. "Thanks be to God," she cried softly, then took one step and fell to the floor in a faint.

Chapter Ten

G ood morrow, my lord.''

It was quite early when Morgana entered Ranulf's chamber with a special posset the cook had made for him and found her husband fully dressed. She was not surprised. He was a man of action, most at ease in the company of his comrades or riding hell-for-leather over the countryside. Despite the harrowing crisis only recently undergone, he seemed no worse for wear—although his keen features were more finely chiseled and hawk-like than ever.

Eight days of recuperation and idleness amidst embroidered linen sheets had rubbed Ranulf's temper a bit raw about the edges, but he was almost restored to health—and ready to do battle today, at least verbally. He eyed the porringer with loathing and made a curt gesture as she came toward him.

"I thank you for your solicitousness, but you may send that dish away, madam. I am done with being wrapped in swaddling and fed infant's pap. This morning I shall ride out with the hunt."

For all his manly height and weight, Morgana thought Ranulf looked, for just a split second, like a sulky and defiant boy challenging his nurse. Although she was concerned that he would overtax himself it took an effort on her part not to smile. "As you wish, my lord."

Strolling closer, he took the porringer from her hands and set it down atop a chest. He had been expecting more of an argument and her ready agreement threw him off balance. His deep blue eyes searched her face with a hint of suspicion.

"You are very meek today."

"Yes, my lord. I have lately made a study of the virtue."

He grinned at that. "Little minx. You know as much of meekness—or as little—as I do. I have become so used to your flaying tongue that this change in you fills my breast with misgivings."

Now they were both smiling, but as the moment stretched out they were enfolded in a sudden sense of intimacy. *This,* Morgana thought, *is what it should be like between a man and a woman. Ease and laughter and gentle teasing ways. And, please God, there will be many more such times.*

It was Ranulf who broke the spell. It always was these days. Abruptly he swung around and went to look out one of the windows. Sea and sky blended together in shifting shades of blue and gold, but far to the northwest a line of dark clouds was forming. She followed his glance.

"It looks to rain again before nightfall. Dame Elva assures me it will fall much sooner, for she feels it in her bones."

"Rain or shine it will be good to ride out with the hounds. I have a taste for fresh venison."

Morgana made no answer but busied herself in folding the robe he had left lying upon the bed. Any excuse to stay near him, while she tried to find the magic words. The words that would erase the scars of the past and enable them to start over anew. Perhaps they would find it made no difference in the end, that they were unsuited in every way—but she doubted that greatly.

During these days of convalescence she had learned much about her husband: that he had a quick mind and an ability for estate management that surprised and gratified her; that he was an excellent player at tables and draughts, although not yet her match; and that the hair at the nape of his neck curled delightfully. That he had as high a regard for learning as he did for skill in battle; that he preferred highly spiced foods and had a weakness for sweetmeats of all kinds; and that his years of wandering had instilled in him a deep yearning for one place to call his home. The worst she had uncovered thus far was that his temper was as fiery as her own, something she could hardly fault him for.

She longed to make her apology over the matter of Owain ap Griffin's harp, but did not know how to escape the awkwardness of bringing the subject up. In the back of her mind, she was very aware of the legend concerning the man who owned and played it. Ranulf whistled a merry tune, thinking of the coming hunt and it gave Morgana the opening she sought.

"My grandfather used to sing that roundelay to me," she said. "It is good to hear it again, but it would be even better to hear it played upon the harp."

He did not meet her eyes. "Daffyd shall play it for you at supper tonight."

The matter was closed like a slamming door and Morgana saw that the subject still rankled. As she searched for some reason to prolong her presence, she noticed that a gust of air down the chimney had scattered bits of ash and burned wood upon the floor. She took up the small broom to sweep them away, but Ranulf stopped her with an impatient gesture.

"Leave it," he said with a touch of his former asperity. "There is no need for you to do servants' work for me, when there are tasks of your own, waiting."

It was polite and of course true; but Morgana had no doubt that she had been dismissed. She covered her disappointment and took another tack. "There are indeed. Today we shall turn out the linen chests and make fresh inventory of supplies in preparation for the festivities in two weeks' time.''

Each summer the knights and minor nobility owing allegiance to Morgana came to Castle Griffin. They would renew their oaths of homage and fealty in a ceremony in the great hall. The guests stayed for several weeks amid music and feasting and general jollity, and a tournament would be held as part of the celebration.

She replaced the broom. "Later, Lady Winifred and Bronwen will ride out with me to visit the good brothers of St. Tristan's and bring them supplies of which they are sorely in need.''

Ranulf's golden brows met in a straight line. "It is not wise to venture out so far yet. Unidentified horsemen have been seen in the vicinity.''

"Traveling merchants or pilgrims to St. Yseult's Shrine, no doubt. Sir Desmond assures me there is no hazard.''

"None to a man of Desmond's size and experience. But a lady of gentle birth is quite another matter." His voice was very firm. "You will take an escort with you.''

"Certainly." She went to the door and opened it. "Daffyd will come with us.''

"Daffyd!" Ranulf's voice was still firm but much louder. "A mere boy. I forbid you to wander about the countryside without protection. You will take Cerdic and several men-at-arms with you.''

"As you wish, my lord. I must go now, or Lady Winifred will be kept waiting." Morgana retrieved the porringer and exited.

Only when she was in the passageway with the door closed, did she let her smile break out again. For the first time in many days she began to hope her prayers would be answered: a man wishing to be rid of his wife would not concern himself with her safety or insist on an armed escort. That left only one conclusion: he was not as indifferent as he seemed.

She hurried to her chamber, barely seeing the two young servants whom she dazzled with her radiant face.

From the wind-whipped battlements of the east tower, Ranulf watched the small cavalcade of riders vanish into the forest. They would be out of sight of the castle until they reached the clearing in front of the monastery gates, and he intended to continue as unscheduled lookout until they were safe inside them. It was easy to distinguish Morgana in her cloak of blue wool bordered with vere and panels of silver thread, and he could not but notice that she rode as well in her woman's saddle as she had ridden astride dressed as a boy.

He would have preferred her to put off the visit until he could accompany her, but there was no sense in creating another angry incident between them. At least she had not defied him by going without an armed escort. That seemed out of character for the tart-tongued woman he had married, although it was true that this past sennight she had softened her ways. *And* her tongue. She had some trick up her sleeve, he was sure, to account for her honeyed voice and this sudden purpose of visiting the Monastery of St. Tristan on such a blustery day.

There was no accounting for the wiles of any female, most particularly his wife. She was a woman like none he had ever known: on one hand, soft and gentle and womanly and drawing all his protective instincts to the fore; on the other, brave and bold and as responsible as any man he could name. And as ready to do battle, using sharp words in place of a sword. He bore the scars to prove it.

Yet it was no wonder that she resented him. By birth and breeding she was far above him. Her lineage could be traced to ancient royalty through the Celtic line. In addition, she was intelligent, well educated and richly dowered. A prize for a prince, and marriage had given him legal precedence concerning all her possessions and rights, except for the right of inheritance: Castle Griffin would go only to her children, or failing that, revert to other blood heirs. It was of small import. At this point he wanted only peace of mind.

No, that wasn't exactly true. He still wanted *her,* God help him!

From the start there had been little likelihood that a woman of great wealth and beauty would dutifully submit to marriage with someone like himself. And only a fool wanted a wife who did not want him. In their case it was more serious than that—for friction between people in their positions was more than antipathy between man and woman, it was a wedge that could split their followers into two opposing camps, creating ill will and eventual chaos. They had started off on the wrong foot, and perhaps it had been his fault as well as hers. In retrospect the wisest course would have been to woo her properly and get her with child, as the King had so baldly suggested. A tiny heir would consolidate their people into a unified whole. It was the politic route to take.

"Strategy be damned!" Ranulf hit the stone wall with his closed fist. Morgana was like a thorn or burr that stuck to his flesh, pricking him and drawing blood at every turn. Try as he might, he could not root her from his brain, nor turn his mind from her for more than a few short minutes. He was wrenched from his thoughts by the sound of someone approaching.

"By the Mass, man!" Desmond exclaimed as he came around the projecting bulk of the tower. "I have searched for you in every quarter."

Ranulf turned from the windy parapet to face his cousin. "I was in need of fresh air and wished to speak with Owain myself. And after keeping to my chambers and the hall for so many days I thought it best to show myself about my usual duties to quell any awkward conjectures."

Desmond shot him a worried glance, but was apparently satisfied with what he saw. "The wind cuts like a knife up here," he said more mildly, "but it makes no matter to an old war-horse such as you. As to the other, no one suspects aught has been amiss with you since Lady Morgana kept to your chamber so much—they understand the ways of a man and woman during the honey-month of marriage."

Desmond paused and took a few paces back and forth along the battlement. "But there are rumors abroad that will concern you."

Instantly Ranulf was alert. "And what may they be?"

"Witchcraft, they say. A village man struck his wife and she fell against a rock and died. Two sailors were lost at sea in yesterday's storm."

"Tragic events. But surely more the fault of a violent temper and an angry sea, than the black arts."

"So I thought, also." Desmond slapped his fist into the palm of his other hand. "But think back to your wound which would not heal. And now come tales of sightings of a two-headed dog near the village." He lowered his voice. "Last night a witch, clothed in blue fire, was spied dancing upon the south castle wall."

"Fool's tales!" Ranulf wrapped his cloak closer against the wind. "I do not understand why you are bothered by such superstitious nonsense. If we make inquiries, we shall find that no person actually saw either event—they will have heard it from someone who heard if from another."

Desmond shrugged uneasily. "This time, Ranulf, we have a witness who swears he has seen the witch clothed in blue fire."

"Who is this jester who claims to have seen such an amazing sight?"

"A most credible person." Turning his gaze seaward, Desmond heaved an unhappy sigh. "Myself."

Morgana, accompanied by Bronwen, Lady Winifred and their escort, reached St. Tristan's gates without incident. The porter let them in and Morgana was gratified to see that much had been mended and the inner court cleared of debris. After conferring with Ranulf and Sir Dyllis, she had sent a contingent of smithies, carpenters and workmen to assist the good brothers in repairing the damage caused by Lindsey's men. The sound of hammer on wood and the clang of metal were evidence of their continued industry.

Morgana noticed that some of the monks and lay brothers who had taken refuge in the forest had made their way back and were tending the remains of the trampled kitchen gardens. They were gaunt and their worn habits hung loosely on their lean frames. Many of the elderly or invalid monks who had made up their ranks were dead, victims of ill health and exposure. The work force of St. Tristan's monastery had been cut to half its previous strength and it would be many years before the life was restored to its old ways.

The elderly abbot and his assistant hurried out into the courtyard to meet the arrivals. "Welcome, Lady Morgana, welcome! And Lady Winifred, welcome to you, also."

"Greetings, good brother. I see much has been put to rights since our last visit, when you offered us shelter in our time of need."

"Aye," Brother Ewen replied, "Because of your good offices and your lord's. We have remembered you and Sir Ranulf and all your brave soldiers in our prayers, my lady, and will do so every day as long as one of us remains upon this earth."

Morgana thanked them warmly. "I have brought gifts for the monastery, in gratitude for your assistance and in thanksgiving for our deliverance from the enemy."

She handed a purse of gold and silver coins to Brother Ewen and motioned for the other gifts to be presented. There were bags of grain, a cask of brandy, baskets of plump vegetables and precious dried fruits to replace those taken by the raiders, in addition to salted venison, wicker hampers of game birds and fish fresh from the mere.

"We thank you, Lady Morgana, most heartily, and will offer a special novena for your continued health and happiness."

They escorted the visitors into the main building and offered them refreshments. Afterward, Morgana expressed a wish to visit the Lady Chapel, where she had spent the night with Bronwen under Ranulf's protection.

While Lady Winifred oohed and ahhed over the stained glass window put in since her last visit and Bronwen admired the painted statues with their gilded wooden halos and crowns, Morgana gave thanks for Ranulf's recovery. Then she, too, began wandering about the chapel, admiring the fine wood carving and elegant stonework that she remembered so well.

She remembered the last time she had been inside the chapel. When Ranulf had begun his plans to rescue the castle, she had seen only a man intent upon salvaging his possessions by marriage. How much she had learned, how she had grown and changed since then! The difficulty lay in making Ranulf recognize and accept the changes as genuine.

Having been exposed to the intrigues and seductions so common among certain of the Court ladies, he had developed a mistrust of feminine wiles. Although they had spent many pleasant hours together, he was still wary of her and seemed not at all disposed to take any steps to break down the barriers between them. Morgana fell deep in thought. Only one plan came to her. The more she examined it, the better it appeared. If Ranulf would not take the initiative, then it was up to her to do so. She must set aside her pride and take the first step.

With the decision made, she suddenly felt lighter, younger. Like a girl in the throes of first love. The sunlight sparkled through the jeweled panes, no less joyous and brilliant than the certainty that flooded her soul. She was impatient to return and implement her plan.

She looked around for the others. The castellan's wife was at the back of the chapel, laboriously deciphering an inscription on a marble stone set in the wall. Lady Winifred had not learned to read or sign her own name until Morgana realized the lack and had offered to teach her. Now the castellan's wife felt herself as learned and accomplished as the Queen herself.

A clank of spurs announced Cerdic's arrival. He bowed to Morgana. "My lady, a cold wind is rising full strong. We had best return to the castle with all due haste before the storm is upon us."

"Certainly. I will fetch the others and meet you in the courtyard."

Within a short time she had made her goodbyes to the friars and was riding out through St. Tristan's gates. The sky had grown darker and the bite of the wind was keen as they made their way down the forest trail. The women drew their hooded cloaks about them tightly. As they skirted the village, Morgana directed Cerdic to stop. "I wish to obtain more of the special ointment from the herb woman. I shall not detain you long."

"As you will, my lady."

Both Cerdic and his men were too disciplined to show their boredom with sedate rides about the countryside while the women visited religious houses and peasant hovels; but a few reined short and crossed themselves when they saw the particular place their new mistress chose to visit. The cottage was isolated from the rest of the village, and the forest grew close at hand. They had heard of the two-headed dog and the appearance of the blue witch upon the ramparts. As for the old biddy who lived alone outside the strict confines of the village, there were rumors aplenty.

Lady Winifred looked around in disgust and disavowed any wish to accompany her mistress. "A low place it seems, and sure to be full of fleas and noisome odors. I do wish you would ride on, Lady Morgana. I do not like the look of it."

"A messenger was sent ahead to have the ointment ready for me. I will be but a moment."

No sooner had the party of riders pulled up, than the old woman was at her cottage door. She waited while Cerdic helped a woman dismount. Because time had dimmed her sight, she mistook her new hooded visitor for Bronwen, who stood just behind her mistress.

"So, my fine lady, ye've come back. Come in, come in. I can guess what brings ye here. Another love potion I'll be bound."

"Love potion! I have come for no such thing. 'Tis more of your healing ointment that I require, good wife."

Morgana and Bronwen stepped inside. The hovel was even dirtier and more disordered than the girl remembered from her previous visits, and a fat goose waddled in the filth, honking and nipping at the herb woman's skirts.

"Begone, imp!" The crone seized a twig broom and shooed the fowl out the door, then brought out a clay pot with a sealed lid. "Here, I have just readied a new batch, my lady."

"Excellent."

"There is word about that your new lord is ailing, my lady. I hope ye may not be in dire need of it," she added, closely watching Morgana from her rheumy eyes.

"Nay, but it was so effective I had hoped to keep some by in case need arose on another occasion."

Her words seemed to surprise the woman and she chewed her toothless gums in silence a while. "Well then, is there aught else I can give ye? I have unguents to keep a fine lady's face white as snow. Not that ye have any need for such."

When Morgana did not show any interest, the old woman sidled closer and lowered her voice. "Be any ladies of the castle in need of a potent love philter? It was given me by a merchant traveling through, in exchange for some rare herbs. It do come from Cathay, he vowed, and has never yet failed in softening the hardest heart."

Morgana shook her head. "I have no truck with such magic arts." Taking the little pot, she placed it in her purse and started for the door. As she passed through the threshold, a decorative metal boss from her habit caught on a protruding nail. The coin-sized bit of metal, adorned with a circlet of pearls and her crest, was swept to the floor by her long train, to lie unnoticed among the dirt and debris.

Morgana went out but Bronwen lingered. She was in her mistress's confidence and aware of the truce between her lord and lady. Over the course of the past week, Morgana had fallen deeply in love with her husband. It was in regard to Sir Ranulf's feelings that Bronwen was unsure. Truces could be broken, and once Sir Ranulf was fit to travel he might leave as he had threatened. And if he went away he would take his men with him, to the detriment of her own hopes and plans. She looked uncertainly at the old woman.

"This philter you spoke of, is it stronger than the substance I purchased from you?"

"Aye, young mistress. The difference is like a candle flame compared to the brightness of the sun."

She hobbled over, not to the rude shelf holding an array of jars and pots and baskets, but to the raised pallet that served her for a bed. Lifting the mattress of dried grasses she extracted something wrapped in a piece of coarsely woven linen. When she returned, the woman thrust a small glass vial into the girl's hand. Inside was a pale lavender fluid.

"Five drops in ale or water today, then two more each day for seven days. On the eighth day, administer the remainder in one dose."

Bronwen nodded. She unbuttoned the inside pocket of her cloak and took out a little velvet purse and a piece of silver shone in her hand. To her surprise the woman backed away. "Keep your coins, my lady. Who else would use it, for 'twould be wasted on these lusty village lads."

After several attempts Bronwen gave up arguing, merely thanked the woman, placed the coin on the deep windowsill and went outside. It was a relief to be in the cool, fresh air, after the smoky squalor of the cottage. Buttoning the velvet purse inside her cloak once more, she remounted with Cerdic's assistance and they headed toward the coast road.

As the calvacade rode toward the castle, a man dressed in a forester's garments stepped from among the trees. Instead of keeping to the verge, he came out upon the track so suddenly Morgana feared he would be run down. Cerdic halted his double column and made a swift gesture. The lead soldiers had their lances pointed at the man's heart.

"Move aside, varlet." The forester ignored them. He stood proudly for a peasant, Morgana saw, and although his air was vigilant, it held no tincture of fear or awe.

"Lower your lances, lads, for I mean no harm. I bear a message for the Lady Morgana of Castle Griffin." He held up one thick hand to show a roll of leather tied with a string and sealed with a thick blob of green wax.

Morgana recognized the seal and was so surprised that she scarcely noted the man's smooth speech. "I will take it," she said out of curiosity.

A sergeant took the roll from the man's grasp. "Be off with you, now." The forester stepped back from the road.

Morgana accepted the leather from the soldier and hesitated for only an instant. Normally she would have placed it inside her cloak pocket and taken it back with her, but wary instinct warned her to read it now. She broke the seal and unrolled the leather. Inside, was a sheet of fine linen paper. In black ink, a bold masculine hand had written:

To the beautiful Lady Morgana, my fondest greetings.
I have heard that your marriage displeases you greatly.
If this is true you have only to send word to me, my
love. Fear not. I shall rid you of Sir Ranulf, for remembrance of the love we shared.

Ever yours,
Lindsey

The letter inside also bore Lord Lindsey's seal, just below his sprawling signature. She had no doubt it was genuine. The man's arrogance was incredible! Narrowly eyeing the messenger, Morgana suddenly recognized him: Guy of Mikelsbury, a swaggering knight who was Lindsey's bosom friend. It was a brazen act, but so like both men she should not have been caught off guard.

Sir Guy stood there under her silent scrutiny and watched her discomfiture with cynical amusement. One word from her and he would be a dead man. They both knew it. Under the rules that men had contrived to cover such matters, a messenger should not be restrained from leaving. To identify him under the circumstances would be unchivalrous by the code of behavior, and if any violence occurred to him, Castle Griffin could come under sanction by the King and Church.

Morgana did not know these men-at-arms well enough to judge their reaction, and if Cerdic and the others learned his identity they might slaughter Sir Guy upon the spot. He knew her quandary and his smile grew. All this flashed through her mind in a matter of seconds and she came to her decision.

"This is my reply." She tore the brief document into a dozen pieces and scattered them in the wind.

Suddenly the sound of horns announced the return of the hunting party from the other arm of the forest. They broke onto the open ground of the meadow with Ranulf and Sir Dyllis in the lead, laughing and shouting. The hunting had been good. There would be venison roasts and stews tonight, and hares with turnips and carrots in pastry. Spotting Morgana's party, Sir Dyllis wound another blast from his horn.

That was all the distraction Sir Guy required. He faded back into the forest to where one of Lindsey's men held his horse at the ready. "Too many of them," he muttered as a dozen others joined him. "But there will be another time."

Meanwhile, Morgana and her little group rode toward the others. Garth, one of the new men recently taken on by Sir Dyllis, called out that his horse had a stone in its hoof and he would catch up with them when he was able. Cerdic nodded and Garth fell behind, pretending to examine his mount's shoe; but the moment the little party wended its way around a curve in the track, he hobbled the beast and scouted along the trail for the torn bits of paper that Lady Morgana had thrown to the wind.

He was uncertain as to what use he might make of the scraps, for along with most of his fellows he could not read or even write his name. Deficient in learning though he might be, Garth was a man of cunning, with an eye ever open to the main chance, and something told him he might make use of this opportunity one day. Perhaps it was the odd feeling that he had seen that forester somewhere before, and not long ago at that.

He chased the pieces of paper along the path and into the forest itself. Some danced and swirled as the wind gusted and blew, but by the time the others reached the hunting party he had gathered up the pieces—all but two long strips from the outer edges, which seemed to have vanished off the face of the earth. Their pale color should have shown up well against the tangled green foliage or the dark gray rock, but no matter how hard he looked or how far he searched, there was no trace of them.

'Tis a waste of time, he thought, returning to where his mount was patiently cropping grass. *The wind has surely carried them out to sea or an animal had snatched them up to line its burrow.* The horse swallowed a mouthful of green and whickered as its rider put the paper pieces in the leather bag inside his padded doublet and mounted.

Garth was new to the district and had no established loyalties. At thirty-one he had made his way with only the power of his good right arm, but did not intend to grow old and spend his life following someone else's orders. He would bide his time, find someone to read these scribbles to him, and then he would decide what to do. He set his mount to a gallop and blended in with the tail of the hunting party. There was one of the chambermaids named Melva who had been making up to him the past few days. She had boasted that she could read and cipher, having been taught by the Lady Morgana herself. The wench might be able to tell him what he had in these torn bits of paper—and then he could decide how he could benefit from them. No one seemed to have noticed.

Ranulf reined his steed in before Morgana and greeted the ladies with a bow. "Well met, ladies! We have been successful, as you see."

"We shall dine well this eve," Morgana replied, satisfied that the exertion had done her husband no harm. Unaware of the hand Fate and Garth had taken in her affairs, she passed on news and messages from the monastery, and made no mention of the strange encounter along the trail.

Lady Winifred was thinking of her dinner, and that the stag and two does would give the castle tanners more work to occupy their time. She would ask Lady Morgana if she might claim some for a new pair of boots. Perhaps two.

As they drew near the castle, there was not much talking. Morgana was busy mulling over her meeting with Lindsey's disguised henchman. Lindsey might have meant nothing more than to plead his cause with her via the letter but she feared Ranulf would doubt her loyalties because she had not ordered the men to take Sir Guy prisoner. It might be necessary to devise a likely story to answer any questions that might be asked. The last thing Morgana wanted, at the moment, was for Ranulf to be angry or suspicious. It would ruin everything.

In her feminine wisdom she realized Ranulf was but a man and would likely think she had been exchanging messages with Lindsey all along. She well knew that men were strange and unreasonable creatures, apt to take severe umbrage at any rival. Even a rival pursuing an estranged and unwanted wife.

She looked at Ranulf from the corner of her eyes. Outlined against the darkness of the distant storm clouds, his hair was a golden halo of light and his profile so beautifully carved it made her breath catch in her throat. He was a man's man, not the kind to waste his time in pretty speeches or writing love poems to a woman's eyes. He had far better qualities: he was quick to think and act, honest and just in his dealings, both ardent and tender in his lovemaking. He might never play the loving admirer beneath a woman's moonlit window, but he would be ready to defend her honor and estates with his good right arm. Jesu, how she loved him!

At the same time, Ranulf was reflecting upon how tiring yet exhilarating the hunt had been—and how beautiful his wife looked, with her cheeks flushed rosy with cold and her eyes sparkling like aquamarines. He wondered suddenly what she would do if he dismounted outside the great hall, swept her up in his arms and carried her upstairs to his bed. Would she melt against him as she had that one, wonderful night? Would she sigh and whisper his name?

More likely bloody my nose, the little spitfire! he thought and grinned. *Still, it might be worth the chance!*

As they approached the gates, Morgana could not help contrasting her emotions with those on her arrival here from Court. Then she had been angry and rebellious against her husband and in fear for her people. Today peace was restored and her feelings toward Ranulf had been turned completely around. She glanced at him from beneath lowered lashes. Was there another man who could have thrown off the results of this wound and fever and taken to the hunting field again so quickly? More and more he seemed to her like a hero out of the old stories, a warrior prince, larger and bolder than life. Yet she had seen a gentler side of him.

He was a man of authority, and in all his dealings he demonstrated a justice and wisdom that reflected the strength of his character. He had humor and wit, as well. And those battle-scarred hands that brought such sweet notes from a harp were as sensitive and sure when they had touched her.

At the memory of their one night together, she felt a pang of longing to return matters to their former status. She had been obstinate and foolish, blinded by her hasty temper and fear of being nothing more to Ranulf than a pawn in his game of power. She knew now that she had been terribly wrong, led astray by past experience and her own fears of vulnerability.

A second chance was all she needed and her spirits were blithe. Her prayers for her husband's recovery had been answered, and if today's appeal worked, their damaged marriage would be saved. God helped those who helped themselves, it was often said, and she meant to work hand in hand with Him.

Morgana rode across the drawbridge in a sunny mood. She would have been less sanguine knowing that a few feet away in the leather pouch at Garth's waist lay a few scraps of paper that would one day hold her happiness—and, indeed, her very life—in the balance.

Chapter Eleven

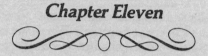

Morgana discovered a hustle and bustle when she rode inside the gates: wagons and horses, servants and men-at-arms in green-and-yellow tunics milled about the inner ward. Sir Dyllis seemed alarmed and Lady Winifred scanned the yard anxiously. Instantly Ranulf braced for trouble, every sense alert.

"Sir Vaughn has come over from Llangfrod," Morgana explained to him, leading the way to the stable yard. "He was not expected for another fortnight."

Morgana hoped he bore no ill tidings. The middle-aged knight was wed to the fair young Alys, the only child of Sir Dyllis and Lady Winifred.

As they dismounted Elva came hurrying to meet them and ease their fears. Although she addressed Morgana and the new master as was right and proper, her words of comfort were aimed at the concerned parents.

"Sir Vaughn has come, bringing Alys and the children with him. There is summer sickness in the valley near Llangfrod and they thought it wisest to leave their home before the illness reached the manor."

Everyone relaxed. "It will be highly agreeable to have more of their company," Morgana said with heartfelt warmth. "And I hope they may stay as long as they wish, until all trace of the sickness is gone from their vicinity."

The Llangfrod family were indeed welcome. Morgana valued and admired Sir Vaughn for his loyalty, integrity and kindly disposition, and she had known and loved his wife, saucy little Alys, all her life. Morgana had been a girl of six summers when Lady Winifred had given birth to her only child, and until adult life and fate intervened, the two had been close friends and chief companions.

As for Alys's three rambunctious boys, some ladies might shudder to find them hanging over the battlements or hear them screaming through the corridors and across the great hall, but Morgana found their antics amusing. They reminded her of herself at a like age, when she had been Elva's joy and despair, and of the strapping sons she had always hoped to bear some day. And still would, if her prayers were answered.

"I trust that you have seen well to their comfort, Elva."

"Yes, my lady. Alys and the children are installed in their usual apartments and resting after their journey."

Daffyd joined them. "Sir Vaughn has brought some prime steeds with him," he announced with shining eyes. "Arabian-blooded. He is wishful to hear your opinion of them. He is presently in the tiltyard, putting them through their paces for Dal."

"Let us go then without delay," Sir Dyllis suggested eagerly, "and leave the ladies to see to Alys and the boys. My son-in-law has a keen eye for horseflesh."

Ranulf smiled down at his wife. "We shall join you shortly."

Morgana smiled back warmly, holding back the laughter that was very near. As the men headed for the tiltyard, the women started back toward the keep, exchanging knowing glances. "We shall not see them again until the dinner horn blows," she chuckled to her companion.

"Aye," Lady Winifred acknowledged. "When menfolk get to talking of horses and exchanging stories they lose all sense of passing time." They entered the great hall, chattering happily, and Morgana spied her seneschal on the opposite side of the chamber.

"I must consult with Arvil and see to household matters first. Do go up to greet them, as you are no doubt longing to do. Give Alys my fond love and tell her I shall extend my welcome to her in person when we meet in the great hall later."

"To be sure I will, my lady."

The castellan's wife bustled off with Bronwen in tow, anxious to reassure herself that her daughter and grandsons were in good health. Morgana spoke with the seneschal and found that all was in order. "Send for fresh ale for Sir Ranulf and the others. And bring out the cup that was my father's and grandfather's for Sir Ranulf's use. It is fitting that it be used by the master of the castle."

As Morgana crossed the hall to the staircase to the upper floor, Arvil brought out three fine goblets, each with its own design of chased metalwork. The fourth was silver washed with gold, its entwined scrolls set with amethyst and topaz. It would be good to see it on the high table again, in its rightful place.

Near her chambers, Morgana encountered two serving men who had just brought up water for Ranulf's bath, after receiving word of his return. It would be quite cold again before he returned from the stables. There was no sense wasting the hot water. After so long out of the saddle, her muscles were tender.

Entering her own chamber, Morgana gathered up several items. A short time later, she slipped into Ranulf's room. Beside the fire a tub of steaming water waited, and the servants had drawn a high, square tapestry screen between it and the door to protect against drafts. Perfect.

First scattering a handful of dried herbs and rose petals over the water, she next unpinned her hair and shook out her elaborate plaited coiffure. With a quick few twists she lifted the shining red-gold mass atop her head and held it in place with a large jeweled comb. She would bathe quickly to shake off the chill and slip into her best robe of aquamarine silk trimmed with knots of rose and white ribbon. Then when Ranulf came for his own bath, she would be refreshed and ready to assist him with his, in the accustomed mode. The intimacy of the moment might further ease the strain between them. She would let him know she was ready and willing to resume her wifely duties. More than willing.

In the time of their estrangement she had discovered many things—one of them, that pride was a cold bedmate. But it was not only that. Day by day, Ranulf had become more and more an integral part of Castle Griffin. He had taken grave responsibilities upon his broad shoulders and lifted them so adroitly that she felt, not usurped as she had feared, but relieved.

The changes he had made in the military structure, based on his experience and knowledge, had certainly improved their security and peace of mind. It was good to share the burden of rulership with someone she respected and trusted. Morgana knew now that the gifts of leadership, intelligence, strength and goodness that Ranulf brought to their marriage in abundance were worth more than titles or fine estates. If only she had realized from the start that he was not her antagonist but her partner, capable of all the affection and passion her lonely heart craved, how different things would be!

Morgana discarded her wet habit and slipped out of her chemise and undergarments. As she stepped over the rim she heard booted footsteps in the corridor. They passed by and she climbed in, feeling the welcome warmth of heated water swirling around her legs. Settling in the deep tub, she felt her muscles relax and slid deeper, until the tiny ripples lapped about her throat. It was soothing and she lost track of time as she lathered herself with sandalwood soap Lady Winifred made each year. The crackling of the fire and the soft splashing of the water muffled the sound of the opening door.

It was the sudden rush of cold air that alerted Morgana to the fact that she was no longer alone. The drying cloth she used was just out of reach, and in any case there was no time. She could only cross her arms over her breasts, draw her knees up modestly and shrink down beneath the water as much as possible.

A firm masculine tread came toward the screen. "Who goes there?" Her voice was husky with embarrassment.

"It is I, Lady Morgana," she called out, meaning to warn any servant of her presence. The footsteps stopped. Morgana's heart bounced against her ribs. "Leave me. I do not wish to be disturbed."

There was no sound, not even that of breathing. She looked up and found Ranulf looking back at her, his head and shoulders rising above the screen. There was no wariness in his face now, only a great and growing hunger. All power to move, to think rationally evaporated from her, and Morgana stared at him while the steam rose around her in a cloud.

Ranulf was a man in a dream as he came around to stand beside the tub. This desirable creature, this languorous mermaid was still his wife. The waterline clung to the upper curves of her breasts and circled her bent knees, and beneath the shining surface Morgana's body was rosy and luminous as a pearl. Although her arms were crossed upon her breasts, he could clearly see one taut nipple, delicious and enticing.

He inhaled deeply. Through the scent of the sandalwood soap and aromatic herbs and petals, he thought he could distinguish the womanly fragrance of her skin. He wanted to scoop her up from the water, carry her dripping wet to that soft feather bed and forget everything except that they were man and woman. The temptation was almost overwhelming. What would she do? he wondered.

While he pondered her probable reaction Morgana kept
her eyes locked on his. She had seen his rising desire and felt
a warmth grow and spread through her body in ever wid-
ening waves. And when he smiled that crooked smile, her
bones grew weak from the hot rush of longing that followed. She moved her arms away from their protective posture and let them fall gracefully to her sides. The risk was
hers: she had made the opening gambit. The next move belonged to Ranulf.

Ranulf saw the arousal in her eyes, the way her lips softened and parted. He could not mistake her mood or her
meaning. Bending swiftly he scooped her up into his arms,
ignoring the water that soaked his doublet and hose. It
didn't matter. He didn't plan to have them on much longer.
He carried her to the bed and set her down gently upon the
fur throw. Against the rich, dark background, her vibrant
tresses had the glow of smoldering embers and her creamy
skin seemed as translucent as precious white jade. She took
his breath away.

He shed his garments, unaware of the splendor of the
flames outlining his body in fire, tracing the rippling muscles, the wide chest and shoulders, the powerful thighs,
narrow hips and flat sculpted plates of his abdomen. Morgana watched him through half-closed eyes, one arm flung
languidly above her head. She had no shyness or false
modesty to inhibit her now, filled as she was with love and
anticipation. How beautiful he was, how golden and manly.
She held out her arms to him as Ranulf leaned over the bed.

Instead of joining her upon the mattress he smiled and
shook his head. Picking up the towel he moved near the bed
and began to blot the beads of water from her body. His
light touch sent chills of pleasure racing across her skin while
her blood heated. He dried the delicate arch of her feet, her
slender ankles, the curve of her calves, and where the towel
went his lips followed. They trailed across the front of her
thighs, over the rounded softness of her abdomen and along

her sides. He brushed her breasts lightly with the cloth causing exquisite ripples of delight. Only then, when her need was as great as his, did he lay beside her and pull her into his arms.

His kisses were deep and thorough. Oh, how she had missed his touch! Morgana's head was spinning with sensation as his hands stroked and tantalized and renewed their intimate acquaintance with her body. He remembered everything she liked, every caress and touch, until she sighed and trembled and ached with the need to meld and merge with him.

Circumstances had forced her to be alone so long, and for years she had had to be strong for others. With Ranulf she could be just a woman. A woman in love. Her fingers traced the lines of his form she had unconsciously memorized: his chest, covered with crisp golden hairs; the winged blades of his shoulders; the solid strength of his back. Here was the tiny star-shaped scar whose history she did not know, and lower—near his left ribs—the smooth ridge of scar tissue from the wound he'd received in the battle for the castle. A few inches higher or lower and he would have been dead.

She clutched at him, pulling him closer, closer, as if she could shield him from injury or death with the strength of her own body. Ranulf responded to the change in Morgana, meeting her urgency with his own. Their joining was a union of body and spirit and soul. He plunged inside her, restraining his enormous power for fear of frightening her. Morgana's fingernails raked his back, spurring him to thrust harder, deeper and she arched up to meet him. The moment came and they soared together rising higher and higher in a burst of light and joy, then came spinning back to earth in a blaze of glory that left them satiated and fulfilled, still clinging to one another, almost afraid to let go.

Ranulf buried his face alongside her neck and gasped for air. Beneath his chest he felt her heart beating in rapid time with his own. He kissed her temples and her eyelids, the high

sweep of her cheekbones and the full curve of her mouth.
She smiled and arched her neck, almost purring with pleasure. But after a while the palms of her hands began to push
at his chest. He raised his eyebrows questioningly.

"You are squashing me, husband," she said in a husky
whisper, smiling up at him.

Husband! That one word, spoken low and lovingly, told
him all he wanted to know. He did not care why she had
changed her attitude toward him, but he was glad she had—
whatever the cause. After one last kiss he rolled onto his
side, but his arm held her tightly against his side.

She snuggled next to him, safe and secure with his arm
around her. As she was drifting into sleep, Morgana realized Ranulf had not spoken one word the entire time. It
didn't matter. He had spoken with his eyes, his hands, with
the tenderness and passion of his lovemaking. Without a
thought for her duties or her guests, she fell asleep in his
arms.

It was the sunlight on her face that woke her, golden and
filled with warmth. Ranulf slept soundly, his breathing deep
and even, one strong arm and leg thrown possessively across
her body. With a sigh of pure happiness she turned her head
toward the window and saw a cloudless sky, as deep and
pure a blue as Persian turquoise. While they slept the un-
seasonable cold and rain had been vanquished by summer.

Elation filled her. Morgana had been raised to believe that
heaven sent signs and portents to guide earthly souls, and
she saw the change in weather as a harbinger of good times
to come and smooth sailing through once troubled marital
waters. Basking in contentment, she could not know that
this halcyon interlude was not an omen for the future but
merely the calm before the storm.

"How handsome Sir Ranulf is!"

Sir Vaughn and the other men rode ahead of the ladies,
and Alys could not help throwing a wistful glance in her new

lord's direction. A dark-haired girl, she had inherited her mother's tendency to full curves and her father's quickness of mind. She rode side by side with her hostess while Morgana's merlin circled high in the sky, preparing to snatch its prey in midair. Much as she had learned to love her own husband, even the fondest eye could not deny that Sir Vaughn had a decided paunch or that his days of physical prowess were on the wane.

It was not unusual for a mere girl to be wed to one of her father's contemporaries, or even to a man old enough to be her grandfather; but for just a fleeting instant, seeing Ranulf look over his shoulder to smile at Morgana, Alys wondered what her life might have been like with a younger man, or one of her own choosing.

"You are a fortunate woman, to have the love of so seemly a knight."

Morgana readily agreed. "We are both blessed in our husbands. I must admit to great relief that Sir Vaughn's indisposition on your arrival night proved to be nothing more serious than the colic. The severity of his pain caused me to fear something was greatly amiss."

The remembrance of that terrible night sobered Alys as they rode back to the castle. Sir Vaughn had been so racked with agony at one point they had despaired for his life, but after a course of purgatives he had rallied with the coming of dawn. Whatever had caused the illness had taken quite a toll from her aging knight, but although he was still tired easily his strength increased from day to day.

No one else in the castle had fallen ill, although Ranulf and several of the men had complained of intermittent stomach pains for several days, thought to be the fault of some salt pork gone past its prime. Alys crossed herself, thanking God once again for sparing her husband and silently vowing to cherish him as she ought.

Morgana's spirits remained high, basking in the sunshine of Ranulf's open affection and esteem with every passing day. She entertained Alys for the rest of the way back with plans for the coming tourney and for entertaining the children in the meantime.

The days that followed were magical for Morgana, the mornings and afternoons filled with hunting and hawking with their guests, the evenings with music and laughter in the great hall. A group of wandering jongleurs came to the castle, delighting everyone with their songs and juggling and acrobatics until the page boys yawned and the candles guttered in their holders; but after, when the merriment stilled and night held sway, came the best times of all. She and Ranulf talked and made love, and their private Eden had no contact with the outside world except for the intermittent "all is well" calls of the guards making their rounds.

It was only her dreams that were dark and disturbed. Visions of vines growing in the night, black twisted things that scaled the castle walls and slithered through windows and doors, filling up chambers with their foul growth. Reaching out to catch and strangle her, while voices whispered and laughed. Many a night Morgana awakened in a panic, only to find the peaceful silence and her head cradled against Ranulf's shoulder. She could find no reason that such a joyous time would be troubled by nightmares and during her waking hours put the memories from her mind. But they lay just below the surface, casting a shadow on her sunlit days.

The enchantment of their lovemaking lasted as the days wore on, although their different duties frequently parted them. On a bright Tuesday, gowned in embroidered silks of jonquil yellow, Morgana went off to check the progress of the weavers and Ranulf departed for his second meeting with Brother Lewis, who had come from St. Tristan's to take on the task of mapping the castle precincts. Desmond and Sir Vaughn had taken the boys to the archery butts to watch Owain's bowmen at their practice, and he planned to join them later.

Ranulf ascended a winding set of stairs that led off a gallery. A room in one of the towers had been set up for the monk, so that he would have good lighting from all sides, and Brother Lewis was hard at work. One long table was stacked with sheets and rolls of parchment and a newer book of paper leaves stood open on another. When Ranulf arrived, the old monk was unrolling the older parchments and comparing them to the more recent ones. He was a quiet man, tall and thin, with the gaunt features of a martyred saint and a gentle, otherworldly smile.

"Ah, Sir Ranulf. There are some interesting discrepancies between the newer plans and the old. Portions omitted, walls misplaced, no doors recorded where doors most certainly were put."

"I imagine in three hundred years there have been many confusing alterations and repairs."

"Not as much as you would expect, I vow." The milk blue eyes glinted. "I believe these changes to have been made a-purpose, with intent to deceive."

Ranulf came over to compare the drawings. "Yes, this one does not show the lower wing beside the north tower—and if I am not mistaken, there are now no chambers along this wall."

"Exactly so, my lord. But I believe there may be chambers *within* the wall. But hidden for what reason? They serve no defensive purpose."

A chuckle escaped Ranulf. "For deviltry as well as defense, I vow! From what Sir Dyllis tells me, these Griffins were a bold and lusty lot." Brother Lewis looked puzzled.

"The second lord," Ranulf explained, "built the original keep. He is said to have brought his mistress and their children to the castle and kept them hidden from his wife for ten years before the lady discovered his deceit."

He scanned another set that the monk indicated and went on. "The fourth lord feared assassination by his loving relations, and had secret tunnels and hiding places added when he built on to the existing structure. Even Lady Morgana's grandfather added to the maze, but whether from necessity or habit I do not know. We shall not realize the whole until you have completed your enormous task."

"And interesting work it is, my lord. Look here." The old man led him to the other table and spread out his drawings, to date, with blue-veined hands. The outward elevations of the castle were drawn in masterful strokes, the details finely and accurately rendered. A series of floor plans were equally well done. Ranulf was considerably impressed.

"I did not hope to find so excellent a draftsman among the good monks. You have had training in architecture, Brother Lewis."

The monk nodded. "I was a master builder in England before taking the vows," he said in his thin, melodic voice. "Apprenticed at a young age, my early years were spent helping to build churches and abbeys. Ten years of my life I gave to one cathedral alone, before being acknowledged a master by my guild."

Ranulf was surprised. "And through this work you discovered your true vocation."

The cowled man smiled and shook his head. "Now I realize that this is where God always meant me to be, but in the pride of my youth I thought only of material things."

"Then how came you to St. Tristan's?"

The brother smiled faintly, as if recalling days long past, while his gnarled fingers carefully unrolled the parchment. He smoothed it flat and began to unroll another.

"I was employed to build a new manor for a great lord. There was a beautiful woman—there always is in these matters, is there not? She was his daughter, and as wanton as she was lovely. Unfortunately, or so I thought at the time, the lord found us together. Knowing she had ensnared me with her wiles, he offered me a simple choice: the church or the gallows."

Ranulf nodded and stifled a smile. He could scarcely imagine this wizened ascetic bedding some lusty wench. "And the lady—was she also punished?"

"I was only the last of many caught in her toils. She was contracted in marriage and wed to a man of great wealth and power, which she now wields with his blessing." He shook his head. "Beware of women, for in their greed they will use and discard many a better man than you or I."

"Not all women can be judged by the actions of such a one. A woman can be loyal and true as any man."

The monk gave Ranulf a sad and steady look but did not refute him. In a few minutes he was deep in his work, comparing the parchments and making notes, so engrossed he did not know when his visitor left.

Ranulf went down to the great hall and out to the tiltyard. How unlucky Brother Lewis had been in his choice of women—and how blessed he was in his. There was no other woman who could hold a candle to Morgana. She was a jewel beyond price.

But while he dwelled contentedly on such lover-like thoughts events were already in train to bring disaster.

Five miles to the north, Lord Lindsey sat near a tall window in the estate room of his fortified manor and brooded. A brightly plumaged bird trilled a series of notes, hoping to attract its master's attention, but its efforts were in vain.

"Quiet, Mogwedd!" The bird tilted its head to one side, bright eyes alert with malice as Lindsey pulled the cloth covering down over the cage. The lord was in no mood for annoyances. Morgana had torn his message to pieces. Still, Lindsey had expected to hear from her in secret, for his spies—and he had several—had reported her initial keen dissatisfaction with her new husband.

Every quarrel and sharp word uttered in public came, in time, to his interested ears. But more recent accounts told quite another story, and Lindsey knew his hopes for a rift between them had failed—as had his careful plan for disposing of the hated Dane.

By All that was Holy, if the old woman had taken his gold and played him false she would be made sorry! Now he must take matters into his own hands. His fingers curled unconsciously, as if they held his rival's throat between them. His hatred of Morgana's husband was profound. Even now he did not see the beautiful chests and rich hangings of his own room, for his mind was filled only with visions of what he did not possess.

He cursed Ranulf to the torments of hell. The usurping Dane had won the woman Lindsey had always coveted and the castle that would have been his if the English system of male inheritance had been followed. Sir Ranulf had tricked and outflanked him, decimating his private army in the process. And the worst insult yet: the Dane had not even bothered to attack Lindsey's fortified manor in retaliation. Well, if Sir Ranulf should change his mind, he would find a great surprise—for although the place was a third the size of the Griffin stronghold, it was in reality a small castle and well defended.

A servant entered and bowed. "There is a man at the gate claiming speech with you, my lord. He is from the castle."

"Send him up at once." Lindsey tapped his long fingers atop the table.

A message from Morgana, no doubt, saying she had at last come to her senses. She had loved him once and there was no reason to think she might not love him still. Her marriage to Lord Hartley had been a farce, with the man's infidelity known from the Scots border to the English Channel.

He caught a glimpse of his face reflected in a bowl of polished brass. Lindsey had been favored at birth with handsome face and form, and no one had ever doubted his cunning or bravery. Women came at the beckoning of his jeweled finger and melted at a smoldering glance from his heavy-lidded eyes, thinking themselves honored by his attention. It was no wonder that his pride had enlarged his vanity and hardened his character until it was stiff with arrogance. The aggressive warrior and lover had become a grasping, jealous man.

The servant returned with a tall fellow dressed in a countryman's simple hose and tunic, but his posture had a certain military bearing that brought Lindsey to his feet, dagger in hand.

"What villainy is this? You are no peasant!"

The stranger fell to his knee. "Hear me out, my lord. I was directed to come to you by a maid called Melva, of Castle Griffin."

"Say no more." Lindsey dismissed the servant and did not speak again until the heavy door shut behind him. "We are alone. State your name, rank and business."

"I am called Garth, my lord. My home is in the north and I came to Sir Dyllis this spring as a mercenary. Several days ago Lady Morgana rode back from St. Tristan's monastery. I was among the guard. On our return, a forester stopped our party and delivered a message to my lady. After reading it she tore it into pieces and scattered them to the wind."

Lindsey raised his brows and eyed the man steadily. "What had this to do with me?"

"I do not know, except that they bear your cipher. I showed them to Melva, the serving maid who is my paramour. She told me to bring them to you."

Carefully Lindsey took the torn bits of paper and arranged them on the table before him. Parts were missing. Important parts, yet a message could still be made out. He smiled as a plan formed in his mind. Where force of arms had failed to win his goal, trickery might prevail. Then Morgana would have nowhere to turn, but to him.

The smile widened. "I knew Melva would serve me well and faithfully. She is a creature of enterprise." He gathered the torn papers up and gave them back to Garth. "Give these scraps into her keeping and have her arrange to 'discover' them among the Lady Morgana's belongings. Have you any other messages?"

"Only that a monk, Brother Lewis, is drawing up a map of the whole of Castle Griffin. Using old plans and measuring each area he has already discovered a secret room beneath the east tower and a stairway that seems to lead nowhere between the walls of the inner keep. Melva thought this might interest you."

A small pouch of coins made its way across the table and into Garth's ready hand. "You have done well. Keep an eye on Brother Lewis and any further discoveries he might make."

A short time later, with the bag of coins hidden inside his doublet, Garth rode back toward the castle, wondering what torn letters and strange monks had to do with Lindsey. He did not have to wonder long.

Chapter Twelve

"What ails you, Desmond?" Ranulf cried, putting down his sword. "You are off your stride today and have no rhythm to your strokes."

Desmond wiped the sweat from his face with his sleeve. "I slept ill last night and the night before. There is a restlessness upon me that I have never felt before. More witchery, no doubt, from this accursed place."

Ranulf laughed aloud. "The only spell upon you, my friend, is that from a pair of shyly downcast eyes. I have seen the way you look so often to the fair Bronwen."

His cousin flushed to the roots of his red hair. "You are mistaken. The maid is too young—and too far above me in rank and fortune, in any case."

The hound, watching eagerly from a sunny place, decided the mock swordplay was done and bounded forward, only to be waved back by Ranulf. "Ready, Desmond?"

The other man nodded and gave the signal to begin again, trying to push the image of Bronwen from his mind. The Lady Morgana was aware that he looked upon her changed ways with suspicion and she would never countenance a match between him and her young ward.

Ranulf countered Desmond's blow, lunged smoothly and knocked his cousin a solid whack against his padded ribs. As Ranulf thrust again to follow up his advantage, Desmond stumbled back. "God's Eyes, Ranulf, but you have regained your strength and more."

"Aye! I've suffered many a worse wound in battle in my time, but this one nearly did me in. Now, thanks to the nursely skills of my lady wife I am more fit than ever." To prove his words Ranulf slapped the side of his sword over Desmond's shoulder, following up with another lightning thrust.

His friendly opponent let his sword drop. "Enough!" He rubbed his forehead with the sleeve of his doublet. Desmond set his mouth stubbornly and lowered his voice. "You are strong as ever, but I still say 'twas only witchcraft that could have brought you so near to death."

Seeing Ranulf did not attach any credence to his theory, Desmond pressed his point. "Have you forgotten Giles of Longleat? The flesh melted away from his bones between Michaelmas and Christmastide—and when he died, they found the stub of a candle wrapped in a piece cut from his best linen shirt."

Ranulf could not decide whether to laugh or be annoyed. Desmond seemed obsessed with talk of witchcraft and saw it manifested in every accident or illness that came to his attention. "Sir Giles," he rebutted, "died of a wasting disease, as did his father and grandfather before him."

"Exactly. When three strong men waste away and die before their thirtieth year there is sorcery afoot."

Taking a long pull from his water flask, Ranulf shook his head. "The Moors claim such wasting sickness is a disease, carried in the blood from father to son."

"Do not speak to me of Moors. You know the witch was seen outside the village before dawn this morning, bathed in blue fire. Perhaps the witchcraft has affected your brain."

"Witchcraft! You are as bad as an old peasant woman, Desmond, blaming what you cannot explain on spells and faerie folk."

He was distracted from this sermon when his hound, snuffling interestedly among the blocks and bales, found something near the foot of one wall and began whining and scrabbling at the stone. Ranulf whistled him to heel. The animal came toward him with great reluctance and he wrinkled his nose in distaste. The dog's sleek and shiny coat carried the foul and distinct odor of rotting fish.

"Whatever have you gotten into, you old scamp?" Ranulf crossed the yard with the hound trotting eagerly alongside until they reached the wall behind a short buttress. Something glimmered evilly in the shadows. Dim blue fire, glowing within a small drainage hole. Thrusting his big hand in, Ranulf drew the object out. A hooded cloak of dark cloth, smeared with decaying bits of matter. The smell of rotting fish was overwhelming and the dog capered and whined in excitement.

"Come, Desmond, and view your 'witch'!"

The Orkneyman hurried over, frowning. "What does that rancid heap of rags have to do with anything?"

For answer, Ranulf thrust the piece of cloth back inside its hiding place. The crumpled cloth once more shone with pallid blue light. "There is your mystery! Nothing more than putrescent slime from dead creatures of the sea. Not the glow of sorcery, but that of simple decomposition."

Abashed, Desmond rubbed a finger along his lean jaw. "A prank?" He made a face of disgust. "Who would employ such an odorous trick . . . and for what reason?"

"Not a prank," Ranulf answered deliberately. "Deep mischief is abroad, or I am greatly mistaken. Someone means to rouse superstitious fears. But as to why, I have no clear idea yet. Meanwhile, keep your eyes and ears open. Discover if anyone has been seen here who has no business in the tiltyard."

As he washed his fouled hands with water from the rinse trough, an eerie wail suddenly split the air, growing and swelling from a terrible moan to an ear-splitting, inhuman shriek.

"'Tis the *ban-sidhe*, howling!" Desmond exclaimed.

Ranulf cuffed him in the shoulder, laughing. "Superstitious fool! 'Tis one of the hounds baying."

A series of sharp barks preceded the next howl, accompanied by low growling and the angry shouts of one of the kennel lads. A dogfight was imminent, and the two cousins set out for the nearby kennels. The growling grew louder and the howling changed to piercing yips and whimpers. Another voice, deep and penetrating, added to the din.

"Damn your eyes, Lunger, get down! Down, you sorry benighted son of an imp!"

They rounded a high wall and found a scene of milling confusion. A large black hound had cornered another which was bleeding from a gash on the flanks and a partially severed ear. Presently the fierce animal also held a freckle-faced lad at bay; the boy was backed against the wall, cradling his bloody right arm in his left. An older youth assisted Floyd, the deep-voiced kennel master, who cursed and prodded at the black hound with a pole as long as a lance.

"Here now, you witch's spawn, you hound of hell!"

The attacking dog turned on Floyd and assaulted the end of the pole, splintering the wood with his pointed fangs. Ranulf instinctively went for his sword but stopped when the kennel master raised his hand.

"No need, my lord. He's only a bit riled up over a bitch in heat." Floyd gently teased the dog away from the other. "Now, then, that's a good lad. Steady Lunger. Steady."

The dog lowered its ears and released his death grip on the pole. A long pink tongue came out and he pranced playfully toward his master, who patted his head and scratched behind his ears. "All's well now. Easy, easy."

Floyd grinned at Ranulf and Desmond. "Ah, there's nothing like a female to set one male at another's throat."

He caught the quieted beast by the collar and nodded to the uninjured boy, who took the hound and led him away.

Ranulf assisted the wounded lad to a more comfortable sitting position in the angle of the wall. "'Tis a nasty gash you've got there, lad. I will ask Lady Morgana to send some of her special healing salve to you, and Master Floyd will give you something to ease the pain, as well."

He stepped out of the archway looking for a servant to send on his errand, and spied Melva, one of the young maidservants.

"There has been an accident," he said. "I have need of the special healing salve Lady Morgana prepared for me."

She took in his sword and gear, his sweat-streaked face and grim expression. Once before he had reopened his wound during arms practice. "What is the injury, my lord?"

"'Tis only a scratch, but the salve will do some good."

"Yes, my lord. I will go and fetch it at once. I know where it is kept."

She ran out of the yard, eyes shining with a strange dark light, chuckling to herself. It seemed that Fate itself connived to further Garth's schemes. Here was just such an opening as he had instructed her to look out for, and she planned to use it to the full. Lord Lindsey paid well. With winged feet she hurried to complete her task.

Desmond went off to the stables to confer with Dal, while Ranulf stayed behind with the boy. Newlyn was in a good deal of pain and suffering from reaction, but he was brave. Floyd quickly stitched the edges of the wound together with a needle and boiled thread. Nephew or no, this was a signal honor, as the kennel master ranked among the highest and most valued servants: without his skill at breeding and training the hounds so excellently, the castle folk could well starve. That he tended to his nephew himself was due less to their blood relationship than to the fact that Floyd considered the boy valuable in his job.

"You have things well in hand, Master Floyd." Ranulf stood. "There is naught for me to do but apply the salve and let nature do its healing."

Melva returned, bearing the pot of ointment which she handed to Ranulf. The kennel master held out his own hand. "I'll do it, my lord. No need to keep you from your duties."

Melva bit her lower lip but gave the earthen container to Floyd. After a moment she turned on her heel and left, glancing worriedly over her shoulder before vanishing around the corner. Floyd took the opened pot from her and daubed the ointment over the kennel boy's stitches. His gnarled fingers were scratched and Ranulf noted a large abrasion on the back of his wrist.

"Do put some on your own scratch, Master Floyd. 'Tis a wondrous medicine."

"Aye, that I will. Happen 'twill heal my nicks and cuts. Might do the hound a deal of good, too."

Ranulf laughed, and seeing that the boy was comfortably settled, went in search of his wife. He found Morgana in the solar, surrounded by her ladies. In their flowing gowns and sparkling headpieces they made a charming and colorful domestic scene. Embroidery frames were set up before Lady Winifred and Bronwen, and their needles and bright threads flashed. Morgana and Alys sat together turning the pages of a gilt-edged book, and old Elva dozed in a sunny spot on the window seat; in the background, Daffyd sat softly plucking his harp and worshipping Morgana with his eyes.

When Ranulf appeared, the harper gave his master a startled look before he lowered lashes to screen his fine dark eyes. *The impudent young pup,* Ranulf thought in chagrin, *has been weaving his daydreams with my wife for his heroine.*

He greeted the women courteously, but his voice was rather stern when he addressed Daffyd. "I have no wish to deprive the ladies of their pleasure, harper, but Cerdic tells me you missed sword practice this afternoon."

The youth flushed. "I thought it would not hurt to miss a session when I was otherwise engaged."

The sunlight streaming through the window struck bright fire from Ranulf's hair and outlined his square jaw. "You did not acquire your skill at music by practicing when the mood was upon you, but by steady application. If you wish to develop skill at arms, you must do the same; if you do not, you may convey your wish to Cerdic. He is in the smithyard with the armorer."

Daffyd set his harp aside, knowing Sir Ranulf was right. "If it pleases my lady, I will ask to be excused and seek out Cerdic."

Morgana smiled at him to take the sting from her husband's reproof. "Go, with my blessing. A bard must be prepared to defend himself—in case his music pleases not." The ladies laughed at her sally as Daffyd went out, crimson with embarrassment.

Lady Winifred watched Bronwen comparing silks, trying to choose the perfect shade of rose for the buds she was embroidering, and Alys had moved to the other window seat. Morgana rose and went to her husband. "Surely you were a bit harsh with Daffyd, my love."

Ranulf took her hands in his and kissed them, first one and then the other. "He is a good lad, but I will not encourage any moonling to hang about your sleeves like a lovesick calf. In any case, these are restless times and you are more precious to me than my life. If ever Daffyd is called upon to defend your life or honor, I wish him to be able to do so."

He looked at her mouth, smiling softly and forgot his lecture. If not for the interested audience he would sweep her up into his arms and kiss her until she laughed and cried mercy. Then he would carry her up to their chamber and make love to her over and over again. Duty be hung!

Ranulf drew her away from the others. "For the first time it strikes me how pleasant it would be to live alone together in a simple cottage, with no servants or troops to oversee and only ourselves to please."

"Your tongue is changed from brass to silver, my lord, and sweet words drip off it like honey from the comb." She gave him a saucy look. "But if this is what you have come to tell me, alas it is too late, for there are some three hundred souls under our roof, all demanding a portion of our time."

His sigh brought a bubble of laughter to her throat. "We have this great pile of stone instead of a cozy little cottage. But we will have tonight."

Once again, he raised her fingers to his lips and kissed the tips. "Then let the night fall swiftly," he said, smiling down into her eyes.

The next morning Morgana awakened from rose-colored dreams to find Ranulf gazing at her with great tenderness. It was not quite dawn, but the light was pink and pearly, flooding their room through the east-facing window. She smiled, unabashed by her nakedness, and stretched out a hand to tickle the stubble on his lean jaw.

"Good morning, my love."

For answer he kissed her once, and then again. He was a man more comfortable with deeds than words, and still could not completely trust his luck: no man could enjoy such happiness without paying for it somehow. The old tales were full of stories of fools lured by the enchantment of beautiful women to their destruction. Yet he did not doubt Morgana.

Her hair spilled about her like a cloud of flame. During the day it was confined with nets of gold and silver cording or snoods of silk and satin to match her various gowns. The artfully arranged coifs, jeweled chaplets and elegant headpieces suited her beauty and position; but if Ranulf had his way it would always fall free like a red-gold waterfall shimmering down her back.

Now it was loose as he favored it, silken tendrils streaming down across her shoulders, curling about her arms and clinging to the satiny curves of her breasts. As he pulled the embroidered coverlet down, sunlight streamed in the window, gilding her body with light.

"How beautiful you are!"

He cupped one white breast in his big hand, rolling his palm against the tip until it drew into a hard, little bud. Her indrawn breath was his reward, telling him once more that he had the power to stir her passions to their depths. To pleasure her was his greatest joy.

Ranulf pressed his mouth against her other breast and ringed the rosy nipple with his tongue. Morgana felt as if she were drifting away on a river of sensual delight. When he suckled her breast she arched against him, raking her nails over his shoulders and along his back. She shifted her legs apart, becoming fluid and pliable beneath his touch, responding to his growing heat.

He lifted his face to watch her as his hands moved lower, seeking to bring her pleasure. There was magic in his fingers, in the way they could stir from tantalizing gentleness to driving urgency, bringing her from civilized sensuality to the edge of violent primal instinct. The air was filled with the scents of love and she wanted him with a fierceness so intense it was almost pain.

Her fingers twined in the curly golden hairs covering Ranulf's muscular chest, and she touched and stroked him in return, until he was giddy with joy and swiftly surging hunger. He pulsed with desire and the need to possess her again, and could no longer hold back.

Morgana reached out to him, welcoming him. They were lost in their love, moving and breathing as one, transcending the boundaries of time and space. They moved in rhythm, achingly slow at first to savor each sensation, lost

in delight, then more quickly, as desire drove them to mutual frenzy—the ultimate, delirious pinnacle. The world
went whirling out of control, shook and trembled and exploded in showers of red-hot fire.

Afterward Ranulf held her close, kissing her soft mouth
a dozen times. His lips trailed along the angle of her jaw, the
sensitive curve of her throat. He had not realized how alone,
how lonely he had been until they had come together. It
seemed of utmost importance to find the right words to explain how infinitely precious she was to him.

"I never knew it was possible for a man to be so happy or
so content. You are everything a woman should be," he
whispered against her throat. "Everything I ever wanted,
but feared to even dream for."

Morgana ran her fingers through his tousled hair. "If this
is a dream, I hope never to awaken; if this be a spell, love, I
pray it is never broken."

Dawn was still new when Ranulf slipped from the bed,
leaving his wife curled up to daydream awhile beneath the
silken quilt. He bent to press a kiss to her temple and left the
room in search of his cousin, with whom he had made plans
to ride out. His favorite dog, a lean-flanked gray ratchet that
kept guard each night outside his master's door, greeted him
with joyful yelps. "Down, Lightning. Good boy."

With the hound bounding along at his heels, he strode
along the corridor, immensely pleased with life and the hand
Fortune had dealt him. He met Desmond at the head of the
stairs.

"Why the fierce scowl? Have you tried to woo Bronwen
again and been sent packing?"

Shaking his head, Desmond scanned the hall below,
where the servants were stirring and men already breaking
their fast with bread and ale. "We must be private, Ranulf.
Let us step into the solar."

With the hound at his heels, Ranulf followed him. He had
seen Desmond angry, impatient or enthusiastic a hundred

times before, but he had never seen him so grave and intense. Something was greatly amiss. "What's afoot? You are like a stag with the wind up."

"Aye, and 'tis an ill wind. The kennel boy injured yesterday is in profound delirium, the kennel master too ill to rise from his bed—and the two hounds both dead."

Ranulf was shocked. "The lockjaw?"

"Nay. Nor the rabid disease. They were poisoned."

"Poisoned! By what?"

"By the Lady Morgana's ointment. Don't you see, Ranulf? 'Tis an evil plot. That ointment was intended for you!"

"What profit is in it? Who could wish to poison me?"

Desmond paced a few steps away, then swung back abruptly. "You are a powerful lord, and power breeds enemies: a madman with a grievance, an enemy within the walls, an agent of Lord Lindsey."

He leaned down and gripped the edge of the table. "Or a woman wishing to rid herself of an unwanted husband!"

Ranulf's eyes blazed with fury. "Be careful what you say! Any other man but you would find my dagger at his throat for less."

"Do you think I have not considered this carefully? Hear me out—unless you are so caught by her witchcraft that you cannot hear what you *must* hear."

"Enough, I tell you! The village woman could have poisoned the ointment for some reason of her own. You have nothing against Morgana except these ridiculous suspicions."

"You are under her spell, blinded by her beauty. You went to your wedding with dire reservations and when she ran away on your wedding night, they seemed confirmed. Then, only a few days later, you risked your life for this same woman. If that is not witchcraft, I do not know what it is."

They stood glaring at each other, the sinews and cords standing out in their necks: Desmond determined to save his cousin despite himself; Ranulf equally determined to prove the other horribly mistaken. It was the sound at the doorway that made Ranulf look in that direction. A figure had been standing there for some time.

Ranulf frowned. "What is it, Garth?"

The mercenary watched them with quick, interested eyes. His hands held several torn pieces of paper. "One of the maids—Melva, by name—dropped these from among Lady Morgana's embroidery things when she removed them from the solar, my lord, and she did not know what to do with them."

"Then, see that they are returned to Lady Morgana."

Garth paused, as if unaware of the tension in the room. "I cannot read them, but the device on this seal is familiar to me. I think, my lord, that you will wish to see it also."

Garth had their full notice now, and reveled in his part in the little drama. At Ranulf's gesture, Garth stepped forward and gave the papers to him. The insignia pressed into the dangling wax seal was imprinted clearly—the crest of the master of Lindsey Keep. Ranulf gave the man-at-arms a sharp look.

"You may go. Say nothing of this to anyone."

"As you will, my lord."

When the man was gone, Desmond and his cousin exchanged glances. Ranulf put the pieces down upon the table, glancing over them quickly. One stood out—the one with Lindsey's scrawling signature. Moving slowly, like a man in a nightmare, he smoothed the crumpled pieces and matched them up one to another like the parts of a puzzle. A large and irregular portion of the left-hand border was missing and smaller sections in a few places. But there was enough to make out a damning message:

Lady Morgana, my fondest greetings...your marriage displeases you greatly...love. Fear not. I shall rid you of Sir Ranulf, for...of the love we share...

Ever yours,
Lindsey

The only sound in the room was Desmond's sharp intake of breath as he peered over Ranulf's shoulder and read the incriminating words. His breath came out in a sigh that sounded more like a hiss. "As false as she is beautiful...!"

Ranulf didn't seem to hear. When he looked up, his face was pale and stern, his eyes cold and hard as granite. "Say nothing to anyone. Nothing! Take Cerdic and ride to the village. Find the herb woman and bring her to me."

Desmond stood erect, watching his cousin's face. Once, while fighting in the north, he had received a stunning blow to his helm. It had left him numb and partially senseless. He had known he was hurt but could feel nothing at all for several minutes—until the pain had come crashing down upon him like a stone wall. Ranulf seemed to be going through a similar experience. There was no more life to him than to an iron mask.

He wanted to say something and see the old, familiar light in his comrade's eyes. "Ranulf?"

Ranulf seemed surprised to see Desmond still in the room. The hound whimpered and was ignored. Ranulf walked to the window.

"Leave me, Desmond. I must think, and I would be alone."

Desmond returned in better time than Ranulf had expected, and found his cousin with the estate books in the armament room, his favorite greyhound curled at his feet. Castle Griffin was fortunate in its servants: Sir Dyllis had been an honest and efficient steward of its properties and men, but Ranulf found his concentration poor. Too many thoughts and possibilities tumbled out of control through his mind. He looked up now at the jingle of Desmond's spurs.

"Where is the woman?"

"Among the laundresses outside the gate. I thought it wiser not to bring her inside until we had spoken."

They were interrupted by a slight cough from the doorway. Brother Lewis stood outside, a roll of parchment in his bony hands and the light of excitement in his pale eyes.

"Your pardon, my lord Ranulf. I have uncovered some interesting discrepancies in the measurements of the main keep. If you have the time, perhaps you might care to go over them with me now? I am sure you will be quite fascinated."

Ranulf's face gave nothing away. "Alas, I have other responsibilities that cannot wait, good brother. If you will be patient, I shall discuss them with you when my duties are less pressing."

"Very well. In another day or so I will have even more to show you." His ascetic face took on a sterner expression.

"There is one other matter. I discovered one of your men, a common soldier, in the room designated as my scriptorium. I do not mind answering his questions from time to time; but I will *not* have him meddling among my papers and putting things quite out of order."

"Would you recognize this man again?"

"Aye, my lord. I've quite a memory for faces."

"Thank you, Brother Lewis. I shall look into the matter."

The monk bowed and withdrew as quietly as he had come.

"Well," Ranulf commanded. "What have you discovered?"

"The old besom confirms our worst suspicions." Desmond opened his hand to reveal a decorative gold boss with Morgana's crest centered in a circle of pearls and emeralds. "This costly bauble, she claimed, was given in payment."

Ranulf rubbed his eyes wearily with the back of his hand. "All women are false, so Brother Lewis tells me. It is in their very nature. And to save himself from their wiles, he has buried himself away from the temptations of the world in his monastery."

Ranulf leaned back against a low chair made in the Roman style and tried to put his thoughts into complete order. There were decisions to be made. Immediately. But he must see Morgana . . .

"There is no benefit in making judgments without first gathering the facts. I will speak to Lady Morgana."

He pushed past Desmond and went to search out his wife. In the hall he encountered Bronwen, who shuddered at her master's thundercloud look. She had never seen him so stern or forbidding.

"Where is the Lady Morgana?"

His tone sent chills of fear up her spine. What had her mistress done to invoke such icy fury? "At this time of day she takes a turn in the rose arbor, my lord. If she is not there now, she will be there shortly."

Ranulf spun around and took the steps two at a time, leaving Bronwen filled with apprehension. She was glad she had sent him on a fool's errand. Morgana was not in the garden, but in the stillroom among her herbs. She hurried in that direction, her mind in a whirl.

The last time she had seen Sir Ranulf so angry was when he had threatened to leave and seek an annulment. *That* rift between the newlyweds was supposed to have been private, but there were few secrets in such a household as this. Had there been another falling out between her lady and her lord? But they had seemed so happy, cooing like doves these past weeks. Still, there was no doubt that something terrible had happened to raise Sir Ranulf's ire. She fingered the small bag attached to her silver-link belt. The love potion was still there, she could feel the slender vial. A sudden resolution came over her.

She found Morgana distilling a clear fluid from foxglove to make a medicine that strengthened the heart and aided dropsy. Only the fact that her mistress was measuring out

the precious liquid into tiny bottles kept Bronwen from
blurting out the reason for her visit to the stillroom. Morgana caught a few drops into a tiny bottle of dark glass with
a steady hand and smiled.

"Good news, Bronwen. I wrote to Sir Meridith at Caer-
philly and asked if he wished to send his twin daughters to
me, as their mother died six months ago—they are lovely
girls, close in age to you."

With great care she poured off a dram into another small
bottle. "His reply came today. He will bring Gladys and
Deirdre when he comes to take his oath of fealty, 'that they
may learn the womanly arts of managing a great household.'"

Ordinarily, Bronwen would have been happy and excited
to know she was going to have female companions of her
own age, but right now that was last thing on her mind.
"My lady! Sir Ranulf is seeking you. He...he is greatly
disturbed. I sent him into the rose garden in...in hopes the
beauty would ease his mood."

Morgana wiped her hands, wondering what could be
weighing so heavily upon his mind. "I will put this aside and
go to him at once."

"Perhaps you would like to take a...a cup of wine to him.
I will fetch it to you at once."

Not five minutes later, Morgana wound her way through
the rose arbor in search of her husband. Damask roses
nodded in the sun and yellow blooms from Arabia perfumed the breeze. It was too perfect a day to be out of temper. She would soon calm his disposition by listening with a
willing ear and offering advice. A few wifely caresses would
follow. That prescription had never failed to soothe him in
the past.

She spotted Ranulf striding up and down by the high
stone wall that marked the garden's boundary, his gray
hound lazing beneath a plum tree. The sun shone brightly
on his golden head and upon his handsome new doublet of

dyed leather. Just to look at him gave Morgana pleasure—
a soldier's physique combined with kingly grace. Every day
she loved him more. It was hard to keep her secret from him,
but it was early days yet. Best not to say anything until she
was sure, as her old nurse had counseled.

She wondered what had put him into a pet. Perhaps it was
Daffyd, again. It was well and good to be the inspiration of
a poet or musician, although she did nothing to encourage
it; but lately the harper's adoration of his mistress had become so transparent that it was the butt of many a joke in
the great hall and the solar. Smiling a bit ruefully, she hastened down the walk, but as she neared she realized Bronwen's assessment was accurate. This was no matter of minor
annoyance: someone or something had stirred Ranulf anger to boiling. His back was to her as she approached, although he must have heard her footfalls along the walk.

"I have brought you some wine, my lord, newly decanted."

He pivoted slowly to face her without replying, and she
stopped dead in her tracks when she saw his face. It was
rigidly set and pale as death, his eyes deeply shadowed.

"What is this, my love? You are in great distress!"

"Aye, lady! More than you know."

She held out the goblet and he took it from her. His hand
gripped the stem of the goblet with near crushing force.
"Wife, there is evil within the walls of Castle Griffin.
Charges of a grievous nature have been brought to me, and
I would hear what you have to say in answer."

"Charges of what nature?" She thought he must be teasing her, yet his face was utterly serious. "Explain yourself,
my lord."

He took a deep breath. "Charges of base treachery!" He
stepped forward, flinging the goblet away, and caught her
by the shoulders. "Charges of attempted murder!"

Morgana stared at him in white-face amazement. The
lines of his face settled into a mask so alien, so frightening

that her heart thundered with alarm. "I don't understand . . . against whom?"

"Against you, Morgana."

Ignoring the drama unfolding beside him, the hound snuffled at the fallen goblet. It lay on its side among the dropped rose petals, a portion of wine pooled in the center of the lower side. Curious, the ratchet lapped at the red liquid a few times, then backed away, whimpering.

From the other end of the rose garden Desmond whistled to the beast. "Come, Lightning."

The dog looked at him inquiringly and made a move as if to obey. Suddenly it stiffened in every limb, and a mewling sound came from its elegant throat. Ranulf whirled around in time to see the ratchet fall to the ground, quivering and jerking uncontrollably. He knelt beside the beast, but it was already dead. The animal's muzzle was flecked with wine and foam.

Not till Desmond joined them did Ranulf look up. He indicated the dead hound. "There is more danger than we knew. That cup was meant for me."

Chapter Thirteen

Morgana, dazed and shocked, reached out toward Ranulf as he rose to his feet. "Who...what...oh, what is happening?"

Ranulf did not meet her eyes. "I will soon get to the bottom of this. You will be safe, never fear." He assumed his crisp military manner. "Desmond, you will escort my lady wife to her chambers. See that she is guarded well at all times."

Cerdic materialized nearby and stooped to retrieve the fallen goblet. Desmond took her by the arm, and Morgana went off with them, bewildered. "Will you kindly explain what this means?"

He gave her a cool look. "It is quite clear to my eyes, lady. Sir Ranulf's wine was poisoned."

"Poisoned? Impossible!"

"No, my lady. There is no doubt of it. But whether by accident or design I cannot say, as yet."

Morgana was stunned. "Surely it must be by accident— who would do such a heinous thing?"

Her question hung on the air, unanswered. Desmond and Cerdic exchanged an enigmatic glance. But it was not until they reached her chambers, that all the ramifications became clear to Morgana. Only two persons had handled that cup of wine—Bronwen and herself. And she no more doubted her maid's innocence than she doubted her own. The girl called Melva was inside the chamber, building up the fire in the huge hearth.

"Send Bronwen to me at once," Morgana instructed.

"Yes, my lady." Melva hurried to obey, but not before speaking briefly with one of the men outside.

Time passed and she did not return. Morgana opened the door and looked out. Two sturdy men-at-arms controlled all access to her chamber. She took a step out and one of them moved to bar her way. "You are to remain in your chamber, my lady, by orders of Sir Ranulf. He will report to you shortly, and begs you to be patient."

She smiled. It was reassuring to know Ranulf was looking out to her safety at such an unsettling time, yet these brawny fellows had the look, not of guards, but of wardens. Dismissing such ridiculous thoughts, she closed the door again. She would not openly disregard her husband's express request. If only Ranulf would come and soon explain things. But more time passed and no one came at all. Worry and hunger began to wear on her and she was glad when at least one of the serving lads arrived with a tray laden with stew and cheese and bread from the morning's baking. After, there was nothing to do but wait. Unaccustomed tiredness came without warning. She stretched herself upon the bed and fell into uneasy sleep.

It was dark when Morgana awakened to the sound of voices just beyond her door. *Ranulf*! She was disappointed when it opened and Cerdic entered and bowed.

"My lady, Sir Desmond has sent me to beg you to come to him at once on a matter of grave importance."

She was weary, and her head ached with fatigue. "Can he not come to me?"

"There is something you must see with your own eyes, mistress. It is most urgent."

"Very well." Morgana rose to follow Cerdic.

"Best take a warm wrap," he murmured. "'Tis cold where we be going."

Taking a woolen cloak from a peg in the wardrobe, she threw it over her shoulders and followed the soldier out. The guards stood at attention, eyes bright with curiosity.

"Where is Sir Ranulf?"

"I do not know, mistress. I have been with Sir Desmond these past hours."

"And where is he now, then?"

"In one of the lower storerooms, my lady. Near the south tower."

They went along the deserted gallery and down the stairs to the hall. Two torches burned by the entrance, and fires flickered in the great hearths at either end of the room. The sleepy menservants bowed as they went by, and Morgana realized it was far later than she had thought. What on earth was Desmond doing in the storerooms at such an hour?

Cerdic continued to lead the way. A long corridor led off from the next room, branching north and south a hundred yards ahead. It was dimly lit and eerie. Despite the woolen cloak, the cold seeped into Morgana's bones. A tiny shiver ran up her spine and she looked over her shoulder. How strange, how lonely this corridor was, without daylight and the sounds of life and laughter!

They reached the branching of the ways and Cerdic turned left. "You are going the wrong way," she said more sharply than she intended. "The south tower is in the opposite direction."

"Did I say the south tower, my lady? I beg your pardon. I meant the north tower."

Morgana accepted the answer and continued on with him, her feet hurrying a bit to keep up with his rapid pace. A sense of his urgency communicated itself to her and she began to feel that something was terribly wrong. They passed through the connecting passage and down a set of winding stairs to the base of the unfrequented north tower. It was darker here and had the empty air of places largely unused. It reminded Morgana forcibly of her visit to the Tower of London which was quite appropriate: at the end of this corridor was a door that led outside to a restricted court, and within the court was the great iron door leading to the donjon.

There was nothing below the tower but the old armory, which had been part of the original keep and now stored remnants of antiquated weapons and armor. She expected Cerdic to enter the old armory but he passed by it, never once breaking stride. Ahead was the barred door leading to the court. Morgana was increasingly uneasy.

"What can there possibly be in this peculiar place of such importance as to require my presence at this ungodly hour?"

"I do not know, my lady. I am not in Sir Desmond's confidence."

Morgana hesitated. Perhaps it was some clue regarding the poison in Ranulf's wine cup. That took away her fear. Cerdic had gone ahead and unbarred the door. As he swung it open, she hurried through and out into the high-walled court. Morgana felt small and insignificant as she crossed the pavement in the shadow of the walls and ancient tower. There was no wind here, but it seemed dark as a well. Above, a few faint stars were visible, moving in their slow, majestic patterns.

"This way," Cerdic said, pointing straight ahead. In the glimmer of starlight, she could make out the gleam of the massive donjon door. It stood ajar, the opening a huge black maw.

"We must enter, my lady."

She was suddenly afraid. Her feet slowed and finally stopped. "It is too dark to proceed safely. Where is Sir Desmond?"

"I am here."

His voice came from behind her and Desmond stepped out of the inky shadows. He advanced upon her so quickly

Morgana could not even cry out for help. Her voice was stifled by his hand over her mouth and he picked her up bodily and threw her over his shoulder as if she were no more than an empty sack. Try as she could, Morgana could not free herself. She kicked and pounded on Desmond's back. Biting his hand, she drew blood, and he let go momentarily, cursing. She screamed as long and loud as she could, but it was too late. They were inside, and no one would ever hear her cries through the thick, ancient walls.

Inside the donjon, the air was stale and musty. Cerdic produced a dark lantern and opened its shutter a bit. Light flickered over the massive stones that formed the walls and Morgana had a terrified glimpse of them, slick with moss and moisture.

As Desmond descended the steps, his shoulder dug into Morgana's stomach with every bounce and the grip he had around her ribs cut off her breath. Long before he reached the second door at the bottom, she was dizzy and gasping desperately for air.

She was dumped unceremoniously upon a pile of dirty straw, the wind knocked from her lungs. With the lantern on the ground beside him casting strange shadows, Desmond looked gigantic. Cruel and ominously threatening. When she was able, Morgana tried to speak. Her voice was so hoarse it was a mere croak.

"Why...? Why have you brought me to this fearful place?"

Desmond stood over her, and his hatred could no longer be contained. "Do you not approve of your new quarters, madam? Perhaps that is just as well—after your attempt on Sir Ranulf's life, your stay within these walls will not be a long one."

Horror turned her tongue to lead. Unable to rise yet because of the pain in her midsection, Morgana stared at Desmond blankly.

"Do you not understand, my lady? Then, let me make it clear to you. Whether you sought to free yourself by sorcery or poison or both makes no matter. The penalty for witchcraft or murder are the same—death."

Death...death...death... The words echoed from the cavernous walls and the unseen ceiling high above. Desmond strode away toward the stairs while she struggled to her knees. "You had almost convinced me of your professed love for Ranulf, but I see now that my every instinct was true."

He took the stairs two at a time and Cerdic followed, but at the top he paused and left the lantern on the uppermost step. It left a flaring bar of light on the rough-hewn stone, but the rest of the chamber was swallowed up in the hovering shadows. Then he, too, went out into the court and the great door swung inexorably behind him. A groan of ancient hinges, a scrape of metal on stone, the rush of a bar shoved home, and Morgana was alone.

She got to her feet, still sickened from the jouncing of Desmond's shoulder against her stomach, her thoughts in wild disarray. The panic that blotted out logic and reason in those first traumatic moments was not for herself, but for Ranulf. To be locked away not knowing his whereabouts or condition was intolerable. Why had he not come to her? Was he aware of her imprisonment? Had the whole world gone mad?

For the first time her spirit failed her. Cold, tired, and terribly afraid, she buried her face in her arms and wept. When the flood tide ended, she was exhausted—her eyes swollen with weeping, but her courage restored. Ranulf could not know of Desmond's perfidy. But when he did, he would find her, save her from this nightmare. Until then, she must help herself.

She climbed the stairs and sat beside the lantern in the pale wedge of light. There were two candles inside, one unlit. They would last several hours, possibly till morning. But would the sun's rays ever penetrate this gloom? Were there even any openings to the outside world? If only her ancestors, in their building zeal, had had the foresight to provide her with an escape route from this dismal place!

Morgana picked up the lantern and descended to explore her prison. Once, as a very small child, she had seen this part of the donjon from the open door with her grandfather and had been terrified by the dank, dark yawning space. She had never been tempted to explore it again. Now, she vaguely remembered something to the right, perhaps a passageway, and made her way in that direction. A small creature went scuttling away at her approach with a squeak of alarm.

Her path dead-ended in a series of squalid cells with eye slits in the splintered doors that hung partly open. A grisly but compelling curiosity led her to shine the light in one. Rotted vegetable matter that might have been straw lay in one corner next to the iron shackle attached to the wall. A lone initial had been scratched into the stone. Someone had been imprisoned here a long time, to make so deep a groove! She lifted the lamp higher, and light fell upon something pale and white and round. A bowl? The back of a skull? Morgana did not examine it any closer.

It took quite a while to go through the chamber. It was enormous, with no sign of windows or air inlets but with sufficient remnants of old sorrows and tragedies to make her flesh crawl. How many had vanished through the massive door to disappear in this numbing darkness forever!

There was nothing to do but wait until her ladies raised the alarm. Now that she was calmer, Morgana could examine Desmond's threats more coolly. Surely no one could doubt the genuineness of her love for Ranulf, even those aware of the bad start to their marriage caused by her angry pride. And even if Desmond were fool enough to think it an elaborate ruse on her part, he could not sway her own people to side against her. They would know she was innocent, and once they discovered her whereabouts they would join with Ranulf in releasing her and proving her innocence. It was only a matter of time.

The wisest course now would be to sleep and conserve her energies, but although she was tired to the bone she could not do so. Morgana sat on the steps once more, away from the filth of the floor and the night creatures that swarmed over it. Despite her determination to stay awake, she could not fight off the troubled sleep of exhaustion. When she woke every limb was cramped and so stiff she could scarcely move.

"It must be near dawn," Morgana said aloud, just to hear the sound of her own voice. The high ceiling of the huge chamber was visible, yet the cold gray light barely outlined the salient features of the donjon. She imagined the castle being searched all night by torch and candlelight. It would take considerable time to explore every room and cubbyhole in the various levels of the enormous complex, but eventually someone would think of the donjon and she would be found. She must hold on to her sanity until then.

She dreamed again of vines, their horrid tendrils writhing, reaching for her throat. Danger surrounded her.

She jerked awake and saw everything was as it had been before. She did not know if the vines had been a remnant of her previous dreams, or if she had been given another "seeing." It was like that other time when she had envisioned Ranulf below the salty waters of the mere. The sense of danger grew greater, and she was thankful for the tiny glow of the candle.

Hours passed slowly, underscored by the rumbling of her empty stomach and the changing quality of light. Her candles had long burned out. There had been no use in saving them, since she'd had no way to relight them. It was growing dimmer and she was dreading another night of complete darkness when she heard welcome sounds. The heavy bar was pulled back and the door opened slowly.

"Oh, thank God, thank God!"

Morgana's legs were stiff, but she lifted her skirts and ran upward toward the light. She was so glad to see the sunset sky showing over the three-story court walls that she could have wept with relief. As it was, her eyes were blurred with tears. So blurred she could not make out the faces of her rescuers.

She wiped her eyes, looked around and shivered. These were not her men. They were Desmond's. She glanced at the tight-lipped faces. "I demand to be taken to my husband!"

A grizzled sergeant stepped forward. "You are to come with us."

Two men-at-arms flanked her, one led the way and the rest fell in behind as they marched Morgana across the court and into the lower level of the north tower. They did not answer her questions or meet her eyes.

They led her back the way she had come the previous evening, and with every step her sense of unreality grew. She tried to convince herself that this was an evil dream; that any moment she would awaken in Ranulf's arms. To no avail.

When they reached the main keep, the place was strangely deserted. Torches burned along the walls at intervals, lighting their way, but no servants were in sight. As they approached the hall, it was the same—music and laughter and the low buzz of conversation should have been quite audible along the corridor. Instead the tramp of the soldiers' feet rebounded from the stone surfaces with the rhythm of a death march, and Morgana was filled with increasing dread.

And then they were in the hall. It was not empty as she expected. The stillness was the heavy silence of anticipation: a huge throng waited unmoving inside the great hall. As the crowd parted to let her through she realized that the majority of them were Ranulf's men—and that they were the only ones armed.

She looked for Dal or Owain or Arvil, and wondered and worried at their absence. The soldiers in front of her stepped

aside and she was in the center of the hall, facing the dais.
The canopy of state had been set up, making clear the seriousness of the occasion, but the single high-backed chair
and the two smaller chairs flanking it were empty. She began to tremble. They had brought her here for judgment,
but who would be the judge? If Desmond took the seat of
justice, her life would surely be forfeit.

A fluttering movement caught Morgana's attention and
she spied Lady Winifred, flanked by Bronwen and Alys on
a bench near the side. In this room full of people, they were
the only ones to look at her openly and not from the corners of their eyes. Their faces were white, strained and filled
with emotions that Morgana could not read. Her spirits
plummeted further when Lady Winifred bit her lower lip
and turned away. Here, in the castle of which she was mistress, she had been reduced to the rank of prisoner. Here,
surrounded by her servants, friends and retainers, she was
alone.

The heralds blew their trumpets and the tension in the
room grew. Two men-at-arms led the way for Sir Dyllis and
Sir Vaughn. They stood on the dais before the lower chairs
and stared somewhere over Morgana's head. Her last small
hope crumbled to dust. Even they had been turned against
her. But how? And why?

The trumpets blew again and she turned her head with the
others. A scullery lad blocked her view for an instant or two,
but he was not tall enough to hide the gleaming gold and
sapphire circlet that topped a shining golden head. *Ranulf!*
Now she was safe and all would be explained. The way
cleared and she saw him fully.

He wore royal blue, emblazoned with his device and
trimmed with marten, and the wide gold-and-sapphire collar the King had given him. As he strode across the hall, he
looked hale and hearty and in the pride of his manhood.
Dear God, how she loved him!

Her burst of joy turned to pain when he passed by without a glance in her direction. He took his place beneath the canopy and faced her with stern coldness. Despair crept over her like a shroud. She was so numb now, she could not even think. This was not real. This was some awful nightmare, and in a moment she would wake up, safe and warm, in Ranulf's arms.

But it was real. Sir Dyllis came forward. "The court of justice is convened to rule on the matter of Lady Morgana of Castle Griffin, who stands accused of attempted murder of her husband and lord." He cleared his throat. "Who accuses the lady?"

Desmond came before the dais. "I so accuse."

"Then let the trial begin."

Impulsively Morgana stepped forward, hands outstretched to Ranulf. "My lord..."

He looked straight at her and she could see nothing in them to give her hope: his eyes were those of a stranger, cool and completely indifferent. Two lances dropped and crossed before her, barring her way.

Sir Dyllis pounded on the floor with his staff for order. "The prisoner will have her say in good time." He turned to Desmond. "State your case against the Lady Morgana."

Desmond bowed. "My case is simple. From the first, Lady Morgana made it clear that she found marriage to Sir Ranulf abhorrent. So abhorrent, in fact, that against her holy vows given before a priest of God, she fled his bed rather than consummate the liaison."

There was anger in his voice, and the ring of absolute conviction as he continued. "Arriving in Wales, she found need of his military strengths, and put aside her opposition until peace was assured. That object attained, she then tried to rid herself of her encumbrance through means of black arts and poison."

A murmur ran through the crowd and Arvil banged again for order. "Lady Morgana of Griffin, how do you plead?"

"Innocent! By God and all the Saints, I am innocent and love and honor my husband before all men!" She was shaking like a victim of the ague and appeared likely to faint.

Ranulf spoke for the first time. "A chair for Lady Morgana!"

Someone hurried to do his bidding, but Morgana drew herself up and fought for control. "I will stand," she said, her voice clear and steady with great effort.

Ranulf sat back. "You may call your witnesses, Sir Desmond."

"I call Bronwen of Llandelly to speak." Pale and trembling, the girl came to stand before the dais.

"Is it not true," he said in ringing tones, "that the Lady Morgana did not wish to wed Sir Ranulf, called the Dane, and that she fled the King's Court by night rather than lie with him?"

Bronwen's reply was inaudible. "Speak up, so all may hear," the castellan ordered. "Does Sir Desmond speak the truth?"

"Aye."

But Desmond was not through with her. "And when Sir Ranulf caught up with his recalcitrant wife at an inn, did she not climb down a tree by night in an effort to flee?"

"Aye."

"You may take your seat."

Bronwen burst into tears, sobbing so loudly the seneschal ordered her removed from the room. Weeping hysterically and supported by Elva and one of the maidservants, she was taken from the hall. Desmond nodded toward the ladies' bench.

"I call next Daffyd, harper of Castle Griffin." When he stood before the judges, angry and ill at ease, Desmond had only one question.

"Is it true that you once came upon Sir Ranulf and Lady Morgana in the alcove of the long gallery, and that the lady struggled mightily against the embrace of her lawful husband and master?''

"Aye," he said at last, and was dismissed.

Desmond turned to the crowd. "I call forth Cerdic, captain of Sir Ranulf's own men-at-arms, that he may give report of what he has seen and heard."

Cerdic, dressed in dusty riding clothes, came forward and was sworn. "My lord Desmond sent me to spy out doings at Lindsey Keep. Sir Bryce Lindsey has assembled a large number of knights, sergeants and foot soldiers, in addition to his usual force. It appears he intends to march again upon Castle Griffin."

"To do battle?" Desmond asked softly.

"Nay. It is said the gates will be thrown open and he will be welcomed by Lady Morgana."

Sir Vaughn leaned down. "What proof have you of this serious allegation?"

It was Desmond who answered. "The pieces of this letter provide all we need and more, my lords." He held out a tray on which the scraps of Lindsey's letter were laid out in proper order. "If you will read this aloud, Sir Vaughn."

The knight cleared his throat and did as Desmond instructed.

"Lady Morgana, my fondest greetings. Your marriage displeases you greatly. Love—fear not. I shall rid you of Sir Ranulf for the love we share.

Ever yours,
Lindsey."

A terrible silence filled the room, to be broken a few seconds later by a murmur that grew and swelled like the roar of an angry surf. Morgana was in a daze as Desmond dismissed Cerdic with no further questions. He prowled back and forth before the dais.

"It is plain to see the Lady Morgana had a change of heart and decided to throw her lot in with Sir Bryce of Lindsey Keep—the man who had once been her lover."

There was a collective gasp from the throng, and Morgana felt her heart sink. How they had twisted and misconstrued everything! Was there not one soul among them who believed in her innocence? Desmond turned toward the crowd.

"My lords, I call before this court of justice a woman of the village—Gwynn, by name."

A wrinkled crone hobbled forward and Morgana gasped, recognizing the herb woman from whom she had obtained the healing ointments for Ranulf's wound. What could this woman possibly say?

"Did the Lady Morgana visit your cottage and ask you to provide her with any special preparation?"

"Oh, aye. My lady asked for something and I give it to her, right enough—something to put an ailing dog from its misery, she said."

The shout that went up from the listeners brought the guards on alert, and Arvil pounded and shouted for order to be maintained. When it was restored, Morgana stood in a circle of accusers. Desmond pounced. "Did you not, Lady Morgana, serve Sir Ranulf wine in this very cup yesterday in the rose arbor?"

"I did, but . . ."

"Then let me call my last witness. Master Carey, barber and surgeon to Sir Dyllis, will you come before the court?"

The barber came forward with little relish for his part in this drama. Desmond had only two questions for him: "Master Carey, you are well versed in herb lore and you have examined the remains in this wine cup, as well as the carcass of the dead hound—is that not so?"

"Yes, indeed, Sir Desmond."

"And can you tell to us what was in the wine—intended for the master of this castle—which instead killed his faithful ratchet?"

"I can. 'Twas an extract from the flowers, leaves and roots of certain plants—a combination of foxglove, pennyroyal and witch's weed, compounded with powdered toad skin."

Morgana felt a shiver of dread. She had made a decoction of foxglove only yesterday, as several people—including Bronwen—could attest. With every witness and every word, Desmond was drawing the noose more tightly.

He leaned toward the barber now, like a bird of prey homing in for the kill. "If you will please, Master Carey, what are the properties of this extract?"

The barber's tone was severe. "Such a preparation would cause the heart to cease its beating within seconds. It is universally fatal."

A cold sea of whispers surrounded Morgana. She felt the blood curdle in her veins.

Ranulf leaned down in his chair. "What proof have you that this was in the wine?"

"The proof, my lord, was supplied by your late ratchet, which did lap up the drops of wine from your cup and fall dead immediately thereafter. But we tested it again upon two rats fetched by the stable boys. Both died immediately."

Again the hostile buzz of whispers and mutters went round the hall, sounding like the pattering of hail upon stone. Desmond smiled coldly. "My lords, I rest my case."

It was Ranulf who spoke first. "My Lady Morgana, you have heard the evidence against you. Have you aught to say in your defense?"

Resolutely she faced him. "If I were brought to trial for false pride and folly, my lord, I would admit to the crime and throw myself upon your mercy. As to allegations of poisoning or witchcraft to rid myself of you, ask your own heart for the truth."

She moved closer, head high. "I confess only to loving you so well it blinded me to the hatred of your friends and to my own danger. But I see in your face and the others' that I was judged and found guilty long before this trial began. If you have lost your love and faith in me, I care not what verdict may be brought against me."

Ranulf's brows drew together in a straight line and he stared at Morgana as she stood swaying before him, wrapped in her dignity. He sat back in his chair and she held her breath, waiting. When he spoke after an interminable pause, the words were not what she had expected to hear.

"The Lady Morgana is fatigued and unable to continue this trial. See that she is escorted to her own chambers with all courtesy, where she may refresh herself until tomorrow morning—when judgment will be rendered."

The tension and its sudden release, coupled with hunger and lack of sleep, were too much for Morgana. She fell in a crumpled heap at Ranulf's feet.

Chapter Fourteen

Before anyone else could react Ranulf was out of his chair, swooping Morgana up in his arms. He carried her limp form up the stairs himself and along the corridor to her chamber, where he placed her on the bed. The room was dimly lit by the banked fire he had ordered earlier and the thick bedside candle that burned in its own wrought-iron stand. He stood over her still form, the pale little face with hyacinth shadows beneath the closed eyes. His own features were devoid of all emotion. He had never thought that the road from London would lead to this.

When Bronwen and Lady Winifred came hurrying in, he turned to the men-at-arms who had accompanied him. "Guard her well."

"She'll not escape from us, my lord."

They took up their positions, swords in hand, on either side of the door. When it swung to, Bronwen threw the bolt home. Her eyes were red from weeping and she was frightened half out of her mind.

"What did they say or do to make her swoon so!"

Lady Winifred sighed heavily. "That she sought to murder Sir Ranulf by purchasing a poison potion from the herb woman, and serving it to him in his wine cup."

For a moment Bronwen stood paralyzed. "In...in his wine cup? Oh, no. No!" She whirled around and ran to the door, sliding back the bar. "I must speak with Sir Ranulf at once. There is some terrible mistake. That was not poison but a love potion, which I obtained from the herb woman, myself—and it was I who put it in his wine."

The other woman ran to stop her. "If you go to him, you will stand accused along with Lady Morgana. They will say you did it to aid your mistress, and you will both be lost."

The truth of her words rocked Bronwen. "It does not matter. I cannot let her take the blame for my actions. I would not be able to live with myself!"

Lady Winifred was too upset to stop her. Things had come to a pretty pass at Castle Griffin in the past few days. Bronwen flung the door open and went out. One of the guards closed it again, and Lady Winifred moved to the bed. Morgana was awake, her eyes bleak as she stared unseeingly at the canopy overhead.

The castellan's wife smiled mistily. "What a fright you gave me, child. Would you like something to eat? A little soup or some morsels of roast fowl?"

But Morgana still stared at the canopy with wild, blind eyes. "If I could only talk to him... explain to him. They speak of poison, yet someone has poisoned his mind against me."

The other woman put out a soothing hand, and Morgana grasped it. "You must go to him. Make him come to me. Please, for the love of God!"

Lady Winifred did not like to leave Morgana alone in such a state, but Bronwen had not returned and she was becoming worried. Perhaps the girl was now a prisoner. There were too many strange and unexplained happenings, and Castle Griffin was turned completely on its ear. It was time she got to the bottom of things. Elva might be of help, for she had promised to collect servants' gossip—the household staff always seemed to know what was going on.

She looked down at the strained white face. "Very well, my lady. But first you must sustain yourself with food and good, heartening ale. And you will wish to bathe and change your garments, for you are soiled and muddy and your hair is a mare's nest.''

Slowly Morgana rose and looked at herself in the polished mirror. Her hair was disheveled and her features were smudged with dirt. Her pupils were dilated and her aqua eyes were much too large in her pale, pinched face. A witch indeed!

''You are wise, Lady Winifred, and your advice well taken. I must be at my best for the coming interview.'' She was of the house of Griffin, and would not give in to melancholy or despair. Stripped of her power and protectors, she would fight with the only weapons left to her.

After she supped, Morgana bathed in warm water scented with oriental oils and put on fresh linen, then selected one of Ranulf's favorite gowns. It was of ivory kendal slashed with the same rich green silk that lined the long, open sleeves. Her hair she brushed out but left loose and flowing, crowned only by a gold fillet set with large square-cut emeralds. It had belonged to her grandmother, the first Lady Morgana, and gave her comfort and confidence. She must meet her husband on equal footing, as hereditary Lady of Castle Griffin and not as a helpless prisoner and pawn. She had more than just herself to consider.

When she was refreshed and ready, Lady Winifred prepared to seek private speech with Ranulf. As she left the room she paused on the threshold. ''Do not despair. I shall persist until my lord agrees to see me, no matter how long I must wait.''

The door shut behind the castellan's wife and Morgana had nothing to do but pace the floor. If Ranulf were in conference with Desmond and Sir Dyllis it might be some time before Lady Winifred was allowed to present her petition. Time crept by with maddening slowness, marked by the tolling bells of St. Tristan's. Morgana opened her illuminated prayer book and turned a few pages, but could not concentrate. She touched her lute, but her fingers could draw no music from it.

The ordeal of Ranulf's collapse followed by her sojourn in the donjon and compounded by hunger, sleeplessness and sustained anxiety had gotten the best of her earlier, leading to her collapse. It had seemed like the end of the world—at least her world. Now a cooler head prevailed. Something very strange was going on.

She was in great danger, of that there was no doubt. Danger bold-faced and direct, as well as cunningly masked and disguised. But from which direction did it come? Again and again she had observed Ranulf's strong sense of justice in action. Surely a man who listened so attentively to a humble peasant or disgruntled sergeant would hear his own wife out! Yet Ranulf had goaded her to anger and taken advantage of it.

An hour passed, and another. No matter from what angle she examined her predicament she could not discern any clear pattern. She rubbed her forehead, trying to clear her brain. Thunder rumbled, drawing Morgana to the window. The sky was clear and sprinkled with stars. The sound came again, louder this time and very near at hand. Morgana whirled around in surprise.

The Flemish tapestry that hung between the deep window embrasures rippled and fluttered, and a strong and steady current of cool air brought with it the tart tang of the sea.

In another part of the castle, Lady Winifred was pleading her mistress's cause. Ranulf sat in the tower room amidst Brother Lewis's drawings and diagrams, with a full cup in one hand and a container of robust ale beside him.

"There is nothing Lady Morgana can say to alter the facts," Ranulf said shortly.

Lady Winifred stood her ground. "If you would see her, my lord. For only a moment. For the sake of the vows you exchanged before God and man."

Ranulf glanced away impatiently. "It will do no good."

"Please, my lord. She is wild with grief and deeply despondent. I . . . I fear for her life or her sanity."

Ranulf's hands were clasped before him and he studied them for quite a while, as if words of advice or wisdom would appear graven upon them. She wondered what was passing through his mind. The tic at the angle of his jaw told her that he labored under some powerful emotion. He could be cold and hard as steel if necessary, but now she only wished he would soften enough to speak to Lady Morgana.

Ranulf looked up at last. "I would advise you to administer a sedative to ease her mind. I will see Lady Morgana tomorrow when we fetch her to the judgment hall. It is safer that way."

"Have you met with Bronwen?"

"I could scarce avoid it."

"And . . . ?"

"There was nothing I could say. All know of her staunch loyalty to Lady Morgana, that she would say anything to save her life." He quaffed deeply from his cup. "I told her the truth of what happened and forbade her to return to her mistress."

Lady Winifred wiped a tear from the corner of her eye. "Come to her, my lord, if only for a moment. 'Tis right piteous to see her in such straits." Another tear trickled down the plump cheek. "Only assure her that you will not pass judgement until she gives her own account of what has transpired."

Ranulf sighed heavily. "It would be better if I did not see her. I cannot loose the hold she has on me. It is rooted too deep." He finished his ale and looked into Lady Winifred's drawn and weary face. "It goes well against the grain with me, but I will speak with her briefly."

A short time later, and accompanied by two of his men, he came down the corridor leading to Morgana's rooms. The guards who stood at attention outside her door eased their stance at Ranulf's nod. "I will speak with my wife."

They stood aside, and he opened the door. A branch of candles had been lit and the fire stirred until the room was bright as midday. Morgana was not on the bed, nor was she at her dressing table or upon the seat in the window embrasure. In fact, she was nowhere at all.

Ranulf cursed and shouted for the guards. "Find her! She cannot have disappeared into the air!"

The men searched the room thoroughly, then cast nervous glances over their shoulders as they warded off evil with hasty signs of the cross. Lady Morgana *was* gone, vanished from the room like the very witch she was accused of being.

Not ten feet away, behind the massive stone of the wall, Morgana huddled beside the soldier known as Garth, sorry that she had ever doubted Sir Dyllis. *I should have known my faithful castellan would not fail me.*

They could hear muffled voices and movement from the other side; the secret opening in the wall was not entirely closed behind them, leaving a tiny sliver of light along the edge. As the sounds faded away, Garth started down the narrow winding stairs, motioning for her to follow in the light of his single candle. Cobwebs floated in the moving column of air that rushed upward in her face and it was difficult to see her footing in the dimness.

Morgana shook her head in disbelief as they wound their way down. The rumors had been true after all, although it seemed impossible that this secret staircase had been hidden off the great bedchamber all this time without her knowledge. It was true that there was a secret strong room in the outer wall near the armory and a hidden stairway from the solar to the south tower, which was intended as the final retreat in case the castle's defenses were breached, but she had judged the rumors of other concealed rooms and passages to be servants' idle gossip.

This was obviously an escape route for times of extreme danger or treachery. The chamber above traditionally belonged to the lord and lady of the castle and had been her father's apartment. Presumably he had meant to tell her of it in time, but death had come calling for him before his fortieth year—while she was far away at York. What other long forgotten mysteries might there not be within Castle Griffin's walls?

She wondered where this stairway ended and expected to arrive at an opening below the tower and near the sea. Instead, once they reached the bottom, Garth led her on at constantly changing angles until she'd lost all sense of direction. Her feet and the hem of her gown were wet from the puddles of water that pooled on the rough stone beneath her.

Initially Morgana thought their path was man-made, but after a while it widened and she perceived they were in a natural grotto. Icicles of frozen stone hung down from the roof or rose up in graduated tiers from the uneven floor. Corridors branched at irregular intervals, and from time to time the candlelight revealed deep holes or caves near the ragged ceiling of the cavern. It was like nothing she had ever seen before, a frightening underworld that was nevertheless compelling in its unworldly beauty.

Water dripped slowly, monotonously, from somewhere to the left. Underfoot, the going became increasingly slippery, and they picked their way with utmost care. The passageway continued to slope downward at a considerable angle and ended in a long, dark tunnel. She had no idea where this strange route ended, only that it led to freedom and safety.

"Is it much farther?" she asked, but Garth only smiled and put his fingers to his lips for silence.

They moved through the tunnel for a considerable time and Morgana estimated they had covered over three miles, but the way had been so circuitous she had no idea of their present position on the surface. Her heart was heavy with thoughts of Ranulf and his bewildering change of attitude. He had held her and made love to her with a passion that had seemed both deep and genuine. But in the great hall so short a time ago he had been a stranger, with eyes of ice and a heart to match.

By the time the ground canted upward by slow degrees, Morgana's brief surge of energy had ebbed to the point where she was incredibly weary in body and soul. From somewhere ahead came the flicker and glow of torchlight, and her lagging feet sped up the pace to match Garth's. Now she could make out the exit of the passageway, a rectangle of deep blue bounded by the dark walls of the underground tunnel. As they drew closer she could see men waiting.

Garth paused on the threshold. "My lord, here is the lady, delivered to you safely."

Morgana stepped past her escort into a wine cellar. The torchlight was blinding after the netherworld of the tunnel, and as her sight adjusted she looked about for her castellan. "Sir Dyllis?"

A figure stepped forward into the light. "Well met, Lady Morgana."

"Lindsey! Where is Sir Dyllis—and why are you here?"

Lindsey smiled unpleasantly. "Sir Dyllis, I imagine, is preparing his arrangements for your execution. Will it be the sword for your pretty little neck—or the stake and a pile of faggots to burn you for a witch?"

He came close, amused and arrogant. "As to my presence here, my dear Morgana, it is not to be wondered at. This is my home. Welcome, fair lady, to Lindsey Keep."

He tried to take her chin in his cupped hand, but she pulled away abruptly. "Lindsey Keep! What treachery is this?"

"The treachery is not here, but within the precincts of Castle Griffin. No doubt you are confused and bewildered by your sudden alteration in status."

She faced him haughtily. "Say what you mean."

He gestured to the stairway. "If you will accompany me to more comfortable surroundings, I will endeavor to explain it all. And since what I have to say involves your relationship with Sir Ranulf I have no doubt you would rather hear it in privacy."

With all due ceremony, he conducted her to a chamber on the third floor of Lindsey Keep. A young maid, blue-eyed and black-haired, bowed when they entered. "This is Jenet. She will wait upon you and see to your needs."

At Lindsey's signal the girl went out, leaving them alone. Morgana scanned her surroundings, a pleasant room done very much in the English style. Luxurious carpets were layered upon the flagged floor and tapestries showing Leda and the Swan and the Abduction of Persephone covered the walls. They were more explicit than any renderings Morgana had ever seen, and her eyes opened a bit wider.

The rest of the room was equally sumptuous. The cushions on the settle were covered in colorful brocades to complement the hangings of the bed in the far corner. The chamber was obviously designed for a woman's comfort.

Lindsey began opening chests and wardrobes filled with a variety of rich garments: gowns and robes of scarlet and deep sapphire blue, embroidered with gold and silver and pearls; capes and cloaks of wool, figured samite and luxurious fur; and soft linen garments so fine they could be drawn through a gold ring.

There was more. He took a large coffer and undid the hasp. A rainbow of jewels cascaded through his fingers: chains of topaz and citrines, ropes of garnets and pearls, collars and bracelets of amethyst, Persian turquoise and coral. Even a cloak clasp set with ruby spinels the size of acorns and fit for a queen. Gems to outfit a woman for any occasion.

Morgana raised her eyebrows, and Lindsey laughed at her. "There are no mistresses hidden in the closet, my dear Morgana. I had this chamber furnished for the woman who will one day soon share my life." He came up beside her and put his hand on her arm. "For the woman who will be my wife.... For you."

He indicated the magnificent garments and jewels. "These are all yours," he said smugly. "Made to measurement taken from your own garments. As soon as Lord Hartley was imprisoned in the Tower I began preparing for our future together."

She was astonished. "You are mad. I am already wed."

"To a man who seeks to destroy you."

She strode away, but he followed, his voice hypnotic and intense. "Have you not guessed what he is about? Oh, it was a clever plan. One to revenge himself upon the woman who spurned and humiliated him—and still keep your estates and wealth for his own."

Morgana was so tired, her thoughts were snarled and entangled. Lindsey's insinuations only made the situation worse. Her eyes were so heavy she could hardly hold them open. "I am too weary to lock horns with you. State your meaning clearly."

He led her to a cushioned bench. "Very well. You were brought to trial, accused of attempting to murder your husband. I say the shoe is on the other foot. That your woman's instincts, which led you to flee from Sir Ranulf in London, were sound."

Lindsey took her hand in his. "You are too innocent, Morgana. Imagine, for a moment, what it is like to be an obscure, landless knight, yet one who is high in the King's circle—an expensive circle for a man with nothing but coppers in his purse."

"I will not listen to this." She attempted to rise.

"Hear me out. It is an interesting tale."

He tightened his grip on her arm, forcing her to sit again. "Then this knight is given a great heiress in marriage. His financial woes are ended, but he discovers that wedlock is not to his taste. His wife has publicly insulted him by running off, for, try as he might, there is no way to prevent such gossip from circulating. What man could forgive such an affront to his pride?"

Morgana flinched. She *had* been headstrong and foolish in her actions. How differently she would do things, if only she could do them again!

Lindsey went on: "He sets out to capture and punish his disobedient wife. Only when they arrive in Wales, and he learns the true extent of her power and wealth, does another idea come to him: To allay suspicions among her people, he feigns infatuation; that is the first part of his plan. The second is to pretend to be the victim of poisoning."

"I do not believe you. Why would my husband stoop to such a ruse?"

"For one reason: to gain possession and sole control of your inheritance. I know it all, you see. Who else would bribe the herb woman to testify against you, Morgana? What has anyone else to gain?"

"You are either a villain or a fool if you think I will believe such an absurd story."

His mouth twisted in anger. "I see that, despite everything, Sir Ranulf still has a grip on your affections. It is you, my lady, who are the fool. Perhaps dreams will bring you good counsel. I leave you to them. Goodnight."

Lindsey went out, and a moment later she heard the unmistakable click of a key turning in the great iron lock. Morgana realized he was right when he claimed Ranulf still held her heart. Despite everything that had happened, she could not make herself believe that Ranulf was anything other than what he seemed. He was too blunt and straightforward to plan and carry out such a devilish scheme. Either that or she *was* a fool and destined for a great fall when the truth was known.

It was late, and Morgana did not know what to make of Lindsey's theories. What was true and what false? She was sure only of one thing, her flight to freedom had ended in exchanging one prison for another.

"Will you have more wine, my lady?"

Morgana covered her goblet with her hand and Lindsey gestured the serving man away. "You have scarcely touched a morsel."

"I have no appetite."

"And in the garden this morning you nibbled like a bird. Perhaps music will lift your spirits." He signaled a page. "Fetch the troubadours."

She turned her shoulder to him and pretended an indifference she did not feel. Morgana feared Lindsey. He played the genial host, plying her with tidbits and dainty morsels of the choicest foods, but the more time she spent in his company, the more she wondered at his sanity. He was either mad or so morally corrupt that the effect was the same. He had many vices, but the one she esteemed most was his overweening vanity: it was the only thing that had kept him from forcing himself upon her thus far. Lindsey's conceit led him to believe it was only a matter of time—a very short time—until she fell victim to his manly charms.

In his doublet of russet velvet slashed with gold and trimmed with sable, he looked handsome as a prince. The colors suited his dark complexion, and his heavy gold collar studded with garnets added to the effect; but Morgana saw beneath the elegant facade to the rottenness beneath. Even in London or at Robin's manor in the North Country, she had heard stories of Lindsey's infamous lifestyle, his sudden aggressions and enormous arrogance. The reality was worse. He was like a thwarted child. A dangerous child, wielding the power of life and death.

Morgana watched as he took another glass of wine. Tonight he was drinking quite heavily, and his heated gaze lingered on her more and more often—dwelling overlong on the curve of her breasts and the shape of her thighs beneath the rose silk gown he had provided. At first she had refused to change from her own gown, but she had deemed it prudent to give in when Lindsey threatened to dress her with his own hands.

He had selected her garments for this evening's meal from head to toe. Dainty slippers of satin embroidered with seed pearls covered her feet and a pendant of amethyst and gold hung against her soft white bosom. The sheerest of gossamer veils cascaded down her back from a triangular cap of gold brocade silk, and her long hair was caught up at her nape in a large coil that threatened to come loose with every movement of her head. A tiny lock had escaped the ivory comb and trembled at her temple.

"What lovely hair you have, my dear." He reached out and flicked the curl idly. "How beautiful it must be unbound."

The growing lust in his eyes was disquieting. Morgana had used every stratagem she could think of to hold him at arm's length, but the odds were not on her side. She feared he would not wait much longer for her to come round, and that a few more cups of wine might be all it took to make him change his tactics from persistent persuasion to all-out assault.

Lindsey leaned closer. "You are pensive, sweetheart. Can it be that you pine for the husband who would have sent you to your death?" He took her hand in his and kissed it. "I find such loyalty touching, if tragically misplaced."

Snatching her hand back, Morgana glared at him. "And I find your unwanted attentions abhorrent."

Lindsey threw back his dark head and laughed. There were threatening lights in his eyes as he looked at her. "Softly, softly, Morgana. A man expects compliance and sweet womanly graces from his consort."

"Consort!"

She rose so abruptly she knocked over the goblet and a river of wine spilled on his russet doublet and splattered stains over his fashionable white hose. His anger was immediate and displaced. He cuffed the servant who jumped forward to attend to the spill, sending the man sprawling to the floor. The servant picked himself up and continued his efforts to mop up the wine, ignoring the trickle of blood from his nostril and the discolored welt already rising along his cheekbone. He took the blow so in stride that Morgana realized it was a common thing in this tense and violent household.

No sooner had her captor left to change his garments than her quick mind was thinking of ways to use his absence to her benefit. She could not return to her own castle, but neither would she remain here. Fortunately she was aware of the location of the postern gate, hidden near the kitchens: long ago, a much younger Lindsey, wanting to impress his pretty cousin, had showed it to her. And after that, what? The wisest course was make her way to St. Tristan's where the good friars would honor her claim to sanctuary.

Morgana bided her time in case Lindsey lingered in the corridor, and then rose with calm and quiet dignity. The door of the hall was at the opposite end from the dais. It was a long walk past a curious and possibly hostile assemblage but she moved gracefully toward it. A thick silence fell over the room.

Her blood drummed so loudly in her ears she wondered that they could not hear it. Nobody stopped her, but scores of eyes turned to stare. She could feel it in the prickling of her back as she walked by. Head high, she continued on her way with all the air of a lady taking an afternoon stroll through her own garden. Another step, and another. She was almost there.

A few more feet and her hand touched the door handle. The first step toward freedom. She pulled and the door opened inward, but before she could exit her way was bared by crossed pikes. Morgana jumped back in surprise, and the two guards planted on either side of the door held their positions. She knew when she was beaten, at least temporarily, and let the door swing shut once more.

After resuming her seat it was only a short time before Lindsey returned, smiling smugly. "I hope you did not intend to retire so early, Morgana. The evening is young and I have made plans for your amusement."

He clapped his hands smartly. "Send in the musicians!"

The wide doors were flung open and two men entered, one a bold, strutting youth with wild orange hair as dry as straw, the other an elderly hunchback. Their garments had once been quite fine but were now threadbare and none too clean. They approached halfway to the dais and bowed.

"Forgive us, my lord, for coming before you so travel-stained as we are," the gray beard said.

Lindsey smiled graciously. "It is said a barefoot bard may take his place beside a king. Is that not true, Lady Morgana?"

She inclined her head, not trusting herself to speak. An incredible idea was forming in her brain, one so seemingly impossible she could scarce give it credence. The two were given seats of honor and removed the protective covers from their instruments. She watched, openmouthed and breathless, as the fabric fell away to reveal the great gilt harp of Owain ap Griffin. The torchlight caught the ancient carvings and taut strings, and glinted from the gold and emerald ring on the tall harper's left hand as he bowed again to Lindsey.

"What is your pleasure, my lord?"

"A saga of love and betrayal, where the knight searches in vain for his lost lady, is always a favorite with the ladies." Turning to Morgana he added: "But we shall have our lady choose the song."

Morgana took a deep, shivering breath and smiled down upon the two musicians. "Do you know, 'Oh, That My Love Would Come to Me?'"

Bending his grizzled head, the old harper plucked a minor cord and sang in rich, full tones that filled the hall:

"Oh, that my love would come to me
with artless charms so sweet and pure
that I would all the world abjure
and heaven find within her arms.
Quarrels and sorrow fade away
While our affections rest secure.
Ah, if my love cannot come to me
Then I must go to her."

The youth joined in on the chorus as the four verses were sung, and even the servants paused in their tasks to hear them out. Morgana had been watching them closely and her sense of disbelief turned to certainty. Daffyd's new shock of marigold hair and Ranulf's gray locks and disfiguring hump—quite cleverly contrived—at first had tricked her eye. But no matter how padded and altered his form, there was no mistaking the strongly shaped hand that strummed and plucked the strings or that deep honey-smooth voice.

Her mind was alive with speculation and confusion. A man who thought his wife had tried to murder him did not risk his life for her, by coming disguised into his enemy's stronghold. Or was Ranulf here for some other secret reason? It might be that he only wanted to confirm her treachery, that she had fled the castle to the arms of her lover. But it seemed a terrible gamble to take unless.... A little spurt of hope rose inside her chest and she quickly quelled it.

Something winked in the torchlight, green and glowing as a cat's eye. On Ranulf's finger a great emerald blazed, the one she had given him upon their wedding day. The one he had left in her chamber after their first estrangement and had never worn since. The spurt of hope rose again and spread along her veins, warming her entire body. Could the ring be a signal to her? An acknowledgment of faith and commitment? Again cold reasoning intruded. A few short hours ago, Ranulf had believed her a would-be murderess. Nothing could have happened in the elapsed time to show him otherwise, not with such damning testimony against her.

She was aware that Lindsey was watching her closely. Morgana was breathless from the racing of her heart but she dared not show it. If he discovered the true identity of the two "wandering bards" he would have them killed.

"A fine song." Lindsey clapped his hands to summon a hovering servant. "Bring food and drink for our unexpected guests, and we shall have more songs in the meantime."

Morgana pretended a sudden interest in her food, spearing a bit of roast veal and slicing it with her small, silverhilted dagger. From his vantage point, Ranulf observed her every movement and expression. The faint shadows of fatigue and strain beneath her eyes only heightened her delicacy. She appeared, he noted grimly, to be on remarkably easy terms with Lindsey, bending her head to his as they exchanged words. And knowing what he knew only made it worse. His mouth thinned out dangerously in a set, square jaw.

Up on the dais, Lindsey smiled at Morgana. "You seem to enjoy the music greatly, my dear."

Her answering smile was false but he did not appear to notice. He leaned closer and spoke in low, intimate tones. "I must admit to some surprise. I was not aware that Sir Ranulf was so skilled in musical arts."

She pulled back, aghast, then tried to recover. "You speak in riddles."

"Then, I will speak plainly," he replied in the same deceptively soft voice as his hand closed tightly over hers. "Sir Ranulf and that gangling boy were recognized the moment they presented themselves at my gates. No doubt they hoped to come among us unsuspected and spirit you away during the night."

Daffyd had begun a bittersweet lament and Ranulf filled in the countermelody. The listeners were enthralled, unaware of the deadly drama unfolding around them. Morgana forced her voice around the choking constriction in her throat. "What will you do to them?"

Lindsey's arm snaked around her waist. "Why, sweetheart, that is up to you. Say the word and they will be dispatched on the spot. I do not forget how ill he treated you. Or—" a look of cunning crept into his eye "—if you are still enamored of the gallant Sir Ranulf, only say the word and his life will be spared."

She knew he was lying. Testing her. Morgana cleared her throat. "I have given much thought to what you said to me last evening. Painful as it is to admit, I perceive that there is truth in your allegations that Sir Ranulf conspired to put me away. There is no love in my heart for my husband. Indeed, I mean to petition for an annulment as soon as possible."

Unfortunately the song ended and the latter part of her reply carried down the length of the silent hall. Ranulf, who was tuning his harp for the next song, went still for the barest instant and then continued tightening the pegs. He was not surprised to hear such cool sentiments from her lips, yet they struck him like knives.

Watching Ranulf beneath his heavy lids, Lindsey stroked Morgana's arm with his fingertips. Although layers of silk and linen separated his flesh from hers she felt her skin crawl in revulsion.

"I am glad you have come to your senses." Lindsey raised a languid white hand, and several men moved unobtrusively closer to the supposed bards. Morgana drew in a long hissing breath and tried to rise, but Lindsey's hand curled cruelly around her wrist.

"I will avenge you, my sweet. One word from your lovely lips and they shall both lie dead before you."

The blood drained from her face until she was dizzy with the lack of it. "Although my marriage to Sir Ranulf has been little more than a farce, I would not wish to spoil this pleasant banquet with bloodshed. I would much prefer an annulment to another widowhood."

Lindsey laughed. "You are clever, Morgana, but I want more proof than mere words." Lindsey was so close his breath touched her face. "Show me how you do not care for Sir Ranulf. Prove it. Kiss me."

Knowing Ranulf's and Daffyd's lives might hinge on her actions, she had no choice but to comply. Morgana turned her face up and Lindsey's possessive fingers caressed the line of her jaw as his mouth came down on hers, hot and greedy. He kissed her long and hard while she tried not to show the utter disgust she felt.

Even with her eyes shut she was aware of the alteration in the room. Every eye was upon the dais, watching with various degrees of interest while Sir Lindsey treated his highborn guest as he would a brazen mistress or a common whore. Morgana could only guess at what thoughts were running through Ranulf's mind.

When Lindsey broke the embrace she took one swift glance in Ranulf's direction. There was such contempt in his face, such naked fury that she could not bear to see it. She lowered her lashes quickly, and Lindsey chuckled. "Enough of these fool's games."

He pointed sharply to Ranulf and Daffyd. "Seize them!"

Chapter Fifteen

Morgana could not stifle a small cry of horror. Ranulf and Daffyd sat rigidly, their harps still in their hands while Lindsey's men held drawn swords at their throats. The slightest movement and they would be slain on the spot.

The hand about her waist tightened painfully. "Your emotions are transparent as water. You love your husband still. I should have him slaughtered here and now and thus eliminate my rival, as well as any impediment to our marriage."

While she searched her mind frantically for the right words to prevent him, a sly look crept over his smooth features.

"But I would rather not start our life together with such dark doings. If you cooperate, sweetheart, he might yet survive this night."

He pulled her close and kissed her again. His hand crept up along her ribs, brushing the side of her breast. Again she dared not draw away or turn her face from his. Morgana could barely stand to be pawed by him. She was suffocating and nauseated. His very touch was abhorrent and obscene; but she had seen Lindsey's men move closer to Ranulf and Daffyd, hands upon their sword hilts. She tried to master her loathing.

"Ah, that was much better, my love. I knew that time would bring you round to my way of thinking." Still holding her by the waist, he raised the goblet to her lips and forced her to sip the wine or choke.

"We were made for each other, you and I. When you were taken off to London and wed to Lord Hartley, there was black murder in my heart. But soon rumors reached me of his subversive activities. I knew you would be mine if I could only wait. I knew you would return to me."

He was slurring his words. Morgana held the cup and urged him to drink, hoping he would become too drunk to be an immediate menace. Lindsey set the goblet aside. "No doubt you wish me to imbibe deeply, but that would interfere with my plans. Tonight, Morgana, you shall be mine. Willingly."

"Now I know you are indeed insane."

"Insane with desire for you." His hand was on her thigh, sliding upward. "You see I have a bargain to propose. I will set Sir Ranulf and his young friend free, but for a price. One you can easily pay."

The lust on his face was naked and raw. "Come to my bed, Morgana. A small favor in exchange for two lives. Give yourself willingly to me and I will set them free."

He was surely mad. "This is some evil trick on your part. I cannot believe you."

"You have little choice."

Again she glanced at the prisoners. Ranulf was as unmoved and unmoving as a statue, but Daffyd was pallid, and cold sweat shone upon his face and neck and stained his doublet. They were all caught in Lindsey's trap with no other way out.

He signaled his guards. "Remove them to the ward."

Morgana turned back to their captor. Her pupils were widely dilated and her aqua eyes looked enormous in the candle and torchlight. "Swear before God and upon your immortal soul that you will keep your word and set them free!''

''I so swear. And that you may know I have kept my side of the bargain, I will let you witness their departure.''

Morgana looked across the hall as the soldiers marched Ranulf and Daffyd out at swordpoint, their arms bound behind them. There was nothing they could do to save themselves, and nothing she would not do in an attempt to save them.

''You have won, Lord Lindsey. Once I see them sped on their way with my own eyes—then I will complete my half of the bargain.''

''I shall not ask you to swear on your immortal soul, my dear, but on something you treasure as greatly. Swear on your husband's life that you will not cheat me of my reward when he is free.''

''Before God and all the Saints, I so swear.''

''Excellent. But I do not want Sir Ranulf riding back here with his army to carry you off. You must tell him that you stay with me of your own free will. And you must make him believe it, or I vow he will never leave my gates alive.''

He escorted her out of the hall and past the anteroom that led directly outside. Daffyd was on his knees, retching, and a dark bruise was closing Ranulf's left eye. Their desperate attempt to fend off their captors had failed. As Lindsey and Morgana came out into the yard, Ranulf turned to look at them. There were new lines of strain bracketing his firm mouth and a cynical light in his eyes.

''I see your adventures have brought you no harm, my lady.''

Her heart was breaking, but Morgana dared not show it. She prayed for strength to carry out her role. Sliding her arm through Lindsey's she faced her husband. ''I do not know what mischief brought you here unless it was to spy upon me. You need no longer concern yourself with my adventures, Sir Ranulf. Go seek your annulment with all good speed and my blessings. I have found a far more suitable mate, one my equal in station."

There was such hatred in Ranulf's eyes that she flinched before it. "The she-wolf turns to her own kind! Tell me, Morgana, did you ever feel love for me, or was it all false smiles and playacting on your part?"

"All . . . all false!" Her voice broke and the words came out hoarsely.

Ranulf's face was like granite in the red glow of the torches. "I was happy in my life until it became entangled with yours and you ensnared me with your wiles. Once I loved you well. Now I damn you to the torments of hell for the black-hearted witch that you are!"

She could not bear to look another moment at that beloved face, twisted and warped with such powerful emotion. Wrenching herself away from Lindsey, she turned her back.

Lindsey addressed his captain of the guard. "Take the prisoners into the ward. See that they are mounted and ready to be set free upon my signal."

Morgana stood on a windy parapet of Lindsey Keep and watched two riders head from the stables toward the wide gates. She was numb and bleeding inside. Never would she forget the look of loathing on Ranulf's face or his parting words. They were engraved upon her heart in fire and ice.

It was dark and moonless, but as the horsemen passed a row of torches there was no mistaking Daffyd's bleached hair or his companion's width of shoulders. Their harps were wrapped and bound to their saddles and the great emerald ring on Ranulf's finger caught fire as they passed beneath a window and into the darkness.

Morgana held her breath, expecting some last-minute trick. The iron-banded gates were thrown open wide and the riders trotted through at a spanking pace. Once clear of the Keep, they kicked their mounts into a gallop and headed down the coast road that would lead them home to Castle Griffin.

She watched them go with tear-filled eyes. Even if her people rallied to save her, it would be too late. Once Lindsey touched her she would never feel clean again. And if a miracle occurred and Ranulf's faith in her innocence was restored, how would he feel? His pride could not withstand the knowledge that she had lain with another man to save him. Even if he did not discard her as damaged goods, even if he swore it made no matter, day by day he would withdraw more from her until he scorned to touch her for the memories it evoked.

Sick with fatigue and fear she strained her eyes until the last glimpse of the riders was gone. *Farewell, Ranulf! Godspeed, my love, my dearest heart.*

She would have stood there forever, had not Lindsey taken her in his arms in a sudden, crushing embrace. His breath was hot upon her face, his hands moving up to tear away the low-necked bodice of her gown and the filmy linen beneath. He grasped her breasts, and the shock of his touch upon her bare skin made her gasp and twist away.

He let her go and she stood eyeing him warily, her garments rent to the waist, her breasts exposed and heaving with emotion. In the faint torchlight from behind them, he saw how her nipples were the same soft rose as her dress. This was the moment he had dreamed of. Laughing softly, he took her firmly by the arms and shook her until her teeth rattled.

"We have made a bargain, you and I. You swore an oath."

"Better to break my oath than my marriage vows!"

"You no longer have a marriage, Morgana. You played your part too well tonight. He will repudiate you openly as a murderess. And a whore."

He raped her with his eyes. She refused to cringe. That was what he wanted, but it would only inflame his passions more. He was a man spurred on by cruelty, instinct warned her. With what dignity she could muster, Morgana pulled the torn pieces of her gown together.

"To think," he sneered, "that it was your own husband who commissioned Brother Lewis to map the precincts of the castle and to ferret out its hidden secrets. And most convenient for my ends."

"When my people know you have taken me prisoner, they will ride to rescue me. They will not believe Desmond's falsehoods."

"And brave Sir Ranulf's wrath? I pay my minions well. The soldier Garth and his paramour have already proclaimed that you and I were lovers. And the old herb woman, who fears the hangman's noose even more than she loves my gold, will continue to spread word that you tried unsuccessfully to poison your lord."

He laughed at her intake of breath. "Did you not guess that my hand directed the matter? Rumors abound that we used the tunnel between Lindsey Keep and Castle Griffin for our clandestine meetings. There is nowhere left for you to turn, Morgana, but to me."

She was too dumbfounded to reply. He had cut off every potential avenue of escape, but at least Ranulf and Daffyd were free. The thought of subduing her at last spurred Lindsey's lust. A dark tide of blood suffused his face and his breath came quickly. He put his hand inside the bodice of her ruined gown, seeking the softness of her flesh with cruel and avaricious fingers.

"There is no place where you can go, no one you can turn to in order to change your destiny. I have kept my part of our agreement as you have seen. And now, my dear Morgana, it is time for you to keep yours."

Two fierce guards escorted Morgana not to her assigned chamber, but to another—more grandiose in every way. She had never seen anything like it, except in drawings of exotic

lands. It was adorned in the eastern style, with mosaic tiles
upon the walls and floor, glowing silk hangings at the windows and carpets scattered about. Great braziers of pierced
brass warded off the damp and lamps of equal ornateness
hung from the ceiling beams on massive chains.

Morgana looked about her in surprise. Carved tables and
low divans covered with multitudes of pillows were placed
along the walls, but it was the great bed that dominated the
room: a low, raised platform covered with feather mattresses and embroidered cushions. She remembered that
Lindsey had traveled to the saracen lands, and become enamored of their ways.

Inside all this glory, a timid serving maid awaited her, the
black-haired girl named Jenet. When the guards left, she
indicated a diaphanous green outfit draped across the bed.
"You are to put these on."

Morgana looked at the short, sleeveless jacket and bil-
lowing skirt of transparent sea-green silk. Except for the
fringe of gold coins at the waistline, they were no more than
wisps of fabric as sheer as mist.

"What folly is this? There is more to one of my veils than
to this pagan finery."

Picking up the two pieces, the maid held them out. "Do
you not find them beautiful? They are from the Eastern
bazaars and belonged to Alfreda, who was mistress here
before you."

"I do not believe that Lady Lindsey ever dressed in such
scandalous attire."

Jenet shook her head. "Not poor Lady Lindsey. I speak
of Alfreda, who came later from London. She often danced
for my lord in these silken trifles when they were alone. He
wishes you to dance for him tonight in the same raiments she
so often wore."

Morgana waved her away. "He is mad to think I would
go before him in this harlot's costume!"

"Oh, my lady! Do not defy him in this! Alfreda was kind to me in her way and . . . and sure of her place within Lindsey Keep. But not five months ago she angered my lord terribly. She would not dance before his guests . . ."

There was a look of such remembered horror on the maid's face that a chill crawled up Morgana's back. She did not want to know what came next, but she had to. "What did he do to her?"

"He forced her to dance naked, at swordpoint, before his men. And then he gave her to them to use for their pleasure. She did not survive the night."

Morgana was sickened. As unthinkable as the woman's words were, she believed them. She had sensed increasingly that Lindsey lived in a world of which he was the supreme center. If thwarted, he was capable of anything. She could imagine Alfreda's terror as she was touched and fondled by rough hands. Beyond that her mind refused to follow.

Well, it would not come to that. Apparently forgotten by the maid, Morgana's dagger lay in the pocket of her discarded gown. The small dagger that served for an eating utensil as well as being a handy tool for a hundred household tasks might find a more basic and deadly use before the night was over. While the unsuspecting girl brought out a small jewelry coffer, Morgana managed to extract the knife and hide it beneath the bed linens.

She was prepared to use it, but whether on Lindsey or herself she was uncertain. Her promise to Lindsey had been made under coercion and to save the lives of those she loved. In Morgana's heart, this absolved her of any need to honor it. After her convincing performance tonight, she could expect no help from Ranulf. If her plan failed, the odds were great that she would not live to see morning. Meanwhile, she must use any means at hand to further her goal. Morgana stepped into the harem garb.

The top of the filmy skirt came, not to the waist as she had expected, but low upon her hips exposing the soft sensual swell of her abdomen. The gold coins clinked and tinkled like bells with the slightest movement. She put on the jacket and was shocked to discover it scarcely skimmed her breasts and gaped open in front some five inches. Only the tiny gold chain that fastened one side to the other kept it in place.

The maid clasped bracelets around her upper arms, gold and silver serpents with fiery ruby eyes. Other ones of fine gold wire were slipped over her wrists and ankles. Morgana turned to the polished mirror and saw her reflection. A stranger stood there, sultry and seductive in the provocative splendor of the sheer silk garments. Her arms, throat and midriff were bare, and milky skin gleamed between the open front of the jacket and through the transparent silk. The tips of her upthrust breasts were clearly visible like swollen pink buds beneath the cobweb fabric, as was every rounded curve.

The maid stepped back. "Ah, lady! The master will be pleased. You are even more beautiful than Alfreda, and more finely formed." She paused. "I pray you again, do not anger him. His temper grows increasingly brutal."

"You are afraid. Why do you stay here?"

"I have nowhere else to go. I came as tiring woman to Alfreda, and have neither friend nor kin to aid me. I fear Lord Lindsey and ... and Sir Guy. He lusted after my mistress, and now has turned his eyes upon me. But there is no one to help me."

Morgana took off the small signet ring she wore on her index finger. "Do not despair. If you can escape undetected, you have only to make your way to Castle Griffin. Ask for Lady Winifred, the castellan's wife, and give her this ring in secret. She will take you in for love of me."

Jenet took it wonderingly. In her short life she had met with few kindnesses. She could scarcely believe her ears and fell to her knees, clutching Morgana's hand. "Whatever I can do to aide you, lady, you have only to ask."

Morgana shook her head. "There is nothing anyone can do to help me now. But at least my husband has been spared. Whatever happens to me I will endure it, knowing he is alive and free. Go now."

Jenet gave her a startled glance and looked as if she might speak. She changed her mind, curtsied and left the chamber, taking Morgana's discarded clothes with her.

Morgana scrutinized her reflection again. She turned and twisted, watching the effect of the swirling skirts and the way the jacket rose to expose the underside of her breasts. These diaphanous garments were designed to please a man and incite his lust. Morgana had no intention of pleasing Lindsey in any way. But if she could use his lust long enough to distract him, she might find some way of escape.

He was already three quarters gone in drink. If she could encourage him to take more, he might pass out. Then she could make her way to the tunnel and find the surface exit. But not in these scandalous garments.

There were no other clothes in the room but Lindsey's. Choosing a pair of hose, a linen shirt and a hooded cloak that would serve to hide her well in the darkness along the cliff, she hid them under the linens with the dagger. Once at the monastery, she could decide her next course of action. As she laid the clothing out she heard voices in the hallway. Lindsey! Quickly she snuffed the large bedside candles, so the only light came streaming through the ornamental openings of the braziers and the two pierced lamps suspended from the ceiling.

As the door opened Morgana stretched out upon the cushioned platform, trying to still the frightened beating of her heart. Lindsey entered, his gait slightly unsteady and a wine cup in his hand. Stretching languidly, she raised her arms above her head and watched him through half closed eyes.

The goblet fell from his hand, discarded without a thought in his haste to reach her. He ripped his doublet off as he came, and the fine linen shirt beneath. Despite his leanness the muscles of his chest and arms looked strong. Morgana fumbled beneath the covers for her dagger. She had expected to use delaying tactics, to try and overcome him with drink or the strategic application of a brass ornament to his head. His eager rush caught her unprepared. She rolled over and pulled the dagger into full view.

"Do not come any closer."

"Will you plunge the sharp point into your own breast, or into mine?" He advanced on her more slowly. "You have not kept your vow to me. I should be disappointed but I am not. You see, my dear Morgana, that we are evenly matched—for neither have I kept mine to you."

"What?"

In the moment when she was distracted by his announcement, he sprang—gripping her wrist tightly. She kicked and pushed at him with her other hand, but his wiry frame held incredible strength. He pinned her beneath his weight while his grasp tightened on her wrist until her hand went numb. He wrested the dagger from her paralyzed fingers with ease, and knelt over her in triumph.

"Whether you cooperate or not, my dear, makes little difference to me. In time I will tame you. Perhaps you will even grow to love me."

"Never! I will love Ranulf until the day I die."

"Or until he does."

Lindsey's laughter was wild and dark. "How trusting you are, Morgana, and how gullible. That was not your husband who rode away from the Keep or your young harper, but two of my own men-at-arms of similar physiques. Your beloved husband lies wrapped in chains in my donjon."

She was still as death. "You lie!"

"I assure you it is the truth. My first instinct was to slay him outright; then I decided to let him live until dawn, that he might spend his last hours knowing you lay naked in my arms."

Weeping, Jenet ran along the dark corridors of Lindsey Keep, lit only by sputtering rush dips at long intervals. The lady Alfreda had been kind in her careless way, but since that woman's terrible death Jenet had lived in daily fear for her own life. She was too timid and plain-faced to attract lasting attention, but no girl remained a maid long inside these walls and she had suffered her share of coarse tumbles at the hands of Lindsey's men.

A gruff, masculine voice called out in the distance just ahead, and she stepped into a shadowed angle of wall. The tramp of boots came along the cross corridor and she peered anxiously from her hidden place. She recognized them as they passed the head of the passageway. The soldiers who had removed bold Sir Ranulf and his young harper from the hall. That meant the prisoners were not in the dungeons, but in the Black Tower, so named for its dark chevrons of inlaid stone. At sunrise they would be hurled from the parapet onto the great rocks below. Between scavenging birds and scuttling sea creatures there would be nothing left but a few grisly bones.

Jenet wiped a tear from her eye. *Alack, that such brave and handsome men should meet their doom, and none inside the walls to help them!* Or the kind and lovely Lady Morgana, who had offered to help her escape this life of fear and drudgery.

When the soldiers were gone, she slipped away toward one of her favorite retreats, a small room that was used in former times by the keeps' seamstresses but now was used for storage. Here, she had fashioned a rude bed of sacking and old fabric scraps in one corner, and here she retreated in times of trouble. Lying down, Jenet pulled a bit of cloth over her and curled up, feeling safe as a mouse in its hideyhole.

No one was aware of her little sanctum, not even the other servants—although they knew more secrets than their masters ever dreamed. Things like how casks of the best ale and wine might be tapped so that no one could tell. Or how my lady Whitfield was able to admit Lord Lindsey to her bed-chamber at Windsor Castle under her husband's very nose. Or . . . or . . . where a second key to the Black Tower lay, for-gotten by all but a few trysting lovers.

Throwing the cover off, Jenet sat upright. Did she dare? If caught, it would mean certain death. But if she suc-ceeded, they might all go free. The risk was great, but it was worth it. She crept out of the storeroom and moved silently down the dim hallway. Six paces from the tower door, she worked the loose stone from the frame and withdrew the heavy key. She managed to turn the heavy lock and was just pulling the massive door open when she heard heavy foot-steps coming down the corridor.

Lindsey pinned Morgana's arms to her sides and laughed at her helplessness. As always, struggles roused his pas-sions to a greater pitch. He had lusted after her for too many years to rush his long overdue victory. He would savor every taste and touch.

"What thoughts," he whispered silkily in her ear, "be-guile your husband's final hours? What emotions fill his noble breast, as he thinks of us entwined in love?"

"I shall kill you," Morgana hissed through gritted teeth, and the words were more vow than threat. She did not think she could hold him off much longer. His breathing quick-ened, as he tired of his cat-and-mouse game.

"Come, lovely! In the great hall you were all sweetness. Show me some of that honey now . . ."

His hot mouth traveled down the side of her throat and she shrank away. "Let me go! I pretended to be false to Ranulf only to save his life, and now you will let him die believing me an adulteress. He will curse me with his last breath!"

"Little fool. He fought to be free as he was taken away, in order to save you. A man does not risk his life in an enemy stronghold for a woman he despises."

With the blade of Morgana's dagger, Lindsey unhitched the tiny chain that held the jacket over her breasts. She tried to pull away and he overbalanced. Morgana grasped for the weapon with desperate fingers, but although she weakened his hold, her strength was no match for his. The dagger slipped, scratching a thin line over the top of her left breast, but the blood that dripped from the dagger was not hers, but Lindsey's.

He held his slashed palm to his mouth and sucked at the salty blood to stem the flow. "Stupid bitch!"

He backhanded her, leaving another trail of crimson drops over her creamy skin. In his anger, he struck harder than he'd intended. A circle of stars exploded in Morgana's head and she fell helplessly into a black velvet void.

The chamber door burst open, framing Ranulf in the torchlight from the corridor beyond. On the floor behind him lay the prone body of a guard and Jenet leaned against the wall, hands pressed to her mouth.

In a fraction of an instant, Ranulf saw it all: Morgana unmoving on the bed, the scarlet streaks across her breast; Lindsey half stripped and straddling her, the bloodied knife still in his hand. A great pain ripped through his chest, as if his soul had been torn from his body.

"You have killed her, you foul coward, and now you will pay with your life!"

With a fearsome roar, he launched himself at Lindsey. The momentum of his charge and weight carried them both off the bed. Lindsey tried every dirty trick he knew, but he was no match for Ranulf's strength and wild frenzy. They rolled across the floor in their desperate battle. Both knew what the outcome must be: only one of them would leave this room alive.

Lindsey saw a candle stand nearby and hooked his leg around it. The great brass piece fell, catching Ranulf across the top of the shoulders and barely missing the base of his skull. With a cry of rage, Ranulf wrapped his fingers around his opponent's throat and squeezed. His air cut off, Lindsey was quickly weakening. Spots appeared before his eyes and he knew he must vanquish Ranulf or die.

He caught the Dane with a sharp knee-jab to the groin, and when Ranulf's grip slackened, pitched him backwards. Ranulf's head smacked hard against the corner of an iron-banded chest. The blow stunned him. While he shook off the effects of the impact, Lindsey jumped to his feet. There were sounds of pitched battle from the hall and corridor, and Lindsey realized with fear that the men of Castle Griffin were inside the walls of the keep. There was no time to do more than grab his sword from the chest.

Ranulf groaned and sat up, holding his head. Blood coursed through his fingers from the deep scalp gash, but he lunged after his enemy. He blinked his eyes. Once second Lindsey stood before the massive chimney piece, and the next he had vanished. Rising to his feet, Ranulf fought to clear his thoughts. The solution was obvious. Both Lindsey Keep and Castle Griffin had been built and enlarged by the same men. It stood to reason that if one master chamber had a secret escape route, so would the other.

By God, he would not escape! Ranulf's fingers ran over the lines and curves of the chimney breast. There was no sound, but a small black section opened up on one side of the hearth. A secret route, most cleverly concealed. Well, Lindsey would not get far before retribution caught him.

Before ducking into the opening, Ranulf paused for one last glance at the bed. *Morgana, beloved! I will avenge you!*

He froze. Was that a movement of her arm? He flew to the bedside just in time to hear her moan. She was alive! The joy blotted up the black hatred that had taken hold of him. "Morgana!"

She opened her eyes. A dark bruise was forming beneath one cheekbone and the corner of her mouth was swollen from Lindsey's blow. Ranulf leaned down and kissed it lightly. "My love, I thought he had killed you!"

He caught her up against his shoulder, half naked as she was, and enfolded her in his arms. Morgana's return to consciousness was blurred and hazy. She did not know where she was, or why. All that mattered was that she was in Ranulf's arms once more, crushed against the warmth of his chest.

"Ranulf, my love! Oh, I thought you believed all his lies, that you hated me."

He kissed her brow, smoothed the tumbled hair from her temples with his lips. "I will explain all later, when we are out of harm's way."

"But how did you escape?"

"The maid, Jenet, risked her life for ours."

Morgana turned to thank her and the girl smiled bravely. "No one has ever shown me kindness before, my lady. I would do it again, no matter what the outcome."

Morgana rose and touched his bruised cheek. "But Ranulf, why did you come inside Lindsey Keep? There was little hope of saving me with such reckless courage."

"A fine husband I would be, to make no effort to free you! We hoped our disguises would hold until we could unbar the tunnel entrance to let in Sir Dyllis and Desmond with their men. Now, with Jenet's aid, Daffyd has let our troops inside. Desmond and Sir Dyllis are pouring into the keep with the men, but we are not yet safe."

"But we are together. Hold me. Just for a moment. Let me know that you are real and the nightmare is ended."

He pressed her so close she could feel the strong steady beat of his heart, then let her go. "We must not linger, love. Can you dress yourself while I scout the situation?"

Morgana nodded, and Jenet entered the room. "I will help my lady. We'd best hurry. There is a pall of smoke rising up the stairs. They have fired the hall."

By the time Ranulf found the head of the stairway, the smoke was thick and black. Coughing and choking, he made his way back to the chamber and shut the door. "They cannot reach us that way, and the window drop is too sheer. We will have to try our luck in the passageway."

Morgana had dressed herself in a pair of Lindsey's hose and linen shirt that Jenet brought her. "This will be more practical if it leads down to the cavern in the rock."

Morgana was more herself now. She took up dagger and kept it ready in her hand. "Lindsey is armed."

"Aye. He might be a danger to us, but I think he values his skin too well. By now he is surely halfway up the coast, making for one of his allies' fortresses. I shall deal with him later."

Already the room was turning gray and dim, as smoke from the burning timbers seeped around the chinks of the door. Taking a torch from the wall socket, Ranulf stepped into the fireplace. The rectangular opening was on the left, hidden in the thickness of the wall. He motioned for them to follow, and plunged into the darkness. Morgana waved Jenet ahead and took up the rear, with a candle in her hand.

The torch and candle were only of small help, for the way was narrow and winding. They could never see more than a few steps ahead. The odor of smoke and burning materials was strong as they moved down another level, and none spoke the fear they all felt: that the fire had blocked the way below and they would die trapped within the burning walls of Lindsey Keep.

Smoke stung their eyes and it grew hot as they moved along the section abutting the hall. A crash of falling masonry came, muffled by the heavy stones that formed the passage. The roof of the hall had caved in. The narrow corridor took a sudden turning, went down a slippery ramp and

widened. Cool air blew upward to meet them, smelling not
of smoke but of the sea. They all breathed easier.

This route did not seem connected to the way Morgana
had been brought in before. Here, smoothly dressed blocks
gave way, at a lower level, to a tunnel cut through the living
rock. There was a hint of daylight in the distance. Morgana
kept her eyes on Ranulf's shirt, not for guidance but to reassure herself of his presence. There were so many questions in her mind, but no time for them now. It was enough
to know that he still loved her.

"Careful!"

Ranulf held his hand up cautiously. He had heard something up ahead. Most likely some animal that made its burrow in this subterranean world, but only a fool took
chances. The light ahead was growing brighter and reflected from a turn in the passage wall. They were not far
from the sea. A gust of wind tore at the torch and Morgana's candle. Both went out. Now there was only the faint
glow to guide them.

"Not much farther," he said encouragingly, and stepped
into a void. Everything happened quickly, so quickly that
the parts could never be quite sorted out afterward.

"Ranulf!" Morgana cried out in alarm.

"You shall not have her," a voice shouted a few feet away.

And then Jenet screamed, a high-pitched cry that ended
abruptly. Something warm and wet splashed over Morgan-
a's arm, and she was knocked aside. The ground was slippery and she went sprawling. From the darkness grunts and
curses rang out—and a voice called from far away.

A figure came running from the opposite end of the tunnel, torch held high. Morgana had her dagger ready until she
recognized a soldier in her own livery. He drew his sword
and went to help Ranulf but was waved away for his pains.
The wavering torchlight showed a grisly scene. Jenet lay
dead where she had fallen, her throat slit from side to side.

It was not water that Morgana had slipped in, but the girl's blood.

She saw the shallow trough where Ranulf had tripped and fallen. He was on his feet now, sword drawn and ready as he faced Lindsey. His face contorted with righteous fury and his slashing blade made silver arcs in the air. His enemy defended himself well, but he was no real match for a swordsman of Ranulf's strength and skill. Already his wrist was tiring, his shoulder burning with the effort.

Morgana came into Lindsey's line of view and his eyes went wide. She realized that he had struck at Jenet, mistaking the maid for herself. Her fate had hinged on a thread and she had been saved from a bloody end by her mannish costume. She began trembling with reaction.

"Defend yourself," Ranulf snapped as Lindsey dropped his guard a moment.

The crash of steel on steel rang through the tiny cavern. Ranulf had the advantage of strength while Lindsey was hampered by his insane rage. It seemed the outcome was inevitable. Then Ranulf's booted foot slipped in the pool of blood. He skittered across the uneven rock surface, flailing for balance. Lindsey charged into the opening, his weapon gleaming wickedly in the dimness.

"No!" Morgana threw herself forward, knocking his arm aside, and her quick action saved Ranulf. Snarling, Lindsey thrust her away and she fetched up against the limestone wall. The bit of rock she grasped at was deceptively fragile and broke in her hands. Morgana fell to the cavern floor with such force she was stunned, and could only watch the drama helplessly.

Ranulf had regained his footing and now pressed Lindsey hard and fast. Blow for blow, he met each thrust and parry until his opponent was backed into a cul-de-sac. His arm was weary, the muscles burning with continued exertion, driven by fear, was even more tired and sweat and blood dripped into his eyes. He saw that Lindsey, covered with a wet sheen of perspiration.

Again and again sword met sword. A line of dark red showed on Lindsey's shoulder where he had been caught but had pulled back in time. He was congratulating himself on his narrow escape when Ranulf lunged with surprising suddenness and made a brilliant thrust that caught him in the chest. The sword plunged through him until the tip of Ranulf's blade struck stone. The discordant sound rang in their ears like a broken bell.

For a moment Lindsey looked down in astonishment. His own sword clattered from his limp hand. Ranulf yanked back his sword and the dying man blinked once, twice. He opened his mouth as if to speak but no sound issued forth. Blood-tinged foam trickled from the corner of his purpling lips, and then his eyes went blank and empty. Lindsey's corpse slid quietly to the floor.

Ranulf let his sword drop and wiped the sweat from his eyes. As Morgana rose he went to her and pulled her into his arms. Her own arms wound around him, holding him so close he vowed that she was squeezing him to death. "Ranulf! It is over. It is over at last."

He took her face between his sweaty, callused hands and kissed her soft, sweet mouth. "No, my love. We are just beginning."

Epilogue

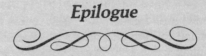

Sun sparkled off the blue-green waters of the ocean below the parapet, rippling like the clear notes that Ranulf struck from the quivering harp strings. Morgana leaned over the protective wall as seabirds dipped and wheeled above the foaming crests, adding their cries and piping to the song.

To the east, bright banners and gaily striped tents ranged between the village and the walls of Castle Griffin. Tomorrow was the great ceremony of oath-taking when those knights pledged to the castle came to renew their vows, and afterward would come a tourney such as had not been seen in years. There would be races and jousts and contests of song and wit, as well.

Ranulf set the great harp of Owain ap Griffin down gently on a cushion and took Morgana's hand. "Enough of singing, my sweet love, or they will find us out."

Morgana smiled and shook her head in agreement. "Yes, and call us back to our duties. But for a while longer we can pretend we are only lovers, and not lord and lady of all we survey."

Hand in hand they strolled along the parapets. From here the ruins of Lindsey Keep could not be seen, but the terrible events of the previous days had left their mark upon her. She was graver now and less quick to anger; at the same time her capacity to love and find joy in even the smallest thing had deepened. Ranulf remembered back to a certain evening in Edward's banquet hall. Who would have thought such happiness could come from such an unlikely beginning?

He spotted something within the castle precincts. "Look!"

Morgana's gaze followed his. Down below, Bronwen crossed a small courtyard and not a hundred feet behind, a red-hair knight came after her. Ranulf sat on one of the benches and pulled Morgana down upon his knee.

"Will Bronwen ever forgive Desmond for thinking you a murderess?"

She smiled and kissed his nose. "Why not? I forgave you."

His dark blue eyes were troubled. "Sweeting, if there had been any way to spare you such anguish I would have done so."

"Hush, I know."

This was old ground, but Ranulf could not help going over it—like someone probing a wound to see how greatly it hurt. "With more time, I could have devised some other way to keep you safe, but I had no choice—someone was trying to see you hung or burned. Once people were stirred up, the danger was great."

He shifted restlessly and she snuggled against his broad shoulder while he spoke. "No one knew of the secret passage leading to your chambers except Brother Lewis—and of course, Lindsey, once Garth brought the plans to him. But I thought you were safe and secure in your own chambers. I meant to keep you safe and protected by pretending you were my prisoner."

She smiled saucily up at him. "I am."

Ranulf cradled her face between his hard palms. "No lady, I am yours. Till death and beyond. You shall never be rid of me."

"I shall never try. To lose you would be to lose part of my very soul."

He kissed her, softly at first and then with mounting intensity that sent the blood singing through her veins. She traced his lips with her fingertips, and he caught them in his hand, pressing them to his mouth.

"You hold my heart in these."

Her response was interrupted when a blast of trumpets heralded an unexpected arrival on the coast road. They peered eastward, toward the bright sun, and as the colorful cavalcade drew closer, recognized the sun-in-splendor device of England's King.

"Edward has come to see how we fare," Morgana murmured. "No doubt to see if we have murdered one another."

Ranulf tightened his embrace. "We shall have a surprise for him on that score. And if we slip away to our chambers quickly, we shall have time for a few more kisses before our royal guest reaches the gates."

Within a half hour the royal procession reached the inner court, and the truants arrived just in time—their cheeks flushed and eyes sparkling. When the King rode through the gates, Ranulf and Morgana stood arm-in-arm, she in rose, with azure and aquamarine, he in white and sapphire. Edward took one look at their glowing faces and knew his plan had worked out more splendidly than he could have ever hoped.

Led by their master and mistress, the whole assemblage dropped to their knees in welcome as the King dismounted, magnificent in topaz velvet slashed with ivory kendal. The sun shone on his regal Plantagenet features and he looked every inch the hero with a great topaz centered in his massive gold S-link collar. Edward was well pleased.

"We had not meant to journey to Wales so soon, but We had great curiosity to see if Our matchmaking has proven itself. It seems this White Rose of Orkney has twined with the flame-haired Rose of Wales to good results!"

"Aye, my liege," Morgana said, as he bade them rise. "And if you had waited but a seven-month more, we should have even greater results to show!"

Ranulf's jaw dropped as her words sank in. "Seven?... What?"

Her rosy blush told him his surmise was correct. "'Tis early days yet. I had not meant to say anything until harvest time."

Heedless of the royal presence, Ranulf picked Morgana up and whirled her around; then suddenly set her down, as if she would break in his hands like an eggshell. He could not believe that his child grew within her, this small woman who had conquered his hardened warrior's heart.

Edward laughed and tossed his golden head. "We have become quite adept at matchmaking, as this happy union proves. Be there other worthy warriors in need of Our assistance?"

Morgana glanced at Ranulf and back at the King. "It seems your Royal intervention might again prove timely. Lindsey Keep stands empty now, in need of rebuilding and a strong hand."

Ranulf joined in. "Aye, so it is. And there is a certain fox-haired knight, loyal to Your Majesty but tangle-tongued in wooing."

Morgana smiled. "Sir Desmond and the little maid, Bronwen, would make a happy pair, if only both parties could be brought to acknowledge it."

The King embraced Morgana first, and then Ranulf. "We see the joyous outcome of your marriage and perhaps will try Our hand at more. It would not do to let Lindsey Keep fall to ruin."

"Perhaps We shall try our hand at matchmaking again. Meanwhile, Lindsey Keep and its demesnes are deeded to Castle Griffin and its heirs, and you may choose your own castellan to oversee it.'' The King surveyed them shrewdly. "There is also the matter of Our a bride-gift, which was overlooked in the haste of your marriage. Ask any boon of Us, each of you, and it shall be granted.''

Ranulf's arm tightened around Morgana. "There is rebuilding to be done in the village; but for myself, I have everything I shall ever want or need here beside me.''

If he expected a similar answer from his wife he was surprised. Morgana was thinking rapidly. Any child born to her, as heir to Castle Griffin, would take precedence over Ranulf, who was only a simple knight. "I have a boon, my Liege. My husband is lord of Castle Griffin in everything but name. That must be rectified.''

Edward's glittering Plantagenet smile spread into a Royal grin. 'We shall do better than that.''

He gestured and a secretary stepped forward holding a parchment signed and sealed in the King's own hand. "Sir Dyllis and Lady Winifred, men and women of the castle, come forward to greet the new Earl and Countess of Griffyth.''

Morgana's heart overflowed. Ranulf's worth was recognized, and the King had even restored to her and her people, the Welsh name that had been altered by the first Edward three hundred years before.

Sir Dyllis and Lady Winifred hastened forward to offer their obiesance and the others followed suit in order of rank.

Much later, when the King had retired to refresh himself from his travels, Morgana stood upon the ramparts again, nestled close against Ranulf's side.

How well they fit together. Two parts of an interlocking puzzle. Two halves of a rare and precious coin.

Ranulf smiled down into her eyes, reading her thoughts. Remembering their shaky beginnings. He had gone into this marriage with the enthusiasm of a man going to the gallows, and had tried to run it like a military campaign. Instead, she had gentled him, shown him a world of love that he had never dared to dream existed. In their union, he had found everything a man could want. Morgana. His love. His life.

Her thoughts were much the same. She had almost thrown away everything for foolish pride. She had fought their union from the start, thinking it would bring her only loss. Instead she had found a wealth of love and goodness and strength. Now she was complete. She smiled up at him as the wind caught at his bright hair. Ranulf. Her Golden Knight. Her love.

Never was a woman so blessed.

* * * * *

COMING NEXT MONTH

#31 TEXAS HEART—Ruth Langan

Young Jessie Conway would stop at nothing to find her
missing father. And although she suspected Cole Matthews
was a veteran gunslinger, she would risk his company
along the Chisholm Trail for her family's sake. But Jessie's
fear melted when she learned her brooding companion
possessed a noble heart she alone was destined to claim.

#32 DELTA PEARL—Maureen Bronson

Jena Veray was alone and penniless, but free at last from
the sadistic clutches of her fiancé, and determined to make
a new start—somehow. But lighthearted Andrew Wade
had plans of his own, and Jena found herself swept up in
the rags-to-riches schemes of Andrew and his
unconventional friends.

AVAILABLE NOW:

#29 ROSE RED, ROSE
WHITE
Marianne Willman

#30 MEDICINE WOMAN
Kathleen Eagle

You'll flip . . . your pages won't!
Read paperbacks *hands-free* with

Book Mate • I

The perfect "mate" for all your romance paperbacks

**Traveling • Vacationing • At Work • In Bed • Studying
• Cooking • Eating**

Perfect size for all standard paperbacks, this wonderful invention makes reading a pure pleasure! Ingenious design holds paperback books OPEN and FLAT so even wind can't ruffle pages – leaves your hands free to do other things. Reinforced, wipe-clean vinyl-covered holder flexes to let you turn pages without undoing the strap . . . supports paperbacks so well, they have the strength of hardcovers!

Pages turn WITHOUT opening the strap.

SEE-THROUGH STRAP

Reinforced back stays flat.

Built in bookmark.

BOOK MARK

BACK COVER HOLDING STRIP

10" x 7¼", opened.
Snaps closed for easy carrying, too.

Available now. Send your name, address, and zip code, along with a check or money order for just $5.95 + .75¢ for postage & handling (for a total of $6.70) payable to Reader Service to:

Reader Service
Bookmate Offer
901 Fuhrmann Blvd.
P.O. Box 1396
Buffalo, N.Y. 14269-1396

Offer not available in Canada
*New York and Iowa residents add appropriate sales tax.

BM-G